VIOLET
GRENADE

ALSO BY
VICTORIA SCOTT

THE COLLECTOR

THE LIBERATOR

THE WARRIOR

VIOLET GRENADE

VICTORIA SCOTT

Entangled Publishing, LLC
2614 South Timberline Road
Suite 109
Fort Collins, CO 80525

Entangled Teen is an imprint of Entangled Publishing, LLC.

Visit our website at www.entangledpublishing.com.

Edited by Heather Howland
Cover design by Anna Crosswell
Interior design by Toni Kerr

HC ISBN: 978-1-63375-687-8
Ebook ISBN: 978-1-63375-688-5

Manufactured in the United States of America

First Edition May 2017

10 9 8 7 6 5 4 3 2 1

For Jessica, my marvelous assistant—
You loved this book first. You loved it best.
Thank you.

"If you cannot get rid of the family skeleton, you may as well make it dance."

—*George Bernard Shaw*

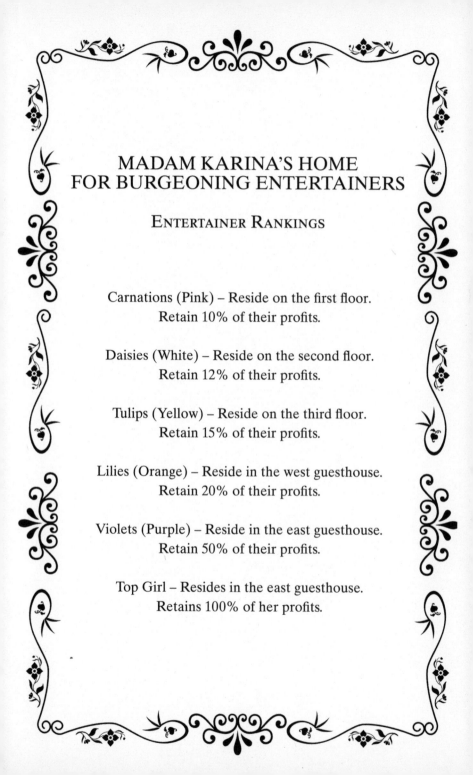

MADAM KARINA'S HOME FOR BURGEONING ENTERTAINERS

ENTERTAINER RANKINGS

Carnations (Pink) – Reside on the first floor.
Retain 10% of their profits.

Daisies (White) – Reside on the second floor.
Retain 12% of their profits.

Tulips (Yellow) – Reside on the third floor.
Retain 15% of their profits.

Lilies (Orange) – Reside in the west guesthouse.
Retain 20% of their profits.

Violets (Purple) – Reside in the east guesthouse.
Retain 50% of their profits.

Top Girl – Resides in the east guesthouse.
Retains 100% of her profits.

PART I

DOMINO'S RULES
FOR LIVING ON THE STREET

1. Stick by people worth knowing.
2. Take care of yourself first.
3. Always wear armor.
4. When in doubt, run.
5. Roll the dice.

CHAPTER 1

PRYING EYES

People say blondes have more fun.

Please.

I snatch the wig off my head and toss it toward Greg. He catches it like a fly ball, his eyes never leaving my face. Leaning over in the chair, I dig through the pile of wigs he's brought me.

Brunette?

Redhead?

My fingers land on hot pink tresses that fall in long, sexy waves. Bingo, my friend, bingo. I slide the wig over my head, pull the straps until it's snug, and flip my head up like I'm a starlet in a soft-core porn. "Well?"

Greg claps his hands slowly, as if he's got all the time in the world. Judging by the lines around his eyes, I'm not sure that's true. "Fan*ta*stic."

"I'll take it." My thighs create a sucking sound against the leather chair as I stand. I like the sound, I decide. It makes it seem as if I have a little meat on my bones like a real woman. But a quick glance in the mirror tells me I'm still the shapeless girl I woke up as.

Greg fidgets as I stare at myself. Finally, in an attempt to make me feel better, he says, "Looks like you've put on some weight."

I smile at the lie and click toward the checkout counter in my super-duper high heels, the ones that make me look a hand taller than the five feet I stand. The second I think about my height, I hear Dizzy's taunting in my head: *five feet, my ass.*

"I am five feet," I grumble.

"What?" the counter girl asks.

I look up at her. She must be Greg's new girl. "Nothing," I answer. "How much?"

She clicks a few buttons on the register with shiny purple nails. I'm pleased that she chose a fun shade instead of the typical pink or red or—dare I speak it—a French manicure.

"Twenty-one dollars and forty-four cents," she announces. I glance at Greg, who's busy replacing the wigs onto creepy mannequin heads. I clear my throat. When he doesn't hear me, or pretends not to hear me, I decide to pay the full amount. He usually hooks me up with a discount, which he should, considering I'm here every week. I dig into my pocket for the cash, knowing Dizzy would give me hell for paying at all.

When I glance up at the cashier, she's looking at the underside of my left forearm, at the crisscrossed scars that nestle there. I instinctually pull it against my side. The girl straightens, realizing I've caught her staring. I think we're done with this awkward moment, but the girl isn't going to let this slide.

"What happened to your arm?" she whispers, as if that helps.

I shake my head, hoping that'll deter her from asking anything else. No such luck.

"It looks like you got in an accident or something."

I meet her eyes, my blood boiling, wanting so badly to shut her up. Instead, I slap the money on the counter and grab my pink wig. The bell chimes as I push open the glass door. "I'll be by next week."

On the streets of Detroit, the heat comes in waves. The pink faux hair dampens from my sweaty palm, and I silently curse the sun. It's so hot in the dead of summer that people are practically immobile. They sit on chairs outside their homes, and on benches near stores, and on the cracked sidewalks. And. They. Don't. Move.

Except, that is, to gawk as I pass by.

They ogle the blue wig falling past my shoulders and down my back, the one I'll replace tonight with the gem in my hand. They stare at my tattoo, the way it slithers down my exposed side. And they narrow their eyes at my pierced lip and wonder where else I may be pierced. What else I'm hiding.

They come to a conclusion: I am a freak.

And they are right.

I head down the sidewalk toward our home, the place where Dizzy and I live. The house doesn't really belong to us, but in this part of town it doesn't matter. No one cares. Certainly not the police. They have bigger problems to worry about than teenage kids squatting in an abandoned house.

Nearing our block, I notice a parked sedan. A guy leans against the side, smoking a cigarette. When he notices me, he nods. I put my head down and walk faster. If Dizzy were here, I'd lift my chin and lock eyes with the man. But he's not, so I don't.

I hear a whistle, and my head jerks back in the man's direction. He's smiling at me. It's not a terrible smile. He's got a mouthful of teeth. That's something. He turns so his body faces mine, and watches as I walk past. The man looks to be in his mid-twenties. He's wearing dark jeans and a proud white shirt, and even from here I can tell his nose is too big for his face. His cigarette dangles between his fingertips as he raises his arm and waves.

I wave back.

His eyes narrow when he sees the underside of my arm. I rip my hand down and walk faster. I don't want to see his reaction, but I can't help looking up one last time.

The lazy smile is gone from his face. A look of satisfaction has taken its place. He pulls a phone from his back pocket and makes a call, eyeing every step I take.

If I didn't know better, I'd think he just found something he'd been searching for.

I rush toward the end of the street, glancing at a nonexistent watch on my wrist like I have somewhere important to be. Behind me, I can feel the guy watching. I don't know why he looked at me the way he did, but I don't like it. Dizzy and I work hard to ensure no one notices us. The tattoos, the piercings, the loud clothing—you'd think it's to attract attention, but it has the opposite effect. It shows the world we're abnormal, and the world looks away.

Twice I look over my shoulder to check if I'm being followed. There's no one there either time, and I begin to feel like an idiot.

No one wants to follow you, Domino.

No one except a particularly determined social worker who's approached me more than once. This neighborhood is part of her territory, and underage strays are her passion.

Just thinking about the woman sends shivers down my spine. Her frizzy blond hair, the way her arms seem too long for her body like she wants nothing more than to snare me in them. Twice now she's followed me as I made my way home, speaking softly in her tweed business suit and scuffed black heels. I could hear what she was saying, but I didn't *want* to hear it. She's a paper pusher. Someone who pretends to care. In the end, I'd be another tick mark in her body count. Another dog off the streets, shoved into a kennel.

That's when they'd find out who I really am. *What* I am.

And then the badness would come.

Standing outside our house, I feel relief. Gray paint peels in frenzied curls, and the front light is broken. The grass is dead and half the windows are covered with boards. But the bones are strong. The house stands three stories tall and is an old Victorian build. This part of Detroit used to be glamorous, where all the rich people lived. But they built too close to the ghetto, hoping against hope that this section of the city would turn around. The opposite happened. The slums grew arms and legs and crawled toward their shiny homes and manicured lawns, and then swallowed them whole without remorse.

And now Dizzy and I have a home that used to be beautiful.

"What are you doing?" someone calls from the upstairs window.

I raise a hand to shade my eyes from the sun. When I see Dizzy's face, I have to stop myself from smiling. Instead, I shake my head as if I'm disappointed to be home and head toward the door.

"It's Friday, Buttercup, you know what that means." Somewhere above me, I hear Dizzy howl long and energetic like a prideful wolf.

I want to tell him not to call me Buttercup, that my name is Domino. But I don't. I just curl my hands into tight fists. I open my mouth wide.

And I howl right back.

CHAPTER 2

SEE DIZZY FLY

Dizzy throws open the door and rushes toward me.

"Stop," I yell, holding my arms out.

"I won't!"

The street-lamp-of-a-guy flips me over his shoulder and barrels into the house. I laugh when he tosses me onto a couch that may or may not harbor the Ebola virus. He places one long, skinny finger on my nose. "Where have we wanted to go for the last two months?"

I slap his hand away. "I don't know. Where?"

He taps his temple and bobs his head, dark curls bouncing against brown skin. "Think, Buttercup. Think."

So I do. My brain goes tick, tick, tick. And then my face pulls together and I crane my neck to the side. "Are you saying what I think you're saying?"

Dizzy jumps onto the makeshift coffee table we constructed and pretends to pound the surface with a king's staff. "Here ye, hear ye. I pronounce tonight the night we wreak Havoc."

"Havoc?" I say quietly. "No one gets in that club."

He nods and his curls kiss his long lashes. "I met someone who knows someone who said he could do something for someone like me."

"We're going to Havoc," I say again, because saying it

again makes it real.

Dizzy raises his arms into the air, and I know that's my cue to react. I stand up and spring onto the couch. Then I jump up and down and he grabs my hands. He leaps onto the crusty couch beside me and we go up and down screaming that we're going to Havoc. That we're going to party like beasts, because we are beasts. I throw my arms around him before I remember that we don't do that. I hate being close to people and he hates being confined and this isn't okay.

"Gross. Get off me," he yells. "I can't breathe. I can't breathe!"

I let go, gladly, and Dizzy leaps back onto the floor. He looks like a spider doing it, all arms and legs. He's certainly as thin as one.

His brown eyes spark beneath thick, caterpillar eyebrows. "Get ready," he orders. Then he dashes up the stairs, each step burping from the weight.

I step down from the couch. Going to Havoc isn't that big of a deal for most people. I get that. But this is my life now, has been for the last year. Sometimes going somewhere new—somewhere that'll let people like Dizzy and me in—is everything. It's a shiny penny fresh off the press, a black swan among white. It's nothing groundbreaking. But it is.

I wash my hair and body as best I can using the bottles of water and bar of soap Dizzy stole from the gas station. The drain slurps it down and sighs as I massage my scalp. Next to me on a rusted towel hook, my pink wig waves hello. She's ready to go, she tells me. She can't wait to be worn like the crown she is.

I tell her to hold her damn horses because I'm washing my hair in a sink.

Wrapping a towel that's seen better days around my head, I step out of the bathroom and into what's been my room for the last ten months. Ten months. I've lived with Dizzy for nearly a year, and I could count the things I know about him on my pencil-thin fingers.

When he was sixteen, his mom put him and his older brother on a plane from Iran bound for America. The pair landed in Philadelphia, and eventually Dizzy ended up here. He never talks about his brother, and I don't ask. I know he enjoys Twizzlers and blue ballpoint pens and crisp, white shoelaces. I know because he steals those things most often.

I've never seen anyone steal something the way Dizzy does. Once before, when I was at a department store, I spotted a pair of kids working together to pinch a yellow Nike hoodie. One kid distracted the associate, asking for help to get something down off the wall, while the other slipped the hoodie inside his leather jacket. They got away with it. I remember wanting to follow them. See what they did next.

Dizzy doesn't work that way. He doesn't distract or scheme. He just slips by what he wants like a ghost, and it's gone. Anything he wants, gone. Dizzy never takes more than he needs, but he needs a lot.

I met him at an arcade. I was playing Pac-Man when I saw him across the room. He was almost as thin as I was, and his nails told me everything I needed to know. He was like me—homeless. I've met homeless people who try to scrub away the streets. It never works. The human body has too many crevices, too many places for grime to settle. You can see it in the small lines of their faces and in their palms and elbows. And you can see it in their nails.

Dizzy's nails were atrocious. He didn't try to scrub away

the street. He embraced it. I needed someone like that. As I watched, the long-legged, dark-skinned man-boy swiped a red can of soda from the bar. The soda was there. The soda was gone. If I hadn't been watching closely, I might have believed he was made of magic—Dracula strikes Detroit.

That day in the arcade, Dizzy met my stare with a boldness I admired. I eyed the place where the soda had been, and he smiled. Then he turned and swept out the door. With the rang-tanging of arcade games behind me, I followed him. I followed him then, and I follow him now. He's my person. Not that I need one.

I startle when I spot my person standing in the bedroom doorway.

His eyes widen as if he just remembered I'm a girl. Tugging the towel around my body tighter, I avert my gaze. "What are you looking at?"

"I forget sometimes," he says softly. "What you look like."

He means without my makeup. Without my rainbow wigs and chains and piercings. He means me as I am right now: Domino, in the nude. "Stop staring at me, perv."

"I know you hate it when I—"

"Stop," I say. "Just don't."

He holds up his hands in defeat. "I'm ready to go when you are."

I move to my closet—a pile of clothes on the floor that Dizzy stole for me—and bend to dig through it. Behind me, I hear him turn to leave.

"You are so beautiful," he says under his breath before he's gone.

I almost charge after him. I almost beat his chest and scratch his face with my dirtied nails. Anything to make him regret what he said. But I just tighten my hands into fists and I count—one, two, three…ten.

Now my blood is even Steven, and everything's going to be okay. It's just Dizzy. His words are easy enough to forget. I smile like I mean it and lay a hand against the wall. It's solid, real. If this wall is treated right, it'll stand straight as the stars long after I'm dead. This particular wall is white with blotches of gray from God knows what.

But my wall, the one in my future house, will be blue.

I walk back into my bathroom, the one uglied by water stains and years of neglect, and pull on a black skirt and tee, lace-up heels, and green-and-black-striped tights like I'm the Wicked Witch of the West. Then I hook in my piercings—lip, ears, eyebrow, tongue—and swipe on enough eyeliner and shadow to cause anyone's mama to shiver. Finally…hello, darling…I slip on my pink wig.

My armor is complete. But then I catch my reflection in the cracked mirror. My jaw tightens as I take in what Dizzy saw. The face of an angel, isn't that what they always said?

They. They.

Them.

I see the same inventory Dizzy does: large blue eyes, soft skin, blond hair kept hidden beneath a wig. But there's more than meets the proverbial eye here. There's something else that he doesn't know about. That no one knows about. There's a darkness living inside me. A blackness that sleeps in my belly like a coiled snake.

His name is Wilson.

CHAPTER 3

MONSTERS

It takes us twenty minutes of walking through the sticky night to get to Havoc. Dizzy leads me to the side of a white brick building and into an alley that reeks of spoiled food.

"What's going on, creeper?" I ask him. "Why aren't we going in?"

"We are." He glances around, searching for something. "There." Dizzy half jogs down the alley and then approaches a window. "VIP access."

"We're going through the window?" I ask, wondering why I'm surprised.

"It's packed every night. They can pick who they want to let in."

And that isn't us. That's what he's saying. If bouncers are allowed to pick, they won't pick us. I stumble toward Dizzy, sure my feet are bleeding from the long walk in my ridiculous heels, and stop when something catches my eye. There's a man sitting behind the green Dumpster. He's homeless. A toddler would know this.

His face is mangled in a way that makes my stomach lurch. One of his eyes is missing, a single slash across the space where it should be. His other eye is oozing something yellow. And along his neck is an angry rash that's slowly climbing its way onto his cheeks.

He attempts a smile. "Evening."

His voice is gentle, and I try to return the gesture as Dizzy calls my name.

"Have a good time," the man says sincerely, nodding toward Dizzy.

Before I can talk myself out of it, I dig into my pocket and pull out what little cash I have. I hand it to the man.

"Domino." Dizzy's voice holds a warning.

I move away from the man and toward Dizzy. "Let's go."

"Why did you give that guy our money? Dude looks like a monster."

I eye the man over my shoulder. "I've seen monsters before," I say. "They don't look like him."

They look like me.

There's a *tap-tap-tap* from behind me, and I turn to see a guy standing inside the window, waving. He slides the glass up and reaches out an arm. Music explodes into the alley as if it's offering a hand, too.

"Hey, big man," Dizzy says.

"Hurry up," Window Guy responds. "It stinks of herpes in here."

Dizzy gives me a boost. Using the guy's arm as leverage, I pull myself through the window. It's a perfect opening. My body slides through the square and lightly brushes the frame. I bet whoever put this window here figured it was immune to break-ins, but they never counted on Dizzy and me.

I land in a bathroom that's covered in magic marker.

For a so–so time, call Trini!
Aiden + Amber = Pimp Juice
Jessika is a LIAR and SKANK

I love it instantly. Just a few more streaks of color and—

Window Guy calls for my help and together we drag Dizzy upward. Halfway through the window, Dizzy gets stuck. In an instant, he becomes a kicking, swinging madman, his fear of tight places overcoming reason.

"Calm down, Dizzy," I yell as I tug harder. "Just. Calm. Down."

I pull backward with all my might, and he crashes onto the floor. Then he bounds upright as if nothing happened. As if he didn't just have a completely unwarranted panic attack. Dizzy throws me a grin, and a girl with short black hair and red lipstick swings through the door.

"What's going on in here?" she asks. And then, "No. Never mind. Whatever it is, I'm in. That's how I roll." Except when she says roll it's more like roooooooll.

Dizzy slams his hand down on the porcelain sink and points at her. "I like you, girl. I'm going to name you Black Beauty."

The girl gallops and slaps her butt as if she's riding a horse. She is, without a doubt, wildly drunk.

Dizzy takes her arm. "I'm also going to let you buy me a drink."

I'm hurt when he vanishes with the girl. Sometimes I feel like our relationship is a close one, or as close as it can be between two homeless people harboring demons. Other times it feels like I'm standing in place as Dizzy walks away, or perhaps trailing behind as he's a step ahead.

I'm overthinking it. Of course I am. Who do we have if not each other?

Window Guy glances in my direction. He's short and thick and built like a closed fist. He smiles with one side of his mouth. "Don't do anything I wouldn't do," he says. And then he's gone, following after Dizzy and Black Beauty.

I quickly recover from being ditched. After all, I enjoy

being alone, and there's no better way to be alone than in a place like this. After straightening my pink wig, I walk through the bathroom door to where the music thumps even louder. The room is dark and the ceiling low. A dozen globes hang overhead, lighting up different colors. It reminds me of one of those Christmas houses that times the lights to the music, each strand taking its turn to shine.

The club, Havoc, is packed. Bodies pulse against one another and, as I pass them by, I am forgotten. It's a feeling like no other—to be present and invisible at once. I don't appreciate that the people are so close, that they are everywhere. But they don't see me so it's okay.

It doesn't take long for me to lose myself in the music. I dance alone, and in my head it feels like I'm normal, like all these people are my friends and they give me space, but they care about me, too. My head falls back, and I raise my arms into the air. Music injects my veins and rushes through my body. It takes me away, far away.

Until.

Until someone grows nearer than the others. An arm wraps around my waist and hips brush my rear.

"Back up," I yell, because there's no way he'd hear me otherwise.

He doesn't back up.

I spin around and the guy—tall, broad-shouldered, eyes that remind me of a Sunday school boy but I know better—pulls me tighter. He leans his head down to my ear and tells me I look sexy. Do I want to dance?

We're already dancing, and the answer is no. It's always no.

"Let go of me," I holler. "I won't say it again."

The guy grins so that I can see every tooth in his mouth. His cheeks are bright red, and his brow is covered in sweat. He isn't unattractive, but I can smell what's beneath his sweet cologne.

He is ugly on the inside. And his hands are on me.

He spins me around and my stomach clenches.

I'm being pulled backward toward a corner and oh my God no one is seeing what he's doing. Or they see and don't mind. My heart beats so hard it aches, and my breathing comes fast. But I don't care about that. I care about what will happen if he keeps manhandling me.

I fear what I will do.

The guy pushes me against a wall so that my belly touches sheetrock painted black. His hands roam over my body, exploring the curveless shape of my torso. If he only knew. If he only knew he had an explosive in his grasp.

He runs a finger over my lips.

He pulls the clip off the grenade.

He pushes his mouth against the back of my neck.

He relishes the danger of the bomb in his hand.

His palm slides down the flat of my stomach.

Seconds left until detonation. Take cover!

Inside my head, I scream. Outside my head, I scream. I thrash against him but he uses my weakness to his advantage. I am shy of five feet tall, and I am built of bones.

He is built of steak dinners and whole milk.

His hands move lower and lower, and deep inside the recesses of my brain, something sinister yawns awake. No, no, no! Nothing to see here! Go back to sleep!

It's no use.

Wilson stretches tall and smiles to himself.

He looks around like he's amused by what's happening to us.

Hello, Domino, he says. *It's been a while.*

CHAPTER 4

SPRAY PAINT SAVANT

I lift my legs off the ground and the guy holding me falters. His grip loosens, and I drop to the floor in a ball. I shoot under his legs and scramble backward, nearly losing my wig. Springing to my feet, I blast across the dance floor like a bullet from the barrel of a gun.

I spot Dizzy near the bar, raising an amber-colored bottle to his lips. Shoving people from my path as best I can, I get to Dizzy. Only then do I turn back to ensure Manhandler isn't following me.

He isn't.

But I'm still here, Wilson says. *And I can help.*

Shut up, shut up! I press into my temples as I lurch forward.

Dizzy notices my face. "Follow me," he orders.

I nod. I know this plan. We've done it a hundred times before when the going stops going, when a store clerk catches me lifting a Snickers bar, or when a fellow street rat harasses us, or when Wilson threatens to surface. Dizzy may not know about Wilson, but he knows I have demons, and he's always ready when they come crawling.

Fight or flight, that's what they say.

Dizzy and I fly. Always fly.

He tips his chin toward the front door, and we swim

through the crowd like eels. Behind us, Black Beauty calls for Dizzy to come back. But he won't. We don't ever stand too close to each other. We don't ever ask personal questions. But when it's time to go, Dizzy and I are in the same flight formation.

He pushes through the heavy double doors and together we head toward the house. I walk fast and don't mind the ache my high heels cause my feet. I want the pain. I want that and more. Anything that will make me forget about what almost happened with the guy. But more importantly, anything that will make Wilson go back to sleep.

Why would you want me to go to sleep? You need me for this. If you'd just go back, we could really—

Go away!

We're almost home, fifteen minutes of treading across Detroit with my hands sweating, my heart racing, when Dizzy pulls me into yet another alley.

"I want to show you something," he says. "I was gonna save it until I could get a few more colors…"

Dizzy doesn't have to continue the thought. He sees the fear on my face, notes the tension in my shoulders. He knows I need a distraction.

"This way, my lady." He sweeps an arm in front of his body and bows like royalty, but the look in his eyes is one of worry.

I walk past him, my fingers itching to close around something I know will push Wilson down. I get to the end of the alley and see that it turns right and left. The butt of a gray wall spreads in front of me, its arms open in an embrace.

My eyes travel the ground and I spot them, five cans of spray paint.

Graffiti art? Wilson asks. *Listen. Let's go back to the club. I'll handle everything.*

I don't think, I just rush toward the cans, pick one up in my shaking hands, and open it. The pop of the cap raises goose bumps on my arms, and quiets Wilson. I hear him shifting inside me, but it's like he's far away.

Dizzy knows I like to dress up old forgotten walls. It started a few weeks after I left home. Exploring the streets of Detroit one night, I saw a kid—couldn't have been older than fourteen—tagging a wall. He was so enchanting doing it, graceful as a ballerina. I watched him from my place in the dark until he'd finished. Before he left, he pulled off a pair of blue surgical gloves and ditched them, along with two cans of spray paint, in a city trashcan.

I still remember what it felt like to pluck his leftovers from the other rubbish. What it felt like the first time I attempted to copy his movements. I was sloppy, unpracticed.

But it kept Wilson away.

I shake the can of orange, ensuring the sediments don't settle. Then I hold it upright, stiff as a prick, and take a deep breath. I know what I want here. I've been imagining it while I should have been sleeping. After giving one last shake, I start to spray.

I sketch the outline fast and rough, knowing I can worry about details later. Then I switch to a can of red and start on the letters, careful not to spray on top of wet paint. When I'm done with that, I snatch a can of black. As I work on outlining my letters, placing shadow in various places for a 3-D pop, Dizzy adds commentary to relieve the tension.

"The artist works with an intensity unmatched by the best in the industry," he says like he's an announcer at a golf game. "Look at the way she moves. I'm telling you what, Ted, Domino Ray is one to keep your eye on."

Domino, Wilson says. *Don't push me away again.*

I'm mute with concentration and, as the colors blend along the brick wall, Wilson's hold on my mind eases, bleeding down the grooves of my brain like wet paint.

Until, finally, he's gone.

I move on to adding flare and shadow to my piece as Dizzy continues broadcasting my steps to an invisible audience. Lowering my can, I step back and tip my head, trying to spot my mistakes. Streaks of orange and red and black wink in the streetlights, and my mood lifts at the work I've done.

I'm improving, but Dizzy won't hear me say that. He says it's impossible to improve when you're a graffiti savant. I love that he thinks you can be a savant at holding a can of spray paint.

I mutter without turning, "Thank you, Dizzy."

"Been picking them up a little at a time," he offers. And then, with sudden intensity, "Domino."

The way he says my name makes me freeze. I know that tone, and already my heart is tap-dancing with anticipation. He sounds as if he may say something that's deep enough to hold on to. Something *real*. Something that will change whatever it is we are. Do I want that?

Blue and red lights flash across my wall, and a distinct *wurp* breaks our quiet alley.

"Damn it!" Dizzy yells.

I spin around to see Dizzy running down the alley. I race after him.

Fly! Fly!

He finds a door and tries the handle. It's locked. He throws his shoulder into it as the sound of a car door opening and closing reaches us. I drop my spray can and start pushing on the door, too. My skin burns with anxiety, and my head screams that I can't go to jail. I can't be alone with myself without any distractions. If that happens, Wilson will return.

I bang on the door with the flat of my palms and yell for someone to open up. Wrong move. Now I can hear the patter of police officer shoes hitting the ground. I glance in the opposite direction, but there's nowhere to go.

Dizzy stops throwing his weight into the door as the pig rounds the corner. The cop looks like a shar-pei, all wrinkles and blond fuzz. His hand is on his gun, and he's got that stance that says he's ready to follow if we run.

"Put your hands where I can see them." He says this like we're children.

Dizzy starts to raise his hands.

He stops when the door beside us swings open.

"What do you want?" someone inside growls.

Dizzy drops his hands and dashes in. I dash, too, and decide then and there that Dizzy is magic, that he can make himself disappear just like he can a bottle of Yoo-hoo.

Inside the building, we're running blind. I slam into a table and it scrapes across the floor. I hear Dizzy crashing, too. We reach the opposite side of the room as the person who opened the door yells for us to get out.

Dizzy and I find another door at the same time. He reaches for the handle and we explode through it.

The cop is right there.

Right. There.

He grabs Dizzy from behind and twists his arm in a way that makes Dizzy scream. I can't stand the sound of hearing him that way. I can't stand it. I throw myself on the police officer to get his hands off my person.

Dizzy groans from the ground.

How did he get on the ground?

"Run," Dizzy tells me. "Go!"

The cop spins around, and I have to let go before I fall. He looks at me like he's trying to figure out how to get us both. His hand reaches for his gun. I don't think he'll use it. It's just to scare me. But nothing scares me more than losing Dizzy. I grab his arm and bite down. He roars, but doesn't let go of Diz.

"Domino, dammit," Dizzy says. "Leave!"

I'm not going to. I don't think Dizzy would leave me, and so I won't leave him. I'm set to plunge my teeth into the cop's arm again when flashing lights stop me. There's a second cop car pulling to the curb.

The three of us pause. I imagine we all think something different in this moment.

The cop: *Thank God.*

Dizzy: *That's it, then.*

Me: *Run.*

CHAPTER 5

VISIBLE

An hour after Dizzy is taken into custody, I return to my wall. I'm terrified the social worker will show up, but I don't know what else to do. It doesn't seem right to go to the house without him.

I press my back against the brick and slide down. Another pig could drive by any moment and arrest me for the same crime I just ran from. Maybe that's what I want. Maybe I want to go where Dizzy is even if it means being locked up with my own head.

With Wilson.

I don't know how long I sit there before I hear soft footsteps. They aren't the cold, hard ones of police heels. These are gentle, like a cautious hand stretched toward a stray mutt.

My head rises.

A woman is watching me.

"Go away," I say. I know her type. The bored housewife who's looking for purpose, who believes she can find it in rescuing people like me.

"Did you do that?" she asks.

I follow her gaze to my wall. "What if I did?"

"It's beautiful." The woman holds her shoulders and head high. She has blushing cheekbones and pearls that dip into her cleavage. Her eyes are gray-blue and hooded, and her smile is a nice one, close-lipped without assumptions. She looks old Hollywood. Even her voice has a slow, regal tone.

"It takes talent to do that." She states it as a fact. "And courage."

I shake my head and roll my eyes, but the warmth of her words seep in anyway.

"You don't believe me?" she asks.

I don't respond.

She gestures to my wall. "Most people spend their entire lives quietly. Never saying what's on their mind. *Sheep*." She says the last word with a hint of disgust.

The woman takes a step closer. I glance up, knowing I should have scrammed before she ever said a word. But I remain where I am, still as death.

"Not you, though," she continues. "You don't just say what's on your mind. You scream it."

I've never thought of my art that way. I want her to keep talking, and I hate her for that.

She moves toward me until we're only an arm's length away. "I'm going to ask you something directly. I don't like a lot of small talk."

Her eyes seem kind and her skin looks nice and I like the way she talks to me, like I'm a human being, but not one she feels sorry for.

"I run an establishment for girls."

"I don't need charity," I say.

"I don't provide charity." She touches a hand to her blond, graying hair. "I run an establishment for girls with artistic abilities. Abilities like yours. It's a wonderful, almost magical place people go to forget their worries."

I laugh. "Artistic abilities? I spray walls, lady."

The woman smiles, and the folds around her eyes

deepen. I try to decide how old she is. Between mother and grandmother, she's leaning toward the latter.

"It's not just walls you decorate." Her eyes rake over my pink wig and the piercings in my face. "I'm offering you a place in my house. You will work with the other girls. And you'll get a percentage of anything you earn."

"I don't need a job."

Lie.

"What are you even doing out here?" I add. "Shouldn't you be at home drinking herbal tea or something?"

The woman bends down, and I lean away from her. She smells nice, powder instead of perfume. "What's your name?"

I search her face and wonder why she cares. There isn't anything to be afraid of that I can see. But who knows what lurks beneath. I've been surprised before. I don't want to tell her my name, but then I decide it doesn't matter. She won't see me after tonight anyway.

"Domino," I say.

She reaches out to lay a hand on me. I jerk back.

"Domino," she says, her words gentle as a cloud. "I don't make this offer often. I'm asking if you'd like to get off the streets."

"I don't need you," I snarl. I don't know why I'm reacting this way. She's trying to be nice. But I don't trust it. Moments ago, I was running from police, watching my person get hauled away. And before that, running from Manhandler. And Wilson.

Now this.

"I think you do." She tries again to place her hand on me, and this time I let her. Why do I let her?

She turns my hand over and offers my forearm as evidence. There are slashes across my flesh as if someone forgot the hugs in their Xs and Os. I stare down at them and then up at her. She thinks I'm a cutter, I can see it in her face, but she's wrong. Those marks are a souvenir from my past, and I'd be wise to remember that. I yank my arm away and rise to my feet. She clutches my wrist as I'm about to go. It feels like an embrace and I hate myself—I *hate* myself—for relishing her touch.

"Take this." She hands me a neat ten-dollar bill and a cream-colored card. "I could help you. I could give you what you want." Her eyes flick toward my wall, the one with fresh paint cast across its gut.

I shove the money and card into my pocket and walk fast.

"You have to call by tomorrow evening, Domino," she says from behind me. "Or my offer will be retracted."

That's all she says. She doesn't try to follow me. I hate her for approaching me at all, and I hate her for not following. As I near the end of the alley, I see a tired gold sedan with tinted windows. It's hard to see inside, but not so hard that I don't recognize the guy I saw on the street earlier today sitting inside, the one with the big nose and white shirt.

He waves, and I freeze.

Is he with the woman?

Standing outside the car is another guy, one I've never seen before. He's closer to my age and is built like a stone giant. Bronze skin, hair shaved close to the scalp, lips pressed tight like he hasn't spoken in months and doesn't plan to ever again. His eyes are brown with two layers, one he shows the world and a second he hides at great expense. I see both.

He straightens, and when he realizes I'm staring, his gaze drops. He's built like a soldier, a king without a throne, but he doesn't want to be seen.

I'm intrigued. Maybe more than I should be.

I force myself to move and wait until I'm sure I'm out of sight before I withdraw the card. It has a phone number and a name, *Ms. Karina*, written in cursive. I want to throw it away. I have to worry about bailing Dizzy out of jail, not the woman in the alley. But I can't stop thinking about what she said. That she could give me what I want.

Anger boils in my stomach. I'm furious that I wrote that word on the wall. Furious that she knows what I dream of every night.

HOME.

A home of my very own. Four strong walls that will never fall.

It isn't until I'm lying in bed, painfully aware that I'm alone in the house, that I allow myself to search my mind. To look for any trace of Wilson. I breathe a sigh of relief when he doesn't surface.

Clutching my pillow to my chest, I cinch my eyes shut and silence my spinning mind. I'm in that twisty place between awareness and sleep, when my body grows heavy, and Wilson's voice returns, a lullaby on his tongue.

Hush little baby, don't say a word.
Wilson's gonna buy you a mockingbird.
And if that mockingbird don't sing,
Wilson's gonna burn the world to the ground.

CHAPTER 6

MAD MONEY

I wake the next morning with Ms. Karina's card wrinkled in my hand. I worked it between my fingers until the lettering smeared, but I can still read the ten-digit number. It doesn't matter whether or not I want to call, I have to bail Dizzy out of jail and that's that. Even if I spent half the night looking out the window expecting to see the social worker. Even though I'm so exhausted it's hard to think straight.

I stand and stretch on Dizzy's mattress. I slept in his room last night. Sometimes I do that. If he stays out too late or crashes at a girl's place he's sure will one day bear his last name, I sleep in his room. I always move if he returns, and neither one of us ever mentions the shuffling.

Sometimes I wish he'd mention it.

Dizzy and I have never hooked up. I guess I've never hooked up with anyone, really. Not in the no-turning-back, you're-a-woman-now way. Still, it seems like we should talk more, even if we don't share a pillow. But he says talking is overrated.

I dig through my wigs until I find a green one, chin length. And I don't bother with makeup, which is saying something. After grabbing a stale bagel, whose origins are unknown, from the kitchen, I head out. I don't have extra cash for a cab.

Even if I did, I'd never spend it when I've got two perfectly good legs.

Rogers County Jail is four miles away, and I'm praying Dizzy is there. By the time I arrive, I'm dripping sweat from the July heat and feeling good about my decision to forgo foundation. I even left out most of my piercings. Look how civilized that girl is who's come for her friend, is what they'll say.

I've got sixty-four dollars and ninety-one cents heavy in my pocket. That includes the ten the lady gave me. If it isn't enough to bail Dizzy from jail, I don't know what I'll do. We rarely have spare cash, because we've never stolen anything good enough to buy much outside of food and Band-Aids and maybe a pack of Marlboro Reds when Dizzy is anxious.

I can't steal like he can, so I need sixty-four dollars and ninety-one cents to do the trick.

I push through a glass door, and a bell chimes. It seems way too cheerful for such a place, but I take it as a sign that things aren't so bad. How scary could it be? There are happy little bells for crying out loud.

A woman sits behind a glass wall. She isn't dressed in uniform, and the knot in my stomach loosens. I'm terrified someone will recognize me from last night. Maybe they'll throw me in with Dizzy. I thought I might want as much, but now that I'm here I know better. I want no part of this place. I want to go back to the house that isn't ours, and I want Dizzy to come along.

The woman slides the glass wall open and leans forward. "Can I help you?"

There's a row of chairs on my side of the wall. A girl sits in one of them with her legs spread wide. She's picking a scab off her thigh, tongue between her lips in concentration. She doesn't look up when the woman speaks.

"I need to get someone out."

The woman cocks her ear toward me. "What's that?"

I clear my throat and speak up. "My friend got taken here, I think. I need to get him out."

"Name?"

"Dizzy."

The woman raises her eyes. "Last name?"

I shake my head. "I don't know."

She sighs and types something into a computer. "Got picked up last night around midnight?"

"That's right." I push against the counter, forgetting my fear. Dizzy really is here. He's locked up, and people are probably invading his space. He's going to drown in his own head.

"He has a warrant out for shoplifting. Third offense. You want to pay that ticket for him?"

Dizzy got caught shoplifting? Three times?

"Can he get out if I do?"

"Mmm-hmm." She hands me a slip of paper. "Take this across the street to Quick Bonds. It's next to the frozen yogurt place. Your friend will still have to appear in court."

The money in my pocket is worthless. It means nothing without Dizzy walking home next to me. Dizzy telling me how it stunk inside his jail cell. Dizzy suggesting we pawn a video game or two for some chili cheese fries and jalapeno burgers, even though I hate jalapenos.

I glance at the paper she handed me. The total is filled in at the bottom.

Pay to the order of Rogers County Jail: $423.52

My heart ceases beating. My foot stops tapping. I'm going back alone. It would take me months of petty theft to save that kind of money. I'm nowhere near as good as Dizzy, and now that he's gone I'll be the one buying the things I need. It'll be a miracle if I can keep myself fed.

I meet the woman's glare. She's tired of me already. "How long will he stay in there if I can't cover this?"

"Until his court appearance, and then longer if he can't pay the fines."

"He won't be able to pay the fines." My voice rises. I no longer care whose attention I draw. "And he can't stay in there, either. He's claustrophobic. He'll go *crazy*."

The woman glances behind her like she's got a live one.

A second woman appears through a doorway. She's in uniform. She doesn't say or do anything, just leans against the wall and looks at me with authoritative eyes.

I lower my voice. "Listen, maybe I can pay in installments. A little now, the rest later. Will that work?"

The woman points to the sheet in my hand. "Just go to bonds if you come up with the money."

My throat tightens. I'm overreacting. I know I am. But I can't leave Dizzy here, confined. I slam my hand against the glass wall, and the woman in uniform strides over. "He can't take being in this place," I yell. "If you just listened. He can't stay here. He'll die."

The officer grabs onto my arm, but I yank out of her reach. She looks angry at first, but then her face softens. "Look, kid. He's fine. He's just hanging out back there, chatting up the other detainees. Save your money, he'll be out before you know it."

"He's *not* fine," I snarl. "I know Dizzy."

I back toward the door I came through.

Do you need me? Wilson asks.

I startle in the doorway, because I'd hoped he'd vanished as I slept. But I know better.

No, never, I say. *Go away.*

...

After I leave the jail, I do two things.

    I try to swipe a camera from Wal-Mart and fail.

I ask for an application at Electrobuzz.

The application asks for my social security number and says I need two forms of ID. Dizzy was right. Electro-whatever doesn't want a homeless chick greeting their shiny customers. And there's no way I'm giving them a way to probe my background.

Because worse than losing Dizzy, worse than Wilson waking up and staying awake, is someone finding out about my parents.

CHAPTER 7

RING, RING

It's almost midnight, and I'm standing in front of a pay phone. There are few pay phones left in Detroit, but Dizzy taught me how to find them. This one has a booth, but I'm afraid to go inside. Even though I love pay phones with booths. Even though they remind me of old black-and-white movies where the hero sweeps a well-groomed girl off her feet after one fated call.

Even then.

I'm not sure what this woman wants with me, but I've spent ten months with Dizzy, and before that was an expanse of Nothing. I can't think about the Nothing. I can't let myself remember my life before I lived on the streets. Because remembering will make Wilson happy. And when Wilson is happy, bad things happen.

Correction: I appear *when bad things happen. Doesn't mean I cause them. Well, not always.*

I shake my head, and an image comes to me as it has several times today. Dizzy screaming inside his cell. Dizzy rocking back and forth, people touching his hair, his face, his stomach. Greg can't help; his store hardly makes enough to stay in business. And there's no way anyone will hire me without transportation and identification and a second set of shoes. So I go inside the booth and salvage the card from my pocket.

I insert fifty cents into the phone and push the buttons.

My heart is in my ears. I can hear it beating louder than ever before, because it's right there in my ears. I pray the phone will ring and ring, give me time to back out. But someone picks up right away.

"Hello?"

It's her. It's Ms. Karina.

I don't speak.

I hear the sound of a lamp being flipped on. She takes a deep breath. I imagine the oxygen leaving her lungs filling me up. "I'm glad you called."

She must know it's me, but I still don't speak.

"I know it's frightening to leave behind the familiar for the unexpected, but you are so very brave. The girls at my home will adore you, and we'll make sure you always have something warm to eat."

My stomach growls imagining these warm things.

"As I said last night, you'll have to work hard. This isn't charity."

I like that. Does she know I like that? I should say something, but I can't. Even though it's ninety degrees outside, I'm frozen solid.

"You are talented, and it's a shame no one noticed how special you are."

That's not true. My father noticed. I can't think of him, though.

"Come and live with me, okay?" Her voice is honey, and I want to drink it down. "Domino?"

That's what seals the deal. Her saying my name like that. Like she's heard a million names before mine but never spoken one so lovely.

I swallow. "Okay."

"Oh, good. That's wonderful." She sounds truly happy, and I have to stop the twinge of hopefulness working its way inside. "I could pick you up near the same alley we met in yesterday?"

"What about money?" I ask, remembering Dizzy. "How soon would I get paid after I started working?"

Ms. Karina pauses. "That all depends on you. There are plenty of different jobs available. The longer and harder you work, the more you'll earn. We can discuss the details of what will be expected of you when you arrive at my home, but you won't be asked to do anything you're uncomfortable with."

I have more questions for her but decide they're pointless. I'm going. I don't have a better choice if I want to bail Dizzy from jail. She says if I work hard and put in long hours, I'll earn quickly. And that's what I need. Because every day Dizzy is in jail is a day he's suffering.

And a day I'm alone.

I squeeze the phone. "I'll meet you outside the alley."

An hour later, I arrive at my destination. The gold sedan is already parked outside, and there's a second car parked in front of that one. The second car looks like a demon—chrome teeth, chrome claws. It's sleek and black and glistens in the streetlights. The huge, way-too-serious boy I saw last night steps out of the driver side and walks around the car. He doesn't look in my direction.

After he opens the backseat door, Ms. Karina appears. She wears a cautious smile, arms folded over her middle. Even from here, I can tell she's tired. A sliver of guilt courses through me for calling so late.

Somewhere in the distance, a train releases a mournful *choo, choo*. Almost immediately, my shoulders loosen. I love trains. I love their sturdy engines and rusted cars. I love the steadiness at which they chug along and how they seem to be going slow until you get right up close.

But the sound is best. I respect a machine that gives fair warning while it's still far away. When something is that powerful, that dangerous, it's only right that people have time to flee. *Here I come,* it says as it screams down the tracks. *Give me room!*

"Come, dear," Ms. Karina says.

I come.

My footsteps echo off the sidewalk. As I approach the car, the man-boy opens the backseat door on the opposite side. Before I step inside, I glance over the hood at Ms. Karina. "I'll need to go by my place and get my stuff."

"You'll get new stuff once you arrive," a new voice says. I glance at the gold sedan parked behind us and see White Shirt guy. He's swinging keys around his pointer finger like he's in a hurry.

"If she wants her things, she'll get her things," Ms. Karina snaps.

The guy straightens and then shrugs. "I'll follow you, then."

Ms. Karina looks in my direction. "Eric can be quite impatient, but I want you to be comfortable. Shall we?" She motions toward the inside of the vehicle.

Glancing around, I take in Detroit in all its gristly glory—the city of motors and lions and brute determination. I didn't grow up here, but it was home for a little while. A better home than I've had in the past.

I sit down in the car, and the smell of leather hits my nose. The interior is dark and stiff, and the cup holders contain a glass bottle of orange pop and a plastic tub of gumdrops.

Who are all these people? Wilson asks. *I don't trust them.*

You don't trust anyone, I hiss, before remembering that replying only encourages him.

"Where to?" Ms. Karina asks.

It's been so long since I've been in a car. I want to touch everything at once. Instead, I tell her where my place is, and the boy in the front seat kicks the beast into drive. It travels down the road like a ghost, feet off the ground, and by the time we make it to the abandoned house I don't want to get out. But I do anyway, gathering my wigs, body jewelry, and makeup from upstairs. I'm too embarrassed to bring any of my other stuff.

The last thing I do is leave a note for Dizzy. If he somehow escapes (he won't), or talks his way out of jail (he might), then I want him to know how to contact me.

Diz,

I'm going with a woman who says she'll give me a job. I'll earn enough cash to get you out of jail, and then come back. If you get this, and I'm still gone, call Greg. I'll keep in touch with him.

    Domino

I leave the paper on the couch. It's hard to refrain from adding more to the letter. Like how I'm feeling with him gone. Or how I wonder if he'd do the same for me if the tables were turned.

Though I think about it, I don't tell the house good-bye. This isn't my real house, not like the one I'll have when I get enough money. So I just grab a T-shirt of Dizzy's on my way out and return to the idling vehicles.

Giant Boy opens my door again.

"Thank you," I say to his two-layered eyes.

He doesn't respond, but I don't miss the way his muscles tighten. I wonder if, when he works out, he uses these cars as bench-press weights. Black one on the right side of the bar, gold one on the left. Three sets of eight reps and he's all warmed up.

I step inside, and the door softly closes.

My makeup and jewelry is balled in Dizzy's T-shirt, but my wigs spill across my lap in a disheveled rainbow. Ms. Karina eyes them and smiles. She seems pleased that this is what I needed to retrieve.

"Let's go, Cain," she says to the boy.

Cain.

I let that name sit on my tongue like a peppermint. It burns with flavor.

Cain pulls out onto the road and, behind us, the gold sedan follows along. I lie back on the headrest and look up at the stars. It's early morning now, but it'll be hours before the sun rises.

"Where are we going?" I ask quietly.

"Texas," she responds. "West Texas."

My heart leaps at this news. I figured we might travel some, but Texas is a million states away. How will I get back? How will I get the money to Dizzy? And what was Ms. Karina doing here if she lives in Texas? Something about this whole thing unsettled me since the first moment I saw her in the alley, but now I'm almost ready to bolt.

Almost.

I wonder what's in west Texas. I've never been to the state before, but I've heard it's big and flat. And friendly. I think I heard somewhere that people in Texas are friendly. And I know for a fact that it's even farther from my past, which is endlessly enticing.

"Have a jelly." Ms. Karina offers the plastic cup of

gumdrops. I'm not ready to accept any kindness from this woman, but my mouth waters seeing the crystals of sugar clinging to the candies. I choose a green one. When she holds out the soda, I take that, too. Both treats taste like childhood. Like pajamas with feet and cartoons on Sunday and my father's arm around my shoulders.

It tastes incredible.

And it makes me forget my concerns.

For the next twenty hours, we travel. We stop once at a hotel and sleep for a few hours. But mostly I feel as if I'm asleep the entire journey. The realization that I'm moving farther away from Dizzy twists my stomach, and it makes me tired. My eyelids are heavy, and my chest rises and falls slowly. I'm walking through a field of REM-blossoms. I gather them into my arms, all the colors of the world right here at my fingertips. Look how much sleep I'm holding. Enough to feed an army of insomniacs.

Wake up, Domino, Wilson urges.

But it's too hard.

Ms. Karina offers me sandwiches if I get hungry, and always the jellies. One after another, gumdrops in my mouth.

Sometimes when I don't even want them.

At some point Ms. Karina says my name directly, like maybe she's said it more than once. "We're almost there, Domino. Are you excited?"

I push myself up, and the woman offers me a new drink. Water, I think. I gulp it down, ravenous after so much tart orange soda. I put the bottle down in the cup holder and glance outside. The ground is impossibly flat with knobby oak trees peppering the landscape. A heavy sun hangs in a cloudless sky, and I can practically see the heat vibrating across the land. Cain navigates our car down a narrow unpaved road toward a manual fence. When we get close, he hops out to unlatch the thing. It groans as he pushes it open, his triceps flexing against the weight.

Cain runs a hand over his shaved head as he walks back. I try to catch his eye, but he won't have it.

"Did you hear me?"

I turn to look at Ms. Karina.

"I asked you a question. I need you to answer when I ask you questions." Her voice is sharper than I've heard it in the past.

"Sorry," I mutter. "Yes, I'm excited."

Her face relaxes, and she smiles like it's perfectly okay. I like it when she smiles at me that way.

Cain shuts the door and pulls the car through the gate, and the woman waves an arm toward the windshield. "This is it, Domino. Madam Karina's Home for Burgeoning Entertainers. Isn't it spectacular?"

PART II

DOMINO'S RULES
FOR LIVING IN A GROUP HOME

1. Remember why you're there, and how to get out.
2. Keep your head down and your mouth shut.
3. Don't be afraid to make enemies.
4. Make yourself useful.
5. Claim your space.

CHAPTER 8

STATUS

The house is white. Or, it once was white. Now it's more of a dull cream color. It's three stories tall, and there are toad-green shutters framing the windows. A porch stretches from the house in a vulgar underbite, and thin beams support the floor above. A bold blue door is suffocated by a rotting screen one, and I wonder what kind of person paints a door blue when the shutters are clearly green.

My home will be much more traditional. Colors that match and a wreath on the front door. I'll paint the siding using long strokes and put on three coats if that's what it takes. In the backyard there will be a swing lounging in the sun. I'll paint that red and watch as the years of rain erode my work. Inside there will be soft couches bought from real furniture stores and a dining table where I'll eat eggs and toast with raspberry jam.

And in my room. In my room I'll have a queen-sized bed with a lavender comforter. It'll be big enough for me to spread out in, small enough so that no one else can sleep there comfortably with me in it. It'll be a room I sleep in. Dream in. It will be my room.

This isn't the house I hope to own one day, but it's better than the place Dizzy and I shared. There are no boards covering windows or broken glass. This home is built of clapboard, and there are three wide steps like enameled molars leading to the porch. A few bushy plants grow snug against the house, browning in the July heat, and there's a single chaotic rosebush near the right corner.

There isn't a sidewalk. No numbers to mark the address. And the entire area is surrounded by a five-foot-tall fence built of wooden posts and barbed wire. The place feels eighty years out of date, and for some reason that makes it less intimidating. Internet, cell phones, security systems—these are things I've lived without for months. But this place feels historic, like it's been here a while and it's not going anywhere anytime soon, thank you very much.

Two girls sit on a front porch swing. When they see our car grumbling toward the house, they dash inside. The screen door smacks shut behind them. Seconds later, silhouettes appear in windows. Their faces press against the glass, hands cupping their eyes for a better look.

I sink down in the seat.

"Don't worry." Ms. Karina has a compact out. She examines herself in the mirror. "You'll fit right in, if you want to."

The car comes to a stop, and Cain opens the woman's door and then mine. Behind us, Eric parks the gold sedan. There isn't much of a driveway, so the vehicles simply squat in the crunchy yellow grass. It's hot outside. Impossibly, mind-blowingly hot. I'm still dizzy from so many hours spent half asleep, but the heat slams into me like a flyswatter.

"Some girls are groggy after such a long trip," Ms. Karina says. "It's understandable."

"I'm fine," I reply.

"I'm gonna take the bags in and then drop the rental in town." Eric has a bag under each arm and is marching toward the porch. He toes the front door open and heads inside.

Ms. Karina looks at Cain. "Go ahead and get started on breakfast. Let's have eggs, scrambled, and turkey bacon. Not that fatty pork kind. Turkey." She turns back to me. "You like eggs?"

I nod. I'm trying not to appear too eager, but I could eat an entire henhouse of eggs right about now.

Cain reaches for my wigs and Dizzy's shirt in the backseat.

"No!" I bark.

He snaps his hand back and stares at his feet.

"It's okay," Ms. Karina says. "He's only going to put them in your room."

It's not her words that change my mind, though, it's the look on Cain's face. He's large enough to cause an earthquake, and his face is carved from a quarry, but he's incredibly skittish. And I know it didn't help that I snapped at him.

"Here." I shove the wigs and Dizzy's shirt into his arms. "Sorry."

He looks up at me. It's only a second, but it's enough. There's a world of hurt behind those brown eyes. And something else, too. Something I feel reflected inside myself. I can't name it. I'm not even sure what it is.

Cain turns and heads toward the house.

"This is my family home. Built by my grandfather in the 1920s. He worked on it for six years to win his sweetheart's hand. Now that my parents are gone, it belongs to me." Ms. Karina says this last part like she's arguing with someone. She puts her arm behind me. Not in a touching manner. Just, there.

I walk beside her, wishing I still had Dizzy's shirt to cling to, questioning whether I've made a mistake in coming here. As we approach the house, I realize how enormous it is. Monstrous, really. I wonder what kind of work they do out here in the middle of nowhere. Maybe they help keep the place from falling apart. I've heard of old houses needing an entire team to keep them functioning. That could be fun. Though it wouldn't explain what Ms. Karina was doing in Detroit.

From the corner of my eye, I catch sight of an empty garden bed. It's positioned on the side of the house and surrounded by smooth stones and railroad ties. The dirt is cracked and barren, telling me nothing has grown there in some time. Ms. Karina sees me studying the garden, and her shoulders tense.

The porch creaks when we step up, and the screen door is even louder. We spill inside, the blue door gaping open. Ms. Karina closes both behind us, and a second later Eric reopens them to go back for more luggage.

Three girls sit on a couch pushed against the wall. One girl, a slim Asian, beats her heels against the floorboards. The second claps her hands together and then the tops of her thighs. And the third sings a playground song.

Went to the market,
To buy me a gown.
All the boys whistle,
And one fell down.
Sway my hips,
Lips stung by a bee.
Keep on walking,
Till he take a knee.

"Girls, come meet Domino," Ms. Karina says.

The girls stop at once and walk over. I notice all three wear silk carnations on their blouses, pink like the fading day. The Asian girl offers her hand, and I stare at it. A second girl slaps her arm down. "You're always so overeager, Siren. Give her a second to breathe."

A thunderous sound rocks the house, and the girl who

spoke rolls her eyes. "They all want to check you out." She leans in close and makes a crazy face. "Show no fear."

I smile in spite of myself.

Two new girls appear in the front sitting room. It isn't a large area, and already the floral papered walls seem to close in. Both girls have dark skin and light eyes. They could be sisters, but I don't think they are. Over their hearts are white silk daisies.

"The others are still asleep," one of the new girls says to Ms. Karina, eyes never straying from my green wig. "Nice hair."

"It's a wig," I say.

"No shit." The girl grins. Her teeth are immaculately white against full lips. She is beautiful. The other girls are, too. Actually, beautiful isn't the right word. They're more interesting, some with oversized eyes, or sweet freckles, or hair that tickles apple-bottom rears. These aren't the girls you ask, do I know you from somewhere? Because one look says you haven't seen a person exactly like this before.

"She dumb?" the same girl asks Ms. Karina.

Detroit Domino might have put this girl in her place, but that Domino had Dizzy waiting at home and Greg a few blocks away. So I say nothing.

The woman drops into a chair and waves a hand toward her own face, trying to cool down. "Go and turn on the air, Jezebel. And if you say anything else you'll be cleaning toilets for a month."

Jezebel bumps her shoulder into the girl she came down the stairs with. "Come on, let's go bother Cain."

As they leave, another four girls enter through the small space. They wear yellow tulips and don't say much. They just run their gaze over my body and head toward the kitchen. I can already smell the bacon frying, and my stomach clenches in excitement.

Everyone leaves the room, giggling and singing their playground song once again.

Ms. Karina sighs. "Run along and get some breakfast. One of the Carnations will show you to your room after you eat."

I don't know what she means, but I know exactly where the food is coming from, so I follow the smell. There's a short hallway that connects to the front entry room. I'm halfway down it, following the tune of pans and utensils clashing, when someone cuts off my path.

He's round and sweaty and has the shortest neck of any human I've ever seen. Dark hair sticks against his forehead, and when he sees me, he grins.

"Well, what do we have here? A little rabbit." He's breathing hard. It sounds like he was outside running sprints, but I find that doubtful.

I tense, and he approaches.

Huff, puff.

Grin.

"What's your name?" he asks.

"Leave her alone, Mr. Hodge," Ms. Karina calls from the entry room. "She's only just arrived."

The smirk leaves his face. He lifts a finger, thick as a serpent, and jabs it into the middle of my chest. "I hope you aren't lazy. Because if you are, you'll answer to me."

I brush past him, and he chuckles.

"Your first shift's tonight, new girl," he says as I move away.

I spill into the breakfast room, my pulse ringing. Mr. Hodge is someone I want to stay away from. Ten seconds with him. That's all it took to know this.

The kitchen is sunny, and there are multicolored Christmas lights strung across the ceiling. Several of the girls are already seated at two long tables. When one of them sees me, she shoots up from her chair.

"Is this her?" she squeals.

"That's her," someone answers.

The first girl races toward me, and I think she's going to—

She throws her arms around me and hugs me close. "Now I'm not the new girl anymore. You saved me. You saved me! My name's Poppet. You can call me Poppet. I'm a Carnation, obviously, but some of the other girls are Daisies and Tulips. The Lilies and Violets live in the guesthouses out back and they eat later, but we can—"

"Take a breath, Poppet," someone says, shaking her head. "Good God."

There's a bar separating the seating area from the kitchen. Cain rounds the counter and appears with a plate in his hand. He lifts it slightly and then places it down at an empty spot next to Poppet's seat. Cain doesn't look at me. He doesn't look at anyone. He only heads back to the kitchen, a Teflon spatula in one hand, and keeps his mouth shut.

"See?" Poppet says with a bounce. "Even Cain thinks we should be friends. That's like the most interaction he's had with anyone all year."

"Serial killers don't speak much, isn't that right, Cain?" one of the Daisies jeers.

Poppet frowns. "I wasn't being mean. It's good that Cain is communicating." Poppet leans toward the back of the kitchen. "I wasn't being mean, Cain. Honest."

Poppet releases me, and I suck in a breath. She straightens, and her breasts expand. She has the largest boobs of any girl her age, ever. Her hair is blond and curly and she wears glasses. She's small, with fine bones, but her voice is like crystal breaking.

"Come sit with me," she says. "I'll show you around after we eat."

I pull my chair out as Poppet eyes my green wig with obvious interest. I like Poppet. I like her too much. It's something I hate about myself. How easily I fall for people. It's why I have to keep my walls strong. It's for other peoples' safety. If they're too encouraging, I'll cling and never let go. Even after they've left me, even after they've told me I should move on too—I'll still love them.

Because they cared.

The kitchen is straight out of a *County Living* magazine, but in every corner there is something unexpected. A fireman's hat. An origami swan glued to a window. A rabbit mount with a lei around its furry neck.

It looks like Grandma went out of town and the grandkids threw a rager in her house. I inspect my surroundings and shove a bite of cheesy scrambled eggs into my mouth. Before I can help myself, I let out a moan of ecstasy. Everyone stops.

Cain looks up from buttering toast.

I swallow the eggs and wipe my mouth with the back of my hand. "Sorry."

Poppet roars with laughter. "It's good, right? I never had food like this before I came here. Cain can cook a mean meal. He puts cottage cheese and sweet onions in the eggs."

She's about to launch into a detailed explanation of her past culinary experiences when the back door swings open. A girl takes two steps inside and puts a hand on her hip. Her eyes roam over the girls eating, and everyone stops to look at her.

She's wearing red lipstick. It can't be later than 9:00 a.m., and she has on cherry red lipstick. "Get the other girls up. Twelve hours until doors open. We've got a lot to do in that time."

The girl glances in my direction. She takes me in, every

last dollop there is, and grimaces. Her chin rises almost unperceptibly, but I catch the movement.

Know your place.

She's wearing a purple silk violet. Her eyes flick to the flower and back to me. If the flowers somehow separate the girls, I have no doubt where she falls in the rank. I'm not sure why the desire arises, but it rears its ugly head all the same—

I want that flower.

"You heard the girl," Mr. Hodge booms, appearing through the hallway again. He stands over one of the girls, his great belly pressed into her back. He isn't smiling anymore. "Eat up. But not too much. Don't need porkers around here."

"Jesus," a Carnation says loud enough for him to hear.

Mr. Hodge grabs a plate from the kitchen and leaves at the same time Violet Girl does.

"That was Lola," Poppet whispers. "She's Top Girl here, which means she makes the most money. But we do all right, too." She elbows me. "Come on. Hurry and finish. Tonight will be here before you know it, and there's a lot you need to learn before then. Madam Karina will take you through the rules of the house, and I'll tell you the stuff you *really* need to know." She elbows me in the ribs and winks.

Though I'm itching to learn what I'll be doing here—and wondering about that word, *Madam,* now that both Ms. Karina and Poppet have used it—what I'm most concerned with is this Top Girl, Lola, and exactly how much she earns. Bailing Dizzy from jail will cost a lot. Does she make that much? What about enough for a house? Could that kind of opportunity exist here? A chance to afford a safe, permanent place in this world?

Hopefulness blooms in my chest until Wilson grimaces.

It's almost all girls that work here. And it's in the middle of nowhere. You know what this place is.

If you're not going to leave, be quiet, I reply. *You don't know anything.*

Out of all the places we could end up, Domino, this is the absolute worst. I remember the things we did, even if you don't. And we shouldn't be here. We should be anywhere else but here.

Maybe he's right. But I can't leave.

Or maybe it's that I don't want to.

CHAPTER 9

AN INNOCENT OFFER

P oppet shows me to my shared room on the first floor, but the girls already living there aren't looking for someone to take up more of their limited space. So Poppet drags me to her room just down the hall. She bunks with two others for a total of three to the small space. One of the girls, a Latina with hair so black it appears blue, stands up from a twin bed.

"This is Domino," Poppet says. "And I was wondering if maybe she could stay with us. The room she's supposed to stay in is, um, full."

"Where was she s'posed to stay?" the girl with the bluish-black hair asks.

Poppet nods toward the hall. "In Raquel's room."

The girl shakes her head and purses her lips. "I'm so over that girl's mess. I'm in charge now. I swear on my mama's grave if she don't learn her place…"

Her words trail off as she storms from the room and marches down the hall.

Poppet's eyes grow large. Or, as large as they can. Though Poppet wears glasses that magnify, her eyes are so small they're almost nonexistent.

The other girl—petite with freckles across every inch of her skin—walks over. "My name's Michelle, but everyone calls me Candy. You can stay with us, I guess, but you'll have to sleep on the floor. If it were me, though, I'd go back in there and stand my ground. Don't be a baby, or it'll get worse."

I look at the doorway and consider what she said. She might be right. I should stick up for myself. The girls will respect me more if I'm not a pushover, and I've never been one to back down from confrontation. But that was when I had Dizzy to back me up. Without him, I can't help thinking it might be best to let them show their dominance. They'll accept me over time if I'm not a threat.

"I'll sleep on the floor," I announce. "I don't mind."

The Latina girl barrels into the room. "Such bull crap. You take my old bed. I'll be sleeping in Raquel's room now."

Poppet and Candy startle at her announcement, but the girl only smirks as she loads her things into a tattered bag. "Teach that diva to open her fat mouth," she mutters. Within seconds, the girl is pounding down the hallway again. Even from here, I can make out the shrill sound of girls arguing.

Poppet starts to say something, but I'm already leaving the room. I catch up with the girl and tap her on the back. She swings around. "What?"

"Thank you for that," I say.

She runs her eyes over my body. "This wasn't a favor."

"It felt like one." I shove my hands in my jean pockets. "And I'll remember it."

The girl laughs like that's hysterical and walks away. Once she enters Raquel's room, the arguing grows louder and I head back to Poppet and Candy. They've cleared the sheets off the girl's bed and bundled them into a tight ball. Candy shoves them in my arms. "Put these in the hallway." She tops the sheets with a pillow and pats the bundle like one would the back of a van.

"Where do I get new ones?" I ask, assuming putting them in the hall means they'll get laundered. Before either girl can respond, Ms. Karina appears in the doorway.

"Aren't you supposed to be in Raquel's room?" she asks.

My cheeks flush, and Poppet opens her mouth to respond. I step in front of her, refusing to let anyone else rescue me today. "I'd prefer to stay in this room."

Ms. Karina has changed into a green pencil skirt and black elbow-length blouse. Her knees are of the knobby sort, jutting away from her legs like they're eager to strike out on their own. The woman shifts her weight to one side and crosses her arms. A smile lifts her mouth, and I notice one of her lower teeth is brighter than the rest. She sweeps her gaze over the room. "Candy, Poppet, get with Mercy about your chores."

The two girls nod, their backs rigid with respect.

Ms. Karina curls her fingers toward herself, motioning me forward. "Come with me, Domino. Let's chat now before my day begins."

I follow her down the hall and hear the girl who snubbed me earlier, Raquel, yelling. I note the name Ms. Karina used, Mercy, and assume she's the girl who helped me out. I make a point to remember her name. I make another point to repay the favor. If there's one thing my waste-of-a-father taught me, it's to never leave a debt unpaid.

The house speaks in tongues as we make our way down the hall and up two flights of stairs to the third floor. It's like it resents being crossed so thoughtlessly. Even the walls groan from the shifting weight, begging for holy water in its pipes and an exorcism in the foyer.

The home's quirks continue across every inch of the space, mimicking the kitchen. A stuffed monkey vulgarly straddles the staircase banister, a plastic pumpkin sits upon a small stand, wicked grin glowing, and the ceiling inside a room we pass is crisscrossed with purple crepe paper. Twice we step over a stack of things—the first time books, the second, records—and when we stop outside a closed door, I notice violets, one day wilted, strewn across the floor.

"We'll speak in my room." Ms. Karina opens the door and ushers me inside, her palm flat upon my back. My skin tingles beneath her touch as if she's burning my flesh. I like her hand there, and I don't. Even before I landed on the streets of Detroit, physical contact was two-sided. On one hand, it's a promise of safety and kindness. On the other, it's a lie. A false hope. Something to believe in that can be hijacked all too easily.

I'd vowed never to let anyone touch me again.

Until now, apparently.

Taking in the ornate gold mirrors and rich red paint, I find myself feeling grossly inferior. The furniture is such a deep chocolate that I can taste the color sliding down my throat. And the wallpaper isn't like the kind downstairs. This sort reflects the shadows our bodies make as we move across the space, while in other areas it appears velvet to the touch. She points to a set of wingback chairs, black with gold stitching. When I sit, my body sighs with pleasure. It solidifies my longing to one day decorate my own room with, on second thought, a heavy hand.

"Do you like the house?" Ms. Karina sits across from me, crossing one long leg over the other. The skin is loose on her calves, but appears soft to the touch.

I sit up straighter. "I do. It's nice."

Ms. Karina cocks her head like she's turning that word over in her mind, nice. In the end, she grimaces, like she's found it lacking. My muscles clench like I've failed an unimportant test, but a test all the same.

"This place seems almost magical, like you said," I try again. "And this room is fit for a movie star."

Ms. Karina leans forward at my praise, and a blush rises in her cheeks like summer tomatoes ripe for plucking. "Why, what a beautiful thing to say. Though you must be exaggerating." She glances around the room, trying to see her surroundings through my eyes. I tuck a leg beneath me and lean forward, too.

"No, really. It's insane," I go on. "Those drapes look like they cost a fortune, and that vanity…?"

Ms. Karina stays quiet, silently urging me to continue.

"I mean, I can totally see an actress brushing her hair there before she goes onstage. And all the throw pillows, the bedposts, the mirrors—I can tell you're classy."

Ms. Karina laughs. She covers her stomach with one hand and her mouth with the other, and she laughs. The sound rushes inside me like I'm a stray cat who's happened upon a birdbath. I lap up the noise thirstily and long for more.

"I like you, Domino. You feel familiar." She flinches like maybe she's said too much. "But let's get to it, shall we?"

Some of the nerves I entered the room with have gone. Now I'm excited to hear what she has to say.

"Each group of girls has a Point. That's who you'll speak with each morning to get your assignment. Assignments range from cleaning the floors to doing the wash to room searches. It can be anything the Point Girl feels needs to be done, really. If you progress to a new group of girls, there will be different chores. The Carnation Point is Mercy. It used to be Raquel, but she wasn't up to the job."

I think about how quick Mercy was to attack Raquel for dismissing me from their room. Maybe she was telling the truth when she said she wasn't doing me a favor. Maybe she was simply cementing her leadership among the girls.

"As you've probably noticed, each girl wears a flower. Carnations live on the first floor, the Daisies on the second, and Tulips on the third. Behind the main house are two guesthouses. The one to the left is reserved for the Lilies, and the one to the right is for the Violets. You will not, under any circumstance, go into those houses."

Ms. Karina shakes her head, and I find myself shaking my own along with her.

"It's a sign of respect, Domino. Those girls worked very hard to have a place of their own, and it would be rude to violate their privacy unless you were invited inside. Do you understand?"

"I understand."

"Of course you do." She walks to her window and gazes out. "I saw you noticing the garden outside. My mother loved it very much. I think maybe she loved it more than she did me." Ms. Karina laughs, but there's no humor behind it. "She used to line these flowers up in neat rows according to which pleased her best, and every year they bloomed she would act as if she performed a miracle."

She checks to see if I'm listening, seemingly wary to continue. When she notes how I'm hanging on every word, she returns her gaze to the garden. "Mother only ever cut the flowers on our birthdays. She would choose her favorite for my sister. Not me, though." She flicks her fingers toward the garden as if she's remembering the blossoms greedily soaking up the sun. "I got the flowers from the first row. Always the first row. Always the ones she didn't care about."

I swallow, unsure of what to say.

"Do you know why I'm telling you this?" she asks.

I shake my head though she isn't looking at me.

"All my flowers are important to me, Domino. This house, it's my garden now. I make it grow, and I love my blooms the same." Now she does look at me. "But it's not always about what I find beautiful. Other people come to see my flowers, too."

Someone knocks on the door, and she calls for them to enter. Cain steps inside holding freshly ironed sheets and a plush pillow. The scent of breakfast clings to his body—turkey bacon and butter melting on the griddle. His gaze stays locked on the linens.

"Would you like new bedding, Domino?" Ms. Karina asks.

There's a part of me that wants to say no. I don't want to take anything from this woman who says she likes me and whose laugh shoots through my bloodstream and whose stories about flowers I don't understand. But if Dizzy were here he'd say to never turn down an offer like this. *If it's free, it's free. Don't be too proud, Domino.*

But pride was never my problem, and I think Dizzy knew that. My problem is I can't handle being crushed when people aren't what they pretend to be. More than that, Wilson can't handle it.

"Cain, come over here," Ms. Karina says.

He does as she asks.

And then he's just there, head bowed, arms full of the sheets I won't take. I'm a jerk for allowing him to stand there like a statue. Every inch of his body is rigid with the desire to flee the room. So I stand up and close the distance between us.

The sheets are white like Dizzy's shoelaces. White with the purity of a second chance.

I take them.

As they are transferred from the boy's arms to mine, his head raises. Our eyes meet for the second time today. He appears guilty, and angry. Behind that dark gaze brews fire and brimstone. It's like he's asking me to read a silent thought, but I'm focused on the hard muscles along his clenched jaw.

Cain releases the smallest of sighs as he turns and exits the room. Ms. Karina asks me to sit back down. I do, awkwardly, with the sheets spilling over my arms. I shuffle my new temporary belongings, and my finger finds an unexpected hole in the chair's ornate armrest. It's large enough to dig my nail into.

The woman stares at the sheets, a smile playing on her lips. She seems absolutely delighted that I took them.

CHAPTER 10

ASSIGNMENTS

Ms. Karina answers very few of my questions, and instead shuffles me back down the stairs when Mr. Hodge says she has a phone call.

"Anything you want to ask me, you can ask them," she says outside my new room. Then she turns and clicks down the hallway.

Candy inspects my sheets and purses her lips. Poppet, however, offers to help put them on. "After this we'll go see Mercy."

I pull the sheet across the blue and white pinstriped mattress and glance around. Poppet and Candy's room is a blinding shade of white with posters of actors and musicians strewn across the walls. Above Poppet's bed is Taylor Swift in a sequined dress, one hand clutching a microphone, the other waving toward the crowd. And over Candy's bed is Channing Tatum, a heart drawn over his chest with Michelle written in the center. Many of the posters curl at the corners, in desperate need of fresh tape.

The only other furniture besides our beds is a small vanity and a single dresser. Poppet notices me eyeing the dresser and says. "You'll get the bottom drawer. Cain already put your things in."

I leave the bed and open the drawer. When I see my wigs, makeup, jewelry, and most importantly, Dizzy's shirt, I smile with relief. I'd almost forgotten about my belongings. But now they wink up at me, reminding me why I'm here.

Candy leaves the room and, when Poppet's back is turned, I slip the sixty-four dollars and change from my pocket—minus the fifty cents it took to call Ms. Karina—into the back of the dresser. Once I'm satisfied that it's hidden, I close my drawer and turn to Poppet. "Can I ask you a question?"

She glows. "Shoot."

"How do we get paid? I mean, what kinds of jobs are available? And when do we get the money?"

The girl pulls her blond hair into a half pony and then removes her nightshirt. Pink nipples the size of silver dollars stand at attention. I blush until she shrugs on a white tank and black Victoria's Secret sweat shorts. "Don't worry, I'll walk you through that tonight. Or maybe Madam Karina will." She claps her hands with excitement. "You're going to love it here, Domino. It's so much fun. Well, the days aren't that fun, but the nights make up for it. Right now, though, we have to get our assignments or we'll be docked. Oh, and you can't wear that. Borrow something of mine until you can get things of your own."

This girl's all right, Wilson decides. *I approve.*

Poppet finally pauses in talking, opens the middle dresser drawer, and pulls out a plain black V-neck.

"Why do you keep calling Ms. Karina *Madam*?" I ask as she hands me a shirt. "And do we get paid for these assignments?"

She laughs her broken glass laugh, and I decide broken glass laughs aren't so bad. "It's just a term of endearment. All the girls use it. And, no, we do our jobs to keep things nice around here."

When I try to hand the shirt back, insisting I have one,

she shoves it into my chest. "I saw what Cain brought in. No offense, but you need something clean. Mr. Hodge will get upset if he sees you out of sorts." She waves toward the stained gray shirt I came here in. It's the best one I've got. The one I wore to try and spring Dizzy from jail. "Come on, we gotta go."

I tear the thing off and stand exposed in my pale yellow bra, the one with wiring that digs into the underside of my left breast, and replace it with Poppet's shirt. It's loose. Not because Poppet is bigger than me, though she is—everyone is bigger than me—but because her chest is three sizes larger than mine. It reminds me of that movie, *How the Grinch Stole Christmas*.

And what happened then? Well, in Whoville they say, her small breasts grew three sizes that day!

I reopen my bottom drawer and pull off my green wig. Grab my orange one instead. Poppet's mouth opens in a circle of black when she sees my real hair matted to my head.

"Your natural color is pretty." Poppet twists side to side like she's three instead of sixteen, or however old she is.

I ignore the comment and bounce on the balls of my feet like I'm ready to go. She takes my cue, and we find the other girls. Mercy, our Point, yells for us to move our rears when she sees us. We jog over as I count the girls. There are ten of us, nine wearing Carnations, one with an orange wig and soft black V-neck that makes me feel like I'm being hugged.

Mercy calls out assignments, which are more or less chores, to the others before looking at Poppet and me. "You two. You're on bathrooms. Next time don't be late or you'll be sleeping outside." She pushes black bangs out of her eyes. There's a scar on her forehead. "New girl, if you finish early you'll help the others with their assignments. And if I see your freak ass slacking for one second I'll deduct a week's pay."

All eyes turn to me, and heat creeps up my neck. "I won't slack."

Mercy sighs. "My God, don't even open your mouth. Just shut up and work. That's it."

I nod.

"Don't nod at me, either."

My teeth snap together as a couple of girls laugh. Mercy is singling me out to prove a point. I wonder how she got to be the Carnations' Point Girl.

And whether someone else wouldn't be a better one.

We would be better, Wilson whispers.

I clean beside Poppet for hours and then help scrub the floors. Every few minutes Mercy barks at me to work harder, leaving muddied footprints in her wake. The girls glare at me with disdain as if it's my fault Mercy is targeting me.

We're almost finished with the floors when Raquel glides over. She has short brunette hair and a long neck. Raquel smirks at me before kicking over the bucket of dirty water. It sloshes over my knees, soaking my jeans. I jump to my feet, fists curled, breathing hard through flared nostrils.

"You'd better keep Mercy off my back, new girl." Raquel turns to leave.

I imagine grabbing her by the hair and taking her to the ground. But I shake the thought from my head. This is exactly what Wilson would want, and I have to keep him quiet at all costs. So I bite my lip, do my internal counting, and crouch down to sponge the water away.

Mercy walks by and sees the mess.

"Jesus, Domino. You are worthless."

Wilson lifts his head, and I grit my teeth.

CHAPTER 11

NIGHT FALLS

When night comes knocking, chaos erupts. Girls run between one another's rooms, stealing lipstick and dresses and nail polish. Someone tests her vocal chords like she'll be singing all night, and somewhere in the house, a piano plays. The pitter-pat of bare feet morphs into the firm click of heels, and Poppet orders me to sit at the vanity.

I've barely digested my dinner—chicken-stuffed ravioli in a bittersweet red sauce—and showered the day's work off my body, and now Poppet is attempting to apply foundation to my face.

I gently push her hand away. "We work tonight, right? For money?"

Poppet dives toward my face again, this time with blush. "Yes, we work tonight. But you won't make squat if you don't let me do your makeup."

I dodge her deft hand a second time and rush toward my drawer. As we scrubbed bathroom floors, Poppet explained what I'm to do tonight. Customers, men and women alike, will come to be entertained. I figured I might be doing something along those lines since the place is called Madam Karina's Home for Burgeoning Entertainers, but before now, I was waiting for the actual job choices Ms. Karina—er, Madam

Karina—mentioned before we left Detroit.

Though it appears there's only *one* position I'll hold here, Poppet assured me there isn't any funny business. "Customers keep their hands to themselves," she said. "They only want to have fun and watch us perform. And to get rip-roaring drunk, of course."

I'll say it once more for the people in the back, Wilson says. *We need to get out of here.*

I ignore him. The job is fine by me. I need the money, and I need Dizzy. Though I'll admit that already I question how long I can live with these girls and their bullying. Every time one of them upsets me, Wilson sits up straighter. If he's going to stick around, at the very least I want him lying down.

Now where's the fun in that?

I grab my makeup and jewelry and return to the vanity. I smear on black shadow and purple mascara and ghostly powder. Then I finger-brush my orange wig, and Poppet lends me a dress. At first she encourages me to borrow a pink one, but I insist on the black.

When I'm done, Poppet appraises my work, sucking on her bottom lip. "All the girls have a shtick. At first I wasn't sure about all this"—she waves toward my piercings and heavy makeup—"but hey, maybe this is your look. It could work."

"That's good, because I'm not changing a thing."

Poppet grins. "Accept yourself and all that, right?"

"Right." I study Poppet's plunging neckline and blond locks made frizzier with hair spray. She has on a fluffy blue dress and looks kick-you-in-the-face sexy. Her eyebrows are thick and three shades darker than her dye job, but she's still beautiful. I tell her so, and she blushes.

"You really do, Poppet," I add. "And you've been nice to me. What can I do to repay the favor?"

Her face scrunches up. "Repay the favor? What do you

mean? We're friends. This is what friends do." Almost instantly, she withdraws into herself. "I didn't mean it like that. I know we're not actually friends. But it seems like we could be."

I reach out to touch her arm. Stop myself when I remember I don't do such things. "I think it's okay if you call me friend. I mean, I'm okay with it if you are."

Now I'm the one waiting for her to laugh. To point a finger in my face and say she was joking and that she'd rather hang herself than make an alliance with the likes of me. But she doesn't. Instead, she throws herself around me. I stiffen and keep my arms pressed tight against my sides as she hugs me. It feels wrong. It feels wrong.

It feels amazing.

"Come on, it's nearly time. We can't be late." She waves me along, and we make our way to the back left of the house. I've never been to this part before. All the rooms are on the right, and the kitchen is left front. We're behind the stairs, I think. There's a doorway with a curtain. Poppet pulls it back, and we step inside.

Nine girls race across the space. One runs to the corner and plugs something in. Instantly, a thousand multicolored Christmas lights flip on. Music starts playing. Big band stuff— trumpets and tubas and soulful crooning. A train cruises around a track that hugs the room's perimeter near the ceiling, releasing a beautiful *choo-choo* every few minutes. On the left side of the room is a bar, and behind it stands Cain, wiping down the counter.

There are beanbag chairs in the corner. A piano near one wall. A microphone. A violin on a stand. And small stations throughout the room with a chair or two and a hint of privacy. The smaller spaces are separated by bead curtains, all illuminated by the Christmas lights. I take everything in, realize I'll be spending an entire evening down here.

And I fall in love.

As the girls scramble across the room, fluffing pillows and fluffing themselves and powering up a retro jukebox, Poppet grabs my arm. More touching. I don't pull away.

"Follow me," she says. "I forgot to show you something."

Right outside the curtained doorway is a metal box mounted to the wall. The contraption has twelve sections like postal boxes, with a horizontal slit cut into each smaller square. There's a number on each one.

Poppet points to a box number. "That one is mine." She points to another one. Number ten. "I think this one is yours. Since you replaced…"

My head whips in her direction. "I replaced someone?"

"Never mind about that." Poppet avoids eye contact. "What you need to worry about is getting the bronze coins customers pick up at the front. Each person receives one coin, and at the end of the night they slip the coin into the box of the girl they liked best. The more coins you get, the more money you'll make."

My pulse races. I figured we'd all be paid the same, and now I learn I basically have to compete with the other girls? No wonder everyone hates me. I'm competition. *Replacement* competition, by the sound of it. I think about the girl I came in after. About where she went and why.

Poppet must see how nervous I am because she adds, "Remember, this place is somewhere customers go to forget their troubles. Just pretend you're in a dreamworld, and they'll dream along with you. There's no room for worry inside Madam Karina's Home for Burgeoning Entertainers." She finishes her speech with a flirtatious smile.

I hear Mercy yelling, and Poppet giggles. "Come on!"

I shuffle after her, lifting the black dress so I don't trip on the fabric. A heartbeat after we enter the room, Madam

Karina bustles in, black marker in hand. She inspects the space and then barks a few orders at Mercy. Then she grabs my arm and tugs me toward her.

Before she says anything, she writes a big black 10 on the back of both my hands. "I'm sorry we didn't get to spend more time together, Domino, but the key tonight is to ensure the customers are entertained. Remember your gifts, and keep a smile on your face." She looks around, licks her lips nervously. "You make them happy, understand? Don't disappoint me." Her grip on my arm starts to hurt, and I'm suddenly remembering how much I hate physical contact. She glances down at where she's holding me and shakes her head. "Sorry. I'm sorry. You'll be great, Domino. Just have fun, okay?"

Uncertainty flickers inside my chest, but I push it down where it belongs. "I'll make you proud."

Madam Karina releases me and stands tall. She's got eight inches on me, easy, but right now she seems tall enough to cast a shadow on the moon. Her face opens, and her head falls to one side. "Well, that was the perfect thing to say. I didn't mean to… I apologize."

"It's okay." I grin to reassure her I'm all right. Because I *am* all right. And I'd do just about anything to keep her smiling at me like that. Her smile makes me feel peaceful. No, that's not the right word. Her smile is soothing? Warm?

Healing.

That's it.

She cups my cheek in her hand and looks at me like my mother once did, and my heart swells like a balloon begging for a needle. Wilson wraps himself around the two red, pulsing halves instinctually and holds them in place. He doesn't want to let her in. And I don't want to fight him.

So I move away from Madam Karina and join the other girls, who have formed a line. The madam marks their hands and claps twice above her head like she's about to perform a dance. Then she swooshes out.

I look at Candy, who's a couple of girls down. She has two perfect circles of blush on her cheeks, false lashes, and white tights. She looks like a living doll. When she sees me inspecting her, she rolls her eyes and jams a *hush* finger against her lips. Totally unwarranted since I wasn't going to say anything.

Behind us, the music picks up. Drums now, beating wildly. A man singing about love under the Brooklyn Bridge.

And then the curtain pulls back.

CHAPTER 12

CUSTOMERS

Customers stream into the room. Some bashful. Some pushing their way forward. I count seventeen in all. Too many for this tight space. Musky cologne and scented lotions assault my nose as the guests make their way to the bar, talking over themselves. There is one female to every four men. And the ages range from a pair of early teen boys to a woman in her sixties.

The Carnations descend upon them like flies on crap, each one donning her pink silk flower proudly. I stand staring at them idiotically, curious as to what the other girls—the ones ranked higher than the Carnations—are doing tonight, and why I don't even have the lowest ranked flower to wear.

Then I recall Dizzy in detail. Dizzy bringing me wild-rice soup when I had the flu. Insisting on feeding it to me bite by bite so he could put a spoonful into his own mouth before giving me a turn. I must have told him a dozen times that he was going to catch what I had. He didn't care. *Soup is for sharing, Domino Ray. And I'll catch what you have any ol' day.*

Later that night he left to try his luck with a new girl. Or maybe it was a boy. Sometimes I didn't know with Diz. A part of me wished he'd stayed home, or that he remembered I was allergic to the mushrooms in his beloved wild-rice soup. But that's not the point. The point is, Dizzy cares.

I straighten my wig and approach the bustling at the bar. Cain is more alive than I've seen him. He's practically grinning as the women dote on his strong forearms and that precious dimple in his cheek. The patrons pay Cain with silver coins, and I spot a teenage girl with a fistful of them. Included in her palm is a bronze coin. The one she'll deposit in the box outside.

No one approaches the teen girl. They're too busy flirting with men in suits and the older women with heavy handbags. When the girl turns and faces me, I realize why. She's missing the bottom half of her right ear. In its place is a flat stretch of hairless skin. I approach her immediately. Not because she's an easy target, but because I can't stand the thought of no else doing it. If she came here to be entertained, it's probably because she's lonely. And that's a feeling I know well enough.

"Hey, my name's Domino. What's yours?" I sound like I'm in kindergarten.

The girl smiles and turns the right side of her face away so that I see only her left. "I'm Katy."

I swallow, unsure of myself. "You don't have to do that, you know."

Her brows pull together in a question.

"You don't have to turn your face away like that."

Katy curls her fingers around her thumbs and glances down.

I'm drowning here. I haven't had much social interaction outside of Greg and Dizzy in the past year, and I have no idea how to amuse this girl. "I've never played the piano before, but maybe we could try it together?"

She points to her scar. "I don't have much of an ear for music."

I cover my gut and laugh once, hard. "Oh, my God. That was really funny." While the other girls drape themselves over the people at the bar, slowly inviting them to certain corners of the room, I motion Katy toward the piano. I'm three steps away when a girl dives in front of me.

"What do you think you're doing?" she snarls.

Heat rushes to my cheeks. "I was going to play the piano with one of our customers."

The girl looks to the ceiling and groans like I'm a complete moron. She has a mustache she's trying to hide under a layer of powder. "You touch only the things you've helped pay for." She flicks her hand. "So go away, little dog. Go sniff somewhere else."

I turn to Katy, trying to maintain a smile. "Umm, maybe we could just talk?"

"That girl reminds me of my sister." Katy watches the girl stride away with visible repulsion.

"Your sister sounds like a swell person."

This time it's Katy who laughs.

I scan the room, looking for a place that we might talk. When I don't find an available spot, I nod toward the bar. It's mostly empty now so we can grab two stools.

For two hours, Katy and I chat about her school and her dad and her affinity for buttermilk biscuits with honey. We talk about anything she wants, really. And it feels nice. I certainly don't want to talk about myself, so this arrangement works perfectly. But after a while I notice Katy's eyes veering to the other girls. The ones offering guitar solos and massages and tango dance lessons. If I don't do something, I'm going to lose her interest. And her bronze coin. But what can I do? I don't have access to any of the instruments the girls bought, and even if I did I wouldn't know how to play them well enough. Then I remember what Madam Karina said about using my gifts.

"Cain, do you have a pen I can borrow?"

Back when I still attended school, I was pretty good with a pencil in my hand. And I can't help wondering how much better I'd be after learning graffiti art. It's different, sure, but it's still translating a picture from my head onto a canvas.

Cain looks at me for a long moment, and then gazes at the curtained door. He seems afraid to lend me a pen, but that's crazy, right? After hesitating, he meanders over and drops napkins and a pen a couple of feet down. I have to stretch to get them.

"He's cute," Katy says.

"He doesn't really talk."

Katy grins mischievously. "I don't need him to talk."

I give her a scolding look like we've been friends for years. She giggles into her soda, the one Cain brought her after she laid a silver coin on the sticky bar. Holding the pen in my right hand, I study the napkin. I have no idea how I can compete with the entertainment behind me, but I'll give it a shot.

I look once at Katy, decide what it is she wants most in this world. Then I draw. My tongue slides between my lips as I concentrate, and I keep my head down, working. She talks as I work, and I prod her with more questions. My drawing is sloppy, and my hand aches to replace that cold lifeless pen with a can of spray paint. I'd paint the entire room with her name if I could. Make people notice her in a good way.

I'm halfway through the drawing when the singing stops. For the last two hours, three girls have shared the microphone, one after another. I assume they shared the expense and that's why they all got a turn. Now someone new steps up. A fresh, upbeat song starts on the jukebox, and I turn to see Poppet tapping her fist against her thigh in time to the beat. The lyrics begin, and Poppet starts singing an Adele song.

Katy cringes beside me, probably without realizing it, and the other girls start laughing. At first, their jeering is quiet.

Then it grows louder, until you can hardly hear Poppet's voice over the taunting.

"Shut up," a girl coughs under her breath.

"Tone deaf," another one says, louder.

I feel myself moving toward Poppet before I even realize what I'm doing. I don't know this song, but I won't let Poppet stand up there alone a second longer.

When she sees me coming, she raises her hands like I'm going to shove her off the mic. Her reaction tells me someone has probably done this to her in the past. I motion for her to stay put and join her in singing the ridiculous song, figuring out the words as I go. Mostly though, I just stand beside her. I can't sing to save my life. I guess Poppet can't either. But she lent me a black shirt and this dress I'm wearing, and she doesn't deserve this kind of treatment.

In the movies, when something like this happens, the taunting eventually turns into encouraging cheers. In this scenario, it gets worse. Girls yell for her to stop the insanity, and a singer from earlier actually tries to sing over us. The guests seem to think it's part of an act, and so they laugh, too. We're almost to the end of the song when someone starts in on me.

"The freak is worse than Poppet," a voice calls from the back. "Look at that lip ring. Who's her father, Charles Manson?

It's the last comment that stuns me. I figured if there were one off-limits topic in this place, it'd be parents. After all, how many of us would be here entertaining customers for bronze coins if we had Mommy and Daddy at home to steer us right?

Another girl joins the fun. "Hey, freak, was your mother attracted to murderers?"

I stumble two steps back. Katy is talking with another girl, and I'm standing in front of everyone, shaking, trying to control the voice in my head that tells me to shut these witches up. To burn them at the stake.

To burn them in their beds.

I'll find the matches! Wilson cheers.

"I have to go," I tell Poppet. I run toward the curtained door, but Mercy blocks my path.

"Get your butt back in there. Now!"

I shove past her and race outside. Once I'm standing in the front yard, surrounded by haphazardly parked vehicles, I gasp for air.

Lean over.

Hands on knees.

Breathe.

I've spent almost a year on the streets, and Dizzy isn't the sort to get too close. But the girls here press in until my brain swells. I'm not used to this. Even at school, before my mother homeschooled me, I never had more than a couple of friends. And now I'm supposed to stand in a room overflowing with bodies and sweaty upper lips and smile when they tease me about my parents.

I can't.

That's not true. I can. Just not right this second.

They don't know anything about my parents. They don't know what my father did. Or what my mother did in retaliation. I realize this, but it still stings. Because what they said back there about my mom loving murderers? It felt like they undressed me. Like I was nude before an audience.

They got close to the truth, didn't they? Wilson says. *But not quite.*

I circle the house and discover an uncovered porch. It's a slab of concrete with a broken ceramic planter and two plastic chairs. On the ground between the chairs is an overfilled ashtray, rainwater turning the butts and ash into a gray pulp.

The chair scrapes across the concrete as I drop down, and my eyes fall upon the guesthouses. One on the left, for the Lilies, and one to the right, for the Violets. They look the same—one story white clapboard, miniatures of the main house, with empty flower boxes on the sills. One of the windows on the Lilies' house is open, and morose music wafts out into the dry Texas night. I wonder what it's like inside those houses. Whether the girls treat one another like family instead of competition.

The sound of approaching footsteps hits my ears.

I slouch farther into the chair, as if I can become invisible.

My heart thumps harder.

Cain rounds the corner, a cigarette dangling between his fingers.

CHAPTER 13

THERE ONCE WAS A BOY NAMED CAIN

Cain doesn't seem surprised to see me there. But he does pause, like maybe he planned to come after me but doesn't know what to do now that he's here. My gaze travels over his frame. Six-foot-four, I'd say. Buzzed hair. Biceps stretching the hem of his navy blue shirt. And those eyes with hidden layers. I lean to the side and kick the other chair. An invitation.

He remains standing, lighting a cigarette with a silver lighter, gaze set on the guesthouses.

Those houses are hard to look away from.

"I'll come back in soon." I'm not sure what his job description entails, but in case it includes ratting out bad investments, I want to make sure he's clear that I have no intention of giving up. Those girls shook me, but I won't stop until Dizzy is out of jail. Hell, maybe I'll make enough after two or three nights to spring him. Who knows how the payment structure works. Maybe each bronze coin you get from a customer is a hundred spot in your pocket. With the sixty plus bucks in my dresser drawer, I'd need only four Katys to put their coins in my box.

Pay to the order of Rogers County Jail: $423.52

When Cain doesn't respond, I keep talking. "Do you

know what day we get paid?"

He sits down. Does that mean he's staying?

"You don't talk much, do you?"

Cain looks at me, and a warm current rushes down my spine. He looks like a mutt that's been kicked one too many times. The question is how long he'll continue tucking tail, and how long until he uses those powerful jaws. Then again, maybe all his biting is over. The second I think this is the second my teeth grind. There's nothing that makes my blood fire quicker than when easy targets get picked on. Like what happened with Poppet inside.

That makes two of us.

Cain looks up at the sky, holds out his silver lighter and says, "I could light a fire if you're cold. I have some lighter fluid beneath the kitchen sink."

I smile at his joke, because it has to be ninety degrees outside, even with the sun long gone.

"What happened to your arm?" he asks, sobering. His voice sounds like tires over gravel. It holds a surprising amount of authority for a boy who keeps his head down. Maybe *boy* is the wrong word. I seldom get the right word on the first attempt. I try again—

Young man.

That's two words. But it fits him better. I'd put him at twenty. Maybe older. Maybe old enough to put a cold beer bottle to his lips in broad daylight.

I don't bother hiding my arms. If you put blade to flesh, you better be ready to show the world, because they're going to see eventually. "It's a body count. Unmarked graves."

Cain chuckles. "You're not as scary as you think you are."

"Who says I think I'm scary?"

He looks pointedly at the piercings in my eyebrow,

my lip, the silver loops climbing my left earlobe like poison ivy. I wonder if Katy felt insulted by my calling attention to my ears when she's got only the one. Man, what a sick thought.

"Thanks for being cool to me," I blurt out.

"I'm not."

"You kinda are."

He stands up like he doesn't like where this conversation is headed. My skin burns with shame. There I go again with my attachments. Someone so much as looks at me and I want to snare them with my octopus arms, suck on their salty skin, and pull them underwater.

You'll stay as beautiful with dark hair and soft skin... forever.

That's a song about someone drowning their companion to keep them for eternity. I've never been one to remember lyrics. Want to play name that song? Don't put me on your team.

But that song I remember.

Cain narrows his eyes like he's searching for something. "Why did you come here?"

I debate whether to confess, and decide it couldn't hurt anything. Maybe he'll tell the madam and she'll advance me the money so I can get Dizzy out sooner. So I explain the situation. I tell him about Dizzy and about living on the streets and about how I need to help him.

The whole time I talk, I stare at my hands. Now I look up and find Cain studying me.

"Your friend, Dizzy, he'd do the same for you?"

"Of course," I say too quickly. "He absolutely would."

Cain doesn't respond. He just studies my face, the cigarette in his hand forgotten. I can't stay still with him looking at me like that. Because by him not speaking, he's actually saying too much at once. Causing questions to pop up in my head like termites chewing through hundred-year-old walls.

Dizzy would do the same for me.

He would.

The front door to the Violets' house opens and a girl's laughter rushes across the space in an unexpected tidal wave. Cain sees who's standing in the entryway, and he leans over and stubs out his cigarette in the untended ashtray. He digs his hands into his pockets, turns a massive back to me, and strides away.

Taking his place is a girl I've seen before. Red lipstick. Commanding gaze.

Lola the Violet. Lola the Top Girl.

Her hair is black and her eyes are lined with a heavy hand and she walks on the tip of her toes. "What are you doing? You can't be back here."

Before I can respond, she leans sideways and spots Cain in his rapid retreat.

"Was that Cain?"

"It was," I say. "Why can't I be here?"

She holds a hand to her forehead like my presence is making her ill. "Because I said so, new girl. And what I say goes. Now be a good maggot and go back inside." Lola analyzes my face and nibbles her plump lip. "You won't be here long, you know. Not pretty enough. So don't stress out about it. That's a favor, me telling you that. Don't forget it."

Anger simmers in my belly, but I can't properly experience it in all its reckless magnitude. Because Lola is exotic, and untouchable, and someone you want to examine in detail even as they torment you. It's like a lion chasing you across an open field. You're going to die, but there's a part of you that wants to turn back and see this glorious creature attack, even if you're the victim.

Lola has a ring on each finger and arms like cattails shooting up from swamp water. She's painfully thin with a high forehead and wide mouth. She uses that mouth to smile at me. "You know why Cain is here, right?"

She pauses so long I feel the need to shrug.

Lola flops down in the chair next to me, rubs her hands over her exposed thighs. "He killed someone. He's a killer." She glances back at the house. "A Bonnie and Clyde kinda thing. But without the Bonnie."

I don't believe her for a second. This morning someone implied that Cain was a serial killer, too. I didn't believe them, either. I know a thing or two about dangerous people, and Cain isn't one of them.

I stand up. "I've got to go."

"Hey, new girl. Don't come back here again." Lola laughs, then grows serious. "Don't come anywhere near my place. You stay with the trash where you belong."

Wilson slams himself against the inside of my skull, stretches toward her breakable body with all his might. Before he can get his way, I follow Cain's path and make my way back toward the main house. Behind me, Lola laughs again. She sounds almost crazy. But it doesn't dampen my interest in her.

I can't help wondering what it is Lola and the other Violets do with their customers in that guesthouse, away from prying eyes.

You know, Wilson says.

But I don't know, not for sure. How could I? They're there and I'm here and that's that. No reason to question things.

Don't be stupid, Domino.

When I push open the door, I stumble across Madam

Karina backed against a wall, Mr. Hodge kissing her neck. The madam sees me and lightly pushes him away, blushes, though she doesn't seem embarrassed.

I rush past the two and back into the entertainment room before the madam or Mr. Hodge can ask why I was outside.

CHAPTER 14

WE ARE SISTERS IN THE DARK

I spend the rest of the night making up for lost time. I do my best to regain Katy's attention, and when that doesn't work, I try my hand with different customers. Shockingly enough, none of them want a picture drawn on a napkin. I need real paint and an easel to have a shot at scoring those bronze coins.

With my conversation with Cain, and then Lola, heavy in my head, the evening ends. It's one o'clock in the morning, and Madam Karina comes in to thank everyone for the spectacular night and to show the guests to the door. As coins *clink* into the money box, I stand still. The other girls do, too, as if we can somehow make out whether a coin fell into our own numbered slot.

Mercy yawns and waves her arm over her head. "We'll clean up Monday. Fifteen minutes until lights out."

The girls file out of the room, and Poppet finds me near the back. "Thanks for what you did, but you know the girls were just being funny, right?"

"They weren't being funny, Poppet, they were being jerks."

Poppet grabs my elbow, and I stop. "No, they were being funny. I've been here almost a year now, okay? I'm one of them. They may tease me, but they also care. I have friends here, understand?"

Poppet's body is locked with intensity, and her fingers dig into my arm. She needs to believe what she's saying is true, even though I know it's not. "Hey, my bad. It's not like I know what I'm talking about. If you say they're your friends, then they're your friends."

She smiles, but the truth lies in her eyes. "You must be exhausted. If I were Madam, I wouldn't have made you work on the first night."

Poppet and I trail after the other girls and enter the community bathroom. It's a white tiled room with two toilet stalls and two showers. Not nearly enough for ten girls. Four sinks line the wall, but only three have running water. "I would have worked tonight no matter what."

"Oh, yeah? Do you need the money for something specific, or are you a lifer?" Poppet is rubbing the mascara out from under her eyes with toilet paper and water. I don't bother doing the same. I leave my makeup on my pillow where it belongs.

Mercy flips the light switch repeatedly. "Five minutes, hussies."

Poppet uses the restroom, and then we go to our room. Candy is already in bed, but she's awake and watches us crawl into our own beds. Poppet puts on matching shorts and tank pajamas with flying pigs on them, and offers to lend me a pair. But I've done enough taking from her. So I pull on Dizzy's shirt and sleep in that alone.

Mercy's voice rings through the night once more. "Lights off."

Poppet reaches over and turns off the lamp on our vanity. The room grows darker as down the hall, other girls do the same thing. Mercy marches toward our room, and every few seconds I hear a spontaneous popping sound. The girl with blue-black hair stretches into our room, grabs the door handle, and slams it shut.

It's quiet in the room for thirty seconds before Poppet resumes our conversation. "So you never answered me, Domino. Are you working here for a reason?"

"Shhh," Candy hisses.

I flip Candy off in the safety of the dark, and say, "No particular reason."

Candy sighs.

"I want to buy a car." Poppet's bed squeaks as she sits up. Because there's no window, and therefore no light, I can't really see her, but I imagine she's smiling. "It has to be black and have a red leather interior. Oh, and I want a double racing stripe that goes down the hood. You know what I'm talking about, right?"

I grin. "I know what you're talking about."

"Jeez," Candy says. "Will you two can it? We have to be up in seven hours."

Poppet's bed squeaks again. "What are you working toward, Candy? You've never told me."

"That's because all I want in this life is seven hours of sleep. God knows I'll never get that with you as my roommate."

I bite my lip and decide to back Poppet up. "I'd like to know, too."

"Like I care," Candy spits.

"Come on, Candy," Poppet urges.

"Yeah, come on, Candy." Even though Candy is mean-spirited, she wasn't one of the girls who booed Poppet tonight, and it almost feels like we're sisters in here, whispering our secrets.

There's a long pause before Candy says anything. When she does, Poppet and I don't make a sound. "I'd like a boyfriend, okay? And that's not something you can buy. But once I have enough money, I can leave and meet someone.

He'll want to be with me because I'll have nice dresses and money to take care of my hair and nails. Stuff guys care about. Then I won't have to listen to the two of you say idiotic crap while I'm trying to sleep."

I lick my lips and think about how to respond. "Candy, you don't need those things for someone to want to be your boyfriend."

"Shut the hell up, Domino," she growls. "What do you know?"

"Nothing," I admit for the second time tonight. "Absolutely nothing."

Poppet lies back down, or at least I think she does. "You sure there's nothing you want, Minnow?"

"Did you just call me Minnow?" I ask.

She giggles. "Yeah, because you're small."

"And because you're the bottom feeder in this pond." There's amusement in Candy's voice. "Even the frogs that come into this place are better than minnows, Minnow."

"Yeah, that's great." I lie on my twin bed and stare at the ceiling. Then—because I know I'll be leaving soon and what does it matter?—I tell them what I've only ever told Dizzy. "I'd like to get a place of my own."

"Fat chance," Candy says.

Heat rushes into my cheeks, and I clinch my eyes against the sting. I knew she'd probably react that way, but it hurts all the same.

"How do you know she can't get a place of her own?" Poppet asks Candy.

"Because I had a place of my own, and I know how hard it was to get there."

I open my eyes and turn my head toward her. "What do you mean?"

Now it's Candy who sits up. She seems more encouraged

by the conversation since the focus is on her. "Listen, to even think of getting a place, you gotta have cash up front. And not just for rent, but for the deposit."

I have no idea what she's talking about, but I hang on every word she says. "And this is to buy a house?"

Candy laughs, and then stifles the sound. No doubt she fears the wrath of Mercy. "A house? Are you crazy? People like us don't buy houses. I'm talking about an apartment, dipstick. Though I guess you could rent a house, too. That's beside the point. You'll never make enough here to do either of those things. And Poppet, hate to break it to you, but a car with red leather interior? That's not happening, either."

"How much is a deposit?" I push.

Candy falls back on her bed with a dramatic groan. "I don't know, Minnow. Maybe five hundred bucks if you got a cheap place. And before you ask, rent would be that much, too. You have to pay the first month in full before you walk in the door. Then there are deposits to turn your electricity and water on. So that's at least twelve hundred bucks. You starting to figure this out in that little brain of yours? Not. Happening."

"Well, how much do we make each night here?" I ask. "How much do we get per bronze coin?"

Candy rolls over, and because my eyes have adjusted, I can see that her back is to me.

I chew the inside of my cheek and think about what she said for the next half hour. Twelve hundred dollars. That's nearly three times what I need to spring Dizzy from jail. Still, once I get him out maybe we could both work here and earn twice as much. All the entertainers are girls, but the madam employs some guys. There's Eric and Cain and Mr. Hodge that I know of.

I turn toward Poppet, whose breathing has deepened.

"You'll get that car," I whisper to her sleeping frame. "I believe in you."

"Don't do that," Candy says, startling me. "Don't you dare get her hopes up."

I'm too surprised that Candy's still awake to reply, so I settle back into my fresh sheets and pillow and try to find sleep of my own. When I finally succeed, I'm plagued by dreams of a quiet boy covered in blood, tired of remaining silent when he'd rather scream instead.

He asks me if I'm tired, too.

CHAPTER 15

HYDRATION

I wake to a hand over my mouth, fingers clutching my shoulders, my legs, my arms. I'm lifted from bed and dragged into the hall. When I realize what's happening, I kick and scream, the sound muffled, but it's no use. There are five Carnations against one measly Minnow and this won't end well.

Mercy tells the girls to drop me when we reach the bathroom.

I land hard on my right hip and Mercy holds a finger to her lips. "If you yell again, we'll make your life a living hell. Got it?"

I nod, because I don't know what else to do. But already—so quickly it causes my head to spin—Wilson is rousing. I can vow to stay quiet, but I make no such promises where he's concerned.

Raquel steps forward. Her neck appears even longer as I look up at her from the floor.

A nice neck for the gurney.

"If you want to be one of us, you have to be initiated." Raquel looks at Mercy, and Mercy grins. The two girls have their differences, but on this point they agree.

Mercy motions toward a third girl, the only one who is

barefoot. Her toenails are painted blue, and she has a glass in her hand. The girl disappears into a toilet stall. There's a plunking sound and then she reappears, the glass brimming with water.

"I don't want to be one of you," I say when I get where this is headed.

Raquel's face softens like she's sympathetic. "Oh, sweetie, of course you do. Now drink up."

Barefoot girl crouches down and offers the glass. I shake my head, but she shoves it into my hand anyway. After getting to my feet, I stride toward the sink, my hands sweating. There's no way I'm drinking toilet water, and what's more, I know doing so won't stop their bullying. Still, knowing this doesn't stop the anxiety from building in my chest.

The fourth and fifth girls block my path. "Drink up," one says.

"Yeah, drink up," Mercy adds.

Raquel pumps her fists. "Drink, bitch, drink!"

"Drink,

    Drink,

       Drink!"

Their voices blend together until it's one solid wall of sound. I can't escape it, and I can't escape them. I drop the glass, and it skitters across the floor unbroken. When I make for the door, Raquel grabs me by the hair. It's the same move I wanted to pull on her earlier. My wig comes off in her hand. "Oh, for crying out loud," she says before reaching for me again. This time her fingers find purchase. "Back on your knees, pig!"

"Oink, oink!" the girls chant.

"Get more water," Mercy instructs the girl with blue toenails. She obeys and scurries toward Mercy, slipping once on the water covering the floor. "Now," Mercy tells me. "You can drink this yourself. Or we can make you. Which will it be?"

"Why are you doing this?" My teeth chatter from shock. I concentrate on select emotions—sadness, fear, surprise— because if I think about the other ones…

—*Anger, rage, fury,* Wilson whispers—

…I won't be able to control him. And though these girls deserve to be put in their place, they don't deserve what Wilson will bring. So, no, I won't drink that water.

"I see how this is going to go." One of the girls grabs my real hair and yanks my head back while another pries open my mouth. I close my eyes and consider calling for help. But if the madam hears me, what will happen? Will she assume I'm to blame? It's five girls' stories against mine.

By accident, the girl with the blue toenails slips a ring finger into my mouth. She was only trying to pry my lips apart, but now it's there, fat and plump and pink on my tongue. Wilson says it once, fast and hungry—

Bite down!

No, I tell him. *I won't!*

Fine, he says, shrugging. *Then I will.*

My teeth come down on her finger, and she howls with pain. Her scream tears through me, puts Wilson back to bed, and brings me—Domino the Gentle—back to the forefront. I open my mouth, and she rips her hand back.

"That's it." Raquel grabs my throat and squeezes. It isn't enough to really hurt, but it's a promise of something more, and I'm terrified of what will happen if it comes to her and me in a full-on fight. "Open. Your. Mouth."

I'm shaking from head to foot, and tears are slipping down my cheeks, tainting Dizzy's shirt.

"We won't leave until you do." I can tell that she means it. That this will grow increasingly violent until someone gets seriously injured.

Won't be us, Wilson whispers from his bed.

Quiet!

I pull in one long, shuddering breath, and Mercy skips in place. She knows I'm going to do it.

"Give me the water," Raquel tells the girl whose finger I bit.

"There isn't much left," the girl replies. "God, she really bit me. I probably have rabies."

"Shut up." Raquel reaches for the glass, one hand still on my throat. The girl hands it to her. "Open up, deary."

I fill my head with things that are good: crunchy leaves falling from trees and a green lizard hiding in a lilac bush. Ducks eating bread thrown from my hand and a train speeding down its tracks, both wild and contained at once. Also, my father. My father shaving his patchy beard and spreading butter on my half-burned toast. My father watching the Patriots play, pointing his hot dog at the screen to make a point the ref can't hear.

My father, there.

My father, gone.

I think of him, because I cannot think of my mother.

I open my mouth, and the water rushes down my throat. One full swallow before I gag and spit out the remainder. Lukewarm liquid rushes over my cheeks and washes away my tears. It swims in my eyes and shoots up my nose, stinging. Above everything else, here's what I think: it tastes the same as water from the sink.

And then Mercy grabs my chin and lifts my face to hers. "Stay away from our clients."

The girl with blue painted toenails throws the rest of the water across my chest, drenching Dizzy's shirt. I'm not sure why, but that's the thing that pushes me over the edge. I jump to my feet, deciding in a careless moment that I'll let Wilson free. There are other ways of making money, and I don't need this. What's more, I'm positive I'm not the only one they've done this to.

When the girls see the look on my face, they sober.

I take two steps toward them, quick, my brain buzzing with nothingness, and then I slip on the wet floor. I fall onto my injured side, and my hip sings with pain.

The girls roll with laughter.

They laugh all the way to the far wall, where they flip the light switch and leave me in the dark. They laugh all the way to their beds as Wilson edges closer.

You almost let me come out, he chances.

I don't answer him because he's right, and there's nothing I can say to convince him or me otherwise. I almost caved. I almost blacked out. I almost let Wilson do my bidding.

Maybe I should have.

CHAPTER 16

FISTS OF SILENCE

The next morning, I debate whether to tell Madam Karina what happened. In the end, I go with my earlier instinct and decide against it. Maybe it's because I don't want her to think I'm a problem, or maybe it's because I don't like relying on others to solve my problems. Either way, I stay quiet. But I do broach the subject with Poppet once Candy has left the room.

"The other Carnations are giving me a hard time," I admit.

Poppet has her back to me, but I don't miss the way she flinches. "It doesn't mean they don't like you."

"That's exactly what it means."

She turns and faces me, tucks a curl behind her ear. "It takes time for them to warm up to new girls."

"It seems like more than that."

"Well…"

I flop down on my bed. "Well, what? Is there something you're not telling me?"

Poppet glances to the doorway like Mercy might be listening. When she's sure the girls are in the kitchen, she says, "The last girl who was here caused trouble for the madam. She had to leave. And I guess Madam Karina made a big show of saying she'd never bring in another girl unless she found someone perfect. Used to be girls came and went all the time. Least that's what I heard. But it had been almost a year and no one."

My eyes widen. "Until me."

"She must see something special in you." Poppet smiles past a blush. "I see it, too. You're nice. And pretty."

Though I despise that word, it doesn't cut as deeply coming from Poppet's mouth. "You think the girls are really worried I'll steal their clients?"

"Some of them. But I think most of us dream of something different."

My brow furrows. "What's that?"

"Top Girl. Highest of the Violets."

There's that title again. "What does the Top Girl get that others don't?"

"They bank all their profits, for one." Poppet gathers toiletries into a basket. "And I guess there are other things."

"Such as?"

Poppet shrugs. "You work with Madam Karina on Sundays. And some girls say this place will be left to the Top Girl when Madam Karina gets too old to run the joint."

My fingertips tingle with excitement. "You mean Top Girl will actually own this house one day?"

"Yep. Course the madam would want it to stay an entertainment center because of the competitive thing she's got with her sister. But I guess whoever inherits the house would decide that."

I hear the part about Madam Karina's sibling rivalry, but that's not what I focus on. Candy told me last night I'd need twelve hundred dollars to rent an apartment, or maybe a house. But Poppet is telling me that this house, the very floors beneath my feet, is up for grabs. What's more, this house is a source of income, and many of these girls could benefit from a leader who ensures everyone is treated kindly and equally.

Maybe this house could serve as a sandwich shop, or a piano bar, or a bed and breakfast. I wonder how far we are from the town center of Pox.

"You've got a crazy look in your eyes." Poppet giggles before remembering my original question. "Why do you think the girls are picking on you? Did something happen?"

"No, nothing." I hesitate. "Poppet, why do the girls stay here? What do they really want?"

Poppet curls a lock of frizzy hair around her finger. "Most of us don't have anywhere else to go, for starters." She lowers her voice. "But I think the real reason we stay is the madam. She's kind, and she cares about us, and who doesn't want to live with someone who believes in them? When Eric found me and brought me to meet her, I just knew I wanted to work for her. You know she told me that I reminded her of a dandelion? Said I was a girl you could pin wishes on."

I smile.

"It's this place, too, I guess. It's easy to forget about my life before when every night is a celebration." Poppet brushes invisible crumbs off her T-shirt. "We should get cleaned up before breakfast. The other girls usually shower after assignments, but because it's Sunday, there aren't any. So we should get in before they do." Poppet eyes my silver wig and the bags under my eyes. "You can borrow some of my stuff, and later today when market opens you can get some of your own." And then, quieter, she adds, "If you want."

I swallow the emotion in my throat. Poppet does a lot for me, and I've done so little in return. "That'd be great. Thank you."

After bathing with some of Poppet's body wash, I towel off and put on a fresh shirt and shorts. Poppet even lends me a pair of flip-flops that are two sizes too big, but somehow feel perfect on my feet.

As we walk toward the kitchen, I drill Poppet about market and what exactly it is.

"You'll see." She beams. "Oh, and after breakfast we'll find out placements."

"What's that?" I ask, but Poppet has already darted to the table we sat at yesterday morning. Now that I've spent a day here, I know these are only the Carnation girls. The others that live on the second and third stories, the Daisies and Tulips, usually eat at different times.

I take my seat and, when I look up, Cain holds my eye. I have no idea why, but I find myself smiling. It's like we both broke a house rule last night, sneaking out back, smoking cigarettes and lounging in plastic chairs beneath a smoldering summer moon. And now, well, now we're criminals in cahoots.

Cain doesn't smile back, but he does hold my gaze for a moment longer before picking up two plates and walking toward Poppet and me. When he sets mine down, his arm brushes the outside of mine. It doesn't cause goose bumps to race across my skin or cause me to fantasize about what he looks like beneath his low-slung jeans. But I don't shrink away from his touch either, which for me is intimacy with a capital *I*.

Poppet stares at the inside of my forearm with a question she doesn't ask. It makes me like her even more for not asking. Just because I don't try to cover up the Xs trailing from elbow to wrist, doesn't mean I want it to spark a conversation.

She bumps my shoulder. "I think Cain really does like you. He totally lingered."

I avoid her stare. "You're imagining things."

"It's rude to whisper at the table." A girl with crooked teeth shovels French toast into her trap and chews with her mouth open. She turns her attention to Cain and holds up her plate. "Hey, King Kong, I need more syrup."

Cain's shoulders tighten, but he moves toward her with the bottle.

As he pours it on, the girl continues talking over her mouthful of food. "How many towers have you climbed, ape?"

The girl sitting next to her mimics an ape call and scratches under her arm.

"Stop it," I mutter.

The girls turn toward me and scowl. "What was that, freak?"

I don't get a chance to respond before Raquel speaks up. "Hey, Domino, you thirsty this morning?"

The room explodes in laughter, and heat rushes through my body. Only five girls pulled me from my bed last night, but right now it feels like a hundred people are laughing at my expense. My fork shakes in my left hand, and I feel myself rising. Why am I standing? What am I going to do? Run? Cry?

And why am I still holding my fork?

Mercy yells something about deep throating and Raquel makes a crude gesture toward her mouth. The laughter grows in volume until it's inside me, eating my insides like an army of maggots. They have to stop laughing. I can't hear myself think and it's too early and they're going to wake up Wilson.

Poppet tugs on my empty hand, the one without the fork, and I look down at her. She's begging me with her eyes to do something.

Hurt them, Wilson says, rising from his slumber. *That's what she wants.*

Is that what she wants?

Is that what I want?

No. No, no, no!

Mercy throws a balled napkin, and it hits me in the left breast. That makes everyone laugh harder. So hard they're pulling in great heaping breaths and pinching the bridges of their noses. Aren't I hysterical? The girl who drank water straight from the place they piss.

Cain picks up his closed fist and slams it four times against the kitchen counter.

One, two, three…FOUR.

The girls are stunned silent. Even I don't know how to react. It's the girl with blue nail polish, the one whose hand is bandaged, who speaks first. "I'm going to tell Madam Karina about that Cain. You can't go trying to intimidate us just because we're having fun."

"God, what a monster," someone else adds.

Though I'm fuming, I sit down. Poppet squeezes my knee under the table, and I let her. Cain is a mystery to me, but I know enough to realize that outburst was out of character.

The girls start to yell over one another about Cain the monster until Mr. Hodge waddles into the room. "What's going on? I could hear your yapping two stories up."

Everyone ceases talking.

"That's what I thought. Nothing in those skulls except cold, dead air. Not when someone asks you a direct question, anyway." Mr. Hodge takes a cup of coffee from Cain and scratches the underside of his belly. "Well, what are you doing stuffing your faces? Placements are up early today."

The girls lunge from their chairs and storm out of the room at once.

Poppet grabs my arm and we run, too.

CHAPTER 17

PLACEMENTS & PAYMENTS

'm not sure why we're running, but it's like herd mentality. The ten of us rush into the entertainment room and watch the digital ticker above the bar. It's blank, just like it was last night. I wouldn't even have noticed the thing had I not been sitting at these stools with Katy.

A moment later, there's a beeping sound, and the board glows with a red light. The color fades, and three names scroll across.

1. Raquel
2. Mercy
3. Georgia

Raquel bursts into a dance and whoops loudly. The rest of the girls glare, but none so much as Mercy. Raquel turns on Mercy and points a finger directly between her eyes. "Better watch your back. I'm creeping up, chica."

Mercy grabs her finger, and Raquel yelps with pain. The girls pull and shove against each another until Madam Karina enters the room. Then everyone falls silent. She holds in her right hand a stack of pink envelopes. In her left are three violets.

The girls line up, Mercy at the front.

Madam Karina whispers words to each girl and hands

each her envelope. Mercy, Raquel, and Georgia—the girl with blue toenail polish—each get a violet as well. I'm last to receive an envelope. Before Madam Karina hands it to me, she takes me by the shoulders.

"I'm proud of you, Domino," she says into my ear. "I just knew you'd be great."

Her words sink into my belly like chicken and dumplings. When she leans back, there's a smile on her face that swallows me whole. She's proud of me. She thinks I'm great. Try as I might, I can't build walls fast enough to keep Madam Karina out. What's more, I don't want to. When she releases me, my rational mind returns quickly enough. I'm no different to her than the other girls, I remind myself. Why would I be?

A memory of my mother slinks in. Soft hands, softer words, guiding me down the basement stairs in our house. I can't take my eyes off her, my mother. She's so charming, so convincing.

Wilson jerks the memory away, and I'm thankful.

The girls have slinked into separate corners of the room to open the pink envelopes. After Madam Karina leaves, I do the same. Inside mine, I find two sheets of paper. The first includes but a few lines.

PERSONAL PLACEMENTS
SUNDAY, JULY 22

Daily Placement: 9th out of 10
Accrued Placement: 9th out of 10

Daily Coins Earned: 1
Total Coins Earned: 1

A grin touches my lips. I wasn't in last place. And I earned a bronze coin. It must have been from Katy. But then again, maybe it was from someone different. She wasn't the only guest I talked to last night.

Around the room, girls are celebrating or groaning. As for me, my mind explodes with possibility. If I can earn a bronze coin after one night, armed with clumsiness and a stack of napkins, what could I do with a can of spray paint? Maybe I could captivate two guests at once. Maybe an entire room.

I look at the second sheet of paper.

PERSONAL EARNINGS
WEEK OF JULY 16

Carnation Total Earnings – $934.77
Total Customers – 17
Coins Earned – 1
Percent of Earnings – 5.88% (1/17th)
Initial Earnings – $54.99

Minus Carnation Household Fee – 90%
Total Earnings – $5.49

*Less Supplies – $10.00
*Sheets, pillow

Total Weekly Earnings – ($4.51)
Total Accrued Earnings – ($4.51)

My head spins and I silently mouth the numbers over and over again. I hardly understand half of it, but in the end, this is what I come up with.

The customers who came in this week spent a total of $934.77 to see the Carnation girls, and I'm assuming, to have drinks. There were seventeen customers in total, and because I got only one coin, I earned 1/17th of that amount. Then, because Carnations apparently retain only 10 percent of their earnings, I get to keep a whopping $5.49. That's not what has my blood boiling though. It's the cost of the sheets and pillow Madam Karina was so thrilled I took.

She charged me for them.

I didn't even know they cost anything, and yet there's the fee.

I melt into the floor, overwhelmed with the realization that I have less money now than I did when I got here. My stomach twists and my teeth grind and I'm about to start screaming for answers when Mercy yells that Angie is here.

The girls scramble out once again.

Something else is happening.

CHAPTER 18

MARKET

Poppet must see how upset I am, because she approaches with caution.

"Don't be upset, Domino. I've been in last place before. Several times, in fact."

I shake my head. "I'm not in last place. It's not that at all." Fury builds inside my chest as I ball the sheet of paper in my fist. "This thing says I owe money. All because I took bedding. This is such a scam! How does anyone make money here?"

"Oh, Minnow." Poppet tilts her head. "Just watch how much you make next week. I mean, you must have already earned a coin. So you only worked one night with no tools, and you made money. That's great! Next week you'll have a positive balance, and you can have Mr. Hodge hold your money. Then you get extra, which he calls interest...or interested...or whatever. So that helps. Anyway, it's not like we have any expenses here."

"Yeah, we do. We pay 90 percent of our earnings toward them."

Poppet thinks about this. "Well, I guess we'll have to work our way up then."

I sigh, some of the anger leaving me at this possibility. "How much do the other girls get to keep? Is it always 10 percent?"

Poppet nods toward where the other girls went, and we walk in that direction. "Well, the next step is to become a Daisy. I think they get to keep twelve."

I groan.

"But their customers are charged more, and they usually spend more at the bar. So they get a bigger piece of a bigger pie."

Dizzy springs to my mind, and frustration returns to me swift as a car crash. I grab Poppet by the arm to stop her. When I realize it's me who's touching her, I drop my hand. "Poppet, we have to become Daisies. For real."

She laughs. "I think you should concentrate on earning your Carnation first. Though Mr. Hodge will probably give that to you soon, considering you earned a coin on your first night. Now come on, it's market day. This is the fun part of getting paid."

Outside the entertainment room, I see the Carnations who received Violets racing up the stairs. When I ask where they're going, bitterness lacing my words, Poppet says, "They're paying tribute to Madam Karina. She gives them violets for doing well with the customers, and they lay them outside her door in thanks for their place in her home."

It takes everything I have not to roll my eyes at this. What's the point?

We file through the kitchen as I stew, and go through a door and down some stairs. When we reach the bottom I see girls with white daisies and yellow tulips pinned on their blouses alongside the Carnation girls.

A cage separates us from Cain, who's busy organizing merchandise, and Eric, who's dressed in a police officer uniform. I didn't realize Eric was a cop. I guess that should make me feel safe. It doesn't, though. It just makes me think of the officer who arrested Dizzy, and about where my friend is now.

Cain slides a window open and holds up a clipboard. Behind him and Eric, I spot a thin woman I've never seen before. She has hard features, small wrinkles around her mouth that tell me she's a smoker, and brown curly hair shaping a makeup-free face. The woman mumbles to herself as she unloads boxes, moving about as if she's sixty when she's probably only late thirties.

My eyes fall to her hands. They look soft, ill-matched to the rest of her. I bet when she holds a palm to your forehead to check for fever, it feels like silky-soft reassurance. I do this thing in my head where I imagine she holds her hand to my own forehead, pulls a blanket to my chin, and tells me I'm home.

Then I roll my eyes and shake my head. I do this sometimes. Imagine entire scenes between me and someone I've never spoken to. I've had boyfriends who brought me peanut brittle, friends who helped me find rare vinyl at an outdoor flea market, and fathers who…well, fathers who did things my real father didn't.

"Come on, Minnow." Poppet guides me into line. "Look at all the cool stuff."

I follow her gaze and spot shelves lined with goods. There's clothing, toiletries, stuffed animals, and bottles of pop to name a few. Farther up are more glamorous items: musical instruments, handbags with brand names I don't recognize, and high heels that make my mouth water. These are all things I can't afford, even if I didn't have a negative balance.

"Do you guys ever go into town?" I ask. "You know, for price comparisons?"

Poppet shrugs. "Nah. The Violets can have Eric take them places, but that's about it. The town is pretty far away, I think."

I look at Poppet, uneasiness mounting in my chest. "You mean you haven't left the house once in the last year?"

"It's not like I couldn't. But you have to help pay for gas

if you want a ride. And I'd rather save my money."

I think about this. That so many of the girls don't go anywhere, and if they do, it costs them their precious savings. I look at the items for sale once more, and then start to leave the line.

That's when my eyes fall on a sketchpad.

It's wrapped in cellophane and includes two sharpened graphite drawing pencils. I stare at it like a cat that's spotted movement among a bed of grass. Last night I held pen to napkin, but with those pencils, that paper…

My fingers twitch imagining holding those pencils.

My mind counts the coins I could earn with them in my grasp.

And my feet, well, they shuffle forward without permission.

Poppet goes first, buying only a dainty bottle of perfume. She asks to see a small hairpin that holds a pink pearl on one end. For several seconds, she turns it over in her hands, admiring the jewelry. Then she hands it back, her shoulders slumped. "Just the perfume this week."

Cain raises his head when I reach the window. Something flashes in those brown eyes, though I can't place what. He flips through the papers on his clipboard until he comes to a copy of my earnings.

"Can I buy on credit?" I ask.

Cain shakes his head, but Mr. Hodge opens the door to the cage and lets himself in. He hears my question, but asks me to repeat it anyway.

"I asked if I can buy something on credit."

Mr. Hodge smiles and pulls his head back like a turtle escaping inside its shell. His neck truly is invisible when he does this. I've overheard other girls calling him The Neck, and there's no doubt why. I briefly wonder what a baby born from him and Raquel would look like.

"Let her do it," he says. There's spittle in the corner of his lip. He licks it off. "She's new. And here at Madam Karina's House for Burgeoning Entertainers, we are hospitable." He laughs like what he said is hilarious. I'm not sure who he thinks he's fooling. I know this will put me further in debt and tie me to the house, but I also know I need it to have any sort of chance.

Wilson sits up. *Domino, you really don't need—*

"How much is it?" I ask.

Mr. Hodge reaches for the sketchbook package. He looks like a bowling ball from the back. "Don't worry about that, rabbit. Leave the math to us men. You just think about all the pretty drawings you can make with this here notebook." Mr. Hodge elbows Cain. "Isn't that right?"

Cain stares at his feet, but I don't miss the way his jaw clenches. He has half a foot on Mr. Hodge and is built to destroy people like The Neck.

"How much?" I repeat.

Mr. Hodge scowls and hands me the sketchpad, muttering for Cain to notate a ten-dollar purchase on his clipboard under my name. I clench my teeth at the price, and then say, "Wait, one more thing." I point to the pearl hairpin. "How 'bout that?"

This time it's the woman—Angie, Poppet said her name was—who hands it to me with a curt, "Three dollars." She hardly looks in my direction because she's focused on Cain. Reaching into her pocket, she withdraws a peppermint covered in lint and shoves it into Cain's hand.

He mumbles a thank-you, but she waves away the pleasantry.

"Gotta load the excess onto Betty," she tells him. Her voice sounds like a tractor rumbling down the road. Yeah, a tractor.

No need to search my brain for a better word in this situation.

I turn and hand the pin to Poppet, and she throws herself around me. I lock every last muscle in my body, but manage not to push her away.

"I'm going outside," I tell Poppet, but she's already racing toward the bathroom to try out the pin I bought her.

On credit.

Because I'm an idiot.

CHAPTER 19

ANGIE AND BLACK BETTY

t's nine o'clock in the morning, but already it's balmy outside. The sun beats down on the cracked soil and gold sedan. Beside it are two other vehicles, a cop car that must belong to Eric, and a black tractor.

Angie, the woman from the market, is loading boxes onto the back of the tractor. Angie, the woman whose voice I compared to that of a tractor, owns a tractor.

I start to sit on the patio bench, but decide I'm being rude by not offering to help. "Is there something I can do?" I call out.

Angie straightens. She must be a touch over five feet. Not so much taller than me. She wipes a hand across her cheek and leaves a smudge of dirt in its wake. "You talking to me, Minnow?"

I startle at her use of a nickname Poppet gave me only last night. "How do you know—?"

"That they call you Minnow?" She lifts another box onto the tractor. "Those girls are loud."

That's all the explanation she gives. Angie appears callous, but she's answering my questions and that means a lot, comparatively. So I keep talking. "You live around here?"

"You need to speak up. You're too damn quiet."

I smile, because no one has ever accused me of being quiet. Especially not Dizzy. Of course, it was easier to be loud when Dizzy stood behind me. "I asked if you live around here."

She stops working and puts those soft hands on her hips. "Yeah, I do. My place is down that way, in the park by the flagpole. Prettiest yellow trailer you ever saw." I laugh when she says the last part, but she purses her lips. "What are you laughing about? You got a place that's better?"

My smile shatters. "No, I…I'm sorry. I thought you were being funny."

We stay this way for a few minutes, her loading boxes, me watching her work. Wanting to ask questions but afraid to say the wrong thing. I thumb the piercing in my eyebrow until Cain walks outside and lights a cigarette. When Angie sees him, she pants harder than she was before and yells for Cain to get his no-good rear end out there and help.

Cain smiles. Not a full-blown grin, but close enough. He tilts his head in my direction without really looking at me. "Her bark's bigger than her bite," he says, that smile still clinging to his lips. Then he stubs out his cigarette, puts it back in the pack, and jogs down the steps. There are only a few boxes left when I work up the nerve to join them.

Angie sees me coming. "What do you think *you're* doing? Too skinny to do a damn thing properly."

Cain chuckles under his breath. "Let her help, Angie. She's new."

"You think I don't know she's new? She's got it stamped on her forehead."

I pull in a deep breath and face Angie. "It's not like you were doing much with these boxes before Cain came along. Huffing and puffing like a bull with emphysema."

Cain throws his head back and laughs long and hard. The sun shines down on his face, and the sound comes from deep in his core. In that moment, it's like he's stepped out of his own body and back into one from his childhood, before the thing that made him the way he is now came along. And I do know he has a thing. Anyone with a thing recognizes someone else with it, too. I like Cain this way—talking, playful.

Cain recovers and looks at Angie to gauge her reaction. She doesn't look pleased, but I see past her frown and spot the amusement in her eyes.

"Here, then." She shoves a box into my arms. "Put this on Black Betty's hood. It'll stay well enough." She pats the tractor and mumbles, "A bull with emphysema."

I help them load what little remains until the screen door slams against the house. Mr. Hodge walks onto the front porch, his steps loud against the concrete. "What's going on out here? Why the hell is one of our girls loading your crap, Angie?"

Both Angie and Cain grow serious, but it's Angie who responds. "It was my fault, Frank. Been feeling under the weather lately. I asked if she'd help."

I start to rebut Angie's claim, but Cain catches my eye and shakes his head.

Mr. Hodge sticks out his chest. "If you can't take care of your own business, I'd be happy to find another supplier."

"Not necessary." Angie pulls herself into the tractor seat and then starts the engine. "I'll be good as new next time you see me."

Mr. Hodge huffs and then turns his attention on me. "Domino, meet me in Madam Karina's room."

He marches inside, and I glance back at Angie.

"Go on," she says. "Don't you keep that man waiting." I rush toward the house, but Angie's voice stops me. "Hey, wait."

I turn around.

She squints in the morning blaze a long time before flicking her eyes toward Madam Karina's mother's empty flowerbed. It's like Angie has suddenly decided against speaking her mind. Finally, the woman says, "Keep your head up in there."

I salute her, and when I do, the corner of Cain's eyes crinkle like he's going to smile again.

Angie shakes her head. Even from here, I can hear her mumble a sharp, "Smart-ass."

I jog up the stairs, into the house, and toward the room where Mr. Hodge is waiting. As Cain and Angie grow farther away, my heart beats faster. I don't know what Mr. Hodge wants with me, but that man makes me more nervous than a snowman in hell.

CHAPTER 20

PHONE CALL

I stare down at the pink Carnation on my blouse. It's been there since Mr. Hodge gave it to me, free of charge if you can imagine that. I poke at it as Poppet gets ready for another night of work. It's been four days since I arrived at Madam Karina's home, and I've missed Dizzy every minute.

I'm getting closer to accumulating the money I need to free him. The first evening I worked, Saturday, I earned one coin. But on Monday and Tuesday, I earned two each night. Eighth place, which Madam Karina assures me is incredible. But it isn't enough. Not when I've barely paid back the cost of my sheets and pillow, and have another nine dollars to repay before I start earning.

I've vowed to not buy another single thing from this place. Instead, I borrow clothing and toiletries from Poppet, and in return I do as many of her chores as I can when Mercy's back is turned.

It's been six days since I've seen Dizzy. And every day the girls grow increasingly abusive as I slowly climb the placement ranks and nab their clients' attention. What's more, I'm not sure I'll make real money unless I move up to a new flower category. And that would take time, more time than I want to spend, with Dizzy in jail.

So it seems I have a decision to make.

1.   Stay at Madam Karina's House for Burgeoning Entertainers and work my way up the ranks quickly.
2.   Count my losses. Find a train. And get myself back to Detroit, stat.

The more I think about it, the more attractive option number two looks. Problem is, I don't want to leave Poppet. And maybe I'm a bit interested in what Cain's deal is. And yes, I like Madam Karina's attention. I like the way she talks to me in that gentle voice. I like the way she lights a candle in her room that smells like oatmeal cookies and asks me how I'm doing.

But even with my sketchpad, I'm not earning enough. And so my decision is clear. Besides, it's not like I tried that hard to get a job. What if I went to five places a day and asked for an application? What about ten?

And then there's Wilson and his insistence that things will only get worse if I stay here. And that he knows, and I know, what awaits us in those guesthouses.

Repeating the past, he whispers. *Manipulation and violence. Is that what you want? Because if so, I'm down. It's just I thought you wanted to forget about—*

I stand up, suffocating Wilson, determined to take action after a week of being pushed around inside this enormous farmhouse that grows smaller by the day. Poppet asks me where I'm going, but I don't respond. Right now, I need to talk to Greg. See if maybe he would hire me even though his shop is struggling.

I shuffle down the stairs to the basement where market is held. The same room I've seen girls pay to use the telephone. Until now, I didn't want to dig myself deeper into a financial hole. But now that I hold the possibility of leaving in my head, I can't think of anything besides hearing Greg's voice. Even if he can't hire me, he may know a good place to start.

When I reach the bottom step, I spot movement behind the cage. I edge closer and narrow my eyes. There's someone sleeping back there. I move closer still and make out a twin-sized mattress on the floor. It's no secret who it is: expansive shoulders, shaved head, tan skin. I cough into a closed fist until he startles and turns his head over on the pillow.

"Little late to be sleeping," I say.

He pops up in bed, his back turned, and breathes rapidly like I've caught him misbehaving. But that's ridiculous. He's a twenty-year-old (don't quote me) boy who was taking a nap before a long night's work. Where's the harm?

When he turns, I see bags beneath his eyes, as if he was fighting in his sleep. If that's true, it'd be a sharp contrast to what he does during the day, which is passivity at its prime.

"Sorry I scared you. I just need to use the phone," I say. "Are you okay?"

He runs a hand over his buzzed, dark-brown hair. "You're supposed to wait for a market day to make calls."

I bristle. "That's bull. I've heard other girls talking down here."

"They're rule breakers."

"So am I."

Cain inspects me. Runs his gaze over my face, my neck. There's amusement in his eyes. "So you are." He leaves and comes back a moment later, opens the cage door, and motions toward a phone.

I don't ask how much the call will cost, because I've pretty much decided I'm out of here. But I need to hear Greg say the words, "Come home." As if there is a home. As if there is a family waiting with open arms that feel good when they touch.

I dial Greg's number on the black rotary phone and turn away from Cain. Meg picks up on the second ring. "Hair Flair and Fun, how can I help you?"

I roll my eyes. What a God-awful name. "Yeah, I need to talk to Greg." I keep my voice low as if that will help. As if Cain can't hear every word I'm saying.

"May I ask who's calling?"

"You may not."

"Oh, oh-kay," Meg stutters. "Let me get him. Please hold for a moment."

Jeez. She really is a good employee. I'm being a complete horse's rear, and she's still perfectly polite. I swallow my guilt and wait to hear Greg's voice. It doesn't take long.

"This is Greg."

"Greg, it's me." I smile into the phone. It's good to hear his voice. It's been only a week, but with so many miles between us, it feels much longer.

"Hey, Dom. How you doing? You coming in to get a new wig today?"

He doesn't even know I'm gone. He'd have no reason to, but it still hurts for whatever reason. I'm about to respond when Greg continues.

"Saw Dizzy pawning some stuff across the street yesterday. I'm guessing that means you've got heavy pockets and a hankering for new locks, am I right? Tell me I'm right."

The floor falls out from beneath me.

One second I'm cool as a mother freaking cucumber, and then Greg tells me he's seen Dizzy.

"It must have been someone else you saw. Dizzy is—"

"No, it was him," Greg interrupts. "He waved to Meg. Him and some other kid."

I close my eyes against the pain of what he's telling me, but at the same time, I refuse to believe it. I left a note for Dizzy to call Greg if he got out early. Surely he would have looked for me immediately.

I clear my throat and force myself to speak again. "Can you give me the number to that pawn shop?"

"What? Why?" Greg pauses. "Where are you calling from?"

"Greg, please."

He must hear the wobble in my voice, because a second later I hear him whispering something to Meg. He gets back on the phone. "You ready?"

I ask Cain for a pen and he grabs one without hesitation. "Ready."

Greg reads the number, and I thank him. He starts to ask more questions, but I tell him I have to go and hang up. I phone the pawn store Greg said he saw Dizzy at. Cain doesn't stop me from making another call.

The guy Dizzy and I deal with at American Picker Pawn confirms Greg's story. Dizzy is out of jail. He's seen him twice in the last couple of days. Running with a new kid, he says. Got out of jail because of inmate overflow, he says. Slapped with a ton of community service time instead, he says. Dizzy mentioned you left a note and were off somewhere. That true?

I want him to stop saying things.

I hang up and struggle to catch my breath. My brain tilt-a-whirls inside my head and my eyes sting. I was alone for two months after I left my parents' house. Two long, lonely months. But then I found Dizzy. I clung to him like he was both father and mother and everything else I needed to survive. But he doesn't *care*. If he did, he would have run straight from our broken-down Victorian house to Hair Flair & Fun and demanded answers.

He wouldn't be visiting pawn shops.

He wouldn't be making new friends who aren't me.

He wouldn't be waving to Meg and not bothering to cross the street.

I can't help what happens next. A sob breaks in my chest.

Just once, but once is enough. Cain rounds my body and stands in front of me. I keep my eyes down and stand still. Won't move no matter what he says. But he doesn't say anything. He just stands there, a pillar when I need so badly to lean on something sturdy and unyielding.

For almost a year, I lived with a boy from Iran with black curls and long lashes. I slept on his blue mattress with the busted spring in the corner. I learned how to steal, and he learned what paint works best on concrete. He was my person.

But now I wonder if I was ever his.

Cain doesn't touch me. He doesn't fast talk like Dizzy or try to make me laugh or say let's nip a pint of Jack Daniels and forget this sadness. He only stands there. Breathing in, breathing out.

Reminding me how it works.

CHAPTER 21

TAKEN

Before the phone call, I was determined to leave. Surprisingly, I still am. There're only thirty minutes until guests arrive, and already Mercy is barking orders up and down the hallway. I should be getting ready like Poppet, Candy, and the rest of the girls, but right now I need to think.

Here, at the house, I have a girl who thinks she's my friend, and a woman who speaks gently, but I have to get out of here before I self-combust. These people can't care about me. No one can. I'm alone in this world, and that's the way it should be.

I'll never leave you alone, Wilson says gently.

For once, I don't push him from my head.

Instead, I check the hallway to ensure no one's coming and rush toward my bottom drawer. Tonight, as the other girls are entertaining guests, I'll skedaddle. My father taught me to always repay my debts. But the biggest favor I can do for Madam Karina and Poppet is to leave.

I pull the drawer out and reach into the back. My fingers spider across the empty space as a clap of thunder sounds through me.

The money is gone.

I lean forward and check again. But it isn't there. I tear

the clothes and wigs and makeup from the drawer and sift through them. Nothing. I jump to my feet and yank the drawer off the rollers, toss it onto my bed. Then I check again, again.

When there's no avoiding the truth, I crumble to the floor and cover my face. Rock back and forth and moan into my hands. I needed that money to get out of here. To pay for a train ticket and food to keep my belly full on my return trip to Detroit. But I'm upset over more than that. After all, I can hitchhike. I can steal food and drink from fountains along the way.

The real reason I'm pissed is because someone in this house *stole* from me.

They've picked on me. Called me names. Poured toilet water down my throat and laughed at me more times than I can count. And now what little I came here with has been taken. First, in the form of my dignity. Second, when they dug through my belongings. Oh, and let's not forget the time they threw dirtied water on Dizzy's shirt.

Of course, what does that matter?

Why would Dizzy's shirt be precious to me when he couldn't take the time to cross the damn street and ask where I went?

Mercy pops her head inside the room. "What are you doing, freak? The guests will be here soon. Get your ugly butt dressed."

I close my eyes. I close my ears. She can't get inside me now.

"Um, did you hear me, retard? Get off the floor and take a shower. You smell like the toilet." She laughs. It's an old joke now, but she hasn't tired of it. "No surprise there, though, huh?"

I shake my head. Back and forth. Keep her out and keep me sane. Don't listen to her words. Nothing can touch me.

"What is *wrong* with you?" Mercy growls. "Get off that floor or I'll get you up myself."

Poppet walks into the room. Sees me rocking, hands over my ears, though I can still hear everything. Too much.

"Leave her alone," Poppet says.

Mercy turns, bares her teeth. "Don't you dare tell me what to do."

Poppet raises her hands. "I'm just asking you to give her some space. You guys pick on her nonstop."

Mercy walks away from me, gets close to Poppet. Her chest bumps into Poppet's chest. Poppet pulls back and Mercy leans forward, fogging her glasses. "I'm not in the mood for this tonight. So I'll do you a favor. I'll turn my head if you will leave this room right now. If you don't, I'll knock your teeth out."

Mercy holds up a finger like she intends to back up the threat.

I uncover my ears, because something sinister is crawling over my mind. It's different when Mercy is talking down to me. I can block her out if I try. But when she's spewing her poison on Poppet, I'm alert. All my senses: ON. Sight, smell, sound, taste: ON.

Wilson: ON.

"Come on, Mercy," Poppet whispers.

Mercy jerks her finger in Poppet's face, pushes it directly against the center of her forehead. "Say one more word. One. More."

Poppet looks down, and tears fill her eyes. It's the first time I've ever seen Poppet truly upset. I should never see someone like Poppet cry, yet here come the waterworks.

And it's. All. Mercy's. Fault.

I stand slowly, rising behind Mercy like a demon shadowing the sun.

Poppet's bottom lip falls open. She says one word though Mercy explicitly told her not to. "Please."

Mercy slaps her.

It isn't hard.

It's hard enough.

I'm on her in a heartbeat. Take her to the floor like an animal and shove my fists into her face.

Wilson springs to his feet. *Oh, damn! It's on! Want my help?*

Yes, I respond. *Yes. Yes. Yes. Yes. Yes.*

Wilson takes my hand, and I am him and he is me. Mercy's screams slip down my throat, thick and foul like cough syrup. Blood covers my hands. The girl beneath me knows how to earn bronze coins. Fine. She can intimidate the other Carnations into following her. Fine.

But she doesn't know what I know, what Wilson knows.

She doesn't know how to inflict fear like this.

I stop hitting her because now I have her attention. This isn't all about pain, after all. My lips graze her ear, and she freezes.

"Listen to me, you sweet, naïve girl. You've had your turn. Now it's my time to reign. And don't think for one second that it's your throne I want. I don't want that. I don't want your status either. I want you. And I'll have you, too. Your mind is mine to hold. Your body belongs to me. Even your soul, Mercy, is gone. I've eaten it. I'VE EATEN IT!"

I scream, and Mercy panics and shoots up. I slide off her chest. She's bigger than me, but she's not bigger than Wilson. I place my hand over her face and shove. Her head snaps backward.

"Give me your crown!" My cries grow louder, more hysterical. "Let it fall from evil and sit upon a head of righteousness!" I don't know what I'm saying. Wilson speaks through me now, and that's fine and dandy.

Two arms grab me and drag me off the girl. Soon, two more join the mission to free Mercy from the crazed Minnow. Four arms against my two. Not very fair, if you ask me.

"Let me go." My chest rises and falls fast, but I've regained some control.

It's the calmness that scares them most, remember? Wilson says.

I remember.

Raquel is hollering in my face and snapping her fingers. She's background noise. All I can think about is Mercy on the ground. Mercy wiping away the red river beneath her nose. Mercy still breathing. Mercy still alive.

My eyes are on Mercy when I say, "You're next, Raquel. When you least expect it, I'll have your head, too."

The girl with blue toenail polish is hollering. Yelling at me and throwing her arms around her head. But all I can think about are three things.

First, that Dizzy doesn't care.

Second, that Candy said it would take $1,200 to get a place of my own.

Third, that a place of my own means I'll never have to rely on anyone again.

Mercy's voice rings above the rest, and everyone turns to look at her. She's screaming something but Wilson is too loud inside my head, and I can't hear her. I clench my eyes shut and push Wilson down far enough so that I can listen to Mercy run her mouth.

Why do you care what she has to say? Hit her again! Wilson is jumping around inside my head, unable to contain his excitement though he was just reminding me to act calm.

Hush!

Mercy's voice rushes in. "…out of here. Just leave, you

freak! Get out!"

"What?" I ask dumbly, because I've missed her rant.

Mercy shakes her head like I'm crazy.

She has no idea.

"I said, get out of this house. No one wants you here. Leave *right now* and never come back!"

The girls look at me. Poppet looks at me. Somewhere in the distance, I hear the sound of heavy footsteps. Maybe Mr. Hodge or Cain coming to see what the uproar is all about.

Dizzy's abandonment.

Madam Karina's affection.

Poppet's kindness.

Twelve hundred dollars.

A place of my own.

I meet Mercy's icy glare. "No," I tell her. "I think I'll stay a while."

PART III

DOMINO'S RULES
FOR DRINKING THE KOOL-AID

1. Strategize.
2. Find favor with the queen.
3. Get out of your comfort zone.
4. Become ruthless in your pursuit of victory.
5. Keep your eyes off the boy who could wreck you.

CHAPTER 22

MY, HOW THEY SHINE

I sometimes do this thing called lucid dreaming. It's where I fully comprehend that I'm dreaming, but the dream marches on anyway, fumbling around like a great ogre. I don't always recognize when I'm dreaming. And sometimes, like now, it's worse when I do.

I'm in my parents' home. I know because the moon shines in a funny pattern through our beveled windows. A cuckoo clock chimes the time, twelve o'clock a.m., though there's never been a clock like this in our house before.

I hear the sound of heavy footsteps, and a door opening and closing down the hallway. A man appears with a bag slung over his shoulder. He's fleeing like a criminal. Or like we're the criminals and the only chance he has to save his own life lies in these few seconds.

"Dad," I whisper. But he can't hear me. He can't hear me because he doesn't have any ears.

He reaches the front door and pulls it open, stops and listens for any sign that we've woken. I reach out to touch him, but my hand passes through his skin. He's wearing a baseball hat. He had time to put on a hat, but not to kiss me good-bye.

"Don't leave," I beg. My legs start sinking through the hardwood floor until only my hips, waist, chest, and head remain. "Daddy, don't leave. If you leave, I'll do the thing I'm not supposed to do."

A storm rages outside our home. I wonder if he planned it this way—to leave with the thunder masking the sound of his engine starting, with the lightning cutting a path from our home to his new, elsewhere life.

The moment he disappears into the night is the second my mom starts screaming. It's like she can actually feel the absence of my father. The clock chimes again, and the bells grow so loud that I have to cover my ears. I can't block the sound of my mother, though. That sound has no beginning and no end. It just…is. I'd do anything to make her happy again if only to kill that dreadful noise.

When I look back toward the front door, it's gone. In its place is a round table with neatly lined knives. All different shapes and sizes, those knives. Gleaming in the moonlight and calling my name.

I don't want to touch them.

But I must.

CHAPTER 23

ANNIHILATE THE ARMOR

The next night, Poppet, Candy, and I are getting ready. Though I'm still on edge from my fight with Mercy, it's my dream I can't stop thinking about. A memory, really, of the thing my father did that led to Wilson's birth.

I haven't spoken to my father in five years. He left me alone with my mother. A woman who grew bitterness in her heart and wrapped it in barbed wire. A woman who loved me and demanded I love her back. Oh, how I loved her, Wilson and I both.

Mercy doesn't pop her head in to ensure we're dressing. She doesn't stomp up and down the hallway or clip orders. Best guess is she's tending to her face, making the cuts and bruises work in her favor. Anything to earn those coins.

Mr. Hodge caught us right after the fight ended and demanded to know whose fault it was. Surprisingly, no one said a word. The girls have all taken sides: Mercy's, mine, or no man's land. But regardless of who supports whom, when it comes to Mr. Hodge, we're an army of ten.

When Candy leaves the room, Poppet turns in my direction.

"Are you sure you don't want to borrow one of my dresses?" she asks for the fourth time. Poppet hasn't thanked me for coming to her defense, and I'm terrified it's because she's afraid of me. But her offering me a dress says all is not lost.

I glance at the door and think about my plan. I've been turning over an idea in my head ever since I made the decision to stay. I need enough money to get my own place, and I want Poppet to get her car. After ensuring no one is listening in, I sit on my bed and lean toward Poppet. "I want to talk to you about tonight. What are your thoughts on teaming up?"

Poppet licks her lips. "How so?"

"There's only one Point Girl per flower. But maybe it doesn't have to be that way. If we showed Madam Karina that we work better as a duo, maybe she'll divide our profits evenly. Then we could share the title of Point Girl and eventually be promoted to Daisies."

Poppet lowers her eyes. "I can only sing."

"Poppet, you're a terrible singer," I say. "What you *do* have is personality. Customers are drawn to you because you're enthusiastic and outgoing. It makes them feel wanted. But you spend so much of your time worried about the microphone that they don't see it. Tonight, if you agree, you stay by my side. I'll ensure no one messes with us and use my sketchpad to provide entertainment, and you keep them talking."

"I'm not that bad of a singer."

"You're the worst."

Poppet laughs. "We're not close enough for you to say that."

I smile and nod. "We're exactly close enough for me to say that. Any less and it would be outrageously rude, any longer and we'd be the kind of friends who lie to each other."

"I don't want to lie to you," she says.

"Okay, so then—"

"My turn to be truthful," she interjects. "This heavy makeup, these piercings, the wigs…it's not working for you."

I cover my heart in mock horror. "How dare you."

Poppet stands up, grabs my hand. "I accept your proposal. But only if I can give you a makeover."

"That's not happening."

Poppet purses her lips. "Look, if you want to be a team, you have to trust me the way I trust you."

I don't trust anyone. We trusted Dizzy and look what happened.

"You get coins because you're real," Poppet continues. "You don't put on an act like the other girls and guests dig that you're authentic. But you need something more to draw them in."

I grin. "That's what you're here for."

"Sit down." Poppet points toward the vanity ottoman. "Either you shed that shell of yours or we don't have a deal."

"No dice."

"Domino, sit down."

I sit.

She leaves the room and returns with a wet washcloth. "I'm going to remove your makeup. It might take me a while since you've been caking new stuff onto old for days. Yeah, I've watched your beauty routine."

I try to feign shock, but I can't move a muscle. My body shuts down as Poppet scrubs away at my face. I don't know why I'm letting her do this. I haven't left the bathroom without my armor in months, ever since I realized how good it felt to have an extra layer between me and the world. But because I don't want Poppet to be scared of me, and because I know she may be right, I let her work. My heart hammers in my chest, and a cold sweat breaks out across my skin.

I feel exposed.

I feel ugly.

"Look how beautiful your skin is beneath all this junk."

Poppet turns the washcloth over.

"Please don't say that," I mutter.

"Say what? That you're beautiful."

I wince.

Poppet squats down so that her head is near my lap. She looks up at me, lays a hand on my knee. "Domino, it's okay to be pretty. And it's okay to be complimented."

My throat aches with emotion. She doesn't understand why this is impossible. She wasn't there when I used my mother's beauty to lure them in and do unspeakable things. She didn't hear when Wilson silenced my tears and offered to take over so that I didn't have to remember.

"I don't know what happened to you," Poppet says quietly, "but I know you're not the only one with a past you'd rather forget." She holds my gaze. "I'm going to remove the rest of this makeup, okay?"

My bottom lip trembles, but I refuse to cry.

As Poppet wipes away my foundation and moves to my ears, unhooking my piercings with tender hands, she says softly, "Thank you for what you did last night. You were right. The other girls don't like me. But that doesn't matter now." She meets my gaze with uncertainty. "Because I have you. My partner."

I grab her wrist and she stops unhooking my lip ring. "That's right, Poppet. You do."

At that exact moment, Candy strides into the room. "Oh, I'm sorry. Am I interrupting a moment?" She shakes her head. "Gag me."

An hour later, Poppet has removed my gold wig, and I've washed out my hair. She's taken a blow dryer and round brush to my mane, and applied lip gloss, blush, and a touch of mascara to my face. Regardless of how many times I plead, she won't add any more. Candy sits on the bed, blowing bubbles with cherry-scented gum, as Poppet hands me a white dress.

I hand it back to her. "I don't do white."

"You do now."

"Put it on, Minnow," Candy urges. "Not like you'll look any worse in that than you do in any other color."

I smile at Candy, because I know she wants to see the completed makeover.

I point the dress at Candy and then start to pull it on. "For you, Candy dearest."

"Bite me." She blows another bubble.

When I'm done, Poppet gives me two silver studs and a pair of nude pumps. Then she walks me over to the mirror.

"We have to go," Candy says. "We're going to be late."

"Can it," Poppet snaps, surprising up both. "I want to see her reaction."

She positions me in front of the mirror, and my stomach churns.

I'm completely and utterly exposed. Blue eyes popping, blond hair shining, thin legs showing, small chest heaving. I turn away and fight rising bile. Poppet takes my chin and turns me back toward the mirror.

"Look at yourself," she says.

I shake my head.

"What the hell is wrong with you, Minnow?" Candy chimes in. "Look in the damn mirror."

"I already did."

"Well, look again."

I do, but only because Poppet worked so hard. When I turn back, I see my parents staring back at me. My mother's cheekbones. My father's nose. They're gone, but I still can't escape them. Though my mask is removed, I remind myself that my serpent tattoo still vines up my side—a token I got after I left home. A lifeline that tells me I am still me, and that though I've done terrible things, I can slither through tall grass unseen if need be.

You know what you look like to me? Wilson says gently. *Strong.*

Mercy chooses that exact moment to round the corner and stick her head in. The skin surrounding her eye is black and blue, and there are bruises shaped like fingerprints on her neck. She sees me, and her mouth parts. Her eyes run over me for an excruciatingly long time. Then she says, "If you were trying to look like a tramp, then you've succeeded." She pauses. "Time to go. Now."

Mercy practically jogs down the hallway so that I can't retaliate.

She shouldn't worry. Last night, after I attacked Mercy, I stayed up most of the night pushing Wilson away. Because even though Mercy may have deserved a good butt kicking, she doesn't deserve the things Wilson wanted to do to her.

There's a big difference between letting Wilson into my head and letting him take control. Last night, I came way too close to letting that second thing happen. And so I vowed, as the other girls slept and my hand ached from smashing into Mercy's face, that I would never, ever let Wilson out again.

But I'm still here, he whispers. *Just in case.*

CHAPTER 24

THE COWBOY

That night, Madam Karina writes a black number 8 on my left hand. Poppet gets marked with a 9. These numbers won't last long.

My sketchpad and pencils are set up in the corner of the room, and music beats through my veins. The songs are faster tonight, more tumultuous. Maybe because it's a Thursday night, and we have to remind guests to relax even though the weekend is one workday away.

Mercy says a few words, staring at me the entire time she talks. Then the curtain is pulled back and seven guests file in.

It's showtime.

I lock eyes with Poppet, and she nods. Pulling her skirts a touch higher than necessary, she bounds in front of the other girls and reaches a guest first. The boy is no older than fifteen, and has angry red acne rolling across his skin. His white sneakers are scuffed and his jeans are torn, and not in a fashionable way. This boy spent what little money he had to come here tonight. He's the exact person I would have approached, which means Poppet and I are on the same page.

Don't approach the guests who have money, I had told her.

Why? she'd asked. *They're the ones who can return over and over again.*

We don't need repeats. We need the most coins, every night. To do that, we need to make a scene. Start with the easy ones, then slowly draw the others in.

Working in this house for only four nights has taught me that the town of Pox isn't a wealthy one. But they say there's a larger city an hour and a half away where townspeople commute. Close enough to earn a payday, too far to face a long drive home after having a beer.

Poppet touches the boy on his arms, his shoulders, comments on his striking smile. The other girls watch Poppet from the corner of their eye, surprised by her aggressiveness, but unconcerned because the boy isn't worth bothering with.

We can't compete with Mercy and Raquel and the others who have built up a clientele. And though they want new guests, they want them only if they're easy, or if they have potential to be added to their repertoire.

But the boy with the red hair and fiery skin?

He's up for grabs.

A part of me feels guilty, like I'm using him. But then I remember he came here to be entertained, to feel special for a little while, and I know the other girls will laugh behind his back and tell stories about his acne after he's gone. I won't do that. Neither will Poppet.

She brings him over to the bar, and I inspect the other six guests. Not many tonight, but that doesn't matter. We only need to secure the most coins. My eyes fall on a young guy and my breath catches. He's stunning. Mid-twenties, blond hair, blue eyes. He has a deep dimple in his chin, and a lean body. I could imagine a cowboy hat on his head and a stallion between his legs.

He sees me looking and smiles. It's warm, but guarded, as if he knows he shouldn't be here. I glance at his ring finger. Sure enough, there's an outline of a wedding band that the sun hasn't touched in years. He probably got married young, and the love has died out. Now he's here, looking to feel wanted again.

I detest him.

I turn away. It's not like we have a chance at him, anyway. I've seen one other young, attractive man come in here, and the girls practically drew blood trying to garner his attention. They'll want to make a repeat out of this guy if only to see that dimpled chin.

Our redheaded boy now has a drink in his hand, and I've taken a seat in front of my sketchpad. Poppet motions toward me, and he nods enthusiastically. He'll go wherever she goes, but it's my job to keep him occupied.

"This is Domino," Poppet says when the two get close. "She's an artist. She can draw you anything you want."

"That's not entirely true." I offer the boy my hand, and he brings it to his lips. It takes everything I have not to recoil. Nothing personal. It's just another level of touching, and I'm not even comfortable with the preliminaries. I jerk my hand back to my side. "I take requests, or I can draw you a surprise."

"Ooh, let her draw a surprise," Poppet squeals.

The boy sucks a syrupy brown drink through a striped straw. "Whatever you think," he says after he's swallowed.

Poppet sits him down on a beanbag and snuggles in close. "Tell me everything there is to know about you."

For the next two hours, I draw and Poppet laughs with such zeal that other customers begin to wander over. When I see girls giving us dirty looks, I warn them with a scowl that says I'll do to them what I did to Mercy. They don't call my bluff, and soon we have two customers lounging on the beanbags instead of one.

Cain watches from the bar. For a second, my attention to my sketchpad wavers, and I think about how he looked at me this morning. When he saw Mercy's face, he eyed me like he somehow knew I was to blame. I wonder if he's repulsed by my behavior. Maybe he's the kind of guy who likes dainty girls who don't mark their own skin and attack people.

To each his own.

"May I join you?"

I glance up and see the blond guy with the dangerous dimple. He's looking at me like I'm the only person in the room. My eyes return to his ring finger, but I smile as best I can and nod toward the beanbags.

He plops down in a red leather one and Styrofoam pebbles shoot out the side.

"I'm not married anymore," he says, causing my face to flush.

I return my gaze to my sketch. "I didn't ask."

Poppet gasps and slaps me on the arm. "I'm sorry. She's not feeling well tonight."

"You saw where I wore my ring," he pushes playfully. "Thought I was a dirtbag, right?"

I'm drawing a picture of the two dudes sitting on either side of Poppet. Now I try to work the new guy in. He's all hard lines, except for his face, which is velvet soft. "I wasn't looking."

"She passed away seven months ago," he announces.

I stop drawing, and Poppet practically crawls into his lap. "Oh, my gosh. How terrible. Tell us about her," she insists.

I would never have thought to ask the man about his wife. It seems like a touchy topic, but Poppet is brazen. The man smiles as he speaks about how they met, and even the other guys listen in on the story. Poppet ensures everyone is involved in the conversation.

Once, as the guy is speaking, a Carnation storms over, her lips pursed in frustration. I shoot to my feet and stare her down until she loses her nerve and returns to the other side of the room. I motion for Poppet to keep the guys talking, and when the night is all but over, we retain their attention.

I show them my finished illustration—three guys who look like the best of friends being adored by a beautiful girl—and the guests praise my work. Poppet asks them to pick a number to see who keeps it, and makes them promise to return this weekend.

Bronze coins fall into slots, and we start to clean up. Before long, Mercy will call for us to get ready for bed, and a new day will dawn. But for now, there's something I want to do. It's been too long since I tasted the night air, and I'm craving a real conversation, one without borders or false pretenses. So when backs are turned, I slip out of the entertainment room and from there the front door.

I count to thirty before the door opens a second time, and Cain appears. I nod toward the back of the house.

He follows without a sound.

CHAPTER 25

THE MOON AND THE STARS

Cain and I sit outside in silence for a few minutes. Not much time at all, but it feels stolen and delicious.

Wilson glares at Cain, wary.

You don't need a guy around, he reminds me. *Have you forgotten about Dizzy? He hurt you. I can't allow that to happen again.*

I glance over at Cain, expecting to see Dizzy's face, but he looks nothing like him. The two are as different as the moon and stars. One boy twinkles and shines with unrivaled energy. The other is solid in his approach; always there, under clear skies and overcast.

I'm not sure how I know these things about Cain. Call it a hunch.

"You hit that girl?" he asks, getting comfortable in his chair.

I turn my face away. "Yeah, I did."

He nods, but doesn't say anything else on the subject. His eyes return to my body and we meet each other's gaze. "Did one of the girls talk you into changing how you look?"

I wrap an arm around myself. "No one talks me into anything."

Cain laughs.

"What?"

He shrugs. "You're different, that's all."

"How so?"

"Most of the girls here are rotten inside. It's not their fault. It's just they let their past turn them. But you took a different approach. You built a wall on the outside to keep the inside intact."

"Don't pretend you know me."

Cain rubs his jaw. "I don't know you, Domino. I doubt many people do."

"What about you?" I say, turning things around. "Why do you work here?"

Shadows cross his face, and he stands. "I don't know what that person told you on the phone, but it wasn't good." He peers at me from over his shoulder. "You okay?"

"You didn't answer my question; why should I answer yours?"

Cain smiles and walks a couple of steps away. He crosses his arms, mimicking me, and stares out at the guesthouses. It's a long time before either of us speaks again. Finally, I ask him a bold question, maybe for shock value, maybe because I'm invincible with the moon standing so close.

"Do you think there's something different for you after this life is over?" I ask.

He steals a look in my direction. "Something easier, you mean?"

"Yeah."

"Like heaven?"

"Sure."

Cain shakes his head and releases a long breath. "Not for me, little lion."

Then he's gone, striding back toward the house, leaving me alone on my plastic chair, knees pulled tight against my chest.

CHAPTER 26

EMBRACE

I've lived inside Madam Karina's Home for Burgeoning Entertainers for almost two weeks. In that time, I let go of the fantasy that Dizzy ever really cared, I've removed the mask I wore for the past year, and I set a goal to earn twelve hundred dollars to rent a place of my own.

It's a goal Poppet and I are accomplishing together.

Today is market day, and I've paid off my debts and now have sixteen dollars to my name. Staggering, I know. Of course Poppet reminds me that if I leave the money with Madam Karina and Mr. Hodge that interest will accrue, so I go that route. It's not like I'm going to chance leaving cash out in the open again.

I buy nothing from the market and, though it takes some persuading, Poppet doesn't either. It's reward enough that we both finished in second and third place this week. Raquel is now in fourth, and retaliating at every turn. So are the other girls. I've woken up to gum in my hair and Poppet's favorite dress in shreds. We've been spit on, shoved, and humiliated. The girls now realize I'm not fighting back, and they're taking full advantage. But yesterday morning, a girl named Shiloh waited until Poppet came out of the shower. She then stole her towel and blocked the door while three other girls pointed out every flaw on her body.

If I'd seen that happen, I'm not sure I could have kept Wilson from returning. But I didn't, and Wilson has been good about lying low. In fact, the closer I get to Poppet and Cain, the less he whispers in my ear. It's as if they soothe something inside me that Wilson usually handles.

Eric descends the stairs and steps down into the basement. Poppet and I are both there. We're not buying, but we're still curious as to what's available and what the other girls are snapping up.

The officer sees me and waves me over. "Come with me to Madam Karina's room."

I glance at Poppet, and then do as he asks. As I follow him up three flights of stairs, nervous energy zipping through my body, I think about why he's here when he should be patrolling the streets of Pox. Maybe he's a private officer hired by Madam Karina. It still bugs me, though. Cops have certainly never done me any favors. I also remember what Poppet said about him being the one who found her. I think it was Eric who first saw me in Detroit, also. Is he some sort of recruiter on top of being an officer? I fidget at the idea.

Eric raps once and Mr. Hodge calls for him to enter. When we stride through the door, Madam Karina is lying in bed, a creamy duvet pulled to her waist. She's propped up by pillows and smiles when she sees me.

Without taking her eyes off my face, she tells Eric, "You can go."

Eric pinches his enormous nose. "What about our payment? The boys are getting antsy, and I'm still waiting for my finder's fee—"

"Did you not hear what she said?" Mr. Hodge interjects.

"She said go. Now get out of here before I bust your head open."

"Oh, Frank," Madam Karina says, as if she's truly horrified by Mr. Hodge's demeanor.

Eric grunts and slams the door behind him.

I stare at the space he once occupied and think about what he said. About his boys getting antsy. Does Eric have sons? Does he mean the other Pox police officers?

Madam Karina opens her arms. "Come here, Domino. Sit right next to me on the bed." Mr. Hodge pulls out a cell phone and stares down at it as I cross the room. I sit where she tells me to and Madam Karina pulls herself up farther. "You know, I've never seen a girl make such quick progress. Not since Lola, anyway. She's our Top Girl. Do you know what that means?"

I shake my head, because I want to hear her explain.

"Top Girl is my right hand gal. I meet with her every Sunday and we discuss the ongoings at the house." She glances at a clock on her nightstand. "In fact, she'll be here soon. We'll have lunch in our room. Might watch a movie when we're done doing business."

She touches my hand briefly. "You know, you're a lot like Lola. Smart, attractive. You figure things out quickly and make them work in your favor. Except Lola is more like a bulldozer, and you're more a rabbit, hopping over girls so no one gets hurt."

"Rabbit. That's what I call you, kid," Mr. Hodge says without looking up.

Madam Karina's lips form a thin line, but she relaxes soon enough. "I'm wondering where the sudden competitiveness is coming from."

"What do you mean?"

The madam touches my bare cheek. "You took off your

makeup, and you're working with that Poppy girl."

"Poppet."

"That's right. So what's your end goal? You know I'm happy with all my girls. Even the ones who stay Carnations forever."

I swallow, decide there's no harm in her knowing a piece of my plan. "I want to become a Daisy."

Madam Karina radiates light. "That's fantastic. But why?"

I avert my gaze. I want to trust Madam Karina, and Poppet, and Cain, but for some reason I don't tell her about wanting my own place. So I say, "I want more time with you."

I disgust myself. First, because what I'm saying is true. Second, because it makes me pathetic. Madam Karina may have her faults, but she's been nothing but kind to me. Except for that one time she lost her temper for a moment. But no one's perfect.

Madam Karina throws her legs over the side of the bed and hangs her head.

"Did I do something wrong?" I ask.

She shakes her head. "No, sweetie." She looks up at me, her eyes glistening. "It's just that most of my girls fight among themselves for status only, and maybe money to fatten their accounts. It feels nice to be needed."

For the first time, I realize the madam and I aren't so different. Maybe we've both been abandoned. Maybe we're both cautious to love, and yet desperate for it all the same.

She holds up a finger. "I have an idea, Miss Domino Ray. Did you know that you have to remain Point Girl for the Carnations for three months, and retain your cumulative top earning rank, before being promoted to a Daisy?"

My heart plummets. No, I most definitely did not know that. I can't survive another two and a half months with Mercy and Raquel and the other Carnations. I'll lose my temper. I'll do something terrible.

"I'd like to see how you do with a little motivation." She stands up. "How about I give you one week to prove you are worthy of being a Daisy? If you can get first placement and stay there until next Sunday, I'll promote you. But only this week. And you should know there's no going back. Once you have taken a step up, you stay there."

My breath catches at this challenge. "Why would you do this?"

She shrugs, makes a face like something smells. "Lola is great. But I need new blood to work with. A sharp mind that can help take my home to a higher level." Madam Karina opens her mouth and closes it. Opens it again. "I told you I had a sister..." She hisses the last word. "She has a home for girls, too. It's in Detroit. I often travel days to visit her, which is how you and I came to meet. While I'm there, she talks only of herself and her accomplishments. Do you know someone like that?"

I nod, though I'm not sure I do.

"Disgusting, really. But my mother adored her." Madam Karina crosses the room suddenly, takes my face in her hands. "Do you know what it's like to be ignored? No, of course you don't. Look at that face."

"I know what it's like," I whisper, thinking of my father, who left me all alone.

Madam Karina studies my eyes as if deciding whether I'm being honest. Then she releases me, goes to her dresser, and pulls something from the bottom drawer. It's a piece of manila paper folded twice, lined and yellowing with age. The madam clutches it in her hands before unfolding it and waving me over.

When I come to stand beside her and look down at the paper, my heart clenches. It's a colorful picture drawn by a child's hand. A young stick-figure girl stands outside a house resembling the one we're in now, and beside her is a smiling woman who must be her mother. The mother and daughter are holding hands, and between their fingers is a bushel of violets. In front of them lies a garden of purple violets spraying in all directions. The mother seems to be offering every last one to her daughter.

Above their heads is one word written with an orange crayon.

HOME

That word is the most prominent part of the picture, as if whoever drew this went over and over it until the sheet nearly tore from the pressure.

"Violets were her favorite," Madam Karina says in a whisper. When she turns and looks at me, there's an unreadable expression on her face. "We're alike, you and I. Seeking a place, or maybe a feeling, we never really had."

She releases me and glances at Mr. Hodge, who's still messing with his phone. "What are you doing over there? Have you heard anything I've been saying?"

He glances up. "Were you speaking to me, love?"

"No," Madam Karina whines. "But you wouldn't have heard a word if I had been."

"Puppy…" he says, tilting his head.

Madam Karina looks back at me with a smile, her sadness tossed aside. "One week. How does it sound?"

"It sounds great, thank you." I pause, raise my chin. "But I need Poppet with me."

"The girl with the glasses and big hair," she says.

I smile. "Yeah, her."

Madam Karina scrunches her nose. "Domino, be careful where you place your alliances. Someone as strong and ambitious as yourself can be taken advantage of by girls who are, well…" She mouths the word "dumb."

I bristle. "I appreciate your offer, Madam, but I don't want to go anywhere if it's not with Poppet."

Madam Karina laughs. "Poppet. What a ridiculous name. Now Domino? There's a name. Makes me think of gambling and placing bets and throwing caution to the wind." When I don't respond, she takes me by the shoulders. "I didn't mean to insult your friend. It's strange, but I suppose I believe in you so much that I don't want anything to get in your way. It makes me defensive on your behalf. Isn't that odd? Me being defensive of you as if you were my own child?"

My chest opens. Maybe literally. Maybe my chest plate has split open and my bloody heart beats for her alone. I'm more vulnerable in this moment than I have been in a long time. I suspect if Madam Karina only reached out, she could take my pulsing heart straight into her hands and I'd go on breathing if she told me to.

Madam Karina acting as if she is my mother.

Me acting as her child.

What could that look like?

No! Wilson snaps, grabbing my heart and shielding it from view. *No.*

"Domino," she coos, bringing her face to mine. "You look as if you've seen a ghost. Could I…? That is, I've noticed you don't prefer being touched. But I wonder if I might hug you. Just this once."

I stand stock-still, but my pulse races. I've never been asked permission to be touched. Will it feel different? Slowly, I nod.

Madam Karina steps forward and even Mr. Hodge looks on, curious as to how I'll react. She opens her arms and before I know it, they are around me. She lays her cheek against the crown of my head and her fingers splay against my back, holding me close. Then she does something that pushes me to my limits. She raises a hand and covers the side of my face with it, presses my head closer to her chest and says, softly, "Shh, child. Shhh."

After I step back, I have to hang my head so she can't see the emotion stretched across my face. A war wages in my mind. On one side, I want to hug Madam Karina forever. I want to be Top Girl and inherit this house and continue running her business to show my gratitude. On the other, I'm too afraid to let my guard down. I can't handle being manipulated again.

Not after my mother showed me her bitterness.

Not after I helped her do the dirty things.

An image of a man weeping springs to mind. He's talking about his daughter, saying her name over and over again as if this will help. My mother stands beside me, eyes blazing. I touch the man's check tenderly, a dangerous hand hidden behind my back. No, not me. I don't touch the man. Wilson does.

Stop peeking, Domino! Wilson pulls an iron curtain closed, and the image fades away.

Madam Karina smooths her green silk robe and touches a hand to her hair. "If you succeed in becoming Point Girl this coming week, and your friend helps, you may both be promoted to Daisies. Now return to your room. Lola will be up shortly."

She turns away from me, and I can't help wondering if she's hiding her own face as well. If that hug didn't mean as much to her as it did to me.

CHAPTER 27

PEPPERMINT

Over the next week, Poppet and I are like bandits. We pick out the guest no one else wants, and show them a good time. Such a good time that other guests wander over. We even pick up a repeat in the form of a blond-haired, blue-eyed, dimple-donning widower.

He says his name is Jack.

Today is Sunday, and Poppet and I stand in front of the placement board. She clutches my hand in hers, and I let her do it even though it makes me itch. It all comes down to today's ranking. There have been nights we've faltered, and nights we swept the room. But we need high placements today to be the top girls overall this week.

The board flashes twice.

And the names scroll across the display.

1. Poppet
2. Domino
3. Mercy

Mercy calls us filthy names, and I give her credit for originality. But beyond that, I don't care. Because we did it. Somehow, Poppet and I have secured a place on the second floor. Madam Karina strides into the room and calls us over, pink envelopes in one hand, three violets in the other.

I take my envelope and flower, and Madam Karina beams. She leans down. "Meet me upstairs in an hour."

I'm all but shaking with excitement, but I glance at Poppet as if asking a question. Madam Karina rolls her eyes but doesn't lose her smile. She nods.

Yes, you can bring her.

I swallow a squeal even though I'm not the squealing type, and race toward the basement. As of today, I have forty-two dollars and sixty-six cents to my name. And I earned it. I've never had a job before, and I'm surprised by how satisfying it is. Poppet races after me, and suddenly I can't help myself. I burst out laughing and Poppet does too and we run down the stairs. The Daisies and Tulips are nowhere in sight, which slays my enthusiasm, because all I want to do right now is stare at each Daisy in turn and decide which girls might be nice.

"What are you two giggling about?" Angie asks as she unpacks a box of toothbrushes.

"We're going to be Daisies." Poppet shimmies. "And it's all because of Domino. She's so smart."

"Uh, it was you who placed first today." I walk toward the open cage and reach for a box. "Here, I can help."

Angie snatches it away and glances over my shoulder. "Back up. Don't be so goddamn overeager."

I bite my tongue, hurt by her words. "Sorry."

"Don't you remember what happened last time?" Angie mutters.

"Stop it, Angie," Cain says. The lack of hostility in his voice reminds me the woman is harmless, and to match her blow for blow.

I fold my arms over my chest. "How's that POS tractor of yours? Still an embarrassment to the auto community?"

Angie bolts upright. "How dare you talk about Black Betty that way."

Poppet laughs. "I didn't know your tractor had a name."

"Nor should you," Angie clips. "Now both of you go away so I can work."

I look at Cain, and he shifts his weight. "You really going to be a Daisy?"

"Yeah," I respond. "Madam Karina offered us a challenge, and we met it."

"She's so nice," Poppet says. "Madam Karina pretty much saved me, and now this."

Angie's face darkens, and a deep line forms between her brows. When I notice how quiet she's being, I lower my voice so that no one upstairs can hear. "What is it?"

Her head whips around. "If there was anything to say I'd say it. Now didn't I tell you to get out of here? I've got five minutes before those girls start screaming for their Sunday haul."

As if on cue, footsteps hit the stairs. Poppet and I watch as the girls line up and trade their hard-earned coins for suede clutches and wide-tooth combs and fashion magazines. I watch the Daisies but they buzz too quickly, and before I know it, they're racing back upstairs with their prizes.

I trail after them, wide-eyed, as they chatter all the way to the second story and out of sight. Excitement blooms in my belly once again.

"This what you want?" Angie asks, startling me. I spin around and take in her soft curls, her dimpled chin, and her small hands that have held more cigarettes than either of us could count. "You want to stay in this house?"

Defiance rolls through me like lava pressed against the mouth of a volcano. "What if I do?"

Angie smiles a sad smile. "Everyone here has such blistering youth." Even though she's speaking plainly, it's as if she's asking me to read between her words. When I don't say anything, she pushes through the screen door and out into the summer heat.

I'm not sure what provokes me to follow her outside. I should be collecting Poppet and heading upstairs. I have a daisy to collect, after all. But I follow her all the same. Standing on the porch, I call out her name.

She turns around.

"You think Cain is nice, right?"

She takes two steps toward me, looks over my shoulder at the house and then back at me. "Yeah, course he is. Why you asking such a stupid question?"

My eyes flick toward the sky, afraid to appear too eager, like she said. "Why does he stay here when the girls are mean to him? Aren't there better jobs in Pox?"

Angie doesn't say anything. She just stands there, breathing hard like she's rooted on a land mine, afraid uttering one word will blow us all to kingdom come. Somehow, this is worse than any response.

"Is it because of the money? Does he need it for something?"

Her hands curl into fists. "If you think that woman is paying him a nickel for his time, you're dead wrong. Now stop asking me things. Ask him yourself if you're so interested."

Angie turns to leave, but then spins back around. She paces toward me and digs her hand in her pocket, pulls out a peppermint. She holds it out and looks away like she couldn't care less if I take it.

But I do…take it.

And when Cain appears through the open door a second later, she shoves another one into my palm.

"For the boy," she says.

Then she's gone, walking toward Black Betty like there's a fire blazing at her back. There are two Dobermans I've never seen before bouncing around the tractor. She brushes them aside, and they bark wildly as she starts the tractor's engine.

"Don't give my dogs the peppermints," she yells over the rumble. "It'll make Kali sick. Damn dog has a sensitive stomach."

I'm not sure why I'd ever give a dog a peppermint, so I stuff them obediently into my pocket and watch as she chugs down the road, dogs chasing behind, her head bobbing in the distance.

I like her, Wilson says cautiously.

Yeah, I think. *I do, too.*

CHAPTER 28

A NOD

It's still early morning when Poppet and I gather our things and head toward the staircase. My blood runs hot when I realize I'll never get back the money I came here with from whoever stole it. Madam Karina said once you move to a new floor, you can't return to the old one. Of course, I don't want to come back here. Especially after the Carnations find out Madam Karina made special allowances for Poppet and me to advance. If the harassment was bad before, I can't imagine what it would be like now.

I start to put on my blue wig, but Poppet tells me I shouldn't. "You've turned over a new leaf," she says. "Embrace it." I agree, but I won't throw them away no matter how much she presses. I'm an addict where my armor is concerned. I may be in recovery, but I still need it there.

In case.

So I carry my wigs, jewelry, linens, and Dizzy's shirt in my arms, and together we climb the stairs. We can't help giggling, anticipating this new chapter. I've never seen the Daisies in their natural habitat. Will things run differently there? Will the girls be welcoming?

We reach the second floor and glance around. To our left are two large rooms. One is open and spacious with couches, a radio, and…a television! Two Daisies are sitting cross-legged in front of it, faces leaned forward, cheeks glowing orange and green and blue from the screen. The other room's door is half open, so I can't see much of what's inside. I make out black paint on the walls, but the rest is hidden.

On our right is a hallway that must lead to the bedrooms. We're about to walk down it when Mr. Hodge yells for us to wait. He marches up the stairs, wheezing and turning red around the collar. When he makes it to the top, he grabs his belt buckle and lifts his khaki pants to hoist them over his belly, but they only slide back down.

The man smiles. There's a piece of spinach from breakfast wedged between his upper teeth. "I'll show you ladies to your room. You're Daisies now, and that means you get more of my attention."

"Thank you, Mr. Hodge." Poppet grins up at him. I try, and fail, to do the same.

As he walks us down the hall, I peek inside some of the bedrooms. They aren't much bigger than the ones downstairs, which is to say they're closet-sized. I bet when Madam Karina inherited the house, she put in extra walls to create these miniature rooms.

Our room has two twin beds with six inches between them, and one dresser I could touch if I pointed my toes while dreaming. A lamp stands on the dresser—a pitiful shade of green—and the hardwood floor is stained in one corner.

"Go on in, girls." Mr. Hodge is talking to both of us, but I don't miss the way his hand pats Poppet's bottom. She freezes, and when his fingers linger, I slap his hand away without thinking. Mr. Hodge's face turns the color of an eggplant, and he flares his nostrils.

"Better watch your temper, girl," he snaps.

"Better watch your hands," I reply. Then, to ensure he

understands never to touch her again, I add, "I know Madam Karina would appreciate it if you did."

He gives me a sinister smile. The spinach is gone from his teeth. Must have swallowed it. "Sure hope you girls don't prove Madam Karina wrong. I'd hate for you to go the way of Ellie."

The Neck storms down the hallway. The second he's out of sight, I swing around. "Who's he talking about?"

Poppet's back is to me. She shrugs as she makes her bed, using the sheets we brought from downstairs. Though there's a pink dust ruffle on each bed that's entirely out of place, the mattresses are bare.

"You don't know a girl named Ellie?"

"No, should I?"

I glance down at the bundle in my arms. "Is it the girl I replaced?"

"Could be. I'm not sure," she says. But that's not what it seems like. It seems like Poppet knows exactly who she is.

I drop my stuff on the bed and sit. Gripping the edge of the mattress, I try a different approach. "Did you know Cain works here for free?"

Poppet meets my gaze. "I did know that."

I laugh, because this place is getting to be too much with its secrets. "So, there's a girl named Ellie who no one will talk about. And a boy named Cain who's probably working here against his will."

"That's not true."

"Which part?"

"Cain stays because he has nowhere else to go."

"That's bull," I respond. "Everyone has somewhere else to go."

Poppet fluffs her pillow. "Well, I've heard he doesn't."

"And you don't know why?"

Poppet smiles like a thought just occurred to her. "Do you think we'll get our Daisy Tuesday morning if we earn a coin tomorrow night?" She touches her blouse. "I feel naked without my Carnation."

"Poppet…"

She throws her hands up. "I don't know why he works here, Dom. Not really. And you shouldn't talk about Ellie. She left the home and it made Madam Karina angry. Angrier than I've ever seen her. Mr. Hodge said we aren't to talk about her or we'll get kicked out. But it's only so that the madam doesn't get upset. I've told you as much."

"You haven't told it to me like that. And what's the big deal if she left? Surely girls leave all the time."

Poppet doesn't have time to answer, because a girl strides into view. "Oh, you two are the newbies, yeah? We're watching TV in the lounge. Want to come hang out?"

My entire body is drawn to this girl with sloping cheekbones and almond-shaped eyes and kind words. Her smile could be seen from Saturn, and she oozes confidence. No, sorry, wrong word. Maybe coolness?

Better.

"We can come with you?" I ask.

Poppet strides past me. "You heard the woman. Let's go watch TV."

As we walk toward the lounge, we learn the girl's name— Ruby. She wears a red scarf, though it has to be a hundred degrees outside. I wonder if that's her thing. Matching her clothing to her name. She has blond eyebrows though her hair is black, and pulls a lip gloss out of her pocket as we walk. She never applies it, just uses it to gesture as she speaks.

Ruby introduces us to the other five Daisies, and as they greet us warmly, and the ice around my heart begins to melt, Lola walks by. She's on her way to the third floor to see

Madam Karina, but she cranes her neck to peer inside.

Our eyes connect, and she pauses, one hand on the banister, right foot already on the next step. The back of my neck tingles, and I raise an uncertain hand in a wave. She doesn't wave back, but she does nod almost unperceivably. Not in a way that she's saying hello. And not even in a way that I've done something right, and she's acknowledging the action. But more like I've followed her plan nicely.

She turns away and glides out of view.

After she's gone, the Daisies pull Poppet and me down to sit with them. They drill us for information on what's going on with the Carnations. They offer us salty buttered popcorn, and Ruby asks if I'll draw something while the others watch. It's one of the best afternoons I've had in a long time, filled with gossip and requests for Cain to bring up frozen grapes and sweet tea. And Cain does bring that tray, quickly, with a quiet smile I return.

We Daisies watch a movie about three teen witches that's supposed to be scary, but makes the girls laugh. I laugh a little, too. When no one is looking. When no one can guess how elated I am to be here among girls who don't call me names.

Soon, I forget all about the look Lola gave me as she passed by.

CHAPTER 29

COME WITH ME

I touch a finger to the white silk daisy pinned on my shirt. Poppet and I earned them after working two nights on the second floor and collecting our first bronze coin.

My time as a Daisy moves quickly. It's very different than the Carnation floor, and it's fun—but something very wrong is happening here.

Ruby, the Point Girl of the Daisies, pops her head in Poppet's and my room. Her smile illuminates the space as she says, "Ready in five, okay, girls? Don't forget to turn off the light when you leave. No reason to waste energy, yeah?"

Poppet doesn't even try to return Ruby's enthusiasm. She just slips into a floor-length dress to cover the mysterious cut marks that have appeared on her legs. As for me, I pull on a long-sleeved gown, one of Poppet's, of course. I have new cuts steadily blooming across my forearms, and I have no idea where they came from. The only connection I make is that we each wake up with a new one every morning.

Two nights ago, we slept in shifts to catch Mercy or Raquel sneaking upstairs to continue their torment. But Poppet fell asleep, and so we woke with a fourth cut. They are shallow and not terribly painful. But that's not the point. The point is the Carnations are sending us a message. They're angry that we left them behind, and they won't let us go that easily.

Last night, I tried a new tactic. I encouraged Poppet to sleep, and then jammed the door with a chair from the family room. When I woke up, a thin, swollen line marked the fifth night.

I vowed to Poppet that I'd talk to Madam Karina tomorrow morning. I have to. But tonight, we have to continue with our plan. Though I sometimes daydream about becoming Top Girl and taking over this house, I know I'm kidding myself. I'm not a business owner. I don't know the first thing about managing money or advertising or whatever else it takes to be successful.

All I know is that I need four strong walls that are mine. For an entire year, I've been on my own. Dizzy entertained me for a while, but in the end, Dizzy was a one-man show, and I guess I don't fault him for that. Then there was Madam Karina's Home for Burgeoning Entertainers, a house of hope and horrors. It's a means to an end, and I know what I want.

I want my own house.

And I want Poppet to come with me.

Poppet is rushing to the bathroom for a last minute makeup check when I stop her. "Hey, I want to ask you something."

Her eyebrows rise.

"You know how I said I wanted to get my own place one day? Well, I'm really going to do it. I'm going to keep moving up in the house until I have enough money. I'll even become a Violet if that's what it takes."

"What's your question?" Poppet's voice is unnaturally soft.

"I want you to come with me. When I get enough money and I leave, I want you to come too."

Poppet is already shaking her head.

"Poppet, listen, we can't stay here. There's too much that's off."

"Like what?"

I glance into the hallway before continuing. "Like the fact that Madam Karina has a police officer on staff, and that girls rarely go into town, and that no one is supposed to discuss the girl I replaced." I trace my fingers over the cuts on my arm that were made by someone else's hand. "Where do the girls go who leave here, Poppet? Why doesn't anyone talk about them?"

She shrugs. "I think most that apply to leave go live in Pox."

"You have to apply to leave? See, that's just it. Why would you have to apply?"

"So you can get paid out." Poppet steps back. "Look, I really like that you're asking me to go with you, but there's nothing bad going on here outside of the Carnations turning on me. On us. Plus, I like it here, even with what's been going on lately. This home is a better one than I've had in the past."

The last part she whispers, and my stomach twists. Maybe I'm overreacting. Maybe Wilson is, too, when he reminds me, late at night as I try to sleep, to be careful.

I don't like it here. Wilson paces back and forth. *It's got me on edge.*

I push my tongue against the roof of my mouth, try to feel the hole that a silver bar once filled. "Maybe you're right. But…"

"But what?"

I hesitate, because I don't want to say the real reason being in this home bugs me. If I say it aloud, then it becomes real. Eyes cast downward, nerves rattling under my skin, I speak my mind. "What do you think the girls in the guesthouses do? The Lilies and Violets?"

Wilson raises his hand. *Ooh, I know! Pick me!*

Poppet puffs out her cheeks and thinks on my question.

"Want to know what my first response to that question is?"

"I do."

"We'd be lucky to find out. Want my second? I'll give it to you. Probably nothing worse than I've done in my past. And maybe a lot better."

I dwell on this. Realize she's right. There's nothing I could do as a Violet that would compare to the thing I did in my parents' home. A memory flashes into my mind. One of my mother plucking a splinter from the heel of my foot. I remember the concentration on her face, the smell of rubbing alcohol. It took her ten minutes to get that sucker out, but afterward she made me apple cobbler with vanilla bean ice cream, and we made a fire in the hearth. It was almost Christmas, only a few short weeks before my father changed our lives forever.

Before he slighted my mother.

Before he made her into a monster.

Poppet is dead-on. Nothing the girls do in Madam Karina's Home for Burgeoning Entertainers can rival the blood on my hands.

CHAPTER 30

INFERNO

R uby reappears in the doorway; the grin on her face is a carefully wrapped gift. "Ready to work, ladies?"

Poppet gathers the length of her dress and follows after Ruby. We're halfway down the hall when she turns and speaks in a low voice. "It's not that I want you to leave," she says. "It's just that I've decided on this place. For however long the madam wants my help, I'm going to give it."

I'm touched by her loyalty, and who am I to say it's misplaced? So I smile and walk beside her in silence. Twenty paces ahead is a full night's work, and though my mind ticks with unanswered questions about this place, one thing is certain—the Daisy's entertainment room isn't like the Carnation's room.

Already, I can hear the psychedelic music and the girls speaking in hushed tones. My pulse races as we grow closer, and my scalp tingles with anxiety. The Carnations' room was simply called the entertainment room, maybe the E-room if we were feeling lazy. But the Daisies arena is different, and appropriately named "The Inferno."

Wilson sits up straighter as we pass by the coin boxes and step inside. And though he's been submissive after my attack on Mercy, he shakes his head and says, *The Inferno? Really?*

Oh, yeah, now I feel better.

    Stop talking, I respond. *And go away.*

    He doesn't go away.

    And as I move farther into the room, I'm glad for it.

    Red starbursts hang from invisible threads throughout the room. The carpet is black, the walls, black, the couches and bar and even the digital placement board—black. Cutouts of crows and ravens mingle with the red starbursts, and the girls weave through them like phantoms, their bodies splashed with white polka dots from a disco ball. Incense is burned in crystal holders shaped like elephant trunks. It smells like human hair caught ablaze, with a hint of sage thrown in for good measure.

    A girl with a fiery braid faces away from me, but I see the way her head falls back, how another girl dangles a white pill above her open mouth like one would a tuft of bread above a koi pond. The pill freefalls, and both girls giggle. Soon, they are hugging and rubbing each other's arms in ecstasy. Ruby leans her head in my direction. "Last time I'll ask. Sure you don't want to try one? You will sooner or later."

    I shake my head. Drugs aren't my thing, though every time she offers, I can't help wondering if they could help me silence Wilson for good.

    Would you really want that? Because without me…

    Ruby places a pill on her tongue and swallows. "Dinner of champions." When I offer a shy smile, she bumps my shoulder. "Come on, Domino. You should try laughing once in a while. You don't have to worry anymore. For most of us, this is where the train stops. We're serious when we say if you're a Daisy, you're family."

    That word is like a bedside lamp in the dead of night. Eerie shadows, sudden creaks, footsteps falling lightly across your blackened room, all soothed with a little switch.

Family.

Poppet refuses the drugs, too, but isn't shy when mingling with the other girls. It takes longer than it did with the Carnations for Madam Karina to arrive with her black marker. I'm guessing she starts on the bottom floor and works her way up.

"Get in line, ladies," the madam says. "Hands out."

We do as she says. I get the number six written on my hand, and Poppet gets a five. She finished well last night, so I knew she'd be ahead of me. Still, we are close to the bottom. There are only seven girls, and my being number six doesn't fare well. We'll have to work our way up the chain. It's the only way to advance again. And I will advance. This is my plan now, and I'm committed. It's hard, though, because my sketchpad isn't as useful here as it was downstairs. Not when dancing is the dominant source of entertainment currency.

Madam Karina glides through the velvet-curtained doorway, and soon heavy boots fall upon the stairs. Mixed with the sound is the clicking of heels.

Our customers have arrived.

Poppet comes to stand by my side, and a silent understanding passes between us. She may not want to leave with me when I go, but it doesn't stop her from desiring a place among the Violets. It's what everyone wants inside Madam Karina's Home for Burgeoning Entertainers, even if they're too afraid to fight for the position.

Eight customers file into the room. They move toward a circular bar that's aglow in a red light. Champagne bottles and plastic glasses await their arrival. There are no silver coins in their pockets for booze. The champagne will do just fine. That's not what they came for, anyway. They came for Poppet and me. And for the other girls.

And they came for the drug buffet.

The customers open their painted beaks like baby birds awaiting their mother. White pills skydive into their mouths and their throats thank them kindly. Ruby approaches a black box perched near the far wall and turns a knob.

The music grows violent.

And the dancing begins.

Poppet and I dance alone for a long time. She's terrible at moving her body, and she'll admit as much, but what she lacks in rhythm she makes up for in energy. When she spots a woman hardly moving to the beat, Poppet takes the lady's sweaty palms in her own. She raises them over her head and shakes them until the woman laughs. Then she guides her toward me, and I dance on the opposite side of her.

I don't touch her, but I stay close.

Swallowing my trepidation, I yell in the woman's ear. Ask her name. Her hobbies. Offer to get her another drink. She refuses the drink, and I'm glad for it. Her eyes are fully dilated and I can hardly understand her responses. But she seems happy to dance between Poppet and me, and a few minutes later, another guest joins us.

Two, I think, but we need more.

A hand touches my waist and I spin around, heart pounding. The man's fingers leave my skin when he sees he's upset me. I take in his solar grin, his lean body, his blond hair.

Jack.

CHAPTER 37

EYES OPEN

I t's too-old-to-be-touching-me-that-way Jack. Too old to put a smile on my face, but I smile anyway.

"Didn't see you downstairs," he hollers over the music. "Had to pay again to come upstairs." He returns his hand to my waist. I'm not sure I like that. I'm not sure I don't like it, either.

I lean forward. "I got promoted."

He raises thick eyebrows to show he's impressed. "That what you want? To stay in this fairy-tale castle?"

I hesitate before answering. "Maybe, maybe not."

"I could help you do that is all." His hand is still on my waist. I can feel it there like a bee sting. "You need those coins, right?"

I nod.

"Tell you what; I'll help you out, but you have to help me, too." He smiles, but his eyes don't smile with him.

I lean close to his ear because I need his coin, and because Poppet has our other two customers entertained. "What do you want?"

He squeezes my hip, his fingers digging deep. "Tell me one true thing about yourself every night."

I forget his touch. He wants me to talk about myself? I

wonder why he cares. I'm one girl among many.

My mind snaps to the house I want so badly, and my reservations slide away. "Show me what you can do to help me, and I'll talk."

His other hand finds my waist, and he lifts me into the air. I'm so surprised that I laugh. The sound is foreign, someone else's happiness. Jack jostles me over his head like I'm a child, light as a snowflake, as the disco ball dances across my face.

"I have here in my hands the most beautiful girl in the room," he bellows.

The smile leaves my face, afraid the other girls won't like what he's saying, but now the other customers are laughing, too. They take a hesitant step in our direction, and when Jack gathers my legs into his arms and clutches me against his chest, they take another. His body feels slight against mine, dainty almost. I imagine him without his shirt, bones above his hips sharp as lightning slicing the sky.

Cain could destroy him.

I don't know why my mind always goes there. Destructive, wicked places. Who's stronger? Who's more dangerous?

I am, Wilson answers.

His voice disappears inside the folds of my mind when Jack hands me to another customer. A boy of fifteen, sixteen at best. He's missing a canine tooth, and there's an insistent freckle in the center of his bottom lip. The boy celebrates the gift Jack has given him, raising me up to show his strength. I'm still being cradled like a doll, and realizing, remembering, I hate people's hands on my body.

The boy's hand trails down my side where a viper slithers in faded green ink.

"Let me down!" I yell.

He lets me down.

I figure I've undone Jack's work, but he's created a ripple

in the tide, and now the customers have circled around Poppet and me. Jack's hand finds the bottom of my back. A gentle nudge, and I'm pressed against my friend. Poppet's small eyes enlarge when she finds me so close.

The room holds its breath, and then Poppet pulls me into her orbit. Now my hands are on her shoulders and her hands are on my hips and Jack reaches over to touch my bottom lip. My mouth opens on instinct, a venus flytrap welcoming a slippery-legged insect.

He tips his glass, and champagne rushes down my throat. Poppet does the same when he balances it over her lips. Jack raises the glass and the music *thrum, thrum, thrums* and my mind goes fuzzy and alert at once. Focusing on everything and nothing, becoming one with the dancing bodies. Flesh of my flesh, blood of my blood.

Oh, Holy Father.

Forgive me my sins.

It doesn't take long for me to understand it was more than champagne I swallowed. Three whirls around my merry-go-mind and I knew. I didn't care that Jack slipped me something as much as I should. It pushed Wilson down the way I thought it might, and now the people that reach out aren't as intimidating as they were before. Poppet grabs hands with a customer next to her, and another one, too. We form a circle and sway side to side slowly, though the song calls for something much faster. Jack takes a piece of my hair in his hand, and I close my eyes to his touch.

I don't know the first thing about him.

But he wants to know about me.

Should I tell him I'm lethal? That I'm as safe as a highball of arsenic? That would go well, I think. Jack's hands find my neck, and I'm pulled away from the pack of customers, singled out like a gazelle, a hyena in pursuit.

I open my eyes, and Jack is everywhere at once. How can a skinny guy take up so much space? Maybe *guy* is the wrong word for him. He's in his mid-twenties, I'd say. But I can already spot the place his hair will thin, like it's holding its breath for an especially windy day.

"How do you feel?" His words slide down my back, sticky-sweet sap oozing from the trunk of a tree.

"Good." I cross my arms over my head and let the music hold me up by the collar. How long have I been dancing? An hour? Three? "You put something in my drink."

He smiles shamefully, shifts to his right.

That's when I see Cain over his shoulder. His jaw is tight, and his hands hang heavy by his sides, the muscles jumping in his biceps. He reaches for me and pulls me away from Jack. But Jack's not one to be abandoned so easily. He makes a grab for my wrist and tugs.

I turn around, and his face blurs in and out of focus.

"You didn't tell me anything," Jack accuses.

I bow for whatever reason. "You haven't guaranteed me anything yet. Tomorrow, we'll see."

"Domino," Cain says low in his throat.

Jack ignores him. "Tell me."

I don't look back at Cain. Instead, I keep my gaze steady on this man who does as he pleases. This man who is laughter and playfulness to Cain's biting truth and solidarity. "Okay, Jack," I say. "You want to know something about me?"

He nods, solemn.

I lean close. "I was born with my eyes open. When I slid from my mother's womb, my eyes were open. I see everything. I don't always pay attention, but I see it."

"Do you see me?" he asks.

"Yes, you," I answer. "One day, you may wish I didn't."

Cain touches my shoulder blade and I spin around, head

downstairs toward our place beneath the stars. My blood kicks in my veins, and my mind thumps recklessly. I answered Jack's question, but it's Cain who has my attention.

Tonight, I'll ask him a question of my own.

Already, nerves fire through my body, anticipating how he'll react.

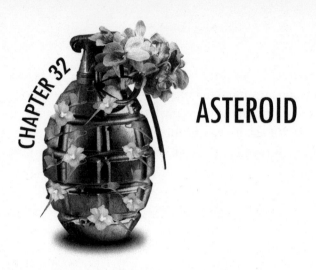

CHAPTER 32

ASTEROID

t's the first night Cain has come for me since I've become a Daisy. I never expected it, but that doesn't mean I didn't secretly hope he'd show.

We head behind the house in silence and take our places in the two plastic chairs. The one I sit in has a back leg that's shorter than the rest. I rock side to side to hear the off-balance thumping. Eventually, Cain reaches a hand over and lays it on my arm to stop me. Maybe that's why I did it in the first place.

He lights a cigarette and we watch the Lilies' and Violets' guesthouses. I think about Lola, wonder what she's doing in there. Question why I care. Then I look at Madam Karina's empty flowerbed. Wonder how often she prayed for her mother to give her a fistful of violets and say she was worthy. As worthy as her sister who moved to Detroit and opened her own business.

I turn to Cain. I've got a bombshell question up my sleeve that I'm ready to toss into open water, take cover and wait for the salty sting. "Why do you work for Madam Karina?"

His cigarette is halfway to his mouth when my question hits him square between the eyes. He doesn't bring the cigarette any farther. It just sits there, wrinkled, crumbling ashes onto his lap. "What do you mean? It's a job."

"Does she pay you?"

"That's a pretty personal question."

My teeth snap together. "Well, let's try being personal for once. We've done enough tiptoeing."

"You don't want to know why I'm here, Domino. If you did, you wouldn't want anything to do with me."

I shoot to my feet, and my head spins. Whatever Jack put in my drink takes full effect. Cain must see how dizzy I am because he stands, too, flicks his cigarette toward the ashtray, doesn't get anywhere near it. "What's wrong with you?"

I put a palm flat against my forehead. "Just answer my question. I need someone to be straight with me. Just one person."

"Well, that person isn't going to be me."

I spin on him and close the distance between us. "Then why are you doing this? Why come out here with me? Why try to protect me?" I point a finger at him. "Don't think I haven't noticed the little things you've done. And don't kid yourself into thinking I need protecting."

Cain lowers his head. "Back away, Domino."

"Why? What happens if I push?" I shove him in the chest. I don't know why I'm antagonizing him. Because of the champagne and drugs, maybe. Because I'm afraid of getting too close, most likely. Better to scare people off than to be left again. I grab Cain's shirt and lean in, so close I can feel the warmth of his body. "Never mind pushing. It's the pulling that scares you most, isn't it?"

Cain's hands are suddenly on my waist. He hoists me up and spins me around. My back presses against the cool clapboard wall, and he slams his hands on either side of my body, pinning me between the house and his massive frame. He brings his lips to my ear and a low rumble sounds in his throat. "You want to know my secret? Here it is. I'm dangerous. I'm a fault line beneath your feet. An asteroid barreling toward the earth. A bomb fuse begging to burn." His lips brush my skin, and I shiver. "Just light a match, Domino, and watch me explode."

He pulls back his head and meets my stare. His brown eyes blaze with pain so deep I could wade waist-high in it. "I keep my head down so I don't snap. Because I snapped once before, and I did something terrible." He lowers his voice. "*I am terrible. And unsafe. So stay the hell away from me.*"

His face softens like he despises himself and instantly regrets what he said. His arms drop away and he strides toward the house. Sweat forms at my temples and my body quivers. Not because of what happened. But because watching him just now—and hearing the poison that spewed from those lips—

It was like looking in the mirror.

I gather myself for a few minutes before going upstairs and finishing the night. The drug in my system eventually wears off, but the conversation I had with Cain sticks. I should be repulsed by what he showed me outside. Instead, I want to open his skull like a can of peaches and sit down with a spoon. Maybe he's as messed up as I am. I doubt it, but it's possible. If that's true, he may be the only person I've spoken to who understands my past and the scars it left behind.

He says he's dangerous.

But I'm not afraid. Not with Wilson slipping quietly into his corner of my mind, circling once, twice, like a tired cat, before flopping down, tail curled around his body.

I saw what happened out there, he says, drained. *I couldn't respond, but I saw.*

Be quiet.

That Cain character… Wilson continues. *Maybe I judged too soon. He's a nice kid. He's got spunk.*

He's got demons.

Spunk, demons. Tomato, tomahto.

Ruby approaches me after the customers have left and we've cleaned up the Inferno. "You okay?"

"Yeah, I'm fine."

"Look, why don't you hang out with us for a while. Calm down a bit. I know that guy slipped you something. Not cool. I may condone recreational candy, but I would never give it to someone unsuspecting."

"Thanks," I tell her. "But I think I'll go to bed."

Ruby pulls me into a quick hug. So quick I don't mind it much. "Domino, listen to me, okay? Just hang out with us. Let's watch cartoons and drink the rest of the champagne."

Poppet glides over and says she's game, even though it's nearly two o'clock in the morning. So I agree. One, because it feels good to be invited. And two, because it's a better alternative to lying in bed rehashing Cain's every word.

"Okay, I'm in."

So I stay up with Ruby and the Daisies. We laugh when The Neck comes down, huffing about the television being too loud. Then one of the girls has the idea to put on a play. She pulls Poppet and me into the production, and we tell the story of a man with supersonic hearing who feasts on other people's happiness. It may or may not have been about someone in the house.

The next day, Poppet and I find out we placed third and fourth, and when Jack returns that night, I tell him something true about myself: my favorite color is yellow. I don't drink anything he gives me, and when he insists on holding my hand as we dance, I do my best to let it happen. Because Jack makes good on his promise—he gets the other customers to pay attention to Poppet and me, and that's all I want.

Wilson doesn't forget what he did to us, though. He's furious that Jack slipped something into my drink that made him lose his concentration. Me? I know Jack didn't mean any harm, even if I don't like what he did.

I try not to think of my confrontation with Cain, or Wilson's anger toward Jack, and instead focus on the girls who are rapidly becoming—dare I think it—friends. It's almost enough to make me reconsider my plan of moving up and out.

But then the night comes. A night I spend entirely awake with two cups of cold, leftover coffee in my belly. So that this time, I hear the shuffling.

It comes from beneath my bed.

CHAPTER 33

ABRACADABRA!

An arm swings out from beneath my mattress, and I swallow bile. There's a person under my bed. She must have come in before Poppet and I did, snuck beneath the pink fringe bed skirts, and waited until we fell asleep. No wonder our assailants still reached us when we blocked the door.

They slept there overnight.

They hate us that much.

I snap forward and grab the person's wrist. Slim, veiny—a girl's wrist. I jerk on it and hear her squeal with surprise.

"Get out from under there!" I yell.

Poppet is awake now, bolting upright. "What's going on?"

I pull on the wrist harder until a face appears from under my bed. Because it's dark, I cross the room and flip on the lamp. When I see who stares back at me from the floor, I gasp.

Dark hair, blond eyebrows, a smile that says she's almost proud to be caught.

"Ruby?" Poppet says.

Ruby gets to her feet and I rush to Poppet's bed, peek underneath. There's no one there. I turn on the Point Girl. "So it's you then. All this time, it's been you. Why?"

Ruby shrugs. "You girls think you're so special. Think the rest of us haven't worked to move up? Think we haven't asked the madam for the same allowances? But here you come and her equality speech goes out the window."

I try to mask how badly the betrayal burns. I didn't see this coming. Not after how kind she'd been, though now I understand why she was always so adamant about keeping the lights off. It was so she could slither under our beds and stay there without being seen. "You've been cutting us! What in the world could that accomplish?"

Ruby strides toward the door like she's finished with this conversation.

"Hey, I'm talking to you," I snap.

Don't let her walk out on us, Wilson growls.

Poppet gets to her feet. "You were the only one?"

I look at Poppet like what does that matter, but Ruby laughs and turns partway around. "Nah. It was a group effort. See, we're friends. But you two are just a couple of holier-than-thou skanks. You're like parasites." She grins and touches a finger to her nose. "One of my girls said she was counting the days until you were gone, and it gave us an idea."

A cold sweat breaks out across my forehead. These girls are worse than the Carnations. At least they were up-front about their resentment. But to hide beneath our beds and torture us while we slept, all while being welcoming to our faces? It makes me sick.

"I want you off my floor." Ruby's voice holds a warning.

There are two beats of silence before our bedroom door opens and another Daisy strides inside. "Oh, crap. They found us out?" She throws her head back and laughs. It's theatrical, that laugh, like she planned for this moment.

Three more girls are close on her heels.

Oh, good. They're all here. It's go time.

"Get out," I whisper.

A Daisy with shiny skin, slick with lotion, crosses her

arms. "Didn't you know? We own this floor, which means we own this room, too. You could sleep in the hallway if you'd like. Right, Ruby?"

Ruby shrugs one shoulder. "Don't ever say we aren't charitable."

"Get out of here," I repeat. My blood pounds behind my eyes as Wilson pulls on boxing gloves, bounces around inside my head, and swings right hooks. He's being funny, but I'm not laughing.

The girl with the well-lotioned face uncrosses her arms and powers toward me. "I'm tired of this chick."

I don't know what she intends to do, but Poppet cuts her off. Slaps her cold across the face and shoves her backward. "You get near Domino again, and I'll hit you a second time. This time with a closed fist."

The girl acts like she might accept the challenge, but Poppet is quick to flinch in her direction. "Try it! Hit me! But you better know where I come from. You better know who you're picking a fight with."

I don't move. Neither does anyone else. If Lotion Face decides to take on Poppet, I'll hit her before she can rear back. But for now, I let Poppet hold the floor. I let her protect me. My body floods with affection for Poppet, this girl with small eyes behind thick glasses. This girl who told me she'd never leave with me, but won't stand by as someone threatens her friend.

The girls in the back of the room are pushed aside when Mr. Hodge bursts into the small space. The moment he enters the arena, the floodgates burst. I don't know how exactly it happens, but it goes something like this:

Mr. Hodge bumps Lotion Face in the back.

Lotion Face collides with Poppet.

Poppet shoves her backward.

Lotion Face makes a fist.

And the room erupts into civil war. I'm taken to the ground, my head slamming into the hardwood floor. Someone is on top of me — Ruby, I think — and she's clawing at my face. I remain calm even though Wilson is bouncing around up there. Instead of defending myself, I let her tear her nails down my cheeks. Then I wait for an opening.

There.

I throw a tight blow to her nose. It snaps and blood gushes out. Her hands fly to her face, and I push her off me with everything I have. Now she's on the floor, and I'm the one scaling this mountain. I'm on her chest for two seconds, enough time to hit her once more in her ribs, before two girls are pulling me off.

The Neck is yelling and trying to hold a Daisy off Poppet, but Poppet is doing just fine on her own until a second girl hits her from behind. Now Mr. Hodge is standing between the three girls — two trying to clobber the third — and I'm left to defend myself against three Daisies.

Wilson positions himself firmly in my mind, whispers sweet nothings.

You don't want to know the things he says.

Or maybe you do.

Get the lamp, he says. *Smash it over her head.*

What does that cord go to? Let's wrap it around her neck.

There's a pillow on your bed. I know exactly what we could do with that.

I try to drown him out and do what I do best when luck has turned its back. I curl into a ball and cover my head, wait while the Daisies get their licks in.

Get up! Wilson yells. *Get up! Get that blanket from your bed. Tie a noose with it. Where are those high heels you wore last night? They'd make a fine blade.*

I ignore him.

Domino Ray, do something. Do something or I will!

Nothing.

I said, DO SOMETHING!

My hands fly out without my permission. I grab hold of a Daisy's ankle mid-kick and yank on it. She's ripped from her feet and lands on her back. I spring on top of her like a chimp. My fingers find my dresser drawer and I rip it open, dive my hand in, pull out a fork. It appears like magic.

Abracadabra.

The girl beneath me stops fighting, and her eyes enlarge. Her mouth forms a black circle of surprise, and it seems to me the best place to sink this fork.

But I can't stop staring at the weapon in my hand.

How did it get there?

When did I nip this from the kitchen?

Shhh, Wilson coos. *Go to sleep, sweet Domino Ray.*

I raise the fork, my arm shaking, and bring it down.

I'm an inch from driving it into the Daisy's mouth—*open wide!*—when strong hands pull me from the girl. I'm no sooner on my feet than another girl is lunging at me. But a wall separates us.

Cain.

I know him by the look of his back alone.

That can't be healthy.

Each time someone grabs for me, each time a girl tries to get in one last shot, he blocks their advance. He doesn't lay his hands on anyone. Just stands there, making it clear whose side he's on.

Mr. Hodge drags Ruby from the room and yells for her to calm down her girls. Ruby shakes her head like a skipping record. But finally she relents and calls for the Daisies to get out of there. They don't listen until she stomps in and pulls two girls out by the elbow.

Though Daisies are still screaming profanities, and Poppet is acting like she might instigate another round, things begin to calm. As for me, I'm shaking. Not my whole body, just my left side. I can't stop thinking about that fork.

About what Wilson almost had me do.

I can't stay in this place much longer. It's not so much about my safety, but the other girls. At the same time, I need more cash before I take off. If I leave with what little I have, I'll end up in the same situation: depending on others, surviving day to day, forming rocky relationships that won't stick.

I need a place of my own.

I need money.

The Neck shoves his face inside and roars for us to stay in this room and not come out. He starts to close the door, but I grab the edge.

"I want to see Madam Karina," I bark, delirious.

He screws his face up like I'm mad. "Out of the question."

"She'll want to hear what I have to say."

"I doubt that."

"I could bring her up," Cain suggests. "If the madam seems upset, I'll take her away."

Mr. Hodge looks back and forth between the two of us for a long time before glaring at Cain. "She's not going to be happy with you."

"Domino, don't leave me," Poppet squeaks.

I turn and look at my friend, at her torn shirt and disheveled hair. She has a purple bruise blooming under her right eye. In any other scenario, I'd tell her it looks wicked cool. But this isn't another scenario, so I launch myself around her in an embrace and then look Poppet squarely in those red-rimmed eyeballs.

"I will never leave you," I say. "Not me. No way, no how."

Mr. Hodge groans. "This is all very touching."

"Let us see Madam Karina." I glare at Mr. Hodge, make him fidget from my silence.

He rolls his eyes upward and waves toward Cain. "Take 'em up there. Better you than me." Mr. Hodge casts a stern look in my direction. "If I hear about you giving her any trouble…"

"You won't."

Cain touches my arm. "Come on."

CHAPTER 34

BOILER ROOM

Madam Karina isn't asleep when we reach her room. She's seated in a wingback chair, one leg slung over the arm. Velvet curtains framing a tall window are thrown aside, and she's looking out across her property, eyes glued on the guesthouses. She doesn't even turn in our direction when Cain clears his throat and announces our presence.

She waves a hand toward the door, telling him to leave. He looks at me, and I nod. The door closes behind us, and then it's just Poppet, Madam Karina, and me. She scratches the side of her neck and I notice her middle fingernail is broken. The other four are pink as newborn mice.

"Heard the scuffle," she says. "Even from up here."

I step forward. "Madam Karina, I'd like to make a request."

She finally turns toward me, and my breath catches. She's been crying.

"Are you okay?" I ask.

Her forehead furrows. "What do you mean?"

I shake my head, realizing she doesn't want to talk about it. "Nothing. It's just that you're awake so late."

"Well, yes, you woke me."

I reap some courage and open my mouth. "I'd like to ask for the same favor you paid me before. I'd like permission to move to the third floor if Poppet and I can maintain the first and second place among the Daisies for one week."

"Why?"

Poppet speaks up. "Because we want to make you happy."

Madam Karina doesn't look at her. "Is that true, Domino? You want to make me happy?" Before I can answer, she says, "Why is it that Lola favors you so?"

"What?" I say, confused.

Madam Karina stands from the chair. Her shoulders slump and she appears thinner than she did only days ago. The woman points a frail arm in my direction. "Lola speaks on your behalf every time we meet. Did you pay her some favor?"

"No, we've only talked once."

Madam Karina flinches as if struck. She holds up a finger and mouths the word *once* as if asking a question. It's then that I understand the madam has been drinking. A burning sweetness reaches my nose, and I locate the tumbler on her nightstand. "It may be that she wants to leave me."

"I doubt that's true." I have no idea what Lola wants, but right now I'll say whatever the madam wants to hear, because I need her to grant Poppet and me this favor. No more chances elsewhere. No more fresh starts. We leave this place with enough cash in hand to survive on our own. That's how this story ends.

Madam Karina spins away. "Could be you're trying to leave me, too."

Her voice causes the hair on the back of my neck to rise. I sense Poppet moving closer to me. Outside Madam Karina's window, I hear a girl giggling. A man's voice chases hers.

"I want only what's best for you, Domino," she says.

The lie slithers from her mouth, sucking on the two of us like plump, slippery leeches.

"I don't want to leave," I whisper, returning the courtesy

she's paid me. "Poppet and I just want to make you happy. Why should Lola get all that alone time with you, when no one wants it the way Poppet and I do?"

"Is that what you told her? That you wanted her place?"

"I said what I said."

Madam Karina covers her mouth like she's overcome with relief. She closes the distance between us, lets her hand fall to her side. Poppet stands behind me like a forgotten plaything. I want to reach out for her, but Madam Karina is looking at me with such intensity that I'm hypnotized, a pocket watch swishing back and forth before my eyes.

Count backward from ten.

"My sister thought she was so successful when she opened that home in Detroit," the madam says. "Left me here in Pox like I didn't mean a thing. Said she was doing me a favor giving this place to me, though Mama and Daddy left it to her. Still, I'm getting my revenge. Girl by girl. Eric finds the best ones before she can, most of them from my sister's own city."

Madam Karina takes hold of my shoulders and lowers herself until her face is inches from mine. She smiles with her whole face. But then, slice by slice, that smile slips away. In its place blooms vulnerability and anger. "You may think you can play me for a fool, girl," she says, "but I know what it is you want."

"Tell me what I want."

She grips my shoulders tighter. "You want that boy. You want to earn enough to leave and get him out of jail. You only want him."

Surprise must drip from my face, because she reaches up with a thumb like she's wiping something away. "Don't look so shocked. You used my phone to make those calls, did you not?"

I recover quickly, try to pull away from her, but it's no use. This thinning, frail woman is stronger than she appears.

"If you know who it is I called and why, then you know what was said, too."

"Yes. He didn't call you after he got out, so why do you need this money so badly? Where have you got to go? Where will you ever have to go? You think you'll make enough here to live on forever? Eventually, you'll need a job. Who would give you one?"

I don't speak, and though my jaw aches from clenching my teeth, my chin still quivers.

"This world isn't for you. But that's okay. It isn't for me, either." She strokes my hair. "Stop dreaming of a life past this one. This is it for you. This is it for me, too."

"Domino, I'm tired," Poppet says quietly from behind me.

"Do you hear what I'm telling you?" Madam Karina pushes.

For once, Wilson doesn't speak. And I really need him to, because Madam Karina is reminding me too much of someone from my past. She's in my head and eating my insides and I can't think because I just want her to smile again. I'm suddenly sharply aware of what Wilson said when we first arrived.

Out of all the places you could end up, Domino, this is the absolute worst.

When I speak again, it comes out as a whisper. "I won't leave you, Madam Karina."

She pushes me. It isn't hard, but I still bump into Poppet and we nearly tumble to the floor. Madam Karina's face opens with alarm when she realizes what she's done. She reaches for me. Stops herself.

"Of course you'll leave me. That's what people do. They leave and leave and LEAVE, LEAVE, LEAVE!"

Madam Karina is crying now, great rivers of pent-up sorrow escaping her soft starlet eyes.

"I won't leave you," Poppet says. "I promise, Madam

Karina. I won't go anywhere."

Madam Karina turns away and sobs into her hands.

It's maybe three seconds, five at the most, before Mr. Hodge is barreling through the door, reaching for the madam. She pushes him harder than she pushed me, but he's unmovable.

"Get away from me!" she yells. "Go back to your precious phone. Go back to calling whoever it is you call."

"Shhh, puppy. Hush, now." He wraps his arms around her and this time she doesn't fight him. Mr. Hodge is grossly overweight, and sweats profusely, and smells like fish left in the sun. But Madam Karina quiets in his embrace. As for me, I'm letting Poppet pull me up and trying to pacify the shock of what happened here.

Mr. Hodge turns to Poppet and me, concern in his eyes. "Go to your room. The Daisies won't give you any more problems tonight. I'll take care of Madam Karina."

"I'm sorry for…" Poppet says, referring to the madam.

"Just go to bed," he replies.

Watching Mr. Hodge care for Madam Karina makes me wonder if I judged him too quickly. The madam showed us she's every bit as explosive and unhinged as the rest of us. But here he is, steady in her aftershocks.

Poppet strides toward the door, and I follow close behind.

Our bare feet crunch over dried violets on our way to bed.

CHAPTER 35

HOLLOW BASKET

The next morning, I find a basket on our dresser. Inside are three things. An uncomfortable apology from Madam Karina asking us to pardon her "inappropriate behavior" and agreeing to our "fine, well-thought-out proposal," copies of Poppet's and my financial statements that clearly reflect a bump from the last time we read them, and—at the very bottom of the basket, covered by a red-and-white checkered cloth—a can of orange spray paint.

Before I do anything else, I make my third phone call from the basement, and when I do, I learn three things from Purple Nails Meg.

1. Hair Flair and Fun will be closing its doors in six days.
2. Greg has moved in with his boyfriend.
3. Meg handles the prospect of losing her job better than I would.

When I hang up, I realize I have only myself to rely on. Truly. And that I will never stop fighting until I have four strong walls to call my own.

CHAPTER 36

THUMB-SUCKER

It takes Poppet and me exactly nine days from the time we received that basket, and from the time I make that call, to break out of the Daisies' control. With Jack's help, I finish the week in first place and Poppet in second. I tell Jack seven true things about myself, and each one feels like a bullet hole through the chest. They are my secrets to have and to hold. And when he takes them from me, they feel less real.

Maybe my favorite color isn't yellow.

Maybe I don't like cinnamon in my coffee as much as I think.

Maybe my parents didn't turn me into an animal that stalks the world, rabid.

I didn't tell Jack about my family. That's one gunshot wound I wouldn't recover from, so why talk about it?

Today is market day, just past lunch on a Sunday, and I'm headed outside and toward the east guesthouse. I want to talk to Lola about what Madam Karina said. There's been little time for that before now. Work to do, coins to earn, chores to complete. But not today.

I wait in the plastic chair out back and watch her territory. I know better than to approach the house, but I also know she'll come out sooner or later. To buy a bomber jacket she'll never wear in this west Texas heat, or a package of popsicles to crunch on, or a paperback romance novel to chase away the godforsaken, ever-present boredom.

It doesn't take long before she appears, but already sweat slides down my temples. Lola swishes toward me, walking on the tips of her toes like she does, and plops down in the second chair. She's wearing oversized tortoiseshell sunglasses and plum-colored lip gloss. A bittersweet scent reaches my nose. It reminds me of the smell I picked up in Madam Karina's room the night she accused me of trying to leave.

Lola pulls her dark hair into a ponytail. "Saw you from the window. You waiting on that boy?"

"I was waiting on you."

She laughs. "Get in line, baby."

"Why are you trying to help me?"

She sobers. "Who says I'm doing any such thing?"

"Are you trying to leave the home?"

Her head whips toward me. "Who said that?"

"Madam Karina."

Lola swears under her breath.

"Are you?"

"That's enough questions, Daisy."

My chest swells though I'm not sure why. "I'm not a Daisy anymore."

Lola raises an eyebrow. "Already?"

"Starting tomorrow."

Silence hangs between us, and Lola sticks her thumb into her mouth. Sucks on it and then pulls it from between her lips with a pop. "I can't stand being here any longer. Might as well tell you, since she already knows."

"Where will you go?"

"Don't worry your pretty little head about that. You just keep the madam happy so I can slip away, understand?"

"Why don't you tell her you're leaving?" I ask. "Don't you have to apply to withdraw your money?"

Lola laughs at this. "Listen, Domino, you're the kind of girl who will stay here until you're dismissed by the madam. Then you'll live in some trailer park and do her bidding until she says you're ready to die. And you know what? That's a better life than you would've had elsewhere. But I've got big plans, and they don't involve staying here."

Anger coils in my belly. "Don't pretend you know me."

"That's the thing. I do know you. Now, will you be a good puppet and keep the madam's attention so I can blow this joint?"

I stare at her, disgusted that she expects me to help her after the insults she's hurled. But then her face softens, and I see the fear in her gaze. She's afraid I'll say no. Afraid she'll be stuck here and those dreams of hers will dead-end. I don't like Lola but, just like Madam Karina, she has a way of tugging what she wants out of you. Plus, I'm still hopeful that if I play by Madam Karina's rules and earn money the way she wishes, I can chase a dream of my own.

Four walls.

A strong roof.

A soft bed that is mine.

Safety.

"You imply that it's hard to leave this place." I say this almost as a question. And part of me is afraid of her response. In order for me to continue here, I need to know that at the end, my goal is reachable. After Madam Karina's outburst, I'm not sure I can trust that.

Lola hesitates. "It's not that you can't leave with a pocketful of cash. It's just that Madam Karina is very persuasive."

Persuasive. I can deal with persuasive.

Can you? Wilson whispers.

"I'll keep her watching me, Lola." I stand and run my eyes over her frame. Then, to return the grace she's shown, I add, "Shouldn't be too difficult considering my competition."

She smiles. "Bitch."

I smile, too. "Trash."

Lola offers her hand.

"Weren't you just sucking your thumb?" I ask.

She shrugs.

I stick my own thumb in my mouth and pop it out. Then I offer her my hand.

She shakes it.

I walk toward the house, and behind me Lola says with a chuckle, "Look what we have here, ladies and gentlemen. The future Top Girl of Madam Karina's House for Burgeoning Entertainers."

CHAPTER 37

RIDERS ON THE STORM

It's my last night as a Daisy, and I can't sleep for two reasons. One, I'm afraid the girls will use this chance to confront Poppet and me before we're officially promoted. Second, because it sounds like the freaking apocalypse has descended upon this clapboard house.

The thunder rolls on top of us like a great ogre stomping his feet. Rain pelts the roof, and I watch a brown stain in our ceiling grow wider and then drip onto the hardwood floor. Poppet is completely out, and I don't want to wake her. But I hate storms. Despise them. They remind me of the night my father slipped away and the world crashed into the sun. When storms tap-danced through Detroit, Dizzy used to let me bring a blanket into his room and sleep at the foot of his mattress.

Like a dog, I realize now.

I pace the floor, dip my big toe into the dripping rainwater. My mind is already where it wants to go, and at a certain point, I feel disconnected from it. So I roll my head and then my shoulders and shoot one last glance at Poppet.

Can I trust she'll be okay alone?

I peek into the hallway and don't hear anything above the storm's fury. Glancing over my shoulder, I remember the way Poppet launched herself at those Daisies. I smile and cover my mouth to keep from laughing.

Then I pad down the hallway in hot pursuit of my lost mind.

I find it on the first floor. Dipping my head inside the Carnations' entertainment room, I watch the toy train roll across its tracks near the ceiling. The lights are off in the room. The girls have swept away the balled napkins and soda straws. But that train still chugs around the room unperturbed.

I smile at the sight.

When the thunder crashes again, I startle and make my way to the kitchen. Twice, I start to turn back, to find my bed and chase elusive slumber. But on the third try, I find my courage.

The door to the basement opens easily in my hand, and I tiptoe down the cool stairs. The lavender gown Poppet lent me brushes the floor, and my hair slides over my shoulders and down my back. I bite my lip when I reach the bottom, desperately wishing, above anything else, that I had thought to wear a wig. I'm too exposed. Too vulnerable.

Cain rolls over on his mattress.

His eyes meet mine.

He doesn't move as I inch toward the chain link wall that separates us. My fingers curl over the metal and I cling to it, my legs shaking beneath me. What am I doing here?

Thunder rattles the walls, and Cain rises like the god who summoned it. He strides toward me, one bare foot in front of the other. His eyes are dark in the dim light creeping through the window. They flash with the lightning, shadows thrown across the room, across his face. He stands a breath away, looking down at me. He is enormous.

Large as a storm cloud.

Large as a tornado.

I take in every part of him—his shaved head, his powerful

shoulders, the bulge of muscles beneath his white T-shirt. His skin is smooth and tan, his lips full. This close, I can see the slightest sprinkle of freckles beneath his eyes. They seem like a false sense of security. Make him seem harmless, when I know that's a lie. Just look how I'm reacting when a wall separates me from him. He's like a caged animal down here in the dark, and though electricity shoots through my fingertips, I want nothing more than to release this beast and see if I am nuzzled or destroyed.

Cain's fingers slip through the links until his hands rest on mine.

He holds my gaze until I can feel him in the very back of my mind.

We stand like that for several moments, my heart beating like a wild, unpredictable thing, and him searching my face like there's salvation to be found there. Finally, he nods toward the door that stands between us and strides toward it. He unlocks the thing and throws it open.

He doesn't invite me inside, but he doesn't need to, either.

I go to him.

He watches as I walk to his bed and sit, folding my leg beneath me. Though his sheets are rough and his pillow hard, goose bumps rise along my arms. He stands across the room, head down, chest rising and falling quickly.

When several seconds pass and he hasn't moved to sit next to me, heat blooms in my cheeks and along my neck. I'm an idiot. I shouldn't have come here. He doesn't want company, and he's too kind to say so.

With my face burning, I start to push myself up. That's when he speaks.

"I don't want to hurt you, Domino."

I freeze. "So don't."

He raises his head. "If you knew the things I've done."

I tug his blanket around my hips. "Tell me."

He lifts his head and lets it fall back, breathes out like he's been holding his breath for three hundred and sixty-five days. And one to grow on. "I killed my brother."

Though I hate myself for the reaction, I can't stop the fear that boils under my skin. I don't speak, and Cain finds my eyes.

"My father was a bastard," Cain continues. "Everyone in Pox knew that. But no one knew it like my brother and I did. He had two loves, and neither were his sons." Cain laughs darkly. He holds up a pointer finger. "My father loved to drink." He holds up a second finger. "And he loved MMA fighters. You know those guys who fight in cages? He thought they were like Roman gladiators." Cain lowers his voice like he's emulating his father and beats a closed fist against his chest. "You boys need to be more like them. You're too soft. You're too goddamn soft."

Cain drops his arm and sighs. "He started making us fight each other. *Training*, he called it. Said maybe his pansy boys could make him some money one day like those gladiators he saw on TV. At first we refused to do it, but my old man found ways to motivate us."

He runs a hand over his head. "My dad wasn't one to smoke cigars often, but occasionally he'd pair them with whiskey. So one day he's smoking one and he got this idea to use them on us after we fought."

My stomach turns hearing Cain's story, and though I don't want to hear more, I'm afraid this may be the first time he's ever told this story. He needs to expel this memory the same way he would poison. So I remain silent.

"He let the winner of each round choose who got burned," Cain continues. "So I fought harder, because even though I didn't want to hurt my brother, it was my father's hand on him I dreaded most. So I won. Over and over, I won. And each time I chose to take that burn."

"Cain—"

He raises a hand like he needs to finish this. "One day I hit him too hard. He fell and slammed his head onto the fireplace ledge. He was dead. He was dead, and I killed him."

Cain's voice breaks, and I can't stand it any longer. I get up and cross the distance between us. He doesn't cry for his lost sibling, only breathes harder like he's trying to prevent a breakdown. But when I twine my arms around him, hesitantly, I feel the change. His breathing slows and I hear an aching sound deep in his throat.

"Your father killed your brother, Cain. Not you." I wrap my hands around his cheeks, force him to look at me. "Your father was a monster. You are not. Do you understand?"

He pulls his face away, and because I know how hard it is to accept forgiveness for something you've owned for so long, I take a different approach. Taking his arm, I guide him toward the mattress. I crawl on and he crawls behind me, keeping a river of space between us. It takes every ounce of courage I have to—gently, slowly—take his heavy arm and wrap it around my body like a blanket made of steel. Several minutes pass before he moves a touch closer.

We stay like that for a stretch, neither of us saying anything. And though I don't prefer being touched, it's okay with him. It's okay.

Can I say something? Wilson asks gently from the back of my mind.

I don't reply.

If I found Cain's father today, he says. *I'd show him what it means to hurt.*

Hush, Wilson, I respond. *Just once, let's focus on recovery instead of revenge.*

I'm just saying…

Cain murmurs in my ear. "Madam Karina knows what happened with my brother. The cops didn't believe my dad when he said my brother and I were just messing around, and that him hitting his head like that was an accident. But Madam Karina said she could give me a place in her home, and that full-time work would make the cops stop asking questions about me."

Uneasiness pulls on me like a noose. "That's why you work for her? Because you think the cops would arrest you if they knew the truth?"

Cain doesn't respond, so I turn and face him. The thunder sounds again, but it can't touch me here. Not with him lying so close. "Cain, your father would be the one arrested. No one would ever blame you."

His face scrunches. "But it was me who hurt him."

"But that's not what—"

"Domino," Cain says, cutting me off. "It was my fault."

I press my lips together and turn back around. I know this guilt. It's the kind we want to hold on to long after the pulse is gone. So I let him have it. Cain may not want a reason to leave Madam Karina's. He knows what to expect here, and it's a big improvement over where he came from. It's a big improvement for me, too. But it isn't enough. Not for me, and not for Wilson.

Ten minutes of silence pass. Ten minutes of thunder and lightning and rain pelting the roof. Ten minutes of warmth and safety and dreadful secrets. It feels like forever before I hear Cain speak again.

"I'm glad you didn't hurt her," he says. "I know she probably did something awful to you, but I'm glad you didn't hurt her."

His heart kicks softly against my back. "Who are you talking about?"

"Mercy," he responds. "When I found you outside her room that night, I didn't know what to think."

I shift until I'm looking up into Cain's face. My insides feel like they're trying to tear their way out. He must see the question in my eyes, because he says, "Don't you remember? It was a few nights after you got here. I saw you outside her room."

Though I'm afraid he'll learn my own terrible secret, I shake my head.

No, I don't remember.

"You were just standing there, Domino." He licks his lips, worry folding the space between his eyes. "You had a butcher knife in your right hand."

CHAPTER 38

MAMA'S GOOD GIRL

When I open my eyes, I'm in my bed. Not in Cain's bed. Not my bed on the second story of Madam Karina's home. Not even on the mattress I claimed in Detroit.

I'm in my bed at my parent's house. My father is already gone. I sense his absence like a missing foot. Like someone has asked me to walk without it for the first time and they say, stupidly, can you feel the difference?

It's light out. Sunshine pouring through my lace window drapes like a rainbow arching over a funeral procession.

"Domino, are you awake?"

My mother's voice. It comes from down the hall.

I curl into a ball and turn my back to my bedroom door. She knocks on it once before opening it.

Would you look at that respect?

She moves inside my personal space, and I clench my eyes shut. It's been forty-nine days since he left us. Forty-nine days since my father decided he wanted a new life. Mama moves closer, and I try not to breathe. Ever since he left, she's been cracking like an egg on the side of a mixing bowl, her innards running yellow down the lip.

"I got us some things when I went out." Her voice is a songbird warbling a falsetto tune.

I don't want to hear about the things she got. They won't be good things. They won't be a new green jacket with gold buttons or a pint of apple juice or body lotion that smells like grated lemon.

They will be bad things.

"Don't you want to see?" she says, sweetly. "We're so much closer to completing our plan now."

Her plan. Not our plan.

"Come on, sweetie. Don't you want to make me happy?" She pauses for effect. "We only have each other now." Her hand comes to rest on my arm. I don't flinch because, at the end of the day, she is my mother. "Who would you have if not for me?"

I open my eyes and sigh.

She takes my sigh as the encouragement she needs.

"Here, I'll lay them on your pillow."

I close my eyes again when she leans over my frame. The mattress groans against the added weight, and then she's gone. Backing out of my room, closing the door behind her. I grit my teeth, remind myself I am brave and good and would never let a man push me around. All the things my mother has told me.

When I open my eyes, I see the gift she's left me.

Two things.

A pair of surgical gloves.

And a shiny, happy knife.

CHAPTER 39

TOP FLOOR

The next morning I tell Cain I need to get out of the house. I don't tell him my plan to eventually *leave*, just that I need a break. I'm on edge after hearing that Cain saw me outside Mercy's room. With a knife. Add to that the fork I almost used as a weapon on the Daisy, and the memories of my mother, and you've got a seventeen-year-old girl who's about to blow.

I need to relax. Feel the sun on my skin without watchful eyes. Poppet said Eric would take girls into town for a fee, and it's a fee I'm now willing to pay. Cain watches me rise from his bed and hesitantly agrees to bring it up with Madam Karina.

I'm about to go upstairs when he stops me. "When are you going to tell me your secrets?"

"You mean, now that you've told me yours?"

He doesn't respond.

"I can't tell you, Cain," I say softly. "It's not like your secret."

I turn and stride up the stairs before the sun has risen. I'm not sure what Mr. Hodge or Madam Karina would think if they found me in Cain's basement, but I'm certain it wouldn't be good. When I near Poppet's and my room, nerves tick behind my eyes. I shouldn't have left her alone that long. Anything could have happened.

When I open the door, though, I find her alone and safe. She's rolling her bedsheets into a bundle and stuffing her clothing, accessories, and makeup inside. Poppet stops and looks at me when I sit down on my bed.

"Where were you?" she asks, cleaning her glasses against her yellow blouse.

I hesitate, but decide against lying. "I slept with Cain."

"Oh, wow." She laughs. "I did not see that coming. How was it? I bet it was good. Tell me it was good, even if it wasn't."

"What? No. No, we didn't sleep together. I just slept in his bed."

Her face falls. "Okay, next time that happens you open the story with, 'I slept in Cain's bed but nothing happened.' It's cruel to get me all excited like that." She tilts her head. "Are you guys like into each other for real?"

"No," I say quickly. "Maybe. I don't know. I think it's more that we understand each other. I don't know a lot about him, really, and he certainly doesn't know me, so there's no concrete reason for us to be attracted."

"So you don't like him?"

I smile to myself, remembering the heat of his body next to mine last night. And the way he makes me feel protected without uttering a word. And our nights spent behind the house, Cain with his cigarette, me with my wobbly chair.

"Oh, God. You do like him. Look at that grin."

I laugh. "It's complicated."

Poppet returns to packing her things, muttering that it doesn't seem that complicated. Then she spins around suddenly and holds out the bottom of her yellow blouse. "See what color I'm wearing? Yellow. Know why?"

I know why. I also know if I stay quiet, she'll spell it out.

"Because today we become Tulips, Domino Ray. I'm so excited I could burst. Top floor and everything!"

I glance at my hands. "What makes you think it'll be any different up there?"

Poppet groans and drops down beside me. "Listen, Minnow, you can't give up on people you haven't gotten to know just because the ones you've already met are lousy."

I nod, and she slings her arm around my shoulders.

I cringe for only a moment before laying my head against hers.

"What's your story, Poppet?" I ask.

She removes her arm. "Why do you ask?"

"I want to know about you. That's all."

She stands up and fidgets with her belongings. "Not much to tell. Born in a trailer park in Mississippi. Mother had four other kids to take care of, and didn't mind one bit when I threatened to run away." She shrugs. "So I did. Came to Texas with a boy who said he'd always be mine. Then he said the same thing to a woman twice his age once we got here. I met Eric in a town not too far away. I was living with an elderly woman who let me stay there so long as I did her chores and let her knock me around when she felt like it. Eric saw me singing in a bar one day and said I sounded like sunshine in Alaska."

"So you came with him."

"Once he brought Madam Karina to meet me, yeah. Couldn't get in her car fast enough."

I smile, but deep down my uneasiness remains. I distrust Madam Karina every ounce as much as I yearn for her approval. It's twisted, and I think she knows it. The thing is, Madam Karina is as messed up as we are. She both loves and detests us at once. Regardless, it feels different when Poppet tells me her story. Both Eric and Madam Karina must have known she was desperate. They took advantage of her.

Or is that too strong a word?

After all, no one lays hands on Poppet here at Madam Karina's House for Burgeoning Entertainers. Not until I arrived, anyway. Sounds like maybe I'm the problem in Poppet's life. Then again, pervy Mr. Hodge did cop a feel the other day. Wonder how often that happens?

"What about you?" Poppet asks.

My hands clench in my lap.

"It's okay," she says. "You don't have to tell me."

"My father left my mother and me, and my mom went nuts afterward." My breathing grows shallow, because I can't believe I said that much aloud. It's more than I've ever told anyone. I'm waiting for Poppet to press me for details or to say that doesn't sound so bad. But she only gathers her things.

"Let's go start our new life on the top floor, shall we?"

I roll my bedsheets, wigs, and Dizzy's unwashed shirt into a ball. I leave the fork where it lays. "We shall."

The sun is rising when we say good-bye to our empty bedroom on the second floor. Right before I close the door behind us, I grab Dizzy's shirt and toss it into the wastebasket.

Nothing but net.

CHAPTER 40

JOYRIDE

The Tulips are unlike the Carnations and Daisies in every way imaginable. They ooze class and pedigree, though I question whether either is more than skin-deep. When I sweep my eyes across the third story family room, I see tight buns, long dresses, straight spines. I hear soft words, smell subtle perfumes. There are windows on the third floor, even in the bedrooms. It casts an ethereal glow over the seven Tulips and the yellow silk flowers they wear above their right breasts.

Even the chores they partake in—polishing silverware and folding linens from the wash—are white-glove. Poppet and I settle into our room and gaze out the small window that overlooks the backyard and guesthouses. The Tulips never introduce themselves. Ignoring us is their unique form of showing us we don't belong. I'll take it over what the Carnations and Daisies dished out.

We've only just begun to ask the Tulips' Point Girl, a mousy brunette with rosy cheeks, what we can do to help, when Cain appears at the top of the stairs. He glances down the hallway at Madam Karina's door and then strides toward me.

"Cain, carry these down to the kitchen, won't you, please?" The Point Girl presents an armful of neatly folded table linens.

There's a yellow sash tied around her waist that matches the tulip she wears. She paid handsomely for it with her earnings, and that tells me what I need to know.

She isn't going anywhere.

She's in no rush to move up, because she's a lifer.

Cain takes the linens and then turns to me. "Can you be ready in ten minutes?"

At first I don't understand the question, but then a smile quirks the corner of his mouth, and I feel myself jumping on my tiptoes. "I can be ready now!"

Poppet walks over. "Where you two off to?"

I turn to Poppet, excitement coursing through my veins. "I'm going into town. You should come."

She eyes the Tulips. "Nah. I want to get to know our new place. Plus, I'm saving my pennies for a dress that'll stop your heart."

Poppet sidles over to the Point Girl and speaks to her in hushed tones as Cain moves closer.

"It can only be you," he says. "Madam Karina said as much."

I roll my eyes, but I can't stop smiling. "You're the one taking me? Not Eric?"

"Yeah, but don't you want to know how much it will cost?"

I wince, afraid he's going to spoil my fun. "Lay it on me."

He curls four fingers toward his thumb, making a zero.

"Nothing?" I yell. The girls glance over, and I lower my voice. "I get to go for free?"

He cocks his chin toward Madam Karina's room. "Not if she changes her mind. Let's get out of here."

I bound down the stairs, nearly taking a tumble twice. Cain keeps pace with his daddy longlegs. I surge outside and clap twice when I see the black sedan we traveled in from Detroit. The one with leather seats, slick with polish, and wheels so mean they bring tears to my eyes.

"I called the guy who lends us cars. He brought her over this morning."

I jump in the front seat and drum my hands on the console. "Start her up, Jeeves."

Cain slides into the driver's seat and tosses a bag into the back. He starts the engine and punches the accelerator a couple of times while in park to really get me squealing. He's about to throw the thing in drive when I grab his arm.

"Wait, why is the madam letting me go for free? And why is she letting you take me instead of Eric?"

Cain leans back. "She said she still felt bad about the other night. Said you should go and enjoy yourself, but to be back by dinner. Oh, and she thought it was fine that I took you. I think she's pissed at Eric right now for whatever reason."

I buckle my seat belt, because who am I to question good fortune?

"One more thing," Cain says. "She said the favor you asked for…"

"Yeah?"

"She said to consider it ongoing."

I grin and clap my hands together again. When I spot the confused look on his face, I explain that it means I can become a Lily sooner if I play my cards right.

Cain's eyes fall on the east guesthouse. "You really want to move out there?"

The smile on my face falters as I follow his gaze. "I have to do what I have to do."

"You say that because you don't know what goes on there."

I look away from him. "I know enough."

I know everything, Wilson mutters.

Cain sits quietly for a moment before lightly punching my shoulder. "Hey, let's focus on the day."

"Damn straight."

He pulls us out onto the dirt road leading away from the white farmhouse with the blue door and green shutters. Then he sends us rocketing forward, dirt spitting from our back tires.

He drives fast and hard with the confidence of someone who's never been told he isn't good enough. On the drive, Cain tells me something about himself. He used to play football. I pry out of him that he was good. *Really* good. Talented enough to get a scholarship to a small out-of-state college.

"Why didn't you go?" I ask.

He stares ahead. "It was before. If they knew what happened, they'd pull their offer. Plus, if I'd left the state, it would've made the cops even more suspicious."

"Because you went to school?"

He waits a beat before responding. "My dad said they'd come after me. He's right."

I turn my entire body toward Cain. "He's absolutely wrong. Do you think you could still get into that college in… wherever it is?"

"It's in Kansas, and I doubt it. That was almost two years ago."

"Think you could try being a walk-on? Isn't that a thing?" I grip my knees. "What I mean is, do you think you can still play?"

Cain looks at me. Our eyes meet, and he's as serious as I've ever seen him. For Cain, that's pretty damn serious. "All I need is turf beneath my cleats and a chump across from me who's ready to meet his maker."

I laugh. "Is that so?"

"It's so."

"You could have majored in something food related. You make a mean meal."

Cain cocks an eyebrow like he's thinking this over. I bite

my lip, terrified of what I'm about to say. I stop myself several times before blurting out, "What if we just went there now? You and I. Kansas. You try to get into that college, and I'll…I'll cheer for you from the bleachers."

Cain glances at me to see if I'm teasing. When he sees I'm not, he looks back at the road. "I can't."

"Why not?" I ask, surprised by how crestfallen I am.

"I just can't."

But I hear the hesitation in his voice. Three beats before he answered. Maybe four. Enough so that I know he considered the idea, if only for a moment. I wonder how long it's been since he thought about leaving Madam Karina's home. Has he ever before now?

I think back to Poppet and the money I've earned that I need to start a new life. I can't leave, either, I suppose. Not yet.

"I was just kidding," I say, but my words ring hollow.

Cain turns on the radio, and I watch as the landscape changes from empty fields and broken down cars to one-story buildings and soda machines on front porches. A stray dog trots in the distance, keeping weight off his back leg, and four children play jump rope outside a white brick house. They could be Poppet's siblings, I think to myself.

Somewhere along our trek into town, the car *thump-thumps* over uneven terrain.

When I look in the side mirror, I realize we just crossed over railroad tracks.

CHAPTER 41

ICE CREAM INTERROGATION

On the way into town, Cain stops at an abandoned building. There isn't a shortage of them around here, but I like the one he chooses best. He digs around in the bag he brought and withdraws my can of orange spray paint, compliments of an apologetic Madam Karina.

"Thought you'd want it," he says. "I remember you tagged that wall in Detroit."

My cheeks warm, remembering him as a stranger in the gold sedan that night.

"Go on," he nudges.

And so for the next half hour, I leave my mark on Pox, Texas. This time, I don't write what's in my heart. I simply draw a fire upon the brown brick wall, flames licking their way upward. It seems the only thing powerful enough to do a bottle of orange spray paint justice.

When I'm done, I stare up at the building and imagine it ablaze, entrails crackling and smoking. I imagine who's on the inside, too. And what their faces will look like when they race into the night, seeking safety from the vengeful heat, their cheeks smudged and their eyes wide.

I don't have to wonder who started the fire.

It's us, right? Wilson asks.

After I've finished, Cain doesn't ask where I want to go, but he does a fantastic job of taking a guess.

In town, we pass squatting brick buildings with generic names—AUTO SHOP and HOME & FARM SUPPLY and POX COUNTY MUNICIPAL. Cain eventually parks the vehicle and motions for me to follow him inside. The door chimes when we enter a shop appropriately called ICE CREAM. It's one of those big, honking red signs that doesn't pretend to care. They know you want what they're selling, and that's all that matters.

Though the sign is tired, the décor inside is inviting. It's set up like an old general store with quirky gifts and jellies on stale crackers ready for sampling. Country music blares over the speakers, and a dozen round tables sit proudly on original hardwood floors. There isn't much light streaming through the single, dusty window, but it's more than enough to peruse the ten flavors of Bluebell ice cream.

"Can I use my credit to pay for this?" I whisper to Cain, knowing I should resist, realizing there's no way I will.

He digs his hand into his jeans. "Nah, this is on me." I open my mouth to object, but he cuts me off. "It's actually on Angie, if that makes you feel better. She slips me some cash for helping her out from time to time."

"Are you sure?" I ask.

He grins. "Will you just pick a flavor, already?"

I press my hands against the glass and stare down, buzzing with excitement. It's sad how little it takes to get me going.

Pick orange sherbet, Wilson says. *That stuff is amazing!*

"Hell, no," I say.

Cain gives me a questioning look, and I gather that I just spoke aloud to Wilson. I wave my hand like it's nothing and return to this critical choice.

"I'll take Cookies and Cream," I say to the man waiting on us. "No, Chocolate Chip Cookie Dough. No, sorry, the first one. Definitely the first one."

The man sighs. "Cookies and Cream?"

Cain leans in behind me. His stomach presses into my back and I try not to think about how enormous he is. Like a tidal wave arched over a fire ant. "Give her a scoop of each in a waffle cone."

I want to tell him that's too much, that he shouldn't spend all his cash on me. But I can't bring myself to do this. Call me selfish if it'll make you feel better. This is ice cream we're talking about.

I smile when the man hands my loot over, and I wait patiently(ish) as Cain orders two scoops of vanilla bean with sprinkles. I rag on him pretty hard about those sprinkles, and he belly laughs the whole time. I think he may have ordered them just to hear me berate him.

"You're the only girl I'd let talk smack to me about my sprinkles," he says.

I take a bite and mutter. "I'm the only girl that'd dare mention it." I mean it as a joke, but the smile slips from Cain's face. "Did I say something wrong?"

He shakes his head. Ice cream drips over his knuckles as we sit across from each other, customers chatting around us. "No. It's just…you're not afraid of me, are you?"

"Are you afraid of me?" I ask.

He laughs once. "No, I'm not."

"Then why would I be afraid of you?"

Cain finishes his ice cream in another few bites. He eats like a blue whale, all that food just sliding down his throat like he's swallowing a fishing boat and a great white shark and maybe a tire or three. After he wipes his mouth, he says, "You really think I'd be scared of you if I knew what you did?"

I'm suddenly colder than the last lick of Bluebell in my hand. I'm solid as the earth. "Maybe you wouldn't be afraid,"

I say, measuring my words. "But you should be."

He scoffs. "Impossible."

For one glittering moment, I consider telling him my secrets. Right here, leaned across this table, squat in the middle of Pox's famous Ice Cream joint. But I hesitate too long, and then it's gone. I open my mouth to fill the void but stop when I hear something said behind me that sets off bells. Like hearing a parent calling for their kid, and then understanding it's you they're calling for, and that's your parent.

I tilt my head so I can better hear what's being said.

"...say Ellie's been there for months, the poor girl. It's not like anything anyone does will help."

A new voice chimes in. "I heard her father came into town looking for her. Said he was taking Ellie's picture up and down Main Street, but of course no one's talking."

I shoot up in my chair and cross the room. Maybe I should form some sort of plan before barreling over there, but I know only that this girl I replaced is named Ellie and is someone I haven't been able to get out of my head. And here are two people finally talking.

I sidle up next to their table and run my hands over my naked hair. I hate Poppet right now for confiscating my wigs. "Hi," I say dumbly. The two women look up. "I apologize for interrupting, but I heard you say my friend's name. Ellie?"

The larger woman leans back in her chair. "And you are?"

"Domino," I answer. When the woman continues staring at me, I add, "I live at Madam Karina's place, and I'm looking for Ellie."

The thinner woman stares across the space at her friend, worry creasing her face. She's clearly waiting for the larger woman to speak. Eventually, she does. "No one knows where Ellie is, dear. She just up and vanished. Upset Madam Karina something awful."

"Madam Karina is a friend of ours," the thinner woman blurts out. "We hated to see her upset. If any trouble came to that little girl, it was well deserved."

"Shut up, Viola," the other woman says. She glances up at me. "Look, go back to that boy over there and enjoy the day. Don't worry yourself with bygones." As an afterthought, she says, "And tell Madam Karina we said hello, and that we'll be sure to bring her some of our canned pears soon."

"And you are?" I say, repeating her earlier words. Behind me, I hear a chair slide across the floor. Three earthquake steps later, Cain brushes up beside me.

"Everything okay?" he asks.

The larger woman ignores my question, pressing her thin lips against a porcelain cup of coffee and slurping loudly. She leaves a red lipstick stain when she lowers the glass. "Domino was kind enough to introduce herself. And now she's leaving."

I'm not sure why it's her final dismissal that pushes me over the edge, but it does. "I heard you talking about Ellie, and I won't leave until you tell me what you know."

Cain's eyes snap to my face when he realizes what I'm asking about. "Come on, Dom, let's get you a Coke."

I glare at him. "Don't patronize me."

The thin woman slumps in her chair. "Just listen to him and get out of here. You're going to make trouble for everyone."

"See, that's what I mean. What *kind* of trouble?" My voice grows more urgent. It's like there's this black seed of uncertainty that rooted itself in place the moment I saw Madam Karina in that Detroit alleyway. As much as I want to please her, as much as I want to believe she loves us girls, that seedling won't go away.

The large woman lifts her coffee cup a second time.

"Trouble is trouble, isn't it?"

"Domino…" Cain urges.

Don't you dare let them dismiss you like that, Wilson sneers. *You can't go back to Madam Karina's without learning what they know.*

He's right.

I slam my hands down on their table. "Tell me where Ellie is!"

A firm hand comes down on my shoulder and spins me around. Eric stands over me, a repulsive grin sweeping across his mouth. "I'll tell you where she is. In fact, why don't I show you?"

I jerk away from him.

"Okay, let's go." Cain practically pulls me off my feet, and suddenly the two of us are soaring through the establishment toward the front door. "Too much sugar," he yells toward Eric in the worst excuse for an explanation I've ever heard. "I gotta get her back before Madam Karina has my hide."

Eric salutes Cain with two fingers, but his eyes never leave mine.

Already, I'm conflicted about snapping at those two women who probably did nothing wrong. I look back to gauge their faces, but instead my gaze lands on Eric.

Eric and his blatant threat.

Eric and his knowledge of Ellie's whereabouts.

Eric and his gold deputy badge that says he's untouchable in the town of Pox.

CHAPTER 42

PINK COUCHES AND ENGLISH TEA

Cain drags me toward the black sedan, and I let him. Not that I have a choice when it comes to his raw strength. He closes my door and climbs into the driver's seat. As soon as his door is closed, I lay into him.

"Tell me what you know about that girl."

Eric pushes open the screen door and watches as we pull away, yellow Texas dust kicking up around the car. I keep my eyes trained on the officer until we're a safe distance away.

Cain watches the road. "I know what you know. That she left a few months back, and it upset Madam Karina."

"There's more to it than that!"

The muscles in his forearms jump. "Yeah, I think there is, too. I also know Eric is in Madam Karina's pocket just like the cops were in her father's pocket, and it isn't good to ask too many questions."

"What does her father have to do with anything?"

"He doesn't, really, except that her father was the mayor of Pox for a long time, and he wasn't a straightlaced kind of guy. My dad said he taxed business owners and then kept the money for himself. Not much anyone could do about it, since he was paying off the deputies. And since Madam Karina is this guy's daughter, that power just sort of slid over to her.

Lot of people want to leave Pox, because it's shady here, but they don't have the means to do it."

"So, what, you're just going to roll over? Cain, if you're living in a house run by a criminal, wouldn't you want to know?" I shake my head. "Something is really, really wrong here."

He laughs, though I don't see how this is funny. "Didn't you know? We're all criminals. It's Madam Karina's House for Burgeoning Convicts. You going to cast the first stone?"

"Stop laughing. What if Ellie is… What if that girl is dead or something?"

The grin on his face vanishes. "If I thought that, I'd be gone."

"So what do you think happened?"

"My honest opinion?" He glances at me, and I nod. "I think she stole cash from the house and skipped town. And I think Madam Karina covered it up by circulating rumors. Better to have people afraid than have them think you got robbed."

"But you seemed worried back there."

Cain straightens. "I wasn't worried. I just know the madam has powerful influence in this town, and sometimes it's better to leave questions unanswered."

"Influence like Eric?"

Cain doesn't respond.

"You know those women said Ellie's dad is looking for her. Even if she's okay, isn't it wrong that her family thinks otherwise?"

I let that hang in the air as the landscape soars past, silence settling between us like a sticky morning fog.

Cain shifts in his seat. "Let's talk to Angie about it."

"Thought you said it was only rumors. No harm, no foul."

"I don't like that her dad is looking for her," he says. "You're right. People shouldn't be afraid of Madam Karina. It isn't right." Cain seems to be telling himself this as much as me.

"You think Angie knows something we don't?"

"Yeah, I do."

"Think she'll tell us?"

"Depends on how much she lost at cards this morning."

A ngie trails outside as we pull up, cussing at her Dobermans to get back. Get back to where, I'm not sure.

An American flag hangs limply on a pole at the top of her trailer, and an old oak tree bows over her home like it's paying homage. Pecan shells and dog feces litter the ground and, though it's a park, the next trailer over is well out of earshot. Angie lights a cigarette and strides toward Black Betty, her beloved tractor. She lays a hand on the machine like she's afraid it may suddenly vanish.

She points her cigarette at us. "Madam Karina know you're here?"

"You know she doesn't," Cain replies.

"Then you best get off my property."

I almost remind her that it's technically not her property. Might be because I'm envious of her dusty trailer with its curtains and mud-caked doormat. It's home for Angie, and that's something.

"We just want to come in for a few minutes." Cain heads toward the front door, but Angie cuts him off.

"I can't let you do that."

Cain peers over his shoulder at me. "She must have lost her ass this morning."

Angie smacks him on his shoulder. "That's got nothing to do with nothing. And I didn't lose my ass, smart aleck."

"How much you win then?" he antagonizes.

She presses her lips together. "I would have won if that old fart Deloris didn't cheat."

"She is a cheat," Cain agrees.

Angie stares at him with one eye narrowed, trying to decide if he's messing with her. She must decide he's not, because she groans and waves toward the trailer. "Well, go on then. Make yourself at home. You're going to anyway, right?"

Angie's dogs rush in before the three us can take a step inside. The woman yells at them without conviction and sits down on a pink sofa that's wildly out of character for her. Then again, I suppose her trailer is yellow. A fact she seems proud of.

"I'll take a glass of tea," she tells Cain. He smiles and disappears into her kitchen. He's been gone for five seconds when Angie yells, "And don't give the dogs any peppermints. You know how it makes Kali sick."

"I know, I know…"

"That damn dog and her damn stomach," Angie mutters to herself before turning her attention on me. "I suppose you're looking for answers."

I sit in a chair across from her, hoping if I stay silent she'll talk more freely.

"Wondering what it is you got yourself into and just how sincere that Madam Karina is?" When I don't reply, she says, "Well, I'll tell you this much. I hope you don't got plans for leaving. Because once you become Madam Karina's property, you're tagged for life."

"What happened to Ellie?" I ask.

Angie sits back and sighs. "You don't beat around the bush, do you?"

"Where is she?"

Cain comes to stand in the doorway, his back to the kettle.

Angie looks at the ceiling. "Mr. Hodge will skin me if he finds out you two are here digging around."

"Angie," Cain urges, his voice gentle. "That girl's dad was here, in Pox, looking for her."

"Well, he came to the right place."

"You think she's still here?" I ask.

"I think you know exactly where she is." Angie directs the statement to me. "And that's all I'm going to say about it."

I swallow a lump in my throat. "Is she dead?"

Angie's face peels back like an orange. "What? No, you twit. That girl ain't dead. What do you think this is, some true crime novel? Madam Karina has a heavy hand, but she's not a murderer."

The woman runs her hand over one of the Dobermans and he lays his head on her knee. "What you need to be concerned with is what you'll be asked to do while working for Madam Karina."

I glance down. "I know what I'll be asked to do."

"Do you?"

I turn my face away. "It doesn't take a rocket scientist to figure it out."

"And are you prepared to give everything you have to Madam Karina? Because that's what happens out there in those guesthouses."

Cain runs his hand over his shorn hair and grits his teeth, his jaw working. "Domino doesn't have to do anything she doesn't want to."

"Like hell she doesn't." Angie stands up.

When Cain spots the anger on Angie's face, he returns to the kettle. But neither of us misses his next words. "How would you know, anyway?"

Angie sucks in air. Opens her mouth to say something. Closes it. Opens it again. "Because I worked in that goddamn house. If you ain't figured that out yet, you're dumber than I thought."

Cain stops what he's doing, and I remain motionless.

Angie sucks on her cigarette, ashes falling onto the floor. "I worked for her then, and I work for her now." Her voice drops an octave. "It's harder than you think to get out. It's like the Sicilian Mafia." She makes a gun with her free hand and fires off a round into my chest. "Bang, bang."

When she sees the look on my face, she waves away the implication. "It's not like she kills you. Jesus, stop going so dark with it."

"So what does she do then?" I ask, growing frustrated. Cain is still staring at Angie like he can't believe she was ever one of Madam Karina's girls, but I'm not sure it's that big of a surprise. She carries herself like she's ancient, but she could have worked in that house as few as ten years ago.

I could see it, Wilson says, nodding. *She's got spice, ya know?*

Angie's eyes travel to a large window and, slowly, her pupils begin to dilate. "Jesus, Mary, and Joseph. That's Eric's car. You have got to get out of here. Now!"

CHAPTER 43

VEILED THREATS

In the distance, a sedan rumbles down the road toward us. It's loud and persistent and a sad shade of gold that brings shame upon its kind. I can't make out who's driving, but Angie is hysterical, shoving us toward the door and yelling to move faster.

The kettle screams from the kitchen, and Cain turns like he's going to take care of it.

"What are you thinking?" Angie roars. "Get out. Go!"

I grab Cain's arm, and we stumble down the trailer steps. Her dogs shoot out the door and nearly take us down. Barking like mad, the two canines race down the dirt road toward Eric's car. The driver taps the brakes when the dogs get within a few feet of the vehicle.

It's all the time we need.

Cain lunges into the car, and I dive in after him.

"Why is it so bad that we're here?" I yell as Cain throws the car into reverse.

"Because they'll figure out what we're doing. Asking questions."

Cain backs up just enough and then slams on the accelerator. We zip past Angie's trailer, but not before I spot her running.

"Stop," I tell Cain.

He hits the brakes, and a second later Angie's face appears on my side of the car. I roll down the window, glancing in the rearview to see Eric cruising closer.

Angie touches my cheek, and I'm surprised by her gentleness. "Do what the madam says, just the way she says it, and you'll be okay."

When I don't respond, anger tightens her features.

"Promise me!" she demands.

Startled by her outburst, I say, "I promise, Angie."

She looks at Cain and waves him away.

That's all the permission he needs. Cain lays on the gas, and we zoom away, leaving that blasted gold sedan in the distance.

It isn't until we're several miles down the road before I ask the question that's haunted me since we sped away. "He wouldn't hurt her, would he?"

Cain shakes his head. "No way."

"How can you be sure?"

"Because I'd kill him if he did."

Just like that. Not a drop of fear or hesitation in his voice. No lowered head or quiet words.

Because I'd kill him if he did.

Cain may keep to himself and let things lay when he shouldn't. But I can tell he's gaining confidence and with it, the courage to fight when something is wrong. Maybe the change is me. Maybe he just needed someone in his corner again.

Am I in his corner?

I study him as he propels us toward Madam Karina's home. Those powerful arms that made me feel safe when lightning tore the sky. That seldom smile that warms my insides. The thing he says to me over and over: *I wouldn't be afraid of you, no matter what you did.*

You're falling for him, Wilson whispers.

I fall for no one, I respond.

Wilson chuckles softly. *You fall for everyone, my rose.*

Wilson's right, but this feels different. Poppet feels like a friend I can trust. And Angie, though she puts on a tough front, feels like a woman who truly cares.

And Cain.

Cain feels like a weather-worn boulder that will stand the test of time. Through rain and snow and flood and fire, he'll remain rooted in place. The earth will move around him. And I will lie next to him through it all and hold on.

He wants me to hold on.

We are opposites, and we are the same.

Me, the girl who needs someone to cling to, and he, the boy who's desperate for someone to protect.

What could the two of us overcome together?

A grenade.

And a volcano.

Cain reaches over and grabs my knee, squeezes. I see the way his jaw works, like he's unsure if touching me is okay. But here's what I do—

I take his hand.

When we get back to the house, Madam Karina pushes open the door and crosses her arms. "Go inside, Cain," she says when we step out of the car. "I'd like to talk to Domino for a moment."

Cain pauses on the front porch and looks back at me, ensuring I'm okay. I give him the slightest nod before he heads inside, bag slung over his shoulder.

"Did you enjoy yourself today?" The evening sun shines down on Madam Karina like stage lights illuminating a rising star.

The way she says it, it's like she wants me to find out her secrets. To dig them from her dress pockets and roll them between my fingers. I meet her gaze. "It was wonderful. Thank you."

"I trust this satiated your wanderlust."

I cock my head, ready to play her game. "I don't have wanderlust, Madam Karina. I only wanted to learn more about the town we call home."

"And why is that?"

"Because one day I'll run this establishment beside you. And knowing your customers is the first step to improvement."

"You think my business needs improvement?"

I move closer, but stay at the bottom of the stairs. "I think between the two of us, we could make that sister of yours itch with envy."

Madam Karina doesn't laugh the way I expected she might. She just stares at me, and I stare at her—two wild beasts wondering whether they could take the other, and also questioning whether they have to be enemies. After all, it can get lonely in these sweltering desert plains.

As I study the madam, I think of Angie.

Do what the madam says, and you'll be okay.

I promised Angie I wouldn't challenge Madam Karina, but I also saw the look on her face. That complete and utter submission that comes from years of fearing someone. I know I can't stay here, but I'll follow the madam's rules and earn the cash I need to leave.

Though if what Angie says is true, she'll probably try to stop me, or at least rip me off.

If she does, Wilson says, *I'll take the cash and I'll get us out of here.*

Steal the money? I ask Wilson.

Take what is rightfully ours.

"I do hope you make the right decision, Domino," Madam Karina says, the lines around those hooded eyes softening. "You are an untamable creature, but that's what endears you to me. Because you remind me so much of myself when I was your age. You are a child in need of a mother, and I am a woman with a hole in her heart. Both of us in desperate need for the feel of a proper home."

That right there.

That's what scares me the most.

That *scares you?* Wilson asks. *She couldn't do scary if I wove marionette strings through her and controlled her myself.*

But I know Wilson is lying.

I climb the stairs and start to pass by, but she grabs my arm and jerks me against her. "I don't like it when girls scheme behind my back. If you ever decide you'd like to leave, you must apply."

I nod, surprised by her strong grip.

"We must trust each other." She lets go and steps back, allowing me to pass. I'm almost to the staircase that will take me to the third floor when she turns in the doorway and says, "I would never keep you from leaving. It's just that I don't like being run out on."

I don't turn around.

Wilson tells me not to.

"I understand," I whisper.

"I pray that you do," she says evenly. "Because I know it'd be extremely difficult for Poppet if you left."

I whirl around and measure the look on her face. She's threatening me. Plain and simple. And I do not respond well to threats. Wilson doesn't, either. I lower my gaze but speak in a clear voice so that she understands I'm serious. "Poppet has nothing to do with the decisions I make. She will live a happy, safe life wherever she chooses."

"Because you'll be here to watch after her," the madam challenges. "Because if you weren't, I'd hate to think—"

I raise my eyes. "She will be happy because if someone made her unhappy, I'd make them pay."

Madam Karina laughs. "Goodness! You are a spitfire, Domino. But one thing you are not is a protector. If you want that girl to have a wonderful life, then be her friend. Be present. Understand? That's all I'm saying."

I turn and head up the stairs without responding. I'm almost out of earshot when I hear Madam Karina mutter under her breath, "The mouth on that girl. Does she expect me to be frightened of her?"

Not her, Wilson replies quietly. *Me.*

CHAPTER 44

SEE ME

It's Saturday night, six days after Cain and I went into town. Jack is back with a bronze coin in his pocket, and it's going to be mine by the end of the evening. He helped me become a Tulip, he said, and he'll help me become a Lily next.

Bold words.

But, so far, he's stood by his promises.

I'm back to drawing in my sketchpad to entertain the customers. I draw their dreams, their lovers, anything they want. My illustrations aren't always good, but that's not what they care about. They care about my hair falling over my shoulder, and that I let them push it back behind my ear. They care that when they pat my knee, I don't kidney-punch them.

And they care that when they speak softly in my ear, I don't pull away.

All the Tulip girls allow the customers to touch them. Not in especially intimate ways, but it's a line I stepped over alongside Poppet. Sometimes it feels like Madam Karina challenged me with this, and each time I let a stranger's fingers brush my skin, I'm showing her I can handle anything she throws my way.

Poppet and I were in third and fourth place last night, which means we'll have to come in first or second tonight to have a shot at finishing the week at the top of the class. The Tulips aren't particularly competitive, but they have a way of stealing clients without using words. It's in the way they look at us, with disgust. The customers see it. Of course they do. That's what the senior Tulips want. And it doesn't take long before our clients wonder if they chose wrong.

Tonight, especially, they seem to know the stakes are high. I don't think any of them want a place among the Lilies. But they don't want us to have it, either.

When an older woman lays a hand on my arm and strokes my skin, asking sweetly for a glass of tea, I bow my head and stand. Jack watches as I cross the room and approach the gold rollaway cart. Upon it is china embellished with hand-painted tulips, sugar cubes, and thick cream. I'm reaching for the teapot when a Tulip cuts me off. She snatches the pot and pours much slower than necessary, then takes her time with the sugar and cream. Meanwhile, my customer is waiting for me to return.

I grit my teeth and wait for her to finish, but once she does, another Tulip blocks my path and does the same thing. I glance over my shoulder at Poppet, and she rolls her eyes before returning her attention to a young boy who's twirling her hair around his thumb. When the second Tulip walks away, I push myself against the cart and grab for the pot. But the moment I have it in my hands, a third Tulip snaps up the sugar and creamer and strides away with both.

"Hey," I say. "I need those, too."

The girl sits down on a suede couch and holds them in her hands like goose eggs. A man on her right lays his hand on her upper thigh and pays no mind to the things she snatched. I close the distance between us and notice the man isn't even drinking tea. Neither is the Tulip.

"May I have those?" I say to her, barely controlling my

anger. "I'm serving tea to a customer."

The girl smiles, but doesn't respond.

I groan. "I know you can hear me."

The man looks up at me and then pats the couch beside him, but I'd rather break his nose than join their party of two.

"Look, I don't want any trouble. I just need those." I reach for the items in the girl's hands, but she rips them away.

She glances at the man and grins. "Do you hear something? I think I must have left a window open. It's like the wind is whistling through here."

"Are you cold?" the man asks, putting his arm around her.

"This isn't funny. Give them to me." I reach for the sugar and cream a second time, and again she jerks them out of reach.

"Hey, Breanne," the Tulip says to another girl. "Do you hear something?"

Breanne shrugs. "I certainly don't see anything."

I turn around and note that the older woman I was making tea for has moved on to a different Tulip. My sketchpad lies open on our empty table, a half completed drawing of her pug, Sadie, exposed to the world. Blood simmers beneath my skin, and Wilson readies himself for a fight.

Want me to hit her? he asks. *Something tells me she'd see you real quick then.*

I can handle this.

Can you? Even your Jack seems unimpressed.

Wilson's right. Jack is talking to another Tulip with long brown hair that shines, even in the dark. She has full eyebrows and a nose that turns up at the end. I hate her. Even though I'm not sure I care about having Jack's attention, I hate her for taking it.

My eyes scan the room. Tulips ignoring me. Tulips laughing at me. Tulips scooping up all the bronze coins and letting them slip between their fingers with carelessness. I need those coins.

I need them because I can't stay here any longer, and I can't start over without more money to my name, either. I'm not strong enough.

I can handle this, if only you'll let me, Wilson coos.

No, I can fix this myself.

My pulse beats inside my neck as I race toward Poppet's and my bedroom. White sheets, white curtains, white slip chair—orange spray paint. I grab it from my dresser and hurry back into the Tulips' drawing room. Once there, I watch on, breathing hard, as the girls and customers and even the moon glowing through the window ignores me.

I'm tired of being a Tulip.

Tired of being invisible.

Tired of unanswered questions and Madam Karina's veiled threats and strange hands roaming across my body without ever seeing my face.

I raise the can to a virginal white wall. I pop the top and shake what little remains—*click, clank, click, clank.* Then I start spraying. Almost immediately, I hear the Point Girl for the Tulips yelling. But I keep going. It takes only a matter of seconds. I'm not worried about shadows or dripping paint.

My arm moves quickly, my tongue pressed into my cheek.

Wilson holds his breath.

When I'm done, I turn and face the room. Every last person is eyeballing me. It's what I wanted, but now it feels unbearable. All those browns and greens and blues trying to burrow inside my mind. The woman whose dog I was drawing stands and smiles. She doesn't come toward me, but she seems pleased by this sudden outburst.

The Point Girl speaks up. "What in God's name do you think you're doing? You've got a lot of nerve destroying property that isn't yours. Wait until I tell the madam what you…"

I run from the room as her voice trails off.

I leave Poppet behind. I leave her behind with the giant block letters I wrote along the wall.

SEE ME

Wilson claps inside my head. *I would have taken a more physical approach, but not bad.*

It's Jack who stops my retreat. He's all smiles and sunshine, and it feels wrong. I need to be alone right now, but his hands slide around my waist like we're two years into a committed relationship. But we're not in a relationship. He's a customer, and I'm a Tulip. That's all this is.

He licks his lips and dips his head. "Domino."

"I need to be alone."

"I understand," he says. "But right now, I need to kiss you."

I stiffen in his arms. It's not like I didn't know where this was headed. Wilson never trusted Jack, not for a moment. And if I become a Lily, I'll have to get over being afraid of a simple kiss. But right now, with fury coursing through my body, I'd be more inclined to disembowel him.

He must sense my hesitation, because he brushes his lips against my ear and says, "I see you, Domino. I saw you the first time I walked into this messed-up place, and I see you now."

I close my eyes against his words, but my heart still thumps painfully from adrenaline. He's saying the right things. Does he know it the same way Madam Karina does? "I've worked hard to ensure you move up. Because that's what you wanted. But now…now I'd like to kiss you."

Without asking for permission, he moves his mouth to mine. I gasp against his lips, but I don't pull away. Not when the tip of his tongue touches my tongue, and not when his fingers crawl down my sides, inching over my serpent tattoo. *He sees me. He sees me.*

But as his hands move closer to my chest than my sides,

my brain begins to spin. Did he really help me because that's what I wanted? Or was it because this was what he wanted? After all, he couldn't be touching me this way if I were still a Carnation. And am I forgetting the way he drugged me when I was a Daisy?

I don't trust Jack.

I don't trust him, and I don't want this.

I can help with that, Wilson says.

No sooner do I think this than my knee jerks upward. I hit him in the junk, and he bends at the waist, groaning in pain.

"What the hell?" he snarls as he fights to catch his breath.

Touch her again, Wilson snarls. *Do it. I dare you!*

I turn and run down the stairs. Behind me, Jack yells hollow words. He cares about me. He's sorry. But mostly, what I hear is the last part.

The part where he says I owe him.

CHAPTER 45

PROPERTY

Near the bottom of the stairs, I hear the muffled sounds of people whispering.

Ignore them, I think to myself. *Find Cain.*

But as the voices grow louder, curiosity gets the better of me. I edge closer, keeping myself hidden. It isn't until I'm outside the foyer that I recognize the voices of Madam Karina and Candy, the Carnation that Poppet and I roomed with. The madam is scolding her for something, but I can't make out what.

I take another step, and the board beneath my foot creaks.

They stop speaking.

Madam Karina rounds the corner and spots me. She grabs my arm and drags me into the foyer. "What are you doing? Spying on us? That's very rude." Her breath smells the way it did the night she pushed me into Poppet. "Tell me what you heard."

"I didn't hear anything," I reply.

Candy sighs. "I'm going to bed. He's not coming back."

Madam Karina swings around and points at Candy. "Don't take another step. You tell me where he is."

"I already told you what I know." Candy throws up her arms. "He left a few minutes after the party started."

"What direction did he go?" the madam presses, growing hysterical.

She's asking about Mr. Hodge, I'm sure. I remember how upset she was when he was on his phone, his attention stolen from her.

Candy appears exhausted, like she's been going in circles with Madam Karina far too long. The white flower on her blouse hangs limply, and her clothing is disheveled. She was one of the few Carnations who was civil toward me, so I decide to help her out.

"Maybe we could try walking down the road to see if he got a flat or something," I say to Madam Karina. "Candy, you can go back to the entertainment room. I'll go with her."

"Thank God," Candy mumbles, attempting to bypass the madam. But the madam has other plans. She grabs Candy by the back of the neck and jerks the girl so she faces her.

"Don't you walk away from me," Madam Karina snaps, "You ungrateful brat."

Candy's face opens with surprise. "Madam Karina, I'm sorry. I just thought…"

"You thought what? That you could watch Mr. Hodge leaving to see *her* and not say anything? Is that it?"

"Madam Karina, I can help." My words are gentle even as my heart shotguns. "Let me take you up to your room." I inch toward Candy so that I'm standing between the two, using my hundred-pound frame as a laughable barrier.

The madam cackles. "Oh, here's the protector, Candy. Come to save you and anyone else I might upset."

"It's not like that," I whisper.

It's exactly like that, Wilson says.

Candy hesitates for several beats and then dashes toward the Carnations' entertainment room. Madam Karina turns to watch Candy flee, and releases a long sigh.

"Did you want to walk down the road and see—?"

Madam Karina wheels around and slaps me across the face using every ounce of her shrunken frame. I'm knocked to the ground and before I can think, she lunges at me, her knees pinned on either side of my chest. She wraps her hands around my throat and squeezes. As my breathing is cut off and the world grows fuzzy and dim, I fumble at her fingers. Head pounding. Mouth gaping. Legs kicking. Wilson roaring.

The madam releases her hold quickly enough, but I still suck in every bit of oxygen the room holds and fight to sit up. Madam Karina shoves me backward and leans her old Hollywood face down until our lips are an inch apart. "My dear child, I don't think you understand your place in this house, so allow me to clarify. You are not my partner. You are not the girls' ambassador. Perhaps one day, you will become Top Girl and sit at my right hand and come to judge the quick and the dead."

She kisses me once, swift, on the mouth as I gasp. "Until then, you are my property." She rises to her feet and steps backward, allowing me room to rise, though I don't. I can't. "Always and forever, Domino Ray, you are mine to have and to hold."

Madam Karina turns and quits the room in a flurry of silk fabrics and graying tendrils unraveling from her bun.

I lay on the ground, my hands protective around my aching throat, my lip quivering because, as much as I saw the warning signs, I'd hoped Madam Karina wouldn't hurt me. Not when it came down to it. Not even after Angie warned me. Not when the madam seemed to think of me as her found pet—the girl who convinced her to try again.

But she did hurt me.

She is my mother incarnate. Whispering lullabies in my ear and then digging in the knife once my guard has fallen away. She even wants the same things from me that my mother did. That's what Wilson meant when he said we shouldn't be here.

All at once, my vines of suspicion for this place, for this woman, weave into a thorny beanstalk springing toward the sky. I have to get out. I have to leave as soon as possible, and I have to get Poppet out, too. I don't know what's happened between Madam Karina and Mr. Hodge, but it's pushed a volatile woman over the edge. And I won't be here when she lands at the bottom of that quarry, bloodied and vengeful.

I have to escape Madam Karina's Home for Burgeoning Entertainers, with or without the money I've earned.

We can't leave here without that money, Wilson says evenly.

We can, Wilson, and we will. I didn't think I could start over empty-handed, but I've done it before. I just need to get away from that woman. That's all.

We won't leave here without that money, Wilson repeats, a nerve-rattling edge to his voice. *And Domino?*

I remain silent, knowing it's what he wants.

Wilson's chest heaves, his wickedly sharp face flashing in my mind as only it does when he grows truly and wholly close to taking over. *That's the last time someone lays a hand on you,* he continues, his eyes storming, voice solid as a casket. *Next time it happens, Papa comes to play.*

PART IV

DOMINO'S RULES
FOR PLANNING A PRISON BREAK

1. Keep your eyes open.
2. Destroy the warden's resources.
3. Understand your allies' strengths.
4. Use the element of surprise to escape.
5. If all else fails, let Wilson out of his cage.

CHAPTER 46

WHAT I DID

It's Saturday. The day my mother brought the first one home.

His name is Tom.

He doesn't have a last name, my mother tells me when he's out of earshot. He is only Tom, and I should think of him that way. The man sits on our couch, adjusting himself, craning his neck to see where my mother went. He's in his mid-fifties, the indention from an absent wedding band on his left finger. I can almost feel the weight of the ring hidden in his pocket. He has thinning hair and a small belly. A bright green shirt hangs loosely on his otherwise wiry frame, and I can smell the scent of cigarettes on him from here.

"I met him at Roosevelt's," my mother explains in hushed tones.

Roosevelt's. A bar clear across town she showed me last weekend. I remember the cars in the parking lot, the cracked red leather booths and dim lighting hardly visible through the dusty windows. Cartoon writing spelled out the name of the bar, but the middle *E* was smudged so badly that it looked more like *Roos velt's*.

"He told me I was the kind of girl he could really fall for," she scoffs. "And as we drove here, he said he wanted a family. To marry a nice woman. As if I don't know he's already married." My mom takes my chin in her hand. "They're all the same, Domino. They will all do to me and you what Dad did to us."

"Why can't we just try to find Dad?" It's a question I've asked a dozen times.

"I tried," Mom hisses. "You helped me look for him. He's gone. He doesn't want to be found." She straightens, smooths her hair. "So we'll improvise. Save other women from experiencing what we did. Better for men like these to vanish in the night than to walk out on their families."

I hate what my mother is saying. Her words crawl over my skin, and my heart beats faster when she sets her gaze on the man, Tom. I want to scream for him to leave. I want to call the police. I want to hit my mother and tell her she's crazy and I won't do it. I won't do this horrible thing.

But then she takes me into her arms. She tells me I am her perfect, beautiful daughter. She tells me she will never leave me, and that we have only each other, forever. And finally, she says the thing that causes my resolve to crumble.

"Who would you have if not for me?" Her words are warm against my ear, her embrace comforting. "Where would you go?"

When she tells me to get our tools, I do.

And when she tells me to open the basement door, I do.

And when she shows me the best ways to cut a person so that they suffer longer, I do these things and more. I am her daughter. I am her good girl. But I cannot stay as this man bleeds and begs for his life. I cannot be present as we bury his body in the freshly churned earth; the same place where, one day, concrete will be poured for a brand new Bank of America. I cannot stand by as Mother brings another man to our home. And another. And another.

I cannot do these things.

But Wilson can.

It was a Saturday the first time Mother brought one home. I was twelve years old.

CHAPTER 47

I KNOW WHY THE CAGED BIRD SINGS

I wake in a cold sweat and realize someone has been saying my name.

Domino…

Turning over in bed, my face bathed in moonlight, I focus on the voice.

Domino, wake up.

When I realize who it is, I pull the covers over my head and groan. *Leave me alone, Wilson.*

He moves in closer. *Why were you thinking about those things? Those things that happened with Mother?*

I can't help it. It's like she's dragging it out of me.

Madam Karina?

I don't respond.

Wilson does something he's never done before. He lays his hand on my forehead. I close my eyes against his touch as he moves his palm over my hair slowly, shushing me. It's almost like if I peek, he'll be standing there, flesh and blood.

But when I do open my eyes, it's my own hand that's petting my hair. I rip my arm down and swing my legs over the side of the bed. Poppet is asleep across from me. Watching her, I'm struck by loneliness. It's been so long since we stayed up late and whispered secrets and wishes for our future and, sometimes, recounted memories from our past.

Pulling on a pair of jeans, I head toward Cain's place in the basement. I find him awake on the foot of his mattress. When he sees me, he opens the cage door without hesitation and takes me into his arms. It's a quick hug, like he did it without thinking. And before I know it, he's put distance between us again.

"Is everything okay?" he asks.

I shake my head. "No. I know where Ellie is. Or at least, I think I do."

Cain raises an eyebrow.

"Want to take a drive?"

He opens his mouth to answer, and then his brow furrows. He takes my chin in his hand and turns my face to the left, examines my cheek, my neck. "What happened here?"

I pull away. "Nothing."

"Domino, tell me." His voice is urgent, furious.

"Madam Karina slapped me. She was drunk." I don't tell him the rest. It's right there for him to see. Cain starts to respond, but I continue. "I have to get out of here. That was my plan for a while, to earn enough to get a place and buy myself time to find a job. But I can't wait any longer. She's cracking, Cain. Mr. Hodge is making her crazy, and she's freaking out about losing anyone else."

Cain stares at my skin like he can will the bruises away. From between clenched teeth, he says, "She's always been like that. Afraid that people will run out on her."

"Will you take me into Pox?"

He hesitates for a beat as if he's weighing the old Cain, who would never risk upsetting Madam Karina, against the new Cain, who cares enough about someone else to come out of hiding. In the end, he pulls on black combat boots and motions for me to head up first.

Outside, the phantom vehicle waits for us, patient as death. It's a stroke of luck that the car hasn't been returned. Cain starts to get in the driver's seat, but I beat him to the punch and take the keys from his hand.

"You know how to drive?" he asks in a whisper.

I nod. It's been a while, but my mom taught me before I left home. Slipping behind the wheel, my senses spark alive. It feels like I've been asleep, and only now have I thought to wake up and see the world for what it is.

I take the car out onto the road slowly and drive a short distance before accelerating. Glancing back in the rearview, I assure myself no new lights have flipped on.

It doesn't take long to arrive in Pox's town square, and never once does Cain question what we're doing. Once, briefly, he looks over and stares at me in the dark. But that's it. I navigate down the roads until I find what I'm looking for. The same place we passed on the way to get ice cream.

Pox County Municipal

A town this size probably doesn't have a separate police station, so I park outside the two-story brick building and kill the ignition. A single light buzzes over the glass door, and moths throw themselves against the intoxicating light.

I get out of the car, and Cain follows me without a word. My palms begin to sweat when we step inside because, in my eagerness, I never thought through how we'd enter the jail area without being questioned. But the woman behind the counter is painting her nails a bubblegum shade of pink to match the teddy bears on her sweater. She hardly glances up as we pass by.

"The jail cells?" Cain asks me under his breath when we're a safe distance away.

"Yeah, do you know where they are?"

He waves me along. "Follow me."

We stride down linoleum hallways scuffed black, and Cain

pauses outside a heavy door that reads POLICE in an arch across a glass window insert. Cain peers through and holds a finger to his lips. The we crouch to the floor, and he brings his mouth to my ear. I shiver from the unexpected touch. "There's an officer on duty. He'll go in the back at some point."

"How do you know?"

"Because I've delivered stuff to Eric before, and they rarely keep anyone up front at night. Too little happens around here."

Just as Cain predicted, the deputy sitting behind the front desk eventually moves to a door on his left and exits. We wait five minutes to ensure he's gone to the lounge and isn't returning. Then we go inside. Cain pushes a button beneath the desk and the door on the opposite side clicks.

I grab the handle and smile when it opens.

"I've always wanted to push that button," Cain says with a sly grin.

I head down the narrow hall, jail cells lining the right side. They're the old-school kind with actual bars and rusting toilets and steel benches that serve as beds. Not sure what else to do, I quietly call out her name.

"Ellie? Are you here?"

When no one responds, I tiptoe past the first cell that lays empty and move to the next, but there's no one here. I was wrong. I figured, with Eric's involvement, that if Ellie were being held anywhere, it'd be here. I look at Cain and shrug, shaking my head. He lays a soft hand on my upper back, ready to guide us out, when the air kicks on. The breeze rushes out through floor vents, and a soft *thump* sounds from behind us.

I turn on my heels, narrow my eyes. And though I'm staring right at it, it's Cain that really sees it first.

He strides over, surprisingly quiet on his feet, and spiders his fingers along the hardwood floor. Near the grated air return, his hand finds purchase. He lifts a flap in the floor and glances at me, his features twisted with concern.

I dash toward him but, when I make for the descending stairs, he blocks my path, holds up a *wait* hand. We listen, and then Cain takes the stairs before me.

Uh, we totally could have gone first, Wilson says.

Below the floor of the jail cell is a buzzing light, concrete floors, and second set of jail cells. I swallow, my throat thick. When I spot a thin girl lying on the bench, her back to me, I'm sickened but not surprised. I steal a glance at Cain, wet my lips, and say, "Are you Ellie?"

There's a long pause that wraps around my throat. Finally, the girl says, "What does she want now?"

My stomach touches my feet, and the wind is ripped from my lungs. It's her. This is Ellie, and Madam Karina put her here, and maybe I've known all along but was too afraid to admit it. Most girls leave and become like Angie, forever toiling for their master until they are one day, maybe, released from servitude. But Ellie tried to escape. And now she is here.

"How long have you been here?" I ask, choking on panic.

Ellie turns and faces us. When I see her, I have to look away. Cain brushes my arm, but I recoil from his touch. It's too much to be comforted when she's the one who needs help.

Her face is shallow and bruised, and her skin has a sickly pallor. A light sweat coats her upper lip and forehead, and blood cakes her bottom lip. "As long as I deserve. And I'll serve the remainder of my time and debt to Madam Karina with gratitude. Being here has given me time to reflect on my mistakes."

My entire body goes numb when I understand why Ellie is talking this way. She's consumed by fear. "We're on your side. You don't have to be scared."

She stands up, greasy brown hair falling over her left eye.

Her body shakes from the exertion, and bile rises in my throat. "I love Madam Karina," she insists, shuffling toward me. "I wish only to return to her home and make her happy for the rest of my days. I was wrong. Can you tell her I was wrong?"

"Screw this." Cain spins on his heel and searches the space, no doubt looking for a way to open her cell.

"It's no use," a new voice says from farther down. A girl's arm appears from between the bars of the next cell. It's gut-wrenchingly thin, with blue veins rising to the surface like earthworms in the rain. "She won't tell you anything useful. But I will."

I race to where the second, older girl stands and stumble upon seeing her. She's in even worse condition than Ellie.

"My name is Viviane Roth, and I was caught by Eric and his pigs thirteen hours after I ran away." She raises her head as if she's proud of what she's about to say next. "I've been here for one year and forty-seven days."

Disbelief and horror crackle through my body, and I find it takes everything I have to keep my legs beneath me. "Tell me what I can do to help you."

She laughs and digs a finger into her ear. "You can't. And if you're one of Madam Karina's girls, you better get out of here."

"How did they catch you?" Cain asks, startling me.

"We're not sure. But one way or another, they always do."

"Paula made it the longest, I think. Three days before they found her."

"Four," a quiet voice says at the end of the aisle.

"Okay, whatever, four." Viviane continues talking, but my ears ring so loudly that I can't absorb what she's saying. Because now I'm moving down the cells, one by one, and trying not to lose control of my breathing. In each cramped space is a female, some young, some old. Their faces are shadowed and accusatory. Some are like the first girl, their bodies turned away, and all of them look broken, their spirits long buried. That doesn't stop a handful from announcing the time they've spent imprisoned.

"Fifteen months," one says.

"Two years and two months," says another.

"Four years, four months, and thirteen days," declares the winner.

My heart hammers against my rib cage, and my fingers fly to my temples. Wilson tries to speak, but I push him down with everything I have. I can't think beyond what I've just learned. I can't think beyond three simple truths.

I am Domino Ray.

I am afraid of nothing more than being alone with my mind.

If I try and escape Madam Karina's clutches, that is exactly what will happen to me.

CHAPTER 48

SNAP

I race up and down the aisle, frantic, searching for anything that will open their cells.

"Domino, we have to go," Cain says.

I stop and look at him like he's crazy. "Are you kidding? We can't leave them here."

"You can if you want to live outside these walls," Viviane says, but then her face falls like a thought has occurred to her. "Though...though maybe you can call someone. Tell the governor or something?"

A girl at the end laughs. "The governor? Oh, yeah, he'll totally believe this chick."

"The FBI then," Viviane says, her voice growing more urgent. "There has to be someone."

"No one cares about Pox," the girl jeers. "Lie down and go back to sleep."

But now Viviane is shaking the bars. Her body is coiled tight and her once-tired eyes are alert. "There has to be something we can do!"

I rush to her cage and clasp her hand through the bars. "I'll do something. I'll get you out of here."

"Domino," Cain says. The way he speaks my name causes me to turn. He's standing next to the stairs and motioning for me to stay silent. My scalp tingles as I weigh how long we've been down here.

"I thought I heard something," he whispers. "We have to leave."

"What about them?" My voice quivers.

"I thought we could get one girl out." He glances at Ellie. "But we need a plan to help them all."

He's right, I know he is. If they caught these girls within days of them escaping Pox, then how quickly would they find us if we ran together? I glance once more at the cells and say, "I will come back for you."

Cain rushes up the stairs, and I follow him, closing the trap door silently. After ensuring the officer is still gone, he pushes open the door. We hurry past the desk, my chest tightening so that my vision blurs. I can feel the caged girls behind me, can feel their eyes watching my abandonment. If I were smarter, I could figure out a way to save them now. If I were braver, I'd try something. The only thing that allows me to keep going is what I told them. I will get them out of there if it's the last thing I do in this miserable life.

The woman with the bubblegum nails is nowhere in sight when we fly by. We've made it into the parking lot before Cain looks back at me. "Want me to drive?"

My hands shake as I offer up the keys.

They're almost in his grasp when the door behind us bursts open. Cain spins me behind him so that he's blocking me. The police officer barrels toward Cain, his hand withdrawing a Glock and taking aim. Before I can think, I lunge out from behind Cain and throw myself in front of him. We look like idiots, the two of us clamoring to take a bullet first.

Mine!

No, mine!

I'm not sure what causes me to look back at Cain's face.

Maybe it's the growl I hear in his throat. Or the eerie stillness that's fallen over our circle of three. But when I do, I see something in him that makes my blood run cold. Rage twists his features until he's unrecognizable. Gone are the wrinkles around his eyes that show themselves when he shyly smiles. Gone are the shadows that darken his features as he hangs his head. Now his chin is held high. And his eyes storm with unbridled anger.

"Pull the trigger," Cain says.

His voice causes a shiver to engulf my body. In this moment, he's not the boy I've grown to care for. He is not gentle or sympathetic. He is not fearful. Cain takes a step toward the police officer, and the cop yells for him to get back.

Cain tells him again, his words as unwavering as a stretch of pavement, to pull that trigger.

The officer's arm begins to tremble, and when his eyes flick to me with indecision, Cain lunges. He slams into the cop in a heartbeat, his arms wrapped around his waist in a bear hug. He takes the man to the ground and pins his body there. The officer has only a moment to grunt his surprise when Cain springs on top of him and jerks his fist back.

He hits him twice, quick like pop rocks hitting the sidewalk. *Crack, crack!* The officer fumbles for his gun. Grabs it.

I charge toward the two, screaming. I yank on the cop's arm to keep him from taking aim at Cain, but the officer yanks his elbow back and slams it into my nose.

There's a sickening *crunch* as pain explodes inside my face and along my neck. I fall back, clutching my nose, blood seeping through my fingers. Cain pauses a beat, his eyes widening at the sight of me. And then all the rage I saw in him shatters and falls to the ground, broken. In its place is a mask of calm that rattles me to the core.

Cain's gaze returns to the officer, to the gun in his hand.

With my vision blurring, I think to myself how Cain looks like a doll in this moment: vacant eyes, unfeeling skin, cold, lifeless expression. It's like he's kissed his mind good-bye, and so anything that happens from this second on cannot be blamed on him alone.

Cain wrestles the gun from the officer and flips it over in his hand. He slams the Glock against the officer's head once, twice, three times. He's like a machine, a robot working on commands.

"Cain, stop!" I holler.

The officer tries to shield himself, but it does little to help. Cain tosses the gun and rears back for another blow. His closed fist drives into the officer's ribs, his chest, his gut.

"You locked those girls up," Cain roars, though his face doesn't mirror the frustration. "You held them there like dogs!"

Cain hits him again, and I scramble forward, pleading for him to stop.

Please stop. Please stop. Please stop.

Cain works his left fist now, pummeling the officer on his uninjured side. I reach Cain at the same moment that he says to the officer, "You deserve to die."

The stone giant locks his hands around the man's throat, and I scream Cain's name. When he doesn't respond to the sound of my voice, I form a fist with my own hand, cock my arm back, and drive it across Cain's icy face.

His head snaps back from the impact, and he whips around to see where the blow came from. For a moment, I'm afraid he'll attack me next. I can see in his eyes that no one is home. He's gone. Checked out. Au revoir.

But slowly, Cain returns to me. The muscles in his face relax, and his hands drop to his sides. He glances down at the barely conscious officer, and then back at me.

"We have to go," I tell him, pulling on his arm. "Someone's going to come."

A weakness strikes my knees as I guide Cain to his feet. He stares down at the officer like he doesn't understand how he got there. And then, as a second thought, he points at the man and says, "You heard a sound outside and came to check it out. Someone in a mask beat you up and took your wallet. That's your story, understand? Because if Madam Karina finds out you aired her dirty laundry, you'll be hurting a lot worse than this." Cain nudges the man's shoe with his. "Say you understand."

The man clutches his side and groans that, yes, he understands.

Cain rips the man's wallet from his pocket and shoves it into his own. Then he picks up the car keys off the ground and places them in my hand. My skin prickles at his touch, and the back of my neck burns. Blood has stopped flowing from my nose, but pain and shock still course through my body.

I open the car and get in the driver's seat, and Cain drops down on the opposite side. It's a long time before either of us speaks, the car moving silently through the night. I glance over at Cain and find him staring at the thin layer of dried blood on his knuckles. He seems surprised and horrified by its presence.

I want to comfort him, but at the same time, what I saw back there is enough to keep me quiet. It's enough to keep Wilson quiet, too.

"My father taught me to turn things off," Cain whispers. "It's like a light goes off in my head, and all I can feel is anger. And then I feel nothing at all."

I try to form a response, but Cain speaks before I can.

"I would never hurt you, Domino." His voice catches, like the thing he's most terrified of is someone being afraid of him.

I lick my lips. "Is that what you think? That I'm scared of you?"

"You should be."

Though it takes me time to recover from the whiplash of his transformation, eventually, I regain my bearings. After all, I've seen the dark sides of enough people to know everyone has one.

"How are you so sure?" I finally ask. "How are you sure you wouldn't hurt me? Because back there… Cain, you really lost it."

"Because I chose to," he says. "I pulled the switch. When I took those burns for my brother… The only way I could do it was to turn everything off. Survive." His voice grows small. "I still hurt my brother in the end, though."

"You didn't kill your brother on purpose," I say. "And you *pulled your switch* back there because that man had a gun, and he's doing a very bad thing by keeping those girls locked up."

Cain wipes his hands over his knees. Gently at first, then rougher and faster like the officer's blood is a venomous thing, like it'll rot the skin from his bones.

My scalp tingles when I realize what I'm about to do, what I'm about to admit. But if I don't do it now, here, I will never do it. I'll carry around my secret like a cancer, let it eat me whole, one mutated cell at a time. "Cain, I'm going to tell you about my dad. And how him leaving changed my mother, and then me, into something terrible."

CHAPTER 49

I WON'T ABANDON YOU

As we drive—the sky purple, the stars quiet as they eavesdrop—I tell Cain everything. Wilson wails inside my mind the entire time, making it difficult for me to recount the story. This isn't something he wants me to share.

I can hold this for you, Wilson complains, wounded by my admission. *You don't need anyone but me.*

Though he is insistent, I speak past his complaints. I tell Cain how my mother brought unsuspecting men home, how I learned the best way to make a person writhe in agony, the best way to cover their screams so the neighbors didn't hear. The graphic details...I can't recall. Wilson keeps them hidden in the recesses of my brain. He swirls the key around his index finger like he's taunting me, but the look on his face speaks the truth.

He doesn't want me to remember the worst bits.

He doesn't believe I can handle them.

Cain doesn't interrupt me once during my midnight confession. He only stares ahead, his hands still on his knees.

When I'm finished, I ask him for one single favor. "Please don't tell anyone. I know you won't want to be around me anymore, but don't tell, okay?"

Cain pulls in a deep breath and lets it out. He runs a

hand over his shaved head, and his face scrunches. "Is anyone looking for you? Or your mom?"

I shake my head. "Not that I know of. Mother was always careful."

"And you don't know what happened to them in the end? Those guys?"

"I know," I say, my voice hardly above a whisper. "I just can't remember."

"You were twelve years old," Cain states.

"I was sixteen before I left."

"Holy shit, Domino." He shakes his head back and forth. "Holy shit."

"Now you know why I can't possibly think of you as a monster." I've held back as long as I can, but now tears thicken my voice. "Because I see one in the mirror every day when I wake up."

Cain looks at me as I drive, as tears slip down my cheeks. I peek at him from the corner of my eye and see that the color has leached from his face. His jaw hangs open, and he stares at me as if I'm someone he's meeting for the first time. His gaze travels to my hands, no doubt envisioning the things they've done. The tools of suffering they've held. He runs his own hands over his head and mutters "Holy shit" over and over until the words lose their meaning.

And then something happens. He falls back in the seat and stares up at the roof of the car, pulls in long breaths through flared nostrils. The nervous energy leaves him, and in its place settles a calm sort of resolve.

"Listen to me." Cain's voice is heavy and sure. "What happened to you was messed up in the most horrific way possible. When we leave here, you'll need to talk to someone. I probably will, too. But this was not your fault. It was your mother, for crying out loud. Your *mother*. She manipulated you. She didn't give you a choice."

"No," I argue. "I had a choice. And I did the wrong thing. It's unforgivable."

"To who? To who is it unforgivable?"

I gasp for air, trying to stop the emotion from welling up again.

Wilson, I need you, I think.

I'm here, he responds at once. *I've got you.*

Wilson tows my memories back toward him like a sailor hauling a rusted anchor from the sea. Relief washes over me, making my body feel light and warm.

"I'm not going to abandon you," Cain says softly. "So you can get that thought out of your head right now."

I briefly clench my eyes against what he's saying. It's almost too much to hope for.

He reaches over and grabs my elbow, squeezes it awkwardly. A soothing current engulfs my entire body at his touch. "I mean it. You and I, we've started something, even if it's only in each other. I feel different when you're around. I feel like maybe I could move past the things I've done and focus on the things I could do." He hesitates. "Do you feel the same way?"

I don't know how to respond. Cain does make me feel different. If I can tell him that I partook in *torturing men* and he can stick by me, that's got to be something. Then again, maybe that's the definition of being screwed up. That we're so damaged that regardless of what the other person says they've done, we just shrug and say, *Hey, as long as you don't leave me, we're square.*

Instead of answering him, I say, "What are we going to do about those girls, Cain?"

He studies the side of my face, and my knuckles whiten from gripping the wheel. "We need cash to get out of here.

If those girls were caught quickly, it's probably because they stopped too soon. We need gas money to get us far enough away, and extra in case something happens to the car along the way. No chances."

Cain grabs the wallet he took from the officer and looks inside. He frowns and shoves it in his pocket. "Empty."

I sigh. "The only way I can get access to the money I've earned is by applying to leave."

"And you can't do that." Cain rubs his jawline. "Maybe we could ask Angie for help."

"No way. We can't drag her into this." I focus on the road ahead. Madam Karina's home rises on the horizon like a corpse pulling itself from the earth. Chills race down the back of my neck as we move closer to the place I fear most. But this is one thing Cain and I are in agreement on. We must return to Madam Karina's Home for Burgeoning Entertainers. Until we have a proper plan to escape and decide how to free the girls from their cells, we have to play our submissive roles.

"Do you have any ideas?" Cain asks.

I do, but I don't want to say it aloud. I don't want to think about what Jack will ask me to do for a pocket full of cash versus a bronze coin.

"I'll get us the money we need," I say.

Cain glances at me in the safety of the dark, his brow furrowing when he understands what I mean.

"Domino, I don't want—"

"You really aren't going to leave me?" I ask, my voice so small it could be swallowed by a crow.

Cain resumes rubbing the officer's blood off his palms. "I'm here as long as you want me to be. For better or worse."

Me, too, Wilson adds quietly.

I pull in a deep breath. "I'll get us the money. You just

convince Madam Karina that nothing has changed."

Cain tells me to park the car in the exact spot we found it, and after I kill the engine, we both stare up at the house, dreading going inside. I'm about to speak, to reassure him we'll be okay, when another vehicle pulls up alongside ours.

It's a red Honda Civic, and there's a woman in the driver's seat. When I squint, I make out who's in the passenger seat. "Duck!"

Cain follows my lead and lies down flat against the leather seat. Our bodies cross each other, my face pressed against his taut stomach. Slowly, Cain wraps his arm around my waist. Almost immediately, my pulse slows. I hear the sound of a car door opening and closing, and then quick steps leading away. The car backs over the gravel drive and out the gate.

Cain and I wait five minutes before lifting our heads and checking to ensure Mr. Hodge went inside. Even after I see that we're in the clear, fear still racks my body, sending tremors through my limbs.

"What does he think he's doing?" Cain says. "It's one thing to do it on the sly. But to have that woman drop him off in front of the house? Madam Karina will kill him."

Would that be a bad thing? Wilson asks.

Hush.

No, really. You should ask him. I'd like to know his response.

I roll my eyes at Wilson, and remember that though I've told Cain the secrets I carried about my mother and the things we did together, there's still one I've kept to myself.

Don't you dare, Wilson warns, hurt flooding his voice. *Don't you tell him about me. Please.*

"Hey. Are you okay?" Cain asks.

I gaze up at the house. "We've got to be quiet when we

go inside. No one can know we were gone."

"Domino, about what you said. About getting the money?"

"Don't worry about it," I tell him. "I can take care of myself."

I open the car door and float toward the house like a ghost. Like I left the real me back in that Pox county jail.

CHAPTER 50

LULLABY LIE

The next morning, the rankings scroll across the Tulips' digital placement board. I'm awarded top rank for the week, but Poppet falls into third place. I guess the customers were as tired of the stuffy atmosphere as I was. They wanted some excitement, Poppet tells me, and I gave it to them.

She pretends to be happy for me, but I can tell she's afraid of being separated. I reassure her that it won't be an issue for much longer, and when she asks what I mean, I cave and tell her what Cain and I discovered the night before.

Poppet and I are standing on the front porch when I share the news. The sun shines merrily, ignorant as I speak in a hushed tone. Poppet rocks on the porch swing, the chains squeaking in time with her movements.

When I'm done explaining, she says, "So when do we leave?"

I can't stop the smile that parts my mouth. "You mean you'll come?"

"Well, yeah. I'm sure as hell not staying here. Did you think I would after you told me this?"

"I wasn't certain," I admit. "I wondered if you'd believe me."

Poppet moves her jaw side to side as she thinks. "I would never have believed it before I saw the madam the way she was the other night. She shoved you, Domino. And she was acting crazy." Her voice grows small. "And I see the bruises. Are you okay?"

I rub my hands together. "I'm fine. But I think things will get worse. Mr. Hodge is seeing another woman, and when Madam Karina finally catches him in the act, she's going to tighten her hold on her remaining assets."

"So what do we do?"

I can't help but love Poppet when she asks this. She's so ready to believe me, so ready to follow where I lead. "We need some cash before we run. I don't think we're in *immediate* danger, and though those girls looked pretty bad, I believe they can hang on a little longer."

"How will we get the money?" Poppet asks.

My gaze travels to the Lilies' guesthouse. I can just see it from where we stand.

Poppet must follow my line of thinking, because she says, "I can't go with you. I don't think Madam Karina ever cared about my advancing. It was always only you."

As strange as it is, I'm struck by the urge to correct Poppet. To assure her that Madam Karina cares about her as much as she does me. But we both know I'd be lying. The madam selects her favorites on impulse, without much reasoning other than a gut reaction. And why should we care who she favors, anyway?

"Will you try to convince the customers to pay you in cash?" Poppet asks.

"Just one."

She scratches her cheek. "I've heard of girls doing it before. Just mumblings."

Poppet seems like she's about to add something else when the screen door swings open. My stomach clenches, and Poppet's mouth snaps shut.

Madam Karina steps into view.

The woman's face lights up when she sees Poppet. "Oh, sweetie, I thought Domino was alone out here. I saw you finished third in this week's rankings."

Poppet sucks on her bottom lip, instinctually ashamed. "I can do better."

Madam Karina rushes toward her, bends down so that their faces are even. "What are you talking about? You did wonderfully! How many girls can say they climbed to the top of their class in one week?" Madam Karina lays a hand on Poppet's knee. "The clients tell me you are the most captivating girl in the house. You have an energy about you, did you know that?"

Poppet smiles, and it makes me want to kick the madam in the spine. She can manipulate me all she wants, but not her. Not Poppet.

"As a matter of fact, if you go downstairs to market, you might find you have a bit more credit than you thought."

Poppet glances at me, and then back at Madam Karina. "You mean it?"

Madam Karina bolts upright, and her voice booms with cheerfulness. "Go on then. Go and pick yourself out something special. You deserve it."

Poppet throws a cautious look my way. With the madam's back still turned, I nod over my shoulder, telling Poppet she should go. I don't miss the excitement in her eyes as she bounds toward the house. We may be leaving soon, but old habits die hard, and it's difficult for girls like Poppet and me, who have known real poverty, to turn down an opportunity for something new.

"What do you want?" I ask the madam. No use in pretending I'm not upset. If I soften too easily, she'll know I'm planning something.

"I should apologize for last night," the madam says. "But I know that won't be enough."

I pass by her and take Poppet's seat on the swing. Play the part of a fuming child who wants nothing more than for her mother to grovel.

"As you may have guessed, Mr. Hodge and I are working through some things right now. But that doesn't change the way I feel about you or any of my girls. I just get low sometimes, and when I do, I drink too much."

"You were drunk last night?" I ask, as if I don't know this. As if this warrants her abuse.

Madam Karina wraps her arms around her slim frame. "Might be time to admit I'm struggling with it. It's not okay to medicate ourselves just because we're feeling down. That's why the doctor's going to call on me this afternoon. I might have him see to you as well."

I don't understand what she means, until her gaze travels over my face. My nose got busted so thoroughly during the fight with the cop last night that I woke to find two blue-black rings beneath my eyes.

"You went out with Cain last night," Madam Karina says. It isn't a question. The porch seems to drop out from under my feet, and I grab onto the bench's chain, thankful for the support. "I have little spies everywhere."

She knows where we went. She knows what we found.

I'll never leave this town.

I wear a mask of indifference while fighting a wave of dizziness. The madam nods toward the empty end of the bench, asking if she can take it. I look away, communicating that I don't care what she does. When her weight settles in next to me, the entire half of my body that she touches goes numb.

"I know the temptations boys present, but you must trust me when I tell you they bring nothing but trouble."

I turn and face her, confusion tightening my features.

She raises a hand and strokes the delicate skin beneath my eyes. "But I suppose you learned that the hard way."

Understanding dawns on me. She thinks Cain and I snuck off to be together last night, and that he inflicted the damage to my face. Relief floods my body, and I find the courage to breathe again. Knowing I need to respond, I say, "I feel like I can't trust anyone."

Not entirely a lie.

"Oh, Domino." Madam Karina slides her arm around my shoulders. "Don't say such things. You can trust me."

I touch a hand to my throat. To the place she sent me a message. That's what it was. She was showing her dominance— like an alpha wolf pinning a pack mate to maintain the hierarchy.

She withdraws her arm and folds her hands in her lap. "I've already apologized for what I did to you. And I told you the doctor is calling on me. I'm sick, sweetheart. Can you understand that?"

Ellie's face springs into my mind. Her bruised face, her busted lip. A figure that must have once been voluptuous and healthy, now shrunken from inadequate meals. She clung to those bars and begged for this woman's forgiveness. Said she'd work for Madam Karina for however long she wanted, if she'd only let her out.

The woman who's soothing me with her false words is the same woman who'd throw me away like a used tissue if I upset her enough.

"I understand," I whisper, fury swirling inside my chest. "But how can you be sure the doctor will make you better?"

Madam Karina reads my question as true concern and replaces her arm around me. "Don't you worry about that. Not for one second. I will get better. I'm not going anywhere, and neither are you." She opens her free hand on my thigh, and I stare down at it. Bile rises in my throat as I place my own hand in hers. She squeezes and lays her head on top of mine. We rock in silence as crickets violin their legs and the bench creaks back and forth. My muscles are clenched and my mouth painfully dry when she says in a lullaby voice, "You're Mama's sweet girl, aren't you?"

I clamp my eyes shut and try not to scream. Wilson folds himself around my mind in a protective barrier, growling.

"Yes," I say. "I am."

CHAPTER 57

PINK ELEPHANT

Moments after Madam Karina leaves me alone on the porch, Angie steps outside. She doesn't look in my direction, but she doesn't head toward her tractor, Black Betty, either. She just shoves her hands into her pockets and scrunches her face like she's solving a riddle.

"I'm okay," I tell her.

"That's not why I'm out here."

"Yes, it is," I say. "It wouldn't hurt you to be more direct about your feelings."

Angie huffs. "Feelings. What good they do anyone I'll never know."

I roll my eyes and attempt a smile though I'm rattled to the bone. Angie's Dobermans jump around near her tractor, nipping each other on the back and rolling in the dirt like newborn pups. My eyes are still on them when she takes two quick steps toward me and withdraws a peppermint from her pocket. She won't even look at me when she hands it over.

I take it from her. Roll it between my palms. "I found the girls, you know."

Angie shoots a glance toward the house.

"They're in jail cells in the basement of the municipal building," I whisper.

Angie curses under her breath. "I figured that's where they were, but I wasn't certain."

"Why didn't you do something if you knew, Angie?" I can't help the accusation in my voice.

"Because I would have ended up like them if I had, and none of us would be better for it." Angie turns her face away, ashamed. I can feel the fear and regret rolling off her, though it does little to lessen my disappointment. I can't imagine not trying to help.

I have to help.

Angie looks once more at the house and lowers her head toward mine. "If you have a chance to leave this place unnoticed, you do it. You do it, and you don't ever look back, not for nothing and no one." Angie surprises me then. Grabs my arm and pulls me up from the bench and into an awkward hug. I feel her hand lowering, but before I can register what it is she's doing, Madam Karina bursts through the door.

"Get off my girl, Angie," she booms.

Angie leaps away as if electrocuted and sidesteps Madam Karina. She jogs down the steps, and her dogs lunge toward her at once.

Madam Karina flicks her fingers "That's right. You play with your pets, and I'll play with mine."

I shoot Madam Karina a disgusted look, but she doesn't notice. Angie's dog Kali sniffs at her pockets, desperately trying to nab a peppermint. Angie shoves her away and climbs onto her tractor.

"Have you loaded everything?" Madam Karina yells.

Angie waves. "Enough for now. Be back next Sunday." She keeps her head down as she rumbles up the road, no more than three boxes on the back, her dogs yapping at the oversized tires.

Madam Karina offers me a warm smile before heading

back inside.

When are we leaving? Wilson asks in a snarl.

Soon.

I go inside and spot Cain coming up the stairs. Understanding passes between us, though I have trouble thinking past the way his red plaid shirt clings to his shoulders and biceps. The way it pulls tight across his chest. Strong, calloused hands emerge from the cuffs of his shirt, and for whatever reason, I'm gripped by an urge to feel those same hands on my hips.

I'm not sure why I'm suddenly struck by desire. Maybe it's because I told him my secret, and he didn't run. Or maybe it's because he told me his. I'm comfortable with him now, and with that comfort comes a sensation I've never allowed myself to feel. Cain is unpredictable, and unstable, and if I ever admitted it to myself, I'd realize he is exactly what my hearts yearns for.

"You going to buy something today?" Madam Karina asks.

My head whips around, and I find her sitting on the sofa. The same sofa where three Carnations sat the first time I entered this house. They were happy, playful.

Went to the market,
To buy me a gown.
All the boys whistle,
And one fell down.
Sway my hips,
Lips stung by a bee.
Keep on walking,
'Till he take a knee.

"I'm saving up for something special," I tell the madam. The corners of her mouth turn down in disappointment, so I add, "The day I become Top Girl, I want to dress the part."

Madam Karina grins. "Good things come to those who wait."

"That's right." I return her smile, and then think to say, "May I have one more night as a Daisy? I'd like to say good-bye to Poppet."

"So you will be leaving her behind? I figured you might fight me on this."

"It's time she made her own way," I reply, not meaning a word I'm saying. "The ends justify the means, yes?"

She tilts her head. "Who said that?"

"Someone you'd admire." I bow my head. "May I stay with Poppet?"

She sighs. "You may, but tomorrow I need you in that guesthouse. Besides, I'd think you'd be eager to earn your lily as soon as possible."

"I'll earn that lily and more," I respond.

That night, after I've washed my face and checked beneath the beds, I climb under my sheets and look across the room at Poppet. She's holding a pink stuffed elephant against her chest as if she's afraid of the dark.

"Did you get that today?" I whisper.

She squeezes the stuffed animal against her chest. "I told Madam Karina once that I saw a pink stuffed elephant in a grocery store. Told her I begged for it for my birthday, but my mother said we didn't have the money for such useless things. I don't know why I remember that toy among all the others I wasn't allowed to have." Poppet holds out the elephant and inspects it. "It's crazy how Madam Karina can be the same person who remembers these things about you and the same person who can lock girls away."

"She didn't give you the elephant, Poppet," I say in the

gentlest voice I can muster. "She had Angie find this for you, and then she stuck it up on those shelves behind the cage wall. She knew exactly what would make you spend your money, and she knows that every dollar you spend lessens the chance that you'll leave. There's a reason they hold our money for us. And it isn't so we can earn more."

Poppet scoots down in bed until I can hardly see her frame. "I know."

Guilt twists inside my chest. As much as I want Poppet to accept the truth about Madam Karina, I also don't want to hurt her. I imagine it wouldn't be easy for any of the girls living here to learn how twisted the madam really is. We all want to trust again, and Madam Karina's Home for Burgeoning Entertainers provides a perfect mirage.

"I need you to be ready at a moment's notice," I tell Poppet. "But don't make it too obvious, either."

Poppet doesn't respond.

"Poppet, you're not having second thoughts are you?"

She shakes her head. "No, I know we have to get away from this place. But it doesn't make it any less scary to start over again. And I haven't even thought about what'll happen if we're caught."

"I won't let anything bad happen to you," I say quickly.

And I won't let anything bad happen to you, Wilson whispers.

I stand and cross the distance between us, pause at the side of Poppet's bed. She realizes at once what it is I intend to do and lifts her covers. I slide in next to her and wrap her in my arms. Pretend she is my daughter and I am her mother and I'll die before I let harm befall my child.

"All we need is a little money and a plan to rescue those girls," I say.

"And what about us?" Poppet whispers, her back warm

against my stomach. "How will we escape Pox?"

I bite my lip, trying to form a quick response so she's reassured. But I can't. Thankfully, Poppet's breathing deepens, and I'm afforded complete silence in which to think.

She's right. The biggest obstacle isn't how to rescue the incarcerated girls, because we can convince authorities in another town to come for them, and for the girls still in this house, too. Surely they'll be interested in what goes on in this place, and that several of the madam's girls are underage. It'll take longer than I'd like to save those girls in the jail cells, but we can do it. I'll make the police listen. And I feel sure I can collect the money I need for gas and any necessities we'll need to run fast and far.

But how will we escape Pox and remain untraceable?

I think of Madam Karina's borrowed vehicles that sit shiny and promising in the front drive. I'd bet my right arm that most of the girls before me attempted that route. Cars can be reported stolen, and if they're rentals, surely the owner has a way to track their whereabouts.

Some girls may have fled on foot. But how far could you get before being found? I think of those two women in the ice cream shop. How wary they seemed of Madam Karina. It'd be difficult to escape Pox on foot with all those loyal eyes keeping watch.

So how will we do it?

How will we be the three people who manage to escape, to get help, and to stay out of Madam Karina's clutches?

It isn't until late in the night, as the promise of sleep stalks forward, that the solution comes to me.

CHAPTER 52

THE FEAR BENEATH HIS HEEL

Night falls before I find the courage to leave the main house. I'm eager to escape Madam Karina's clutches, but that doesn't mean I'm ready to make the sacrifices it'll take. Poppet is quiet as I fasten the same bra I've worn and washed over the last several weeks. The same one that came with me from Detroit.

Poppet walks over to me silently with something clutched in her hand. As I watch her in the vanity mirror, she unfolds the blouse—black with a plunging neckline. I stand silently, and she slips it over my head. Together, we inspect my slight figure. I have a small chest, and hips that would insult a real woman, but this sinful number still screams seductive.

My scalp tingles with anxiety as Poppet hands me her makeup bag. I withdraw what I need and lay it out on the counter, draw in a breath before I begin working. It takes me a full half hour to complete my masterpiece. When I'm done, I cross the room to the middle dresser drawer. An old, familiar chemical-laden scent touches my nose, and when I close my hand over my treasure, a shiver works its way down my torso.

Hello, old friend.

I withdraw the hot pink wig and clutch it to my stomach.

It's the last one I bought from Greg's shop, and the memories of being there in that store, with the fragile safety it brought me, are almost too much to bear.

I wonder how Greg is now. His shop is gone. But he's sharing a place with his boyfriend. Maybe he traded one dream for another. Sometimes, I let myself believe there's room in his life for me. But if there's one thing I've learned from living in this warped house, it's that I must depend on myself first and foremost. It's okay to let others help. But it's time for me to stand on my own two feet, however unstable that may feel.

With careful fingers, I slide the wig onto my head. When I flip back the tresses, Poppet's gaze lands on me with a weight I want. She needs me. Not the other way around, though I do want her in my life. But this time, I am the one who must do for another. I am not a girl awaiting Dizzy's arrival home.

Tonight I am someone else's hope.

It feels good.

"I won't let you down," I tell Poppet. "Give me three days, and we'll be out of here. Maybe sooner."

"Cain, too, right?" she says, wringing her hands.

"Cain, too."

"I could do this, you know," Poppet says in a rush. "I could earn the money the same way you're thinking."

"No," I snap. Then, realizing how harshly that came out, I let my face fall. "No, it needs to be me. I have a customer I can ask."

"Jack," Poppet says.

I nod. "And I'll be in the guesthouses where more money is spent. And more…activities are allowed. The Tulips would never let you get away with doing anything more than first base stuff." I gaze out the window to where the west guesthouse lays waiting. Only a shack, really.

Poppet throws herself into my arms. "Are you sure?"

"I'm sure." I pull back so she can see my face. "Don't take any crap from the Tulips, understand? If it gets too bad, you find me. Promise."

She hugs me again. "I promise."

I let go of her before I lose the nerve, and stride out of the room and toward the staircase. I leave my other wigs behind. I only need the one now. My freshest, hottest baby. Something to remind me I am Domino Ray, and I can handle anything.

What is it you're planning to do, Domino? Wilson asks as I descend the stairs.

I almost laugh. *Look who's avoiding the truth now.*

Wilson pretends to be hurt, presses himself into the corner of my mind and pouts. I push open the back kitchen door and glide through it, spotting the black demon car and Eric's gold sedan in the drive. I pray the officer Cain beat up hasn't ratted us out, but if he has, there's nothing I can do about it now.

Behind me, I can hear the sounds of house girls readying themselves for a night of customers and bronze coins.

I am not one of them anymore.

I am this.

I tear the tulip from my chest and throw it to the ground. The sky presses down on me as I walk, and I press back. Tilting up my chin, I set my gaze on the west house, on the shutters and miniature porch. The house can't consist of more than three bedrooms and one bathroom. I doubt there's a full kitchen, or a dining room, or any more privacy than what's afforded in the main house.

But as a Lily, I'd be awarded safety from Mr. Hodge's constant pressure to earn more, perform better, make the customers happier. And Madam Karina wouldn't be able to keep quite as close an eye on me, either. And there's more money to earn, and a place that must feel secure.

And, of course, status.

I have practically talked myself into thinking this won't be so bad. Until I leave, the days will be improved. And the nights…the nights I will turn to Wilson for comfort as I earn a fistful of cash that Poppet, Cain, and I need to start again. It's true I've never slept with anyone. And when this is all over, I won't count this as my first time. If I ever have a true first time, it will be with someone I feel safe with. Someone I trust. He will go slow and tell me he loves me and I will love him back.

I will love him back.

"Domino."

His voice is as sharp as it is deep. He moves toward me with caution, as if I'm an animal he's afraid will flee.

Cain opens his hands. "Don't do this."

Three words, and already my confidence falters.

"We can leave without the money," he says.

"We won't get far enough."

"I'll steal it."

"It'd be harder than you think."

Cain shakes his head. "There's another way. You know there is."

"Nothing will get us out of here faster than this," I say.

Cain's words come slower, softer. "Don't go in there. Don't become one of her girls."

I touch a hand to my wig. "I am not hers."

"If you go in there, you will be. Regardless of what else happens, of whether we escape her, she will always know she made you do this."

"And I will know I did whatever it took to save my friends."

Cain takes two powerful strides toward me. "I am not your friend, Domino."

When I see the hungry, desperate look in his eyes, my knees grow weak. Not this. Anything but this. I have to be strong right now, but I can't be if he keeps looking at me that way. When his hand rises to my cheek, my breath comes out in a shudder.

"I want to be the one who saves you," he says, his face so close to mine.

I close my eyes against the feel of his fingers brushing over my face, my neck, my collarbone. "Once we leave here, you can save me. But let me do this one thing first."

"I can't stand by and let this happen."

When I open my eyes, my gaze falls on his mouth. On full, pink lips. His hands wrap around my face and my every fear, my every nightmare, crumbles beneath his heel. There is only Cain now. Only this mountain of a boy who refuses to budge. A boy who is more like a man than any I've met.

"I'm falling for you," he whispers. "If something happens to you, it'll destroy me."

His lips crash into mine.

My body reacts instantly. My arms twine around his neck, and he tugs me against him. And there, in the space between the main house and the smaller one where I'll earn our escape, Cain kisses me. I kiss him back, too. Because that question he asked me in the car. About whether I saw the two of us being different—and better—together, has haunted me. I know the answer.

Yes.

From the moment I saw his two-layered eyes outside that alley. From the moment I recognized his pain as a worthy contender against my own, I wanted him. He knows my darkest secret, and yet he holds me in his arms, his lips moving against mine tenderly.

His fingers clutch my back, rising until they reach beneath

my pink wig and slide into my own hair. Chills rush over my skin, wave after wave, as the stars plummet to the earth. I feel small in his arms, breakable. It's a welcomed difference to the explosiveness I've felt with others. As if I were a moment away from taking their lives.

Cain moves his lips from mine and trails a line of warm, delicious kisses down my throat. Then he lifts his mouth to my ear and says, "Stay with me."

But now, more than ever, after I've admitted to myself how I feel about this boy, I know I must go.

"Give me three days," I say, my head against his chest. "And then I will stay with you. As long as you want me."

"Forever," he answers suddenly. "It's too soon to say that, I know. But right now, I can't imagine a time when I won't want you."

I push away from him, knowing if I don't go now, I won't be able to. "When you put it that way, then three days is nothing." I force a smile and lay a hand on his chest, grip his shirt in my hand. Then I let go and turn toward the Lilies' house.

He says my name three more times as I walk away, each more urgent than the last. But I don't look back.

Do you prefer him over me? Wilson asks quietly.

Don't start, Wilson. Don't ruin this moment for me.

Wilson licks his lips, thinking. *I like him, you know. I just don't want to be replaced. He can't carry your pain the way I can.*

Maybe he could.

Wilson flinches like I've wounded him deeply. He crawls away, cowering.

I don't hear from him again that night.

It bothers me more than I care to admit. For all my talk of being frightened of Wilson's presence and what it means, it scares me far worse to imagine him gone.

CHAPTER 53

WEST HOUSE

I knock on the Lilies' door several times before letting myself in. A girl with spiky black hair laughs when I step inside.

"I wondered when you'd decide to open that door," she says. "Did you think we had a butler or something?"

Another Lily rounds the corner and enters the cramped living room. "You're the new girl, right? Course you are. A few rules before Madam Karina comes to mark our hands. First, you don't have a room. You'll have to sleep out here. You can fight Bridget for the couch." She motions to the girl with black hair. "But most likely you'll end up on the floor. Second, if you need to use one of the bedrooms while a customer is here, tell me in advance."

"How far in advance?" I ask.

"As far as you can."

"I'm going to need a bedroom tonight," I say.

Both girls gawk at me. The one with the punk hair grins and says, "Gotta admire her confidence."

The girl who's laying out the rules crosses her arms. I take in her features—high forehead, cheeks that hint at rosacea, and an underbite that's almost endearing. Her wrists are thin and her ankles thick, and the lazy way she speaks tells me she's been a Lily for a while. And that most likely, she is Point Girl here.

"My name is Marie," she says. And then, as if these two facts go together, "Keep the customers happy however you'd like, but if you were a virgin when you walked in that door, you'll be one when you walk out."

"No pokey, pokey," Punk Girl adds, giggling.

Marie rolls her eyes and acts as if she's annoyed. As for me, I'm reeling from their forthrightness. I expected more behind-closed-doors shenanigans. Like, maybe if I wanted to do more than kiss Jack, I'd have to keep my mouth shut and keep up appearances.

Marie rears back and screams over her shoulder for the other girls to get their butts moving. Then she points at me. "Not sure why you're showing up late, but tomorrow you'll have double duty. We have to keep our place clean *and* the Violets', so don't plan on occupying that room too long."

With that, she turns and leaves the room. I'm stuck taking in my surroundings as Punk Girl studies me. The living area has a floral couch, wood paneling, worn carpet with vacuum lines, and a fireplace that looks as if it hasn't been used in years. Sporadic gold lamps, books, and stock paintings give the place a middle-class homey feel. The home is grossly outdated, but clean.

"You have a regular who you think will follow you here?" Punk Girl asks.

"Yeah," I answer, thankful for the conversation.

She clucks her tongue. "You'll have to start seeing the doctor."

I'm about to ask a question, but before I can voice it, the front door swings open. Madam Karina steps inside, and Punk Girl yells for Marie. Seconds later, Marie emerges with three other girls in tow. With me, we make six Lilies.

We line up and Madam Karina marks our hands with her black magic marker. When she gets to me, she smiles, excitement rolling off her. I flinch when she wraps me in a hug and says, "You're almost there, Domino. But this is where you will be tested. Are you ready?"

My throat clenches, but I manage a nod.

"Good," she says, before letting herself out.

Marie claps her hands twice, and the girls spring into action. The lights dim, and music plays softly, and the room holds its breath. Less than five minutes later, customers stream in. One by one, three girls take customers by the hand and disappear into the back. Marie chats with a girl her age who looks like she could buy the town of Pox. They're thigh to thigh on the couch, the girl's hand on Marie's inner thigh.

Try as I might to play it cool, I'm still surprised when they kiss, the gesture more emotional than physical. Marie must sense me watching, because she breaks the kiss and glares at me. "You have ten minutes before your room goes to someone else. And don't forget you'll owe Madam Karina a fee for using it."

Did she mention that? I don't remember. My eyes fall on the coin box attached to the wall and wonder what happens if I rent the room and my customer still awards his coin to someone else. It doesn't matter, I decide. That balance sheet is dead to me. Pleasure washes through me when I realize that, already, Madam Karina is losing her hold on me.

It's another fifteen minutes before Jack arrives, his face both hopeful and wary. He wears a brown corduroy blazer, though it's hot out, and beneath that, a white shirt. His face is clean-shaven and his blond hair slicked back. He looks older in this light, older than the early-to-mid-twenties I'd pegged him at.

I swallow my fear, my hesitation, my pride. Remember why I'm doing this.

Cain.

Poppet.

The girls in those cells.

And secretly, a place of my own. If he gives me enough, maybe it will cover first month's rent somewhere.

I don't owe *him* anything. But I will do this for me.

I adjust my hot pink wig and strut toward Jack. I've never felt like a real woman. Never fancied myself a seductress. But with this music playing, inside this house of sin, I allow myself to become someone else. A vixen who always gets what she wants.

And what I want, I tell myself, is Jack.

He sees me coming, and anger flitters across his face. After all, the last time I saw him my knee greeted his groin. But he's here, and I know it's me he's looking for. So I play this hand like a World Series poker champion, the winning card stiff in my palm.

"Jack," I breathe, curling myself around him.

He grabs me by the arms and pushes me back, not ready to forgive me. "I don't know what you think. But I didn't come for you."

"That's unfortunate," I pout. "Because I came for you."

He eyes me warily, shoves his hands in his pockets.

"Want to go in the back?"

His eyes travel to the narrow hall that leads away from the living area. "The guy at the front, Mr. Hodge, said a girl would have to reserve a room or something. You wouldn't have done that."

"But I did," I say, brushing my fingertips over his chest. Over the same place I touched Cain minutes earlier. "I had to think of a way to make you forgive me. Because even though I was nervous before, I can't stop thinking about the night you kissed me."

"And?" he says, taking the bait.

"And I want more."

He grins, but glances away, his gaze landing on the two interlocked girls on the couch. "Maybe I want to explore my options."

Marie takes that exact moment to glare at me. She's communicating, again, that I'm running out of time on my room and to give her privacy. Desperate, I snake my arm around Jack's and bring my lips to his neck. My stomach rolls when my mouth brushes the rough skin there. "Tell you what, I'm going to our room. If you follow me, I'll make it worth your while." And then, remembering how he pressed me for details of my life, I lose the act and try to reflect real sadness. "Jack, please. I just want to get to know you better without everyone watching."

I turn and go before my face betrays me. Not knowing my way around, I grope the walls along the hallway and find two closed doors. They must be the rooms already taken, I decide. Farther to the left is a small kitchen with a green linoleum floor and yellow cabinets. And across from that is what appears to be a laundry room. Only when I move closer, I see that there's a twin bed shoved inside. Nothing else occupies the space. No pictures, no lamps, no masquerading. There is only the bed.

Fighting the sickness rising in my throat, I move toward the bed. There's hardly enough space on the mattress for two people to lie side by side. But I guess that's not the point. The Point Girl, Marie, said if I came here a virgin, I'd leave here one. Well, I suppose I am a virgin. But I'm not so innocent, and I know there are plenty of other things a man and woman can do that skirt the line.

I'm still surveying the area when someone raps twice on the doorway. I spin around and find Jack blocking the light from the kitchen.

He moves toward me like a beast of prey, eyes locked on my body.

CHAPTER 54

COST OF SUPPLIES

Before I can speak, his hands are on me. He buries his face in my neck and mumbles that he hated the way we parted the night before. His body pushes against mine until I'm walking backward. Until the backs of my knees hit the mattress and I sit down.

My heart pounds inside my chest, and I struggle to catch my breath.

I was sure I could do this, but now my body won't cooperate. If I don't do something to lessen my anxiety, I'll die of a heart attack. Jack sits next to me and slides his arm around my waist. His other hand squeezes between my knees.

"There's still so little I know about you," I manage to say.

Jack nuzzles my neck. "We have all the time in the world to get to know each other."

"Is that what you want, Jack? Truly?"

He pauses and looks into my eyes. "Yes, it is. I may have come here to forget my troubles, but the moment I saw you was the moment everything changed for me." He strokes my face, and it feels like blisters form beneath his touch. "Such an innocent face. So vulnerable."

What did he just say? Wilson snaps. *Innocent? Vulnerable?*

This guy is living in his own head. You're just a prop for his twisted fantasies.

I don't push Wilson down like I usually do. I'm relieved he's back, because I may need him if this gets out of hand. I'm sure I must do this. But I'm also certain I don't want to.

"What's wrong, baby?" Jack grips my hand and looks at me as if we are a couple on our fiftieth anniversary, and he knows me all too well.

"My mother is sick." I don't know where this lie comes from. Maybe it forms so quickly because it's not a lie at all. "She needs money to pay for her prescriptions, and she doesn't have it."

"Can't you send her some of your earnings?" he asks. "Surely you have money after how many nights you've worked here."

"It takes too long to apply for a withdrawal, and it makes the madam wary when we do."

Both truths.

Jack rubs his jawline. "I'd give you money, Domino, but that house manager said if we ever did that we'd be fined and wouldn't be able to return. I'm not sure he could actually fine me, but he might be able to keep us apart." Jack grabs my hands like a thought has occurred to him. "Do you want to stay here? I mean, long-term?"

The hopeful glint in his eyes softens my resentment, and I decide that just this once, I'll tell him the truth. "No, Jack. I don't want to stay."

"Then maybe I could pay off your debts."

My entire body goes cold. "My what?"

"That manager guy—Mr. Hodge?—he said if I had enough cash he might be persuaded to let me take one of his girls. Would you ever want to…? What I mean to say is, how would you like to come and live with me? It would take me a few months to get that kind of cash but—"

"I'm for *sale*?" I ask, stupidly.

"No. Of course not. Well, not exactly." Jack's face pulls together. "You didn't know? They said you were working off a loan and that most of your earnings went to that debt. But that we could pay it off for you, and that'd release you from your contract."

I rub my hands over my arms, fighting nausea. Of all the messed-up things I expected to happen tonight, this was not one of them. How dare Madam Karina? How dare Mr. Hodge? To pitch us as products? To tell the customers we are but bodies to be traded for cash? This house is a mass burial site. The further I dig the shovel in, the more skeletons I discover.

I shoot to my feet, knowing if I don't get fresh air, I'll lose it. But first, there's one thing I want to clarify. "You would want that? To pay off my debt and take me as your own?"

Jack stands up, thinking I'm shocked at his thoughtfulness. "More than anything."

"You don't even know me," I whisper.

"Like I said," Jack coos. "We'll have time."

I spin around and face him, every ounce of pity gone from my mind. He doesn't want me. He just wants a body. Maybe my face pleases him in some way, or maybe I remind him of his ex-wife. Who knows? I only know I'm a placeholder. "I need cash for my mother's medications, and I need it now. If you can get that for me soon, then I'll tell the madam myself that I want to leave with you."

"As soon as I have the money to pay for you," he clarifies.

I cringe at his choice of words, but refrain from showing my disgust. Instead, I pull him against me and touch my mouth against his chest and say thank you, thank you, more times than I can count.

"How much does she need? Your mom?" he asks, his hands moving down my back.

I swallow, grip him tighter and say, "Two thousand dollars."

"Two thousand? That's not much less than what you owe the madam."

Once again, my stomach revolts. Is that how little I'm worth? I choke on emotion, and Jack misunderstands the sound as fear for my mother.

"Shh. Come here, let me hold you." He pulls me next to him on the bed though I desperately need that air. "I'm going to help you, but… Well, how old are you, Domino?"

He must want to ensure I'm not underage, which I am. I open my mouth to lie, knowing I need him comfortable in this transaction. In the end though, I say, "I'm seventeen. I turn eighteen in four months."

At first I'm afraid I've blown it. That he'll hightail it out of here and choose a different girl to spend his bronze coin on. But a slow, shy smile parts his mouth. "So young," he says. "Do you know how old I am?"

"It doesn't matter to me."

Twenty-three.

Twenty-four.

Old enough to know better.

"I'm thirty-one."

He pauses as the floor falls out from beneath me. Thirty-one. *Thirty-one?* He's almost twice my age. What is he doing here? And why is he grinning that way?

"Does that bother you?" he asks, slipping his hand inside the waistband of my jeans.

I shake my head to conceal my rising fear. I can't name

why his age makes me afraid of him. But it does.

Sensing my alarm, he says, "I can bring the money for your mother tomorrow. It won't be easy to get together, and it'll mean waiting longer before I can get you out of here. You still want that, right? To go with me?"

"More than anything," I whisper.

Jack clears his throat. "We should commemorate this somehow. I mean, tomorrow when I bring the money. We should do something special." He licks his lips. "Do you think you could reserve this room again tomorrow night?"

I know what he's asking. Will I reward his generosity? I decided this before I walked into the Lilies' house, so why am I hesitating? I pull in a deep breath. Two. Three.

"Yes," I say.

He hears my hesitation. I hear my hesitation. The girls in the living room probably hear it. Yet he still replies with a cool, "Perfect. How about tonight we do something a little more low-key? It'll help build suspense for our special night tomorrow."

He can barely keep the giddiness from his voice. He sounds like a twelve-year-old boy, knowing he'll commit a petty crime the next evening and wanting to relish the still moments before the excitement unfolds.

"Can I hold you?"

I smile and tell him I'd like nothing better. Jack lays himself out on the side of the bed, his back pressed against the wall. Just like I suspected, there isn't really enough room for us both. But we try anyway. Jack wraps his arms around me, and we share the single pillow. Light continues to shine from the kitchen.

We never even closed the door, I think to myself. Nothing to worry about.

But tomorrow night that door will be closed. And after

it does, I'll never be the same again. But I won't be trapped by another woman promising me love when she has nothing but ugly hate to give. This time, I will escape.

As Jack rubs his anxious hands over my hip and thigh, something catches my eye. A movement in the kitchen. No, not in the kitchen. Outside the kitchen window.

The figure is there.

And then it's gone.

CHAPTER 55

ILLUSION

The next day flies by in a blur. I work alone on cleaning dishes and floors and emptying wastebaskets in the Lily house. Then I walk over to the Violets' home, because Marie reminds me we have to clean their space as well. I'm not sure what I expect it to be like. I've built it up in my head so that nothing can compare.

But when we finally go inside, I'm surprised to find it's a replica of the Lilies' home: wood paneling, outdated décor, worn furniture. I suppose there's no use in pretending these homes are used for anything other than what they are. Still, for some unknown reason, my heart falls. I guess I clung to the idea that if I had stayed, when I finally became a Violet, I would be rewarded.

It's strange, seeing it for the first time this way—the Violets at breakfast, me walking over red bras and lacy robes and thigh-highs in the unforgiving daylight. I always imagined I'd see it at night, music thumping, Lola dancing on a table with a glass of champagne in her hand. I'd look at her and imagine I could be her, not a care in the world. I could take her place when she left this house of mirages and reign as Top Girl.

But this place is not the dream I created. It's just a dusty house where girls trade their virtue for bronze coins they'll never touch. When I complete my chores and leave their home, it feels anticlimactic. *That's it?* I keep thinking. The holy grail of Madam Karina's Home for Burgeoning Entertainers? I watch from the Lily house window as the Violet girls walk back from breakfast.

They stretch in the morning and smooth their tangled hair. Their faces are free of makeup and their clothes mismatched. The oldest can't be more than twenty-four. One girl reaches down and scratches her crotch while yawning. And Lola walks in the back, mumbling to herself about who knows what.

They don't look like the glamorous, untouchable girls I've seen in fleeting moments at market or outside the main house window. In this light, they aren't Violets. They're just girls who were nudged, little by little, to become what someone else wanted.

As I let the curtain fall back into place, and Marie yells for me to get my lazy rear moving, the last of Madam Karina's illusions is broken.

CHAPTER 56

HUCKLEBERRY

My hands sweat as I wait for Jack to arrive. I've already reserved the room, showered, and pulled on a pair of snug jeans. Even my hot pink wig is in place.

The Punk Girl with spiky black hair, Amy, is watching me with interest.

"Tonight the night, Cinderella?" she asks.

I rub my damp hands on my jeans and stare at the ceiling.

"Yeah, it is." She laughs and elbows the girl next to her. The other girl makes a crude gesture with her mouth and hand, and the two crow harder.

Marie comes in and sees that two of her girls are heckling me. She smiles and says, as if I asked for her help, "They're not going to treat you any differently than they were treated."

"I don't expect to be treated differently."

Marie cocks her head. "How'd you move up so quickly anyway? You got a magic vagina?"

Amy slaps her knee and bends at the waist, howling. Then she shoots upright. "Nah, that's not it. Look at that face she's hiding. Men want to wreck her. She's got that scared, skinny, victimized thing going on. Makes them want to rescue and ravage her at once."

I curl into myself, imagining what they're saying is true. Is that all it comes down to? Men like Jack want to steal that fragile innocence away? If so, I wish I could spoil the surprise. Whisper that I've helped end a half dozen men's lives as I bring him to completion. Maybe I will.

Wilson taps his fingers inside my brain, waiting. I won't let him come out and play. Not tonight. Every time he raises his voice, I push him back down. Last night I wanted him close, but I've decided that this is my battle, and I need to do it alone.

I rub at the six written on the back of my hand. It would be harder to move up here than in the main house. Glad that's not a concern anymore. I'm still rubbing circles over my hand when Jack arrives. He's wearing a charcoal gray suit that has him sweating like a pig on the spit. He's carrying limp red roses in his hand and a bottle of champagne in the other. I almost feel a twinge of sympathy over the look of excitement on his face.

Until I remember that he basically wants to buy me off someone. And that he doesn't find that problematic. And that he is a thirty-one-year-old man bringing flowers and sinful expectations to a seventeen-year-old girl in a desperate situation.

The sweat on my palms breaks out across my entire body as he moves toward me. He takes my hand and, without asking if I'm ready, directs us toward our tiny room across the kitchen. A laundry room. A place where things are cleaned and reused.

Jack puts the roses and champagne in the hall, already forgotten. "I brought your money," he says, withdrawing an envelope from his pocket. "Had to sell my father's guitar to get it." I peek inside and see tight green bills. My heart picks up when I realize this is really happening. Jack doesn't seem to have the same hesitation, because he tucks the money away and leads me toward the bed.

"Tell me you can't wait until I take you away from here," he says against my neck.

"I can't wait," I whisper.

He runs his hand under the back of my shirt. "Tell me you've wanted me from the first day you saw me."

"You know I have."

"Say it."

"I've wanted you."

I am a puppet playing Simon Says.

Kiss me like you mean it.

Ha, ha! You didn't say "Simon says."

His lips move up my neck and toward my mouth. Two thousand dollars. That's my price. No, my price is freedom. My price is enough money to get my friends to safety. To find help for girls being kept in cells. To give two stiff middle fingers to Madam Karina.

Jack's mouth is warm against mine, but I can't bring myself to close my eyes. He forgot to close the door. I can see his face in the kitchen light, clenched like he's constipated, as he gropes my chest.

Maybe I could steal the money from him and run without going through with this, I think in desperation. Hit him over the head with that bottle he brought and use the few seconds I have to grab Poppet and Cain and run, baby, run.

Even as I think this, I know it's stupid. I'd never have enough time. I have to do this.

I concentrate on the end game as my pulse races and dizziness overwhelms my senses. He smells like aftershave and tastes of Angie's peppermints. I focus on this and not the fact that his hand is sliding between my knees.

"Tell me you like this," he says.

"I like this."

He pauses. "Tell me you love me."

A chill races down my back. I won't say it. I won't. I'm not sure why this is the line I won't cross, but it's like a fault line that can't be disturbed. Should I attempt it, earthquakes would rumble the house. Aftershocks would bring down the roof.

"Don't ever leave me," I try, hoping that'll suffice.

He bites the tender flesh above my collarbone. "Tell me you love me."

I shake my head, and tears spring to my eyes. He's crazy. We've spent mere hours together, and he thinks I could love him that quickly? He thinks I could love him at all? Jack's hands slide down my arms until he finds my wrists. He pulls them up and over my head.

"You want to tease me?" he says playfully. "Well, I know just what to do with that."

Dread rumbles in my blood as he releases my wrist and strides toward the door, peeling off his suit jacket and shirt as he moves.

"Jack," I say in a whimper.

I hate the sound of my voice. The pleading tone that silently begs him to give me the money, no strings attached. There's no such thing as a free lunch, isn't that what they say? My body begins to shake, and I cry openly.

"Shhh," he says, closing the door. "Don't be sad. I'm not leaving."

When I see him move toward me—completely ignorant of my distress—is the moment I snap. I can't do this. Not for any amount of money. Not for any amount of freedom. Because this isn't freedom. Cain is right, if I do this, I'll become one of Madam Karina's girls. No matter how far away I get.

I've already let Jack kiss me. But I won't let this go any further.

I stand up. "I can't do this."

"You're scared I won't come back," he says soothingly. "But I will. You don't have to worry."

"No, Jack. I don't want to be with you. I thought I could, but…"

"You thought you could?" The confusion that crosses Jack's face swiftly morphs into sadness. He shakes his head once. Twice. Three times. A thousand times, trying to figure out my sudden change of heart. "You thought you could because I was going to pay you?"

I don't respond.

"Do you want to leave with me?"

"Jack…"

He sighs, shrugs. "No. You don't want to leave with me. You want to leave with you."

I expect him to exit the room. Or to yell. Or to report me to Mr. Hodge. But instead, he takes a single step in my direction. "And what if I said no? What if I told you that you don't know what you want? Young girls seldom do."

This isn't going to end well. I look at his stance, at the way he's blocking the door.

"Come here, Domino, and give me what you promised."

I back up, my knees hitting the edge of the mattress.

Wilson?!

Here! I'm here!

Jack reaches out, slowly at first. As if he expects I'll come to him easily. Realize my mistake in rejecting him. When I dodge his hand, the sadness on his face changes, slowly, slowly. The anger twisting his face is so unnerving my head spins.

And then—

Jack grabs my wig and rips my head toward him. His other hand covers my mouth.

Terror seizes every muscle in my body. I was prepared to give myself to Jack. But not like this. Never like this. He lifts me up and throws me onto the bed. My back hits the mattress, and I cry out against the springs.

Did I ask for this?

Have I made Jack into this monster?

No! Wilson answers inside my mind. *No, no, no, no, no!*

Jack reaches down and tears my shirt with the hand that held my hair. The other remains over my mouth. I cry out against his clenched fingers.

Say the words, Wilson pleads, leaping around inside my head. *Say them, Domino!*

I won't be able to stop you, though.

Wilson pulls his hair out. *We don't have a choice!*

Jack tells me not to scream. Uncovers my mouth and reaches for my waist. But I do scream, and when I do, he delivers a blow to my cheek so hard the world spins. Fear shadows his face, like he's surprised at his own assault. He reaches for me gently as if he can make it better. That's when I scream a second time.

Jack tackles me, both hands pushing down on my mouth so hard I think he'll break my jaw.

Where are the other Lilies?

Why isn't anyone coming?

Domino, Wilson says. His voice is so reasonable. So reassuring. Let him take over. That's all I have to do. But I have to be level-headed enough to get us out of here, too. And if Wilson takes over, there's no telling what will happen.

So I make a decision.

I bite down on Jack's fingers.

He hollers and tears his hand away from my mouth.

"Wilson!" I yell over Jack's complaints. "Help me!"

Wilson steps firmly into my mind, cracks his neck, sets his gaze on Jack. *So you want to play rough, tough guy? Well then, I'm your huckleberry.*

CHAPTER 57

ANIMAL

*C*ome at me! Wilson screams. *I* scream.

And Jack does. I spring onto the bed like a wild animal, crouched on hands and feet. I grab the pillowcase and then leap up and over Jack's hunched form. The part of me that's still me makes for the door to escape, but Wilson is controlling my body, too, and he has no plans of leaving quietly.

Jack turns as I wring the pillowcase into a tight stretch of fabric.

"You want to touch me?" I say.

Not my voice.

Not me.

"You want to own me?"

Jack lunges for the second time, and I let him take me this time, keeping my hands above my head. As soon as he closes his arms around me I let my knees collapse and drop to the ground. Surprised by the weight, Jack falls to the floor.

We lay side by side, lovers whispering in the dark.

That is, until Jack attempts to crawl on top of me on the freshly mopped floor. Wilson waits for the opportunity. *Wait, wait. Don't panic.* Even though Jack's on me. Even though he's tearing at our clothes and panting between gritted teeth.

Don't panic, Domino Ray.

There.

Now.

I shove my hand down fast and hard, a viper strike. I grab onto the same place that burns so badly for me. I watch as his eyes enlarge and spittle flies from his mouth, and I pull with all my might.

He howls loudly. Loud enough that now I'm sure someone must be coming to help.

I know that.

I'm reassured by that.

But Wilson doesn't want anyone coming.

I shoot out from under Jack as he groans in pain and leap to my feet. With breakneck speed, I step on one end of the pillowcase and wrap the rest around Jack's neck. I pull back with every ounce of strength I have.

Jack's back straightens and he gasps at the noose around his neck.

No matter.

I lean away and pull harder, keeping my feet planted firmly on the other end. This is how a hundred-pound girl can kill a grown man in a laundry room. Just one way of many.

My personal favorite, Wilson says hysterically. *Look how red his eyes are. Look!*

"What's wrong, Jack?" I say, grunting against the effort to end his life. "Do I take your breath away?"

Wilson, stop! I scream inside my head. *I won't take another human life!*

Then don't. Go away. Let me take over.

Jack's face turns a sickly shade of blue as he thrashes his

arms, trying to break my grasp.

That's what's so beautiful about strangulation, Wilson booms. *Turns strong, capable adults into raging idiots. Look at him. All he has to do is take out your legs, or grab onto the pillowcase with both hands and pull. But nope! He'll just keep flopping around. Flop, fishy, flop!*

You have to stop, Wilson. Please!

No, he answers. *Shan't.*

Almost as if Jack read Wilson's thoughts, he rolls to his left and shoves my ankle. I stumble just enough for him to inhale a lungful of sweet, merciful air. Wilson tries to regain his death hold on Jack, but now the man is reaching for me, despite his purple face and lack of oxygen.

I leap back, and Jack rips the pillowcase from his throat. He coughs for several seconds as Wilson examines the room, searching for his second option. He remembers the champagne bottle and lunges for the hallway, but Jack grabs me, and I'm thrown back onto the bed.

This time it's his hands that wrap around my throat.

I gasp, claw at his fingers.

Wilson laughs like this is the funniest thing he's ever seen.

You really think that's how easy I'll go down?

Wilson prepares himself for another assault, but before he can do anything, the laundry room door bursts open.

Cain stands in the doorway, chest heaving, fists clenched.

Jack spins around.

"Oh, good," Jack says, speaking to Cain, and pointing at me. "This little snatch—"

Cain hits him. He hits him, and it's the shot heard round the world. Jack's head snaps backward, and he pauses in the air for a fraction of a second, a beast on his heels. And then he hits the floor.

He's out.

No pillowcases or fancy moves or strategizing.

Just one blow from the stone giant and he's one, two, three, down for the count.

But Wilson hasn't had his fill. He doesn't want Jack unconscious. He wants him dead. I lunge on Jack, the pillow in my hands. I shove the pillow over Jack's face, but Cain is telling me we have to go. We have to go now.

Cain pulls me backward, but Wilson fights against him. He's not done with Jack. He won't stop. He can't. Jack hurt us. He must be punished.

"Domino!" Cain yells.

Two Lilies appear in the doorway, yelling for Marie. They see me on Jack, scratching at his face.

Wilson, stop, we have to go, I plead.

No, never!

"Domino, you have to come with me." Cain grabs me around the waist and hoists me up. I spin around to face him, Wilson's anger pulsing through me. "I won't make you come," Cain says, "but if you want to, we have to go now!"

"Where do you think you'd go?" one Lily screeches as the other girl rushes to Jack's side.

Marie shoves her way into the small room. "What's going on in here?"

Wilson analyzes the situation, and decides he can still end Jack's life. What's more, he wants the money we were promised. The same envelope one of the Lilies now holds in her hand. She tucks it behind her back, and the other Lily who sees her do it blocks my path. Seems they both want to cash in on my private deal.

Though I know we don't have time for this fight, Wilson makes me lunge toward them.

But this time I'm able stop myself before impact.

I am here, too, Wilson. I didn't leave. And I'm telling you to back down.

But you need me, Domino. I can get our money and finish him, too.

BACK DOWN!

Wilson hesitates just long enough for me to grab Cain's hand and yell, "Run!"

CHAPTER 58

SEE DOMINO RUN

Cain and I bolt from the Lilies' home and race toward the main house. I have only two objectives now.

Get Poppet.

Run.

A voice rings out in the night, stopping me. "You're running, aren't you? Morons!"

I turn to see Lola staring back at me, the red lipstick on her mouth smeared. Swallowing my apprehension, I call out the first thing I think of. "Come with us."

She blinks in the dim light. "You're crazy."

Cain pushed my lower back. "We've got to go."

"Will you tell?" I ask.

Lola looks up at Madam Karina's window. "Yeah, I will. But I'll throw them off. It'll give me time to run while they're looking for you."

"We're headed that way." I point down the road, to the right.

"Well, I saw you go that way." She points to the left.

I tip my head at her, and then race toward the main house. Mr. Hodge isn't at the front like I expect him to be, so I fly up the stairs. Cain is one step behind me. When we get to the third floor, I sweep into the Tulips' entertainment room.

Poppet is sitting in a white high-back chair, speaking with an older gentleman. When I see that he's holding her hand, drawing circles in her palm, I have to once again fight Wilson for control.

She sees me, sees the sweat on my forehead and the expression on my face, and she's on her feet. She zigzags through the customers and bolts past me toward her bedroom. I take off after her and then watch as she fills a bag from her closet. Each thing has its place, and it's as if she went over this a hundred times in her head.

"I've got it," Cain says when she's done. "Can you run in those?"

She kicks off her high heels. "I grew up barefoot. Why change now?"

Cain hurries down the hall, and Poppet and I rush after him, adrenaline firing through me. The three us storm down the stairs, turning corners and hearing girls yell in our direction. We sound like a herd of water buffalo moving through the house. Between stealth and speed, we choose the latter.

I think we're in the clear until I see Mr. Hodge standing at the bottom of the stairs.

Cain sees him and drops Poppet's bag. Mr. Hodge readies his short, massive torso in front of us like there's no way we're getting past him.

Jack appears from the side door, holding his jaw. Behind him are a half dozen of Madam Karina's girls, doting on the injured customer.

"You're going to pay for this." Mr. Hodge narrows his beady eyes. "I'm going to make sure—"

He never gets the rest of the sentence out, because suddenly Cain is moving. He rushes down the stairs like Usain Bolt and skips the last three steps, opting to lunge through the air instead. His fist connects with Mr. Hodge's face and, déjà vu, Mr. Hodge goes down.

Unlike Jack, though, he's not out.

"Come on!" Cain urges.

"Oh my God," Poppet laughs as she grabs her bag and leaps over Mr. Hodge. "You punched The Neck!"

The three of us sail through the front door, and Cain digs keys out of his pocket. We dive inside the black demon car, and Cain starts the ignition and steps on the gas. On our way down the drive, we pass Eric's gold sedan.

"Where to?" Cain asks.

"You don't have a plan?" Poppet shrieks.

He shakes his head. "Not past keeping the car keys and hitting that prick, Jack." Cain glances at me. "I watched you through the kitchen window. I won't apologize."

"Turn here!" I yell.

Cain jerks the car to the right and pushes the car as fast as it'll go.

"Where'd you learn to hit like that?" Poppet asks Cain, bouncing in her seat.

"Keep driving until I say." I stare forward, trying to gauge how far we are from my intended destination. My body itches for movement, to run ahead of the car and expend some nerves. I'm a ball of tension, glancing in the rearview mirror every ten seconds. If we see Eric's headlights, it's over. As it stands, my plan may not work for a slew of reasons.

My hope rests on Lola and her convincing Madam Karina and the others that she saw us going left down the road. She'll help, because the longer they search for us, the more time she'll have to slip away unnoticed. But Pox isn't a large town, and it won't take long for Eric to decide we went in the other direction.

How can I help? Wilson asks. *I know I tried to take over back there, but I'm better now.*

Just let me think.

Right-o. Thinking is your territory. I'm the doer. Let me know if you need any doing.

We're two hundred yards away when I tell Cain to pull into a field on the left. The property looks deserted, an old ramshackle house and a front yard filled with busted tires and a scarecrow that's missing an arm. I tell Cain to park wherever, and we get out.

Cain grabs Poppet's bag from the backseat of the car, and Poppet props her elephant on her hip like an infant. The two give me a questioning look.

"We'll walk from here," I explain. "If they're looking for the car, or have a tracking device on it, we don't want them to find us in it."

"But where are we going?" Poppet asks, her bare feet disappearing into the tall, dry grass.

I point forward. "We'll skirt along the side of the road, but not on it. It should only take us a few minutes to get there."

It's Cain who finally figures it out. "You want to jump the train."

"I've done it before. It's how I left home." It's something I've never told anyone, not even Dizzy. He knew I loved them, the trains, but he didn't know why. Not the whole truth, anyway. Not the fact that a train often has empty cars perfect for desperate travelers. Not that the horn sounds, to me, like a beacon of hope and renewal. He only knew I loved them as a child. Not that they served as my salvation.

CHAPTER 59

BACK POCKET HOPE

The three of us step over barbed wire fences, and voluptuous cow patties, and deep holes where rattlesnakes might lie. And eventually, we spot the tracks in the distance. Cain, Poppet, and I bunker down nearby, and wait an entire dread-filled hour before I hear the telltale sound of a train approaching.

I run out from our hiding spot, and Cain jogs beside me. Poppet hangs back, ready. Cain and I position ourselves on the tracks, arms waving wildly, ice forming in my lungs. The train travels closer, bright lights cutting through the darkness. It's a unit freight train, no passengers, one type of cargo. I love this type of train—the simplicity, the efficiency. It does one thing and it does it right. And tonight, it just may save our hides.

The red-and-white arms descend on either side, and a yellow flashing bulb illuminates Poppet's face. And then, farther down the road, a vehicle appears. A red siren swirls on the hood, dirt kicking up in a cloud behind the gold sedan.

The ice in my lungs shoots to my fingertips. Eric has found us. Even if the train slows enough for us to jump aboard, we may not make it. Cain and I exchange a look and wave our arms faster. My heart sledgehammers in my chest, and Poppet screams over and over that Eric is coming.

The train engineer spots us and hits the brakes. A

screeching sound blocks out anything else. The sound of Poppet yelling—gone. The sound of Eric's manic siren—gone. Now there is only this metal fiend rocking down the tracks, attempting to slow its momentum. The driver doesn't want to kill us, but he will anyway if we don't move.

This isn't a suicide mission, so I grab Cain's arm and we lunge off the tracks. The *whoosh* of air throws me off-balance, and Cain has to jerk me upright before I lose my footing.

"There! there!" Poppet points to the first open train car she sees, and together we start running. The train hasn't stopped, but it might be slow enough now that we can attempt boarding it.

"Run alongside it!" I yell. "Run as fast as you can, and let the car come to you!"

The light from Eric's vehicle paints everything in red, and though I'm too afraid to look, I can feel the shadow of his car as it approaches and stops, can sense his footsteps as he lunges toward us. A blast rings through the night, and I cry out.

"He's shooting at us!" Cain roars.

"Keep running!" My chest heaves, and sweat drenches my arms and neck. We're close. So close to freedom but I can't think about what Eric is doing. Can't wonder whether his bullets are a warning or something worse.

The train car Poppet spotted approaches, catching up with us as we run, heads back, mouths open.

Another shot is fired, and Eric shouts. No longer able to stand it, I look back. He's running after us, waving a Glock, his face redder than seems possible.

Cain reaches for the handle outside the train car. Misses three times before grabbing hold. He jumps like a natural athlete and barely stumbles before pulling himself inside. In a flash, his arm is back out, reaching for me. I grab the handle with one hand, and onto him with the other.

I'm pulled inside to safety.

Poppet is the only one left, running barefoot, her face painted with fear.

"Reach for me!" Cain says.

The train is gaining speed again. The engineer must be familiar with this, teens teasing his pet. So he brushes off what he saw and focuses again on his precious schedule.

Eric runs behind Poppet, closing the distance between them. He's near enough that I can see the saliva wetting his thin lips. I stretch my arm out, fear wrapping itself around my throat, and beg her to run faster. *Faster!*

Poppet reaches for Cain.

Eric reaches for Poppet.

Cain sweeps her up and into the train car. As soon as she's out of reach, Eric trips and rolls away. Poppet leaps away from Cain and into my arms. The two of us lie on the rusted floor and pant for breath. I don't want to let her go. All my fears at being touched vanish as her heart beats against mine. She's here. She's safe.

We're safe.

That's when I see the pink elephant grasped in Poppet's hand. I can't help but laugh. "You brought the elephant."

Poppet rolls off me and faces the ceiling. Cool air rushes through the opening and sweeps over our bodies, carries our fear up and away. "It's the only good thing I got from that place." She frowns. "I couldn't make it on with the whole bag."

Cain offers us each a hand and pulls us to our feet. "What are we going to do now?"

Poppet brushes off her backside. "Domino will figure it out. If she can get us on a moving train, she can do anything." She slaps my rear playfully. Then her fingers move over my back pocket with intention. "What's in your pocket?"

Cain glances at me sideways, and I shrug. Digging my

finger in, I feel a thick fold of something warm and crinkly. I pull it out, and tears sting my eyes.

"Whoa," Poppet says. "Where'd you get the money?"

I look at Cain, a cautious smile spreading across my face when I remember Angie's awkward hug. "It was Angie. She slipped it into my pocket."

It's not enough to start a new life. But it is enough for a motel room and something to eat. And it may be just the thing we need to make it far enough away to ask for help, for us, and for the girls we left behind.

As the train clatters through the night and Cain and Poppet smile in my direction, I close my fist around the money a quietly defiant woman gave me, and imagine everything will be okay.

Maybe, just maybe, we've already made it out safely.

And that no one got hurt in the process.

CHAPTER 60

VACANCY

We ride the train through four station stops until Texas plains give way to the flatlands of Carlsbad, New Mexico. This time when the train stops, we disembark and jog along the tracks. Then we walk for several miles, my mouth dry and sticky, until we spot a red-and-white motel with a buzzing vacancy sign. Three tin horses sit on springs out front for children to play on, but the paint has long faded, and the horses' grins seem sinister in the fading light.

I pay the desk guy half our money for a room while Cain and Poppet wait outside. If Eric and his guys find out we landed in Carlsbad, I don't want this employee saying he saw three travelers come through together.

The hotel room has two queen beds with a white rose pattern, and a television that picks up six stations. Although for an additional twelve dollars we can have all the adult movies we want. Tempting.

Poppet scrunches her nose. "This place is glamorous."

I plop down on the bed. "Don't act like you've stayed in better."

"A girl can pretend, can't she?" Poppet climbs beneath the covers and tucks that pink elephant beneath her arm. "I'm so tired I feel sick, but I'm afraid I'll never be able to sleep."

I exchange a glance with Cain before approaching the other side of her bed. It couldn't be later than eight o'clock, not even twenty-four hours since we left Pox, but I'm exhausted enough to sleep for three days.

Poppet snatches away the covers when she sees I'm climbing in. "No way. Get your own bed." She lowers her voice so Cain can't hear, and winks. "I'm doing you a favor."

Then she smashes her face into the pillow and tries to hide her grin.

I turn to Cain, heat creeping into my cheeks.

"I'll sleep on the floor." Cain grabs a pillow from the opposite bed.

"Don't be ridiculous," Poppet complains. "You're both adults, sort of. Besides, I know you've slept in the same bed before."

Cain shoots a look at me and, even after everything, I smile.

He smiles, too.

I roll my eyes and climb in, and Cain climbs in after me. The sheets against my skin, Cain's body heat warm under the covers, Poppet giggling from her bed—it's almost too much happiness for one room. The terror that last night brought feels distant when the three of us are here, safe. In a room we paid for with Angie's money.

"It was a nice thing Angie did," I whisper to Cain.

He scoots a fraction closer and finds my hand beneath the comforter. "She's a good person. But I'm worried Madam Karina's going to find out she helped us."

"She won't." I say this, but anxiety still twists my belly. It would destroy me if something bad happened to Angie. Angie isn't perfect, by any means, but she's true. When you look at her, you know what you're getting. And that's no small thing.

Not when you've lived with a mother with two faces, or a madam with three.

Poppet flips off the lamp, and before long her breathing deepens.

Cain holds my hand until I can't keep my eyes open a second longer.

CHAPTER 61

HAPPINESS WITHIN REACH

When I wake the next morning, Cain is watching me. He realizes I've caught him in the act and slams his lids closed.

"Creeper," I say, my voice raspy from sleep.

He grins with one corner of his mouth but keeps his eyes closed.

"Oh, yeah," I whisper. "You're totally asleep."

When he doesn't move, I spider my fingers across the space between us and over his rib cage, feeling courageous. Sometime during the night, he must have shed the plaid shirt he wore, because when I touch him, my fingers feel bare skin. Cain's eyes snap open.

"You wouldn't," he says quietly.

"Dare me not to."

"I won't."

I tickle him, digging my fingers into the sensitive spaces between his ribs. His face turns red from holding in the laughter. He doesn't want to wake Poppet, and I know that. I hold the tickle power. And I am merciless!

Once we've showered and dressed, we'll have to walk into town and find the local police station. Then we'll most likely spend hours telling them what we've seen, and where they can find the imprisoned girls, and the other girls who may be staying with Madam Karina out of fear.

But for now there is only this bed.

And Cain's painfully gorgeous smile.

And my friend asleep in the bed a few feet over.

"You guys think I'm not hearing this?" Poppet groans. "Geez, get a room."

Cain bursts into laughter and bounds on top of me, pins my wrist above my head. "The girl's awake. Your power over me is broken. Do you have any final words before I inflict punishment?"

"It wasn't me."

Cain laughs, and the sound stretches my insides, pours sunshine through my veins. "I believe it was."

My head cranes backward as Cain tickles me, running his fingers up my sides and over my serpent tattoo.

"Say mercy!" he bellows.

"You guys are one moment away from doing it," Poppet declares. "And lucky for you, I want breakfast."

Despite my tickle agony, I see Poppet striding toward the door, throwing a wink my way.

"I'll just be downstairs checking if they have any coffee." She grabs the key card from the dresser. "Might be gone for about twenty minutes. Enough for anything to happen, really."

"Poppet, no!" I yell through my torture. "I'll go with you."

Cain stops tickling me and glances over his shoulder at her. "Yeah, we should stick in pairs when we can."

"No way. I didn't run barefoot alongside a freaking train to live in fear."

She salutes us, giggling, and disappears through the door.

"Should we go after her?" Cain asks, still sitting on top of me.

"Yeah," I answer. But as soon as he swings off me, I leap

on his back and wrap my legs around his waist. Then I am tickle champion once again. Cain groans and falls backward, smashing me between his body and the bed. I think I've won this battle, but in one sharp, smart movement, Cain grabs onto my thigh, pulls me from his back and hurdles over my frame until he's on top.

"What will I do with you?" he says quietly, lust warming his gaze. "I can't even turn my back on you, you villain."

He kisses me.

His lips are soft and urgent and everything Jack's lips were not. My body reacts without hesitation. I am arms and legs around him, back arched, mouth open. Here is the boy who knows my secrets and wants me anyway. The boy who punished Jack for his sins, who flew through the air like a warcraft and delivered retribution to Mr. Hodge.

He is broken like me.

I am broken like him.

But together, we fill our missing pieces—glue and gentle fingers and kisses on bruises.

What destruction could we bring together?

What good could we bring to others who have seen what we've seen?

This may not be the right thing, but it is the thing I choose. Cain pushes his arms beneath my back and pulls me closer, his tongue causing a clap of thunder to rumble through my body. His hands run through my pink wig, and he pulls it away, tosses it to the floor. Good riddance. I don't want it. I don't want anything between us.

Look at my face, Cain, please.

See me.

Almost as if he can read my mind, he stops and stares into my eyes, searching. "I am yours, Domino. And I want to know you. I want to know everything." He buries his face in my neck and kisses me softly. "Stay with me?"

His need heals a sharp, jagged place in my soul. Smooths the edges so it's not as hazardous. It is always me who needs others. But he needs me. I don't know what promises I can keep in this lifetime, but I can't breathe until I say, "I'm staying. Cain." It feels so right to voice the words. A prophecy I'm desperate to fulfill.

I run my hands slowly over Cain's body, taking in the sloping curves of his biceps, the rises and valleys of his muscled back, the swell of his shoulders. I'm swallowed by his body, and it feels amazing. My trepidation at being touched is all but gone when it comes to Cain. Maybe I never had a problem with touch to begin with. Maybe it was the people touching me I feared.

Cain kisses the hollow between my collarbones and then trails kisses up my throat until our lips meet.

"I want you," Cain whispers against my mouth.

I arch my back in response, telling him I'm right here, though nerves shoot through my legs. Do I want this now? Here? I'm not sure I'm ready.

"When we're away from here," Cain continues, "starting our new life in Kansas, there's going to come a moment when I won't be able to stop myself. If you don't want me to, that is."

I smile against his skin. "You want to go to Kansas?"

He nods. "After we finish this, I want to do that thing you said. See if I could still play. Even if I can't, maybe I could try to enroll anyway. Maybe you could, too."

I think about this. About getting my GED and applying for college in Kansas. Watching Cain play football and cheering him on, Poppet and I sucking on sour pickles in the bleachers, our blood running the same color as his jersey. We'll have an apartment near campus with two bedrooms, one for Poppet and one for Cain and me. We'll make friends, have parties, dream about our futures, make cappuccinos for paychecks, and vote for the first time in a public election. I'll learn how to make a proper casserole, and Poppet will meet a boy she admits she loves.

Cain will keep us safe. Wilson will quietly slip away, unneeded, and we'll stretch our arms toward the possibilities that life holds.

And one day, quietly, after Poppet has moved in with her boyfriend of two years, Cain and I will look around us and say, we should buy a home of our own. Cain will insist I pick the place, and I'll do so with him in mind.

The walls in our house will be blue. We'll paint them using long strokes, and we'll put on three coats if that's what it takes. In the backyard there will be a swing lounging in the sun. We'll paint that red and watch as the years of rain erode our work. Inside there will be soft couches bought from real furniture stores and a dining table where we'll eat eggs and toast with raspberry jam.

And in our room. In our room we'll have a king-sized bed with a violet comforter. It'll be big enough for us to spread out in, but small enough so that we can always feel each other there. It'll be a room we'll sleep in. Dream in. It will be our room.

I laugh at my imagination. All I ever wanted was a real home and to be invisible. Now all I want is a home with Cain, and for him to see me, and see me, and see me.

Cain dips his head, touches our foreheads together like he wants to breathe in the sound of my laughter.

We stay like that for several minutes, daydreaming, kissing, cuddling beneath warm sheets, until a single thought occurs to me.

"Cain? How long has Poppet been gone?"

CHAPTER 62

DO THE THINGS I CANNOT

Cain lifts his head and glances toward the curtained window. I can see his mind ticking, calculating the time since she left. He hesitates too long, and my stomach churns. I tap his side and he rolls away from me, gets to his feet.

Cain pulls on his shirt, and I step into my jeans. We're frantic as we dress, and silent.

She's fine, I tell myself. She's just giving us space because that's the kind of friend she is. Thoughtful, kind.

Still, I bolt through the front door and search the parking lot. The morning sun casts a harsh glare across the pavement. I rush toward the concrete stairs and hurry down, Cain right behind me. Poppet said she was going to the front for coffee, but she isn't there when we go inside. She isn't anywhere.

Not in the lobby bathroom.

Not at the gated, drained pool.

Not back in our motel room because we might have missed her.

My ears pound and my breathing accelerates until the world spins.

"She probably went for a walk," Cain says. "She'll be back any minute."

I can't hear his words. I can't think past anything besides

what my eyes have spotted in the parking lot. Near the front tire of a Dodge Ram truck is a flash of pink. Long elephant trunk, sewed on eyelashes, a belly stuffed with cotton.

"Cain…" I point toward Poppet's pink elephant, and a sob breaks in my throat.

He rushes toward the parking lot and, as I stand on the second story walkway—Cain frantically searching for our friend—my fear and horror transform into something else. I was so close to happiness. There it was, cupped in my palm, shivering with excitement. A future so bright and bold it could color a canvas.

I held it in my mind for a moment. All that joy. All that potential. Cain and Poppet and me and laughter and fresh starts. No one getting hurt. No turning back.

Cain yells at me from the parking lot, but I can't hear what he's saying. I'm comatose. Lost in the fog of something that could have been. But they took a crucial piece of my plan, didn't they? They took my friend.

I descend the stairs slowly, robotic. When my feet touch the ground, I stride past Cain and over to Poppet's lost toy. I crouch down and take the pink elephant. Think how silly it is that she took it with her to get coffee. I hand it to Cain and tell him to pull it apart. He does—and there it is. The small, intricate tracking device that told them exactly where to go should we escape.

Madam Karina practically handed Poppet the stuffed animal. But not quite. To do so would have given her away. She's much too sly for that.

"Do you think they took her?" Cain asks. "I didn't hear anything."

My head snaps up. "It doesn't matter."

"How does it not matter?" Cain runs his hand over his shorn head, and paces. "We have to get her back. We have to tell someone." He glances around like he's just now realizing something. "We have to get out of here. They could be close by."

"We're going to get her back ourselves," I say evenly. "I can't risk waiting for someone else to help." Besides, there's a reason they didn't wait to find us, too. Madam Karina *loves* that I'm forced to return on my own or leave my friend behind.

"Domino, if we go back there, we won't stand a chance of leaving again. Madam Karina, Mr. Hodge, the Pox police, the girls at the house… We're outnumbered."

Anger courses through me, a thousand ravenous suns drinking every last drop of thick, red blood. My veins run with fire and sulfur, with vengeance and rage. My happiness was waiting in a field of tall grass, but they burned it down around me. They've taken and manipulated and hurt. They've done wrong, and there's nothing I do better than enacting punishment on those my mother deems unworthy.

And if my mother were here, she would find these people unworthy.

"We won't get Poppet back," I say, standing. "But I know someone who will."

"Who?" Cain holds the elephant's smiling, glassy-eyed head in his right hand.

"Wilson."

Wilson snaps to attention. *You mean it? Do you really mean it?*

Can you get her back? I ask.

I can get her back. Wilson licks his lips, tries to control his excitement. *I'll need complete control though. No sharing.*

"Domino?" Cain touches my elbow. "Who is Wilson?"

My hands cradle my head. *I'm so tired, Wilson.*

I know you are. Let me finish this for you.

The fire in my veins beats in time with my heart. The

pulsing reminds me of what I've lost. So close to freedom. So close to the dreams I had.

Taken.

Wilson? I whisper.

Yes, I'm here. What do you need? Name it.

Make them pay.

Wilson cracks his knuckles, grins until the corners of his mouth touch the bottom of his ears. *Say the words.*

I close my eyes. *Come into me, Wilson. Do the things I cannot while I turn away. Use my body and mind as your own.*

No sooner do I think this than Wilson wraps himself around my head, soothing fingers of black stretching over my brain. He shushes me and hugs me close, reassuring. Goose bumps race across my skin, and my knees wobble.

I'll show them what it means to suffer, he says. *I will avenge you. I will love you. I will protect you.*

Now go to sleep.

"Domino, talk to me," Cain says. "What's happening?"

My head whips backward, and I scream.

Wilson is here. Wilson is here. Wilson is here. Wilson is here.
Wilson is here. Wilson is here. Wilson is here. Wilson is here.
Wilson is here. Wilson is here. Wilson is here. Wilson is here.
Wilson is here. Wilson is here. Wilson is here. Wilson is here.
Wilson is here. Wilson is here. Wilson is here. Wilson is here.
Wilson is here. Wilson is here. Wilson is here. Wilson is here.
Wilson is here. Wilson is here. Wilson is here. Wilson is here.
Wilson is here. Wilson is here. Wilson is here. Wilson is here.
Wilson is here. Wilson is here. Wilson is here. Wilson is here.
Wilson is here. Wilson is here. Wilson is here. Wilson is here.
Wilson is here. Wilson is here. Wilson is here. Wilson is here.
Wilson is here. Wilson is here. Wilson is here. Wilson is here.
Wilson is here. Wilson is here. Wilson is here. Wilson is here.
Wilson is here. Wilson is here. Wilson is here. Wilson is here.
Wilson is here. Wilson is here. Wilson is here. Wilson is here.
Wilson is here. Wilson is here. Wilson is here. Wilson is here.
Wilson is here. Wilson is here. Wilson is here. Wilson is here.
Wilson is here. Wilson is here. Wilson is here. Wilson is here.
Wilson is here. Wilson is here. Wilson is here. Wilson is here.
Wilson is here. Wilson is here. Wilson is here. Wilson is here.
Wilson is here. Wilson is here. Wilson is here. Wilson is here.
Wilson is here. Wilson is here. Wilson is here. Wilson is here.
Wilson is here. Wilson is here. Wilson is here. Wilson is here.
Wilson is here. Wilson is here. Wilson is here. Wilson is here.
Wilson is here. Wilson is here. Wilson is here. Wilson is here.
Wilson is here. Wilson is here. Wilson is here. Wilson is here.
Wilson is here. Wilson is here. Wilson is here. Wilson is here.
Wilson is here. Wilson is here. Wilson is here. Wilson is here.
Wilson is here. Wilson is here. Wilson is here. Wilson is here.
Wilson is here. Wilson is here. Wilson is here. Wilson is here.
Wilson is here. Wilson is here. Wilson is here. Wilson is here.
Wilson is here. Wilson is here. Wilson is here. Wilson is here.
Wilson is here. Wilson is here. Wilson is here. Wilson is here.
Wilson is here. Wilson is here. Wilson is here. Wilson is here.
Wilson is here. Wilson is here. Wilson is here. Wilson is here.

I am here.

CHAPTER 63

HERE COMES THE THUNDER

My name is Domino Ray, but I am not Domino Ray. I am Wilson. I remember the things we did. The torture we inflicted on those men. The ways we made them scream. I remember watching as the last shovel of dirt fell over their faces, as their cars sunk into secluded lakes. I remember cement being poured over their bodies by unsuspecting construction workers and wringing our hands at the sight. I remember all the things we did.

And I will do them again.

I speed down the highway, the sun setting in the distance. Reds and purples spill over one another like a stomach split down the middle, innards everywhere. Look at me. I'm a poet!

Cain sits next to me, stoic. He's holding a backpack full of tools I bought from Home Depot—serrated knives, rope, masking tape…and a can of red spray paint, because old habits die hard. I threw in a few other toys for good measure to produce when the time is right. Cain didn't ask questions as we shopped for these things, Michael Jackson playing overhead while we pushed an orange cart down the aisles. He understands I'm gone. Or rather, that the new me has arrived. What really gets me going is that the dude took one look at my vacant eyes and seemed to disappear into his own head.

Two can play at that game, he said without speaking.

See, that's why I like the kid.

He knows how screwed up I am. That I have two sides. Domino the Gentle, Domino the Feared. And when he saw I'd flipped my switch, it's like he thought, *Screw it. Let's do this thing.*

He could have run.

He could have backstepped out of sight.

But instead he let his crazy flag fly and took my hand.

That's some Romeo and Juliet shit right there.

The car I stole is lime green and one of the front headlights is busted. But the driver left the keys tucked above the sunshade, and they slid into my hand like a favor from above. Or below. Whatever. And you know what I did before we took off across New Mexico on our way back to Pox? Ask me. Go on, ask me!

I spray-painted HERE COMES THE THUNDER on the side of this lime green car.

Unlike Domino the Gentle, I'm one for theatrics.

Cain turns on the radio and finds a song that matches our rage and frustration and fear. Scratch that last word. I'm not afraid. I don't do fear. I'm the one who inflicts pain. I'm the monster beneath your bed, in your closet, in your head. There're some lyrics for you. Name that song.

The hours pass quickly, and the moon takes flight. Not too much longer. Even now I can smell the scent of poverty and lies at the tail end of this Texas summer. Almost fall now. Almost the gateway to death and destruction and bleakness.

"Do you remember what I told you?" I ask Cain.

"I remember."

"You don't have to do this."

He turns toward me. "Yes, I do."

Cain is pissed, too. He's got months of backlogged anger

toward Madam Karina, Mr. Hodge, and Eric. Sigh too heavily and that combustible dude will blow. I grip the steering wheel, and when I see the road that will take us to Madam Karina's House for Bullcrap and Lies, I shiver with delight. As we pass over the railroad tracks, I throw deuces to my old friend.

Thanks for the ride out of this crap hole, even if it didn't stick.

My pulse picks up as we bump over the rocky road, closer and closer. I can hardly contain my excitement. Here comes little ol' Domino to gather her friend. My hot pink wig lies on the side of the interstate. Don't need that protection anymore. Don't need anything but me.

Cain tells me again, for the fifteenth time, that we should roll up on the house slowly. Maybe walk from a distance so we're unseen. But that's not my style.

We're a few yards away when I roll down the windows and press harder on the accelerator. Turn up the volume. Blast that metal. And lay on the horn.

Beep-beep, beep-beep, beeeeeeep-beep, beep, beeeeeeeeeeee-eeeeeeeeep!

I stick my head out the window, suck in a lungful of Texas air, and scream, "Little pig, little pig, let me in!" I laugh at the night sky. "Not by the hair on my chinny, chin, chin," I add in a high-pitched voice.

I jerk the steering wheel and plow through the gate. Then, hitting the breaks too late, we slam into the black rental car and my air bags deploy. Crap. Didn't see that one coming. Not in this piece.

"Come on, come on," I yell at Cain, tossing the keys into the driver's seat.

He grabs the things we need from the car, and I skip toward the back of the house, banging on the windows as I go.

"Come out and play. Come out and play, little girls!"

The sound of the front door bursting open greets my ears. Perfect. I grab one of the white plastic chairs from the back, and Cain grabs the other. We pull them toward the closest window and slide the glass open. Such shoddy security. But of course, who would dare break in to Madam Karina's house?

I would.

Me!

We abandon the chairs and window, making it appear as if we've gone through the Carnation's entertainment room window when in fact it's a diversion. Instead, we jog toward the basement window and push it open. Cain shoves himself through and offers an arm to help me in.

Don't mind if I do.

Then he tugs the black backpack on, and I pat it twice. I am bouncing with excitement, clapping my hands noiselessly, a grin parting my mouth. Cain is my polar opposite—hard lines, firm feet, calculating eyes. We are a pair of misfits if I've ever seen one.

Cain starts to move toward the door, but I stop him.

"Give me the paint samples."

He hands them to me—black and red. I draw two black lines on my face, one beneath each eye, and a red stripe down my nose. I hold them out to him, but he shakes his head. I can't say I'm not disappointed he won't wear his war paint, but hey, to each his own. Cain hands me a length of rope and swings the pack onto his back again. I hold up my fingers and count down.

Three.

Two.

One.

We rush up the stairs and, as God is my witness, the first person I see is Mercy. It's late in the night, almost early morning, and her hair stands up around her head.

"You," she says.

"Me!" I roar.

I leap on her like a lion would a gazelle, take her to the ground. Her head hits the floor, and I wrap the rope swiftly around her hands. She looks up at me, bewildered, but she shouldn't be. She's met me before. Remember the fork? I drag her across the floor toward the entryway and tie her hands to the stairwell. Then I wrap the rest around her ankles as she screams. When I'm done with her, she's on all fours, masking tape over her mouth.

As I work on Mercy, a half dozen girls race through the entryway, terrified out of their minds because they see the emptiness in my eyes. And they see Cain, yelling at them to get out or they'll get worse. He's incredible, that Cain. Growling and throwing his fists into walls and asking if the girls want to tease him now.

We've lost our ever-loving minds, and I couldn't be more thrilled.

Finally, the person I want to see most strolls in from the back room where we opened the first window. The look on her face is one I'll treasure all of my days. She's dressed in nightclothes; the blond hair she usually wears pulled back spills over her shoulders. Madam Karina looks shockingly young in this warm light. Young and susceptible.

I open my arms. "I've come home to you."

CHAPTER 64

MOLARS

Cain grabs Madam Karina from behind and cranks her head back. "Don't say a word," he breathes into her ear. "And make sure no one else comes through here."

Girls continue to dart in and out, screaming, though I don't know what all the ruckus is about. Madam Karina yells for them to return to their beds at once, and they follow her orders like good little ducks.

I slink around Madam Karina until I find her wrists and then bind them. "Let's go in the front room, shall we? Away from this horse here." I kick Mercy in the ribs and tell her I'll catch her later. Maybe Ruby, too, if I can find that wench. Cain drags Madam Karina after him and follows me into the sitting room, the first place I stepped foot when we arrived.

"Have a seat," I tell Madam Karina, and Cain throws her onto the couch.

"You are not what you pretended to be," the madam snarls.

"I am exactly as I am. You have two faces, and so do I." I clasp my hands behind me and walk the space before her. Turn on my heels, and pace back. "You are a manipulator. And you are a liar. You brought us here to serve as your property, and I don't believe you've ever once paid a girl the money she deserved."

Madam Karina averts her gaze and works her arms against the binds. "You stupid, stupid girl. If you wanted to leave, all you had to do was apply, and the money would've been yours."

I ignore her. "You put a tracking device in Poppet's pink elephant, the one you knew she'd take, and you lock up any girl who leaves you." I swivel on Madam Karina. "Is that where she is now?"

Shock colors the madam's face, but not for long. A shadow passes over her features, and her mouth forms a tight line. "That girl had two choices, and she chose wrong. Now she's paying for her poor decisions."

"Where is she?"

Madam Karina smiles. "Not where you'd think."

"Not at the jailhouse."

Madam Karina turns her head away and barely suppresses a smile. It's eerily quiet in the house—all the girls huddled in their rooms, doors locked—when I rear back and slap Madam Karina cold across her face. Her hair whips over her cheek, and she glares up at me, anger boiling behind those blue hooded eyes.

"Feels kind of good, doesn't it?" I say. "The snap of being woken up?"

I glance through the windows that lead outside. Mr. Hodge is no doubt out with his mistress, and Eric's gold sedan is nowhere in sight. It seems luck is on our side. Not that I need it. I motion to Cain, and he opens the black bag.

I select my first instrument.

The pliers sparkle, even in the dull light, and the smile slips from the madam's mouth. "Oh, no more smirking?" I push the pliers toward Madam Karina's mouth and Cain yanks her head back. "Tell me where Poppet is."

Instead of addressing me, the madam turns her attention

to Cain. "I'll tell Eric what you did. Murderer! You killed your own brother. Know what they'll do if they find out?"

Cain's eyes enlarge, but he doesn't release her.

I grab Madam Karina's chin and jerk it forward. "It's time to pay penance for many things. Making Cain believe he's guilty is but one of your sins. Open wide, sugar."

Madam Karina screams.

Oh, she screams.

The front lateral incisor pops out as if it never wanted to be there in the first place. *Good riddance*, it says with a backward wave. I hold the tooth in front of her face as she drools and whimpers. "This one isn't that painful to have removed, believe it or not. And it doesn't contribute much functionality. More a cosmetic concern, really. Next time I'll pull a molar, and let me tell you, that won't be nearly as pleasant."

A Tulip tiptoes down the stairs, the same girl who took the teakettle from me when I needed it. I wave the tooth at her. "You see me now, Tulip?" I motion toward the open seat next to Madam Karina. "Step right up! Got room for one more."

The girl races up the stairs, a scream ripping from her throat.

"You see?" I get close to Madam Karina's face. "No one is coming to save you. So, tell me where Poppet is, and I'll bring you a towel."

Madam Karina, lady that she is, rears her head back and spits on me. "I should have known better than to bring in Detroit street trash. Eric should have left you for my sister to scoop off the sidewalk."

I palm her face and shove backward. She moans and clenches her eyes shut. "I'll tell you a secret, madam. I am more than mere street trash. I'm a killer. Me. Not Cain." I nod to show her it's true. "That's right. These two hands killed half a dozen men. Maybe more. I lost count after a while. One could say I'm a man-killing connoisseur."

Cain growls and throws a fist into the couch near the madam's head. "Just tell us where Poppet is and we'll leave."

I'll do no such thing, but I still raise my hands and wave toward the kitchen. "Get this scoundrel a kitchen towel. I can't stand her drooling."

Cain starts to leave, but I stop him with a word. "Bag."

He pauses, wondering how far I'll go without him there to supervise. In the end, he tosses me the backpack and leaves the room.

I withdraw the smaller knife and lay it across my hands on display. "I'll start by cutting you on the hands and arms. You'll bleed a lot, and it will certainly hurt. But it won't do too much damage. You can trust me on this." I show her the inside of my forearm as evidence—the Xs crossing my skin, the scars that memorialize the men I killed. I kept accurate count...for a while. "Where's Poppet?" I ask, giving her one more chance.

"You'll never make it out of here," Madam Karina growls, blood dripping down her chin. "I'll have you in the end. Another jailbird to sing for me."

I round her body and drag the blade across the back of her left hand. It opens without complaint and drips scarlet onto the wood floor. Madam Karina cries for me to stop. But I can't. Not until there's a matching one on the other hand.

There we go.

Much better.

Cain reappears with the dishtowel and tosses it into Madam Karina's lap.

"Go ahead, pick it up," I laugh. "What, you don't want it?"

Madam Karina hangs her head. "You have my hands tied, you dirt. You filth. Tell me, Domino, did you wonder who took the money from your dresser drawer? Did you think Mr. Hodge wouldn't find it?"

This takes me by surprise for a moment, but the reaction doesn't stick. I flip the knife in my hand like a skilled butcher and take it to her forearm this time, press the point against her age-marked skin, but don't press down. "This is the last time I'm going to ask you. Where is Poppet?"

She shakes her head as her blood drip-drops.

"What I did to your mouth? To your hands? That was child's play. I'm gonna show you how I *really* make people hurt."

I push the knife a touch in as Cain watches, face twisted with horror and desire. He's disgusted by what I'm doing, and yet he wants this as much as I do. Kick a dog one too many times…

I begin dragging the knife up her arm—

The front door crashes open.

In walks Eric, arm around Poppet's waist, gun held to her head.

CHAPTER 65

DEAL WITH THE DEVIL

When Madam Karina sees him, she laughs, blood dripping from between her lips. "What perfect timing, Eric, my dear. Most dramatic."

"Don't touch her." I take a step toward Eric, but he jabs the barrel of his gun deeper into Poppet's side, causing the girl to whimper.

Cain attempts to creep around the perimeter of the room unseen, but it's like trying to ignore an avalanche. Eric points the gun at Cain. "Don't even think about it. I'd like nothing more than to hurt you right now. My patroller told me what you did to him."

"Tell us what you want," I say to Madam Karina.

She grimaces. "You pulled out my damn tooth, and now you want to negotiate?"

There's no telling how sinister a proposal the madam would offer, but now that the idea's presented, I jump. I'm not afraid of her. I'm not afraid of anyone. I'm not even afraid of death, and that's a marvelous thing. You are never more lethal than when you hold death in your lap, kiss its sickly forehead, and smooth back its hair.

"That's right. Let's negotiate," I say. "I want Poppet and Cain to leave here unharmed. I want you to forget they ever existed."

"Domino, don't," Poppet mutters, her eyes closed against Eric's gun.

She knows what I'm offering—my head on a platter for Madam Karina to place on display. Domino the Betrayer. See what happens to those who slight her? Poppet thinks I'm being serious, because she sees Domino when she looks at me. She doesn't know that Domino is asleep, and I'd kill everyone in this room if it meant protecting my sleeping beauty.

"And I want you to release Angie," I add. "Tell her she's free to keep working for you, or to work elsewhere."

"You make a lot of demands for someone with a lesser weapon." Madam Karina locks eyes with Eric and yanks her wrists against the binds. "Take this off me."

I step between Eric and Madam Karina, jab my knife to her throat to remind him I'm still armed. Over my shoulder, I say, "I'm going to let him untie you as a show of good faith. But I want your word that you'll release Poppet and Cain."

"Enough with your threats. Let me go!" Rage laces the madam's every word. It's the sweetest music I've ever heard. I smile to Eric and bow like he's royalty. Let him release the beast. When she says it's me she wants, I want her to be on her feet. I want to be on my feet, too.

I step away, and Eric releases Madam Karina. Immediately, the madam covers her wounds and puts pressure on the hole in her gums. Her face furrows, and she moans deep from within her core. I understand then how much pain she's in. It isn't enough. It'll never be enough. If Domino were here, she would've called off the torture long ago. But she isn't here. I am. And Madam Karina has another think coming if she thinks I'll die easily.

Madam Karina straightens and then dashes toward me, fury in her gaze. I lift the knife so it glitters between us and shake it back and forth. *Tsk, tsk.* She glares at it and shuffles backward. Her eyes flick to Eric's weapon, and she seems to understand she can't risk it. After all, how quickly could I stab her before Eric put a bullet in my head?

"Tell me what you want," I say between my teeth.

"You know what I want."

I smile and open my arms as if I'm all hers. She eyeballs my knife again, uncertain as to whether I'll use it on her after Domino's friends have fled. If I'm still kicking, I'll use it and then some. Her eyes slide past my knife toward the open front door. She narrows her gaze as a crunching sound reaches my ears. Lights flood the front room and I turn to see what she does.

It's Mr. Hodge, sitting passenger side in the car we saw him in yesterday. From here, I can make out the woman in the front seat. It's one of the two ladies from the general store. The thinner one who acted scared of Madam Karina and who said she'd bring by canned pears.

Mr. Hodge leans forward and peers through the windshield, eyes squinting like he can't make out what he's seeing.

"Get out of the doorway!" Madam Karina yells. She shoves Cain and Eric so that they disappear from view. The madam grabs my free hand and presses it to her chest, folding her fingers around my own. I'm startled by her touch, especially since I could cut her throat from this distance. "You want to make a deal?" Her eyes are manic, and her bloodied lips are curled away from her teeth. She takes a small step toward me, and I lift my knife. Her breath is spoiled milk and rusted metal, and she looks terrified that I'll reject her proposal. "Kill him," she whispers. "Kill him, and I'll let you go. All of you." She squeezes my hand tighter. "I won't chase you. You have my word."

So Madam Karina wants me to kill her philandering lover. She doesn't have the guts to do it herself, and it seems she's decided there's something magical about her favorite girl turned rogue doing the deed for her. Eric could do it much easier. One antsy trigger finger and it'd be done. But I do have a flare for making murder long and interesting, and I've shown Madam Karina a touch of that sinister side.

I kill Mr. Hodge and we go free.

One more X on the arm.

One more man.

I turn and glance at the open door, knowing that in a matter of seconds that Mr. Hodge will come through it. I push Madam Karina's hand away. "Get against the wall and let me work."

She inches away and waves for Eric to follow her and to bring Poppet with him. I nod for Cain to do the same, and he does, though he's looking at me strangely. Domino would care about that look, but to me, his feelings are irrelevant. Besides, I know what's best for him. For all of them.

After tonight, they'll no longer live under the giant's thumb.

Mr. Hodge strides through the door cautiously, one hand on the threshold. His meaty head appears first, no neck to be seen.

He takes a second step inside, and his pupils enlarge.

I'm on him in an instant.

CHAPTER 66

THE PAST IS PRESENT

I knock Mr. Hodge onto his side, feeling like a comic book hero. The beefy man scoots backward on the floor when he sees what's in my hand. But I just slither on toward him.

"She has a knife," he yells to Madam Karina.

She doesn't care.

When he *realizes* she doesn't care, and that no one else does, either, he makes this high-pitched cry that's unnatural for a man his size. I almost laugh. But I shouldn't laugh, right? I mean, the man's about to meet his maker. It'd be rude to poke fun.

"You deserve anything she does to you," Madam Karina shrieks. "You think I didn't know about your whore? You think I didn't notice she drove you home? You wanted to get caught!"

"Puppy," he pleads. The way his mouth downturns, it's like he's more concerned about hurting Madam Karina than he is my blade. Seeing him this way, vulnerable, I almost regret having to kill The Neck.

"Say it again," I snarl, speaking to Madam Karina but keeping my eyes on Mr. Hodge. "Tell me you'll let us go if I end him."

"Yes, just do it!"

"Domino." Cain's voice breaks through my sniper focus. "Don't."

"Shut up," I snap. "That's not my name."

"Listen to him," Poppet pleads.

"I said *shut up!*"

Blood pounds at my temples as I crawl toward Mr. Hodge. He tries to retreat, but his back hits the wall.

"I'll make it quick," I tell him. "And I'll carry the ghost of you on my arm, always."

Sweat drips between his eyes. I watch it slide down his nose and pool at the corner of his right nostril. His eyes dart toward Madam Karina, and then he makes a break for it. I leap onto his back, the knife arched above my head.

Someone behind me closes in. It's Cain, judging by the heavy footfalls. He doesn't reach me in time, though. Not before I drive the knife into Mr. Hodge's side. It's not enough to kill him. I didn't go deep enough for that. But it does get him on the floor.

He moans like a rhino taken down in a safari hunt. As if I'm the cruel, advantaged hunter with a scope and camouflage. And here he is—one of God's innocent creatures. But the truth is, he helped Madam Karina build this empire. Helped seduce girls into selling their bodies and souls so he could lord over this three-story farmhouse. And let's not forget the way he cupped Poppet's bottom. Think that's the first time he's pulled a stunt like that? Please.

No, I won't mourn his death.

Mr. Hodge flips onto his back and blocks his face with his arms. As if that's what I'm going for.

"Don't take another step," Eric yells.

I turn to find Cain a hand's width away from me. He looks like a knight, come to rescue a damsel in distress. But I'm no damsel, and I'm certainly not stressing. Not over someone like

Mr. Hodge. One less dirtbag walking the planet, if you ask me.

Eric points his gun at Cain, but Cain doesn't react. He keeps his gaze on my face, silently imploring me to see reason. To not kill a monster that deserves to die. But it's men like Mr. Hodge who make me sick. They hurt women, leave them, walk out front doors in the dead of night even though their wife and daughter are asleep down the hall. Doesn't he know how they'll grieve the loss of him? Doesn't he care?

Slowly, Gentle Domino slides her hand over mine. Grips that knife along with me like maybe she wants in on this, too. Is tired of being in the back seat at this midnight matinee.

I stumble to my side, shocked. Domino has never risen while I worked before. She may have whispered in my ear, but I could swat away her presence like a gnat.

I shake my hand once, twice, until I regain full control, and then refocus on my task.

Madam Karina clutches Poppet's upper arm, rooting her in place, and tears streak down Poppet's face. I glance at Cain. He's no longer checked out. Now he's present and accounted for, and he's terrified of what I may do. And what about Poppet? Look at that fear. Taste it! Is that what I do? Is that the same look the men I hurt gave me? Yes. Yes, it is. It's different this time, though. It's different, and it's the same.

Domino's two friends don't want me to do this thing. But I guarantee what they want more than anything is for us—for *all* of us—to be safe. To be free. And so I will do this for them. Because it's people like them I want surrounding my Domino.

I turn back to Mr. Hodge.

He must see the determination in my eyes. He must.

Mr. Hodge screams, and I crawl on top of him like I'm scaling Mt. Everest. I hold my knife above my head, ready to plunge it like a flag into uncharted land. My fingers twitch as I eye the soft spot below his chin. It's funny, really, that the fastest way to kill this man is in the one place he's largely missing. But in all seriousness, there's enough neck there for me to work with.

Wilson, Domino whispers. *Wilson, I was wrong. I am strong enough to handle this.*

Nope, I tell her. *Go away!*

The knife in my hand lifts a fraction higher, and Mr. Hodge fights to get my weight off him. I avoid his flailing and zone in on his jugular. My heart stills. My pulse slows. I am calm in this moment. My name is Wilson, and this is what I do.

I kill.

I kill so Domino doesn't have to.

"Do it," Madam Karina says from behind me. "Do it for both of us."

Her words spill over me like heated oil, tangling in my hair, sticking to my skin. It's dangerously similar to something Mother would have said. Mother didn't want to be alone in her hatred, and so her baby girl helped torture her victims. Madam Karina's own hate stretches from her to Domino, an invisible thread binding them. When I assisted Mother, she gave to Domino freely—affection. And Madam Karina will give to her, too—freedom.

Domino hesitates. She hesitates, but I won't.

My hand quivers above Mr. Hodge's body as he writhes side to side. I lose my hold on him once, but regain my place on his chest quickly enough.

Why am I shaking? I don't have a care in the world for this man. I am fearless and emotionless and made of gears and glass.

Because you are me, Wilson. And I am you.

My body freezes. Why won't she just *shut up*? I asked for complete control, and she gave it to me. So why is she here?

Go back to sleep! I growl.

No, she responds firmly. *I won't turn away this time.*

"What are you waiting for?" Madam Karina barks. "Do it!"

At the same time, Poppet and Cain yell for me to stop. To put down the knife.

But it's Domino's voice that stills my arm. *I've closed my eyes to the things I've done for too long. I want to see it now, all of it.*

I spot it then. The dark room. The girl. *My* girl. She has a chain tied around her ankle. Rusted links that stretch from her to me. She's bound to me the same way Madam Karina binds herself to Domino. But it's not the same.

IT'S NOT THE SAME!

Mr. Hodge breaks away and races up the stairs. I can get to him again. That's not my concern. My worry now is Domino and her insistent fingers digging into my mind.

Domino produces something from behind her back. An axe. She has an axe!

"What are you doing with that?" I yell aloud. "You shouldn't be here!"

"Who's she talking to?" Eric mutters.

These are my memories! Domino says, lifting the weapon. *This is my anger. I want it back.* All *of it.*

"Don't do this," I whisper.

"Enough!" Madam Karina snatches the gun from Eric and points it at me. I lunge at the madam, no longer sure who I am. The gun goes off at the exact moment that Cain slams into her. I'm stunned silent for only a fraction of a second, the bullet lodged into the drywall behind me.

Cain pins Madam Karina to the floor, yelling as if he'll never stop. Eric fumbles across the room for something, and Poppet grabs him about the waist, trying to stop him. It isn't until I see the gun in Eric's hand that I understand what he intends to do.

Let me in let me in let me in! Domino screams, bringing the axe down.

Eric takes aim at Cain.

A gun.

My Cain.

I dive across the space between us and sink my teeth into Eric's arm.

He elbows me off and swings the gun wildly. A second shot is fired, but this time it doesn't lodge in the drywall.

It buries itself into my body instead.

Domino hacks at the chains over and over as I scream in anguish, in desperation.

Pain sears through me, and Cain turns his attention to Eric. He rises to his feet and transforms into a battering ram, a plague, a stone giant come to life—and he uses every ounce of his pent-up resentment to take Eric down. Eric's face becomes a blood-soaked sphere as Madam Karina scrambles back toward the wall in horror. Poppet is next to me, putting pressure on my arm and telling me it isn't so bad. But all I can think about is the gun. Where it is? Who has it?

Then I see it in Eric's hand. It's stretched forward and kissing Cain's gut. Eric smiles, white against red, and his finger moves to pull the trigger.

I scream for Eric to stop.

Domino screams, too. Brings her axe down one more time and severs the chain.

Wilson gone.

Domino here, here, here.

CHAPTER 67

FIRE

Eric jams the gun farther into Cain's stomach as I rise on shaking legs. *My* legs. *My* body.

Eric grins. Spits his anger at Cain. "And now you're gonna die 'cause you thought you were a big man."

The wall behind the two tangled men explodes. The madam collapses beneath the rubble, the house thunders with the magnitude of a deadly earthquake, and I decide that maybe God has had enough, that he's reached in and ripped away the walls that shield us.

But then Angie appears, killing the headlights on Black Betty. She's yelling something I can't make out. But as she climbs over the crumbling fragments of siding and drywall and insulation, I understand her perfectly.

"You killed my dog!" she roars, unearthing Madam Karina from pieces of wall and debris. "You killed my dog, and I'm going to kill you!" Angie's remaining Doberman, Kali, is by her side as she kicks the injured woman in her rib cage. "You poisoned them. You poisoned my babies!"

My eyes dart to Cain and Eric, and I see that Poppet has Eric's gun. I don't know how the exchange happened, but she has the blasted thing now, and that's enough for me. I jump to my feet and race toward the kitchen, one hand gripping the bullet wound on my arm.

I find what I'm looking for behind a box of rat poison, exactly where Cain said it would be.

I could light a fire if you're cold, Cain said to me once. *I have some lighter fluid beneath the kitchen sink.*

Wilson is not the only one with anger. I harbor it, too. *Me.*

Pulling in a deep breath, I flip the red cap and squeeze fluid on the rabbit mount with the lei around its neck. Next, I squirt some on the curtain valance and then trail a line of it down the hallway and toward the room where everyone is screaming threats. My knife lays flat against my back, held tight to my body by my waistband. The coolness is reassuring. It makes me work faster, my tongue touching my bottom lip in concentration.

When I reach the foyer, I squirt the remainder of the fluid over the curtains and couch. No one sees what I've done. Angie is busy kicking Madam Karina's bony butt, Cain is distracted beating the life out of Eric, and Poppet is exalted by her newfound weapon and power.

"Cain, give me your lighter!"

He stops slamming Eric into the floor and looks at me. He's returned to his dark place, nothingness behind his eyes. It's a glorious look on him. I'd like to lick that look from the back of a spatula. Cain spies the fluid in my hand and then digs in his pocket. The silver lighter gleams in the low light. He tosses it across the space and I grab it one-handed.

"Poppet, get out of here," I tell my friend. When she glances at me, I say, "Start the green car and wait for us."

She nods and dashes out the door.

Cain throws Eric into the corner and dusts off his hands like that's that. I crouch next to Madam Karina. She's breathing, but she doesn't look good. I grab her hair and pull her head up so she hears me clearly. "Now you'll see if your girls really care about you."

A vein in Madam Karina's eye is busted, filling the creamy whiteness with red. Still, I glimpse the fear in it all the same. It instills me with power and joy like it would any reasonable madman. I flick the grind and a small flame dances.

Stealing one last glance at the farmhouse, I fill my lungs. Then I yell, "I'm lighting this place on fire. You'd better get your butts down here and out the door or you'll burn to the ground, too."

That's enough warning, right?

Right.

I toss the lighter, and the curtains burst into flames. The yellow-red warmth snakes up the fabric. It stretches its long arms toward the furniture and the drizzle of fluid I trailed along the floor. Already the smell of smoke is all-consuming. I could be roasting marshmallows and telling ghost stories and inhale the same scent. But it's not marshmallows I'm roasting.

It's Carnations.

And Tulips.

And Daisies.

It's Madam Karina's hard work, and Eric's scandalous involvement, and Mr. Hodge's philandering. It's my mother's vindictive dealings, and her seductive tongue. Staring into the fire, watching as girls race past me and into the night, their screams filling my head, I remember the things I've done. The men I've helped kill because my mother deemed them unworthy.

Behind Wilson, a door cracks open. He tries to close it, but he's too weak. I glimpse the men behind that door. Men who cheated, men who lied, men who called women filthy names, but who didn't deserve to die.

I killed them all? I ask.

No, Wilson says. *Mother did.*

I nod slowly, accepting for the first time that I was a child. That I was manipulated into performing these horrors, the same way Madam Karina manipulated me here. But the difference is that, this time, I knew better. I saw it for myself in the end. I chose to let Wilson out.

And I chose to come forward and finish this thing.

I'm choosing to remember.

Wilson stumbles inside my mind, his body too heavy to stand. My own legs buckle, too. Strong arms wrap around me and guide me out the door. When I glance back, my vision blurring, I see Poppet lighting the guesthouses on fire, expelling her own demons with a flaming board she stole from the main house. She touches the board to the houses, all four corners, and screams for the girls inside to get out. They race into the night, wide-eyed and half-dressed.

Lola is nowhere to be seen.

Angie guides me toward the car Wilson spray-painted, the engine purring with a promise of safety and renewal, and places me in the back seat. Cain is beside me, and soon, Poppet is climbing in the front passenger seat.

Turning to look out the tinted window, I see Mr. Hodge dragging Madam Karina from the burning house. She tried to have him killed, and yet he saved her. The way he bends over her broken body, calling her name, smoothing her hair back—it's almost romantic. Let them have each other.

Angie is about to drop down into the car when I catch sight of Eric. He has the gun, the gun I figured was smoldering inside the fire. He points it directly at Angie.

Cain yells her name, and Angie straightens. I don't know why she does it. She should have jumped inside and stepped on the gas, but now Eric has a clear shot, and he's going to kill her. Then he's going to kill us all.

Angie utters a single word.

Just one.

It's enough.

Angie's Doberman appears from the smoke like a hound from the mouth of hell. He's on Eric in a heartbeat. The gun fires at the sky, and my heart explodes inside my chest. As Wilson takes himself to bed, covers his frail body with warm blankets, I'm reunited with fear. The fear of losing another person I care about. I scream for Angie to get inside the car.

But Angie stays put.

She watches as her dog tears into the man, snapping jaws and bloodied muzzle. She could pull him off at any moment. It might take only a sharp word to stop the dog's attack. But she doesn't do a thing. She only stands by, overseeing the officer's death. The same man who chose each and every girl who worked this home and hand-delivered them to Madam Karina.

When Eric's fingers stop twitching, Angie pats the side of her leg. The dog trots over, chest damp with blood. With the dog by her side, Angie takes three quick steps toward Mr. Hodge and Madam Karina. The madam's eyes are closed, her checkered dress blackened by smoke and debris, but Mr. Hodge is fully conscious. He scoots backward and drags his lover after him, away from the woman whose dog just killed a man.

Angie points a thick arm at Mr. Hodge and says something. Then she looks at the few girls still crowded around the roaring house, engulfed in flames, and says something to them, too. Satisfied, Angie turns toward our idling vehicle and gets inside. The dog jumps over her and lies across Poppet's lap, dampening her clothes with blood. I wonder how Kali survived being poisoned, but then I think of how much Angie loves those dogs. If anyone could've saved one of them, it's her. As Poppet hugs the animal, my heart aches for Angie and the dog that didn't make it.

Angie breathes hard for several seconds, and then turns to Cain and me in the back seat. "No one will ever hurt you guys again," she says with finality. Angie looks at Poppet next and nods. Then, slowly, she puts the car into reverse and backs out the gate.

Gravel crunches under our tires as I gaze at the house.

Eric is dead, and Madam Karina hasn't opened her eyes in a long time, but it's the girls I watch. They hold one another and look around for someone to rescue them. I hate them for what they put me through. But as angry as I was then, now I pity them. A part of me hopes they, too, find a path leading to a better life.

Cain wraps his arm around my shoulders, and I lean into him. For the next several minutes, we drive in silence. When we near the train, Cain tells Angie to stop. It takes all three of them—Poppet, Angie, and Cain—to talk me out of driving straight to the Pox County jailhouse. But in the end, they make me see sense. We have to get out of town. We have to expose what happened here, and send the authorities—those who can actually be trusted—to release the girls being held and talk the others into getting the help they need to start again.

Angie takes the longest to jump onto the train, even taking into account my injured arm. But with Cain's help, she manages. Cain is last to leap on, one arm around the dog. The Doberman licks Angie's face, leaving slobber on her cheek.

When she calls me over, I don't hesitate. I scoot under her waiting arm, and Poppet leans back on my knees. Cain sits beside me, one hand rubbing my back. After we catch our breath, he leans close, his mouth brushing my ear.

"Are you…*you* again?" he asks, simply.

I nod against his lips. "You?"

"Here," he replies. "Don't leave like that again, okay? Stay with me. You promised."

Cain presses his lips to my cheek, and I smile against his touch, my eyes closing. I don't know where we'll land, but I hang on to the dream that we'll end up in Kansas, Cain on the field and Poppet and I in the stands. Angie will grunt that she's happy at home making chili and cornbread, and it'll be waiting for us when we return. And dammit, be careful walking back, because the sidewalks are slick with ice and she's got enough to do without one of us spraining an ankle.

The train chugs down the track, *thunk-thunking* over the rails and ties, and Angie begins to hum. Kali lies down at our feet and closes her eyes, and Poppet says, "One day, we'll forget any of this ever happened. It'll be all fuzzy, like a dream."

"Yeah," I mumble. "We're just getting started."

It's the last thing I say before the world slips away.

CHAPTER 68

GOOD-BYE

The room is bare, the floorboards cool beneath my feet. Wilson lies in a twin bed, a crisp white sheet pulled tight across his chest. His eyes are closed. A shadow dances over his body, making it difficult to get a firm grasp on his features. It's like trying to recall someone from your past in detail, but all you can manage is a blurred image. Blackness stretches across his cheeks and nose and eyes—a mask I can't see behind. But it's his face. That much I recognize.

There's a wooden chair beside the bed and a little light coming through a window. Dust coats the floor, leaving imprints of my feet as I cross the distance and sit. Wilson opens one eye and smiles, but I can tell he's doing it for me alone. Sweat coats his forehead, and his frame is shrunken. He's not the bull I imagined him as, but there's strength in his steady gaze yet.

His other eye opens and he says, "It's you."

"It's me."

I take his hand. His fingers are thin and cold, but they wrap around my own and fill me with peace.

"I could stay with you, you know," Wilson suggests. "I could go to Kansas, too. Just in case."

I shake my head and squeeze his hand tighter. "I have to

do this on my own."

He turns his face away. "You don't need me anymore."

Tears prick my eyes. "I'll always need you, Wilson," I whisper. "But I need to face my memories and the things I've done. I need to let people in." I clear my throat. "It's time I talk about what happened after my father left."

"Will you remember me?" he asks, turning back.

My heart aches at the hopefulness in his voice. "I could never forget you." I laugh softly. "You know, there was a time when I couldn't even think your name."

Wilson pulls himself up in bed. A grin parts his mouth. "You were terrified of me."

"I was terrified of remembering."

"But then you started to let me in," he says, his eyes dancing. "You finally realized I only wanted to help."

"That's right."

"I still think you should have eaten the orange sherbet at that ice cream shop."

"No, Cookies and Cream was the right choice."

Wilson shivers like what I said is repulsive.

I pull the sheet higher over Wilson's frame, fighting the emotion building in my chest. "I don't want to leave."

"Then don't," he whispers.

I cover my eyes, and a sob breaks in my throat. "You know I have to."

Wilson sighs and leans back on his pillow, releasing my hand. "I know, Domino. It's just…who will protect you now? Cain? Angie?"

"I don't need anyone to protect me anymore."

"So…Cain?"

I laugh through my tears. "Yeah, Cain."

Wilson nods, satisfied.

I stand from the chair and stride toward the door, because

if I don't leave now, right now, then I'm afraid I never will. My hand is on the knob when Wilson's voice reaches me.

"Hey, Domino?"

I stop.

"You think maybe I'll go on to someone else now? Instead of just...ending?"

I turn partway, speaking over my shoulder. "I think anything is possible." And then, because I'm losing my courage, I say one last thing to my friend. "Thank you, Wilson. For everything."

I walk out the door, and sunlight warms my face. I stare into that reviving light for several moments before my eyes open again. When they do, and I find myself half asleep on the train, I know Wilson is gone for good.

But Cain is there, sleeping beside me. And Poppet is leaning against Angie, who is watching over us all. These people are my home now, and I will cherish them all my life.

And what a life it will be.

ACKNOWLEDGMENTS

Violet Grenade is a strange little book, and I'm indebted to many people for bringing its oddity to life.

A giant thank-you to my editor, Heather Howland, for encouraging me to embrace my voice, and for asking if I could make scenes darker, and darker still. You absolutely *got* Domino, Cain, and Wilson, and this book is undeniably better because of you.

To the entire team at Entangled Teen—thank you! To Liz Pelletier, who first welcomed me to Entangled Publishing, and to my production editor, Christine Chhun, and copy editor, Nancy Cantor, for your little love notes. To Melissa Montovani, my publicist, for her lightning-quick responses, and to the entire marketing and foreign rights teams who get my books into the right places—thank you!

Thank you to Dr. Clark Steffens, a fantastic dentist who didn't panic when I asked him what tooth would hurt the most if you, ya' know, held someone down and extracted it. Thanks for lending your knowledge to an important scene.

A special thank you to friends Angee Webb and Melissa Gouge—I remember pitching this book to you girls over lunch—and to Kay Honeyman, who pushed me to keep that last chapter. Thank you to Lindsay Cummings for inspiring me with your creativity, talent, and relentless work ethic. Love to my mom and sister, who have strange, twisty brains like me. And hugs to my dad, brother, and grandma for always asking what I'm working on.

Always, always, thank you to my readers. If you loved this book, if it kept you up late at night and caused chills to rush down your arms, then you, too, have strange, twisty minds. I always imagined it'd take a special reader to truly love *Violet Grenade*. If you did, you're my kind of people.

Finally, thank you to my daughter, Luci, who just called me into her room to read a book about pumpkins four times. Four times? Really? You're definitely my kid. And to my husband, Ryan, who always tries to write his own part in the acknowledgments and prompts me by asking, "Who else is as important to your writing as me?"

Nobody, baby. Nobody. I love you.

To every last person holding this book—a big, cuddly thank you from me!

And from me.

GRAB THE ENTANGLED TEEN RELEASES READERS ARE TALKING ABOUT!

CHASING TRUTH
BY JULIE CROSS

When former con artist Eleanor Ames's homecoming date commits suicide, she's positive there's something more going on. The more questions she asks, though, the more she crosses paths with Miles Beckett. He's sexy, mysterious, *arrogant*…and he's asking all the same questions.

Eleanor might not trust him - she doesn't even *like* him - but they can't keep their hands off each other. Fighting the infuriating attraction is almost as hard as ignoring the fact that Miles isn't telling her the truth…and that there's a good chance he could be the killer.

LOST GIRLS
BY MERRIE DESTEFANO

Yesterday, Rachel went to sleep curled up in her grammy's quilt, worrying about geometry. Today, she woke up in a ditch, bloodied, bruised, and missing a year of her life. She's not the only girl to go missing within the last year…but she's the only girl to come back. And as much as her dark, dangerous new life scares her, it calls to her. Seductively. But wherever she's been—whomever she's been with—isn't done with her yet…

SECRETS OF A RELUCTANT PRINCESS
BY CASEY GRIFFIN

At Beverly Hills High, you have to be ruthless to survive...

Adrianna Bottom always wanted to be liked. But this wasn't *exactly* what she had in mind. Now, she's in the spotlight...and out of her geeky comfort zone. She'll do whatever it takes to turn the rumor mill in her favor—even if it means keeping secrets. So far, it's working.

Wear the right clothes. Say the right things. Be seen with the right people.

Kevin, the adorable sketch artist who shares her love of all things nerd, isn't *exactly* the right people. But that doesn't stop Adrianna from crushing on him. The only way she can spend time with him is in disguise, as Princess Andy, the masked girl he's been LARPing with. If he found out who she really was, though, he'd hate her.

The rules have been set. The teams have their players. Game on.

OTHER BREAKABLE THINGS
BY KELLEY YORK AND ROWAN ALTWOOD

Luc Argent has always been intimately acquainted with death. After a car crash got him a second chance at life—via someone else's transplanted heart—he tried to embrace it. He truly did. But he always knew death could be right around the corner again. And now it is. Luc is ready to let his failing heart give out, ready to give up. A road trip to Oregon—where death with dignity is legal—is his answer. But along for the ride is his best friend, Evelyn. And she's not giving up so easily.

REMEMBER ME FOREVER
BY SARA WOLF

Isis Blake hasn't fallen in love in three years, forty-three weeks, and two days. Or so she thinks. The boy she maybe-sort-of-definitely loved and sort-of-maybe-definitely hated has dropped off the face of the planet, leaving a Jack Hunter–shaped hole. Determined to be happy, Isis fills it in with lies and puts on a brave smile for her new life at Ohio State University. But the smile lasts only until *he* shows up. The threat from her past, her darkest moment…Nameless, attending OSU right alongside her. Whispering that he has something Isis wants—something she needs to see to move forward. To move on.

Isis is good at pretending everything is okay, at putting herself back together. But Jack Hunter is better.